Jessica Stanley was born in regional Victoria and grew up in Canberra and Melbourne. She worked in journalism and politics before moving to London in 2011. *A Great Hope* is her first novel.

a great hope

Jessica Stanley

PICADOR
Pan Macmillan Australia

Pan Macmillan acknowledges the Traditional Custodians of country throughout Australia and their connections to lands, waters and communities. We pay our respect to Elders past and present and extend that respect to all Aboriginal and Torres Strait Islander peoples today. We honour more than sixty thousand years of storytelling, art and culture.

First published 2022 in Picador by Pan Macmillan Australia Pty Ltd
1 Market Street, Sydney, New South Wales, Australia, 2000

A catalogue record for this book is available from the National Library of Australia

Typeset in 11.9/16 pt Adobe Garamond Pro by Post Pre-press Group, Brisbane
Printed by IVE

Quote on pages 118–119 licensed from the Commonwealth of Australia under a Creative Commons Attribution 4.0 International Licence. The Commonwealth of Australia does not necessarily endorse the content of this publication.

The author and the publisher have made every effort to contact copyright holders for material used in this book. Any person or organisation that may have been overlooked should contact the publisher.

For Jude.

Friday, 27 August 2010

God knows he'd disappointed enough women. He'd grown alert to it, at work and at home. The split-second change from hope to pain, from love to hate. He noticed it now. Her eyes grew vacant, the shutters slammed down. Before him the skylight glowed. His route to the exit was blocked. He stepped back, but the gap between them seemed to narrow. Nearly four decades he'd lived in this house. He'd become a man in it, raised a family in it, become a new man altogether. No one could see them up there on the roof. 'Stop,' John commanded, but his command was not obeyed. The push to his chest emptied him of breath. He teetered on the edge in the dark. It became inevitable. He would fall, he was falling. He was gone.

1.

A year later

Stepping through her front door, Grace Clare had the horrible premonition of a smell. John's long black coat was still hanging from its peg in the entry hall. She lifted it down and took a sniff. As she suspected: the collar *reeked* of Ivanna. Ivanna had placed her coat on John's coat, and now the coat of Grace's dead husband smelt like the instant chemical migraine of her cleaner's perfume. On her phone she found the texts they'd exchanged that morning. *I'm going to come home early this afternoon to speak with you about a matter*, Grace had written in the courteous, egalitarian and forthright manner she adopted with everyone from the Prime Minister to the garbage man. *Okay*, Ivanna had replied, with a colon and a closed bracket indicating a smile. Grace tapped to call her. Was it the fragrance? Her head was aching. The call rang out. She placed the phone firmly on the hall table. Well, well.

Upstairs she took no joy in the immaculate tidiness of her bedroom. Every time Ivanna made the bed she put John's pillow back up next to Grace's – every time. She grabbed the pillow and hurled it across the room. Her pulse was still racing when she heard her phone ring. She sprinted down the stairs to snatch it up. Ivanna was standing next to the hall table, black puffer jacket zipped from thigh to chin, two garbage bags of household rubbish on the floor next to her. So she brought her own plastic bags to take the rubbish out – despite Grace's strict policy on non-biodegradables! She drew breath to begin her long-planned frank feedback, but something gave her pause. Ivanna was staring at Grace's phone. Grace looked at it too. The screen flashed with the caller's ID: CLEANER. Ivanna lowered her own phone from her ear and hung up. She said slowly, 'I-van-na.'

'Yes,' Grace said, 'Ivanna –'

Ivanna's hands were trembling as she buttoned her phone into her hip pocket. 'You don't like me to be in your house.'

'It doesn't matter if I *like* having you here,' Grace began. Tears welled up in Ivanna's light blue eyes. 'Of course,' she added hurriedly, 'I do like seeing you, when I get to see you.' She wrenched the conversation back inside professional boundaries. 'But I do have to insist on . . . certain standards. For example!' She pointed at the coat rail. 'I've cleared this peg for your coat.'

Ivanna stared at the peg and then at Grace. 'You want me to put my coat on there?' She fingered the zipper at her throat.

'Yes. I mean, next time! Not now.'

'You don't want my coat to touch your coat.'

'It's not that, it's that I feel ill when I can smell –'

'Okay, Mrs Clare! Okay. I'll put my coat.'

'Ivanna. The reason I asked to see you – some of my toiletries are missing. Moisturisers, two very expensive ones.' Grace tilted up her chin and mimed patting on face cream. 'I wondered if you'd seen the bottles. Sort of whitey-greeny?' She separated her finger and thumb to indicate the size.

Ivanna's eyes crossed to the hall clock. 'I have not seen the things.'

4

Grace was a good and generous person. Having Ivanna clean on a Sunday wasn't even convenient for her; it was Ivanna's choice, so she could work her full-time job during the week. For the past two Christmases, Grace had enclosed a fifty dollar note in Ivanna's Amnesty International greeting card. She would happily have given her cleaner the expensive anti-ageing moisturisers as a gift. If she'd just hurry up and admit she'd taken them, Grace could move on to absolving her. 'Come,' she said. 'Can I show you where they were?' Grace jogged neatly up the formal staircase and was waiting in the large family bathroom with the medicine cabinet open when Ivanna slunk into view. 'Quite little bottles.' She made the size gesture again. 'Two moisturisers, and some foundation?'

Ivanna refused to look. 'No.'

'Right.' Grace shut the cabinet. In its mirrored door she saw a madwoman, the half-grey roots of her dark brown hair more than an inch long. It had started to grey when she had Sophie. When she'd had Toby, five years later, it practically whitened overnight. She'd dyed it with permanent hair colour every month for nearly twenty years. When Toby neared the end of school, and her lovely empty nest was finally in sight, she'd announced to John she was growing out her greys: 'Not that it's any of your business.'

'Definitely none of my business,' he'd agreed. 'But I think you'll look beautiful whatever you choose.' Bastard! A year it had taken her to grow them out, a full year. All ruined in one afternoon with her spontaneous, disastrous decision to dye it all back.

Ivanna was watching her in the mirror, Grace realised. But when she turned around, the cleaner's eyes were on the floor. 'And another thing!' Grace led Ivanna into the large bedroom

5

at the back of the house. She crossed the floor swiftly and bent to pick up John's pillow. When she rose, she could feel the blood rush to her cheeks. 'This doesn't go on the bed.'

'The pillow doesn't go on the bed,' Ivanna said slowly.

'No!' Grace tapped her foot for emphasis. Downstairs, the trill of the doorbell echoed through the hall. 'Oh!' she said, glad of the distraction. 'I must go and see who that is.'

A tall man of Grace's age was standing on the front step, a cap in his huge hands like a peasant in a musical. 'Yes, hello, missus,' he began.

'It's my husband,' the cleaner cried. Rudely she emphasised the 'my'. Ivanna slipped out, took hold of her husband's elbow and made to hurry away.

'I hope you'll remember what we spoke about,' Grace called after them.

Alone again. Still the air vibrated with anxiety and conflict. And look, Ivanna had left her rubbish bags inside! Grace snatched them up and ran out to the street. Husband and wife were on the footpath, huddled in a tender embrace. As Grace approached, she heard the man crooning: 'She has no one now – she has no one.'

'You forgot your rubbish,' Grace said.

Ivanna looked up from the crook of her husband's arm. 'It's *your* rubbish.'

'I'll take, I'll take,' the man was saying.

Grace bundled it into his arms. 'I won't need you anymore, Ivanna.' She nodded towards what she assumed was their car. 'I think you'll find that's a residents-only carpark.' She stalked back inside and slammed the door.

There was no reason at all for her to have John's coat in the hall. She threw it on the floor. Suddenly the solution to the problem of his pillow was obvious. She sprinted up, grabbed it and hurled it down the stairs. She yanked open John's half of the cupboards, plucked the shirts one by one from their hangers and tossed them on the bed. Trousers. Jackets. She dragged open the drawers at the bottom of the cupboard and added all the socks and t-shirts and tracksuit bottoms, his jeans, even his swimming goggles. Grace sneezed from the dust and shouted to the heavens: 'That's your fault!'

It struck her that she missed getting angry at him. Always he'd just listen and *take it*. He'd summarise her concerns neatly, repeat them back to her, committing them to memory: the keys to Grace. Over the decades, her gratitude turned to resentment. How dare he just float above her, waiting for her to calm down? She wrenched the drawers out of the bureau and tipped his jocks into the bin. Cleaning out the belongings of a dead husband – she felt seventy-five, not fifty-five. Toby had left for university only eighteen months earlier. Where was her Act Two? 'You did this to me,' she cried furiously. 'I want my life back.'

Coughing, eyes streaming, she pulled the duvet out from under her own pillow and went round the bed, tossing all the corners into the centre. She grasped the points together, lumped the mound of jumble off onto the floor and dragged it behind her to the stairs. Halfway down, flushed with triumph, she very slightly lost her footing. The physics of it all caught up with her – the enormous Santa sack of stuff loomed and tipped off a higher step. She toppled, and was flying for a terrifying second; she grabbed at the handrail and steadied herself, bracing against the shoes and clothes that tumbled out and littered the steps. Finally, everything in motion stopped. She cleared a space and sat down, trembling.

*

In Brunswick, the big Brotherhood of St Laurence was closed. If she left donations outside an op shop, it was littering, not charity. The responsible thing would be to come back when it was open. As she paused, torn, the pile of John's things seemed to animate, grow and escape the car boot, to slither over to her, twist around her neck and choke her. She couldn't wait another day. Down a nearby alley she spied a row of three large commercial bins. Grace kept the motor running as she shoved it all in, every bit. On the drive back home to Fitzroy her blank mind buzzed with static. She'd been able to forget the whole scene with Ivanna as she cleaned out John's stuff. But, as she parked the car at 99 Greeves Street, she shuddered to recall it. *She has no one now.* Was it that obvious?

At home Grace pulled her scarf up around her ears and stepped out into the night. She pushed open her front gate and froze. The door to her stately terrace stood very slightly ajar. All those years when John had been away for work – three, four nights a week or more – Grace's greatest fear had been the sound of glass breaking when she was in bed, a footstep on the stairs. Now here she was on the outside, and who was inside the house? Burglars? Smith Street junkies? A murderer? She reached for her phone. Absurdly she dialled her son, hundreds of kilometres away in Canberra. She went straight to voicemail. 'Oh, Toby-love.' She heard how breathless she sounded, how weak. 'Look, nothing important. Just a catch-up. Bye-bye.' She'd left two messages on his phone the day before – neither of them were acknowledged. She was glad when he chose to move away for uni. She'd encouraged his independence and relished the promise of her own. But that was before her husband chose death rather than being with her. Before the whole world knew he didn't love her.

Before her daughter literally pushed her away. Before Anton skipped town without a word. *She has no one now.* It was true.

Grace peeped at the door to check it was really open. It was; she wasn't mad. Fine, she'd call the police. Images came to her from the day they found John's body: blue-and-white-checked tape fluttering on the street, Sophie ranting and raving in the silver hypothermia blanket, a man's hairy hand proffering a cup of tea. No, whatever this was, she'd tackle it alone. She pushed the door so hard it smacked against the doorstop. 'Grace,' Grace bellowed. 'It's us! Where do you want us?' Would an intruder be upstairs or downstairs? She stomped past the library without looking inside. She banged the wall on the way to the cavernous kitchen. 'Yoo-hoo!' Surely he would have run downstairs by now and slipped out. Unless he was waiting for her? Should she slide a knife from the knife block? No, she'd just plead. He could take what he wanted, just leave.

'Grace!' Grace mounted the stairs slowly. 'The three big men are just parking the car,' she called. 'They'll be up in a second.' She stormed around, flicking on lights. The big front bedroom: no one. Toby's old room was empty. So was the monastic cell John had used as a study. Grace gasped when she turned on the light in her own bedroom, but *she'd* ransacked it that afternoon, not a robber. Now she stood at the foot of the new staircase leading up to the house's modern extension. She was silent, her hand on the stair railing. She'd shut the door when the police had finished. Could she face it? She'd almost prefer being murdered in her bed. 'Grace,' she shouted. God, this ruse was pathetic and fooling no one. 'Here we come!'

On the threshold of the studio she smoothed the wall for the light switch. The kiln was illuminated, the abandoned work.

A fine layer of neglect-dust overlaid the clay-dust. Her smock. Anton's smock. Girl's smock. The two wheels by the big window looking over the back garden. The soaring ceiling, the skylight John had opened. The large solid worktable, the stepping stool he'd balanced on its smooth pine surface and used to climb out on the roof. Nothing had changed. No one was there.

Back on the landing, Grace sat on the top step and cried. The front door was still wide open. She'd left it on the latch, trip after trip, loading all that stuff in the car. She must have forgotten to lock it – a breeze had blown it open. She was going a bit mad in the house on her own. Now she'd lock up – properly this time. Grace pushed the door shut. She screamed as the expanse of wall behind it was revealed. A message was scrawled there, in deranged felt-tip capitals: YOU KNOW WHAT YOU DID YOU CUNT.

2.

SHE WAS A solo diner and middle-aged. The young waiter couldn't conceal his dismay. 'I'll have the roast,' Grace told him.

'And wine?'

'Red. The shiraz. A bottle.' Grace huddled at her small table and anatomised her terror. Her home had been violated, that was the first thing. Second, of course – the C word. Grace's upbringing had been almost laughably patrician, at least until the age of sixteen. But she was not, and had never been, an innocent. This was Australia; the language was pungent. Her husband had been a trade union leader, for God's sake. The C word had been in the air he breathed and the water he swam in. Still it cleaved her like a blunt axe. YOU KNOW WHAT YOU DID YOU CUNT. Yes, Grace knew. But – the ghastliest question – who else did?

A memory rose to the surface, the day they found John's body. 'You did this,' Sophie screamed. They were not formally estranged, Grace and her daughter. They were distant, yes. And there was a silence between them. But wasn't that the nature of sudden bereavement and grief? Surely Sophie wouldn't write that message? A moan of horror escaped from Grace's lips. Next to her, a young couple looked up from their plates. 'Ahh!' Grace turned the noise into a yawn. 'Exhausted, sorry!' She dug

11

in her bag to hide her burning face. With shaking hands, she dialled Toby's number. Once again, he didn't answer.

Grace and her son had always been close. She'd dreamt of him for years before he finally came into the world, slightly premature, tiny, perfect. His asthma bothered him a lot when he was little, and – Grace closed her eyes; she could feel the weight of him now – they'd spent so many nights sitting upright together in the beanbag in the corner of his room, the only way she could make sure he kept the nebuliser on, his tiny chest rattling next to hers. She wondered for a moment if she was about to – hideously, and surely not? – burst into tears. Allowing herself to feel a negative feeling was like cracking open Maggie Beer's burnt fig ice cream. Once she'd had one spoonful, why not the whole tub? That was why she no longer had ice cream in the fridge, and why she clamped down on her sadness. But everything in her life was going wrong at the same time.

'Roast beef?'

Grace gave the server a curt nod. The dining room chatter washed over her as she worked her way through her meal, far larger and meatier than anything she'd make for herself these days. Food was like sleep: one simply needed less. Of course, until last year, she'd thought the same of sex. There was a lovely rich taste in her mouth as she dabbed at her lips with the paper napkin. The static was back, her mind was nice and empty. She wasn't real, and neither were her surroundings. She signed her bill with a flourish and put away her credit card. She would do it; she would return to her terrifying house.

Outside the pub it was properly dark and properly raining, and wet punters jostled her as she stood uncertainly at the door.

'Grace!'

What now? So hard to focus in the light after she'd been staring into the dark.

'Grace!'

Laughing eyes, a pouty open mouth in a beard. 'Oh, Ned,' she said with relief, as her favourite neighbour rubbed her upper arm and shoulder.

'And it's me, darling,' said Ned's boyfriend, slipping his arm around her too.

'Oh, Brendan, still in your work shorts,' Grace said, more to show she was across the situation than anything else. 'You know, my late husband used to wear shorts like that. When he was a horny . . .' She drifted off, confused by the phrase that seemed to be at the tip of her tongue. Brendan laughed, and she was conscious of a glance travelling between the two boys, although they couldn't be boys really: they were old enough and rich enough to have bought the lovely terrace opposite ninety-nine, and they'd given the Clares a charming hamper filled with produce and cheese, all from Daylesford, where they lived most weekends, to say sorry – although no apologies were needed – for their spectacular renovations, which had been in *Belle* magazine. Of course, she wasn't 'the Clares' anymore. 'Horny-handed son of toil,' Grace landed in triumph.

'Actually,' Ned said, 'we were hoping to bump into you.'

'Ned had the anniversary in his diary,' Brendan said.

'Darlings, if you're here for your anniversary, don't let me interrupt you. I didn't realise this was a gay pub. Oh, it's called the Rainbow Hotel.' She gave a little laugh. 'Obviously!'

'We go to all sorts of places these days,' Brendan said brightly. 'Ah, look, that's what we need.' He picked up a stranger's black umbrella from the stand, pointed it outside and shook it open. 'Come on, tuck under here with me.'

They'd almost reached her front gate, having sung a bit of Carly Simon, when she noticed something new in front of the three-storey fawn brick apartment block next door. 'Oh, who's selling? It can't be Girl's mum, she's a tenant,' Grace said. 'But how odd, the auction's in a week.'

'Oh, yes, I know who it is,' Ned said. 'It's Anton.'

'Yes, it's Anton,' Brendan said, thrilling with gossip. 'The artist is present.'

Grace looked around wildly.

'We haven't seen him,' Ned said, shooting a *calm down* look at Brendan. 'But, yes, that's his flat for sale.'

Up close, the image on the For Sale sign was as bald and glamourless as a crime scene photograph, but even the wide lens and clinically bright lighting couldn't diminish the beauty and simplicity of Anton's living room. Huge windows. Lovely low wood shelves. And the work, of course, arranged just so by Anton's large, gentle hands. She spoke in a child's wondering voice. 'So did he come back?'

'Anton? No,' Ned said. 'Brendan saw the agent, didn't you, Bren? Anton's sent his instructions from *wherever*. To sell the flat, and in a hurry.'

'So he wasn't here.' Grace hadn't missed him. He simply hadn't come.

'Sorry,' Ned said.

'God, I don't care!' Grace laughed. 'I just pray we get someone quiet! God knows who we'll get! Well, here we are.' They were at her front gate.

Brendan extended an exploratory hand. 'The rain's stopped.' He folded the umbrella and shook it at the camellias.

'Kind Brendan.' Grace leaned forward for a kiss on both cheeks. 'So nice of you to drop me home, and on your anniversary.' Ned's face grew watchful. 'Oh no,' Grace said. 'Did I ruin a surprise? But Brendan!' Grace hit him lightly on the arm. 'You *said*, Brendan. Ned had it in his diary.'

'Oh, beautiful.' Brendan cocked his head. 'That's why I love him, you know. He remembers things. It's not our anniversary. It's the day John died, isn't it? Exactly this time last year.'

She hadn't realised. Where had she been a year ago? In her big old empty house, alone. John on some slab somewhere. Maybe that explained her madness, why she'd felt so driven to make contact with her son. A phrase she'd read somewhere: 'The body never forgets.'

'What's that, darling?' Ned spoke with a special alertness. Had she said it out loud?

'That's why we were so glad to see you.' Brendan's forehead crinkled with concern. 'Will you be okay? Here on your own?'

She has no one now – she has no one. 'I'll be absolutely fine.' Grace slipped away and rushed up the path. 'You, on the other hand.' She turned at the front door and waved at the umbrella. 'You're in possession of stolen property! Back to the pub with you this instant!'

Their laughter and goodnights faded as she closed the front door. 'Here I am,' she announced to the hallway. 'Alone again!' She didn't need a light; she'd lived in the house for almost forty years. Anyway, if she didn't see the scrawled accusation, she could pretend it didn't exist. What was vital was that she sleep. She had a vision of the blackness John must have experienced, as he tumbled from on high into the depths below. At what point did the blackness come? She remembered teetering on the steps the day before. What would have happened if she'd just . . . let herself go? A broken ankle, that's what. Silly woman!

She was in the bedroom now, on John's side of the bed. She pulled open his top drawer. They weren't there. She felt as annoyed with him as if he were alive. But she knew he had them; she hadn't thrown them out. She went into his study – the treatment room, as it used to be. There they were, stashed in the desk, multiple blister packs of Temazepam, each with only one or two pills remaining. She gathered some saliva in her mouth to take one but the red wine had left her spitless. In the bathroom she gulped at the tap, popped two pills in her mouth and swallowed them. She put on her nightdress, lay on her bed and waited. Since when did she have a ceiling fan? It spun closer and closer. She wasn't asleep. She'd never sleep again.

She wriggled to the side of the bed, rolled off and hit the floor at a crouch. She went into the study on her hands and knees this time, and took three or four or however many more tablets and put them in her mouth – maybe six, or eight or something. When Toby was little she hadn't allowed him treats; there was that Easter hunt when he'd stuffed himself, his mouth entirely filled with those small eggs, the cheap ones made of compound chocolate, all of them still with the wrappers on. But where was Toby now?

'Dash, dash, time to dash!' she hummed to herself as she skied in thick snow to the bathroom. She let water trickle in around the chewed-up pill powder; she choked them down and sluiced out her mouth with more water; she made sure every last piece of bitter dust sank down into her throat. That ought to do it! Some fresh air, it would do her good. She thrust open the window and leaned out into the cold. Oh, there was the spot! The spot they found her husband's body. YOU KNOW WHAT YOU DID YOU CUNT. She did, she did know. He'd died because of her.

3.

TURTLE POPPED HER head into the room and coyly arched her back and tail against the doorframe. 'Do you want a pat, then, mookie-mook?' Toby said in his high-pitched and deeply private talking-to-cats voice. Turtle ran over to his legs and wove around them. Toby picked her up and soared her over his head. 'Patting time, pookie-wookie, patting time, Turtle-cat.' He zoomed her over to the single bed in Helen's spare room and lay down. Vibrating with purrs, Turtle draped herself across his neck.

The anniversary of his dad's death, and all weekend his phone had been alive with missed calls from his mum, calls he'd watched but couldn't bring himself to answer. He wished he could rush down there, could selflessly give her what she needed from him, that he could be strong for her. Or, actually, maybe she would prefer that he cried? And she could be strong for *him*. Could he cry? He missed his dad and yearned to properly grieve for him. When he thought of the word 'grief' an image flashed into his mind from *Harry Potter* – Harry gazing into the Mirror of Erised, his dead parents looking back. Other people's grieving was noble; Toby's grief was wrong. The last time he'd seen his dad was when it all kicked off at uni, and the two were tangled up in his mind.

Toby had met his mother's oldest enemy only once before he called her from college in disgrace. Immediately they'd struck

17

a deal. He could live with Helen rent free in her small house in Campbell on two conditions. First, he had to be useful in the hospice where she was the long-serving General Manager. On the first day she led him into her office, papered on three sides with Thank You cards and children's drawings. 'This is the Jolly Trolley.' Helen kicked a metal cart with her foot. 'Around ten each morning, put out all the tea stuff and biscuits. If we're running low on the nice ones, use the petty cash to get more. People want the biscuits with filling when they're feeling low, not plain. At four, take all the biscuits off and put this on.' She opened a cupboard under a bookcase to reveal an Aladdin's cave: bottles of vodka and gin and beer and fizzy drinks and wine, huge untidy heaps of potato chips and nuts and crackers. 'Chill the beer and white wine first, obviously. Use the kitchen fridge. Offer it to all the families in the waiting room. If a patient wants one, go for it. They're in charge here.'

Initially Toby had been relieved he wouldn't be changing bedpans. Then he started to feel like a dick. It might be the last day someone spent with their family. How could he interrupt it to offer a tea? But everyone was so glad to see him – he began to like it. There was a cancer kid in Kookaburra, her treatment options had run out. The dad arrived after work every day to spend an hour with the dying girl. The mum left them to it and sat by the lake. One day Toby pushed the Jolly Trolley right out across the grass and she'd smiled for the first time. 'Hit me with a gin and tonic. No, stay there.' She knocked it back. 'One more,' she said. 'Then *my ex* has to go home to his *new family*.' He mixed it up. She drank it. 'FUCK,' she screamed at the lake. 'All right, time to head in. Thanks, Toby. No really, thanks.' She went back into the hospice. Toby pushed the trolley slowly after her.

One day an old guy was sitting on a big stone by the back door. Toby asked him if he was okay. 'Just trying to light a ciggie,' the man said.

'Hold on.' Toby ran into Helen's office. 'That old guy from Lorikeet wants me to light his cigarette.'

'Lawrence? Light it, then, for God's sake,' Helen said. He ran back and lit it, and Lawrence became his friend. Toby was busy and useful at the hospice. It was ten minutes' drive along the lake from the ANU campus, but felt like another world. It was safe. He couldn't afford to second-guess the morality of seeking shelter with his mum's historic rival. That was Helen's second condition: not saying a single word to Grace. He couldn't break his promise – anyway, he didn't want to. If his mother found out about Astrid and why he'd left college, his life wouldn't be worth living.

He stared uselessly at his phone. Someone needed to check on his mum, that was for sure. But did it really have to be him? His sister hadn't had a mobile phone since she blew up her entire life and job the year before. He could call Sam? But he'd never felt that comfortable with Sophie's terminally cheerful boyfriend. Even at the funeral, he'd tried to make everyone laugh.

'Oh!' Toby exclaimed. The cat jumped up and turned her tail to him in annoyance. 'Sorry, Turtle-cat, sorry.' There was at least one person back home who'd drop everything to look after Grace. He could be responsible for his mother without having to see her himself. Perfect. He scrolled through his contacts and composed a message to Geraldine Green.

4.

As an early reader with a long concentration span, Girl Green had skipped prep and gone straight into grade one, so she'd been just ten years old when called upon to make decisions about her high school education. 'I wish you could go to my school,' Girl's dad told her growing up. He taught at a Marist Brothers boys secondary in Coburg. 'Cut your hair short, Geraldine. I'll smuggle you in. Show those boys what real intelligence looks like.' But, as she got older, he stopped saying it, and by the end of her time at primary school he was barely speaking to her or her mother, Belinda. Girl investigated Parkville High herself and arranged to take the entrance exams. On the basis of her results she was invited to join the Accelerated Learning program, the best the state offered. Her father didn't leave on the day she told him – that would have been too neatly symbolic. Instead, a month or so later, he took the job as boarding house head in a Marist school in Queensland. As if starting high school and becoming a child of divorce weren't destabilising enough, her part-time bookkeeper mother revealed an insane and completely random secret ambition to join Victoria Police. The two of them had vacated Girl's grandmother's home in Coburg and moved to the tiny flat in Greeves Street. Belinda started her training at the Glen Waverley academy, and Girl began grade seven at Parkville High, skinny knees knocking in her daggy new Clarks.

Grace would never have remembered the first time they met, but Girl did. She'd knocked on the door to sell Parkville High raffle tickets. 'You're a neighbour?' Grace had asked. 'Which house exactly?'

'The flats next door,' Girl squeaked.

Grace's reply: 'Poor you.' How Girl flushed and stung. Grace dug through her bag at the hall table and offered Girl twenty dollars. As she filled out the stubs, a boy descended the stairs. He was tall, stoop-shouldered, spotty and thin. Grace looked over her reading glasses. 'Don't forget the recycling, Toby-love.' He sighed and stumped down the hall. Grace turned back, her pen poised. 'How many of these do I have to fill out?' Twenty dollars would buy twenty tickets. 'You can do the rest for me,' Grace said. Girl rushed home to copy out, fifteen times more: GRACE CLARE, 99 GREEVES STREET, and as she wrote the name and address her connection to the Clare family grew until she almost felt she owned them.

Soon the rhythms of the Clare family were more real to Girl than her own. John inching the Saab out of the car spot, track marks from the comb still in his wet hair. The days Toby came home late from school and in his cross-country kit. When Grace did her big shop at Piedimonte's and when – later – she started going to pottery. Summer was good because she could see them in the garden. Winter was good because the night came early. 'Why are you sitting in the dark?' Girl's mum said once, returning unexpectedly from work. Girl had leapt up from her bed. Belinda walked over and stared out of the window that ran the length of Girl's room. Across the high fence, the Clares' master bedroom was lit up like a stage. Toby was picking his chin zits in the large wardrobe mirror. 'They need to keep their curtains shut,' Belinda said.

'Yes,' Girl agreed. 'I'd just noticed the same thing.'

Her mother must have thought she had a crush on Toby. But it wasn't like that. From selling raffle tickets she moved on to kerbside chats. From kerbside chats to being encouraged to borrow books, from borrowing books to being invited for tea and cake – somehow she'd stepped out of her own life and into the Clares'. So when she woke up to Toby's text on Monday morning, she felt a sudden paradoxical wave of dejection and exclusion. Girl didn't have to be *asked* to look after Grace. She was family.

Before school, Girl stood in the middle of Greeves Street and took in the formal beauty of number ninety-nine. The perfect white-painted brick. The elegance of the filigree lacework on the balcony and the verandah. The cleverness of the top-floor studio extension, hardly visible from the street behind the tall decorative parapet. The semicircle of stained glass over the glossy black front door. Upstairs, the three windows along the front top-floor room were blank, the blinds pulled down. Maybe Grace wasn't home? Girl leapt up the steps and knocked a deferential knock. She arranged her feet so they were mainly on the black tiles. Then she arranged them so they were mainly on the white. After a full minute she rang one short peal of the bell. No sound at all from inside. She glanced back towards the street. The Saab was in its normal spot. Perhaps Grace had set off early and walked somewhere. One school holiday, the Clare family had gone to Italy for three weeks. Girl had been left blissfully in charge, picking up the mail and watering the plants. Even now she carried the key with her at all times, still on Grace's long leather strap. She slipped it into the lock and turned it.

'Grace!' Her voice echoed in the stillness. Licensed by Toby's text, Girl couldn't resist going inside. During that luxurious three-week proprietorship she'd uncapped all the bottles under the sink, searching for the base note of the house's distinctive smell. It was linseed oil, and Girl loved it still – she wanted to throw herself on her knees to breathe it in from the floorboards. Instead she stroked the bannister of the staircase where it ended in its tight little spiral. The ornate plasterwork high above her was called 'coving'. Those bits under the arch were called 'corbels'. Girl had added all of these details to the bookmarks folder she kept for when she would one day have her own home. She dropped her backpack at the foot of the stairs and turned to go into the library – she jumped in surprise when she saw a scrawled message: YOU KNOW WHAT YOU DID YOU CUNT. Big black letters. Who did this? She shuddered to think of Grace's day being hijacked by it, of the horror she must have felt, the fact she had no one but Girl to look after her, and that she hadn't said a word to her about it. There was no point trying to clean it away. It would have to be painted over in the same smoky grey-green as the rest of the hall. The scrawled obscenity was so shocking it went past scary and became bracing. It was with a straightened back and a lightness of step that she made her way into the library.

Girl tried to view it as an outsider would. A giant sofa bisected the large front sitting room. Behind it stood a table covered with pictures in heavy silver frames. Young adult John, shirtless on a beach, cooking a fish over an open fire. Grace with Princess Diana hair and a baby draped in crochet. Grace and

23

John stiffly posed in black tie. The pictures of Sophie as a child were very *Who* magazine: STARS BEFORE STARDOM. Toby looked sweet and hesitant in his pictures, sometimes a bit unfortunate. Only by grade twelve had he seemed fully formed, even handsome. Girl could remember when the photo of him playing tennis had joined the collection. None had been added since. Girl turned the table lamp on – Grace didn't believe in overhead lighting – and the walls glowed a golden mustard. Angled in conversation with both the sofa and the fireplace were two beautiful chintz armchairs. One was so old that a sort of linen sheath had been tucked around its frayed seat. Both were strewn with balding jewel-toned velvet cushions. Each had a side table for a book or drink. Hip-height bookcases ringed the room. Inside them: books. Above them: art. Over the fire was an oil painting of shapes arranged in a stand-off or confrontation. Girl had tried searching for it online: 'large abstract oil white grey four lonely objects Australian'. (All the Clares' art was Australian; she knew that.) She substituted 'people' for 'objects' and still didn't find anything. One day Grace would explain it to her. Girl leaned over the back of the sofa and laid her cheek briefly against the headrest. She supposed a stranger could find all this slightly forbidding and exclusive. But *she'd* been welcomed in. *She'd* been given the key.

Girl turned off the lamp and continued her prowl along the hallway. Under the stairs was the storage space crammed with boxes, and next to it the small bathroom. The door to the second reception was locked because Grace and her architect had 'done a little trick with it'. Girl burst into the cavernous kitchen and living area and – she couldn't help it – spread her arms out and twirled. The library was special, but *this* was something else. Grace had done it in the nineties, 'bashed out the back' and extended into the garden. Light poured in from the floor-to-ceiling windows and through the huge, double-height French doors. The left-hand side had another massive sofa facing the TV, and the big family dining table. The right-hand side was Girl's favourite place in the whole world. She did her homework up at the kitchen island as Grace cooked; she ate dinner there if it was offered, soups and pasta and Grace's warm salads. From the kitchen you could turn back towards the front of the house and enter what Grace called 'the utility'. The first architect had so disagreed with the utility that Grace had sacked him; Girl heard all about it. He'd wanted the two receptions to be gutted and merged into one vast room that led into a kitchen and dining area. Instead, Grace had kept them separate: the front reception became the library. The back, with its new entrance from the kitchen, became the private engine of the entire home. It had the complex rubbish-sorting system, the recycling, and the small bin Grace emptied every night into the compost. It was part pantry – preserved lemons, anchovies, big screw-top jars of pulses, tinned tomatoes – and part laundry, with a long bench over two washing machines and a dryer, and plenty of space for baskets. The dishwasher and the main double sink were in the kitchen, but there was a sink in the utility for hand-washing. It was also where Grace arranged her flowers, and vases and bowls were lined up two deep on the shelves above. Inhaling deeply, Girl could smell coffee, the parsley spray Grace used for surfaces, the garlic and onions in their basket. Below the big central table were two pallets of newspaper-wrapped quinces collected from the backyard tree. Natural light came in through the open door to the kitchen but, with its thick stone floors, it remained, even in the height of summer, as cool as a Victorian larder.

It was here in the utility that Girl had been stationed for that life-changing Christmas party. When her mother left for her afternoon shift, Girl donned a waiter's black skirt and white shirt. For hours she followed Grace's instructions about ice, lemon wedges, platters, little bowls for olive pips, glasses of one shape or another.

Girl's English teacher, Mr Wallace, had once taken her aside and complimented her analysis of *Pride and Prejudice*. 'You're very perceptive about men and women,' he said. Girl's best friend Millie had *screamed* when Girl told her, and to this day they could make each other cry laughing by putting on a dumb deep voice and saying 'perceptive'. But he'd been right. If there was a subtext, Girl noticed it. Most of the time she couldn't do anything with the knowledge; outside of her mind and her bedroom and her best friendship with Millie she was shy and fairly awkward. But she noticed things: looks, blushes, evasion, *vibes*. She'd seen the way Grace lit up when Anton arrived at the party. She caught the interest that ran between them like a current.

When Grace gave her a hundred and twenty dollars for her help at the party, she spent it on classes at Anton's studio – open classes in the evening, *not* the classes for young people he ran after school. She liked pottery, the way the clay felt natural on her skin. Soon she had a wheel that was 'Girl's wheel', and Anton never again mentioned her having to pay. The trio met up almost every afternoon, first at Johnston Street Pottery and then, when it was built, in Grace's huge, beautiful studio at the top of ninety-nine. 'The apprentice', Grace and Anton called Girl. It had been hard to think of a more perfect life, only possible because Girl's mother worked from 3 pm till at least eleven.

'Mum, remember I wasn't supportive when you joined the police?' Girl asked one day.

'I remember,' Belinda replied dryly.

'Well, I *am* now, and I'm sorry,' Girl said.

Upstairs, the hush and industry of art. Downstairs, the warmth and intimacy of family life: Toby sprawled on the sofa reading a book for school that Girl had already read for fun; John highlighting documents or pacing round the garden on his phone. She teased him for his slow typing. He tried out bits of speeches on her. It was exactly how literature had led her to believe her life should be. In those lovely fertile hours between school and midnight, she ceased being Geraldine Green, by now fourteen, and became someone altogether new: 'My fairy godfamily,' she called the Clares to Millie, who didn't understand.

'Why are your school shoes covered in dust?' her mother asked, but didn't seem to care about the answer.

Suddenly she was overtaken by a physical longing for the pottery studio. She couldn't go there five days a week for months and then *never* go there again. She ran down the hallway and up the old stairs but, when she reached the blonde oak and glass of the new open-tread staircase, her mind filled overwhelmingly with horror. That Saturday morning a year ago – even Girl's mother heard Sophie's screams. Groggy from her night shift, she rushed into Girl's bedroom thinking it was her. They knelt on Girl's bed and craned to see over the fence. Sophie lolled back in Sam's arms as he dragged her heels through the wet grass. Grace stumbled on the patio, retching. Girl's mother made one of her split-second switches from dead-eyed to keen, putting her coat on over her pyjamas and rushing next door to help. Girl followed her mother to ninety-nine. Poor, *poor* Grace. She sat like a statue on the sofa. Outside, her husband dangled from the fence, dead. God, it was horrible. Police cars and vans and medical guys. The officers conducting their fingertip search in the garden. The palpable change of energy when the note was discovered in John's pocket and it became a suicide rather than a crime scene.

Girl stood at the foot of the new stairs, breathing hard. No, she wouldn't go up there. She just couldn't. As she turned to leave, something struck her as wrong about the bathroom. Why was the light on? Grace never wasted electricity. Girl hated that about her mother, but admired it about Grace. Grace did it because she cared about the environment. Her mother worried about it because she was *poor*. Girl was still thinking this over when she entered the bathroom and saw the pool of blood and Grace's sprawled limbs and closed eyes and the in-and-out of her ragged breaths. 'Help,' Girl screamed. 'Help!'

5.

THE GUIDELINES PATRICK used to organise his crime fiction were as idiosyncratic and strict as he was. Agatha Christies, for example, weren't filed under 'C'. Instead they were Tetris-stacked alongside Allinghams, Marshes and Dorothy L. Sayers in an elegant carved oak bookcase labelled: THE QUEENS. Sophie had unlocked the shop on Monday morning to find a note taped above seven towers of second-hand paperbacks: *Dear Sophie – Please do shelve the new acquisitions if you have time. My Saturday shift was not busy. Even so, there are GAPS. All my very best, P.* 'Gaps!' Patrick always called after a few sales in a row. 'Gaps, gaps!' Every book in the shop had to sit square against the edge of the shelf with no spaces in between. It was the rule.

The covers of the second-hand volumes were marked by grubby adhesive from old torn-off price stickers. She dabbed a cloth with eucalyptus oil and buffed the residue away. Apart from the small loft space, there was no storage in the shop, and multiples of each book had to be stashed on the shelf behind the display copies. The new pile contained four copies of *The Moonstone* in different jackets. Sighing, Sophie took down every book from HISTORICAL and separated out VICTORIAN. From VICTORIAN she separated out SHERLOCK HOLMES and moved it to its own overflow section, which she labelled carefully in Patrick's elegant lettering, knowing that, even if he agreed to the new location, he would definitely rewrite the sign himself. By three, every shelf was dusted and every section neatly shelved. She collapsed onto the built-in seat under the elegant arched window overlooking Little Collins Street, where she could see the world going by but no one could see her. It was like being a child, making a den for herself in her parents' wardrobe. *No one knows where I am*, she thought back then, happily. *No one knows where I am*, she thought sadly now. But that was the choice she'd made to keep herself safe. Safe from the real world, where she constantly fucked up. Safe from the internet, where enemies still massed. Besides, the person she most wanted to speak to wasn't around. The shop phone rang, startling her.

'The Unique Crime.'

'Sophie, it's me. Patrick,' Patrick added.

Sophie smiled at the sound of his voice. 'I know!'

'You saw my note?'

'I've done it! All of them.'

'I knew you would. Well done. I've got some post, if you don't mind . . .'

'No, of course.' She'd worked at the Unique Crime since her first year of university. She'd always loved Patrick's courtesy, and how it enabled her own. 'Lock the shop and do it now, you mean? Or wait till you come back?'

'Just sometime before you leave. You'll have to close up tonight, I'll be out for the rest of the day.'

No afternoon tea together, then. No cosy chats. She hung up the phone with a sigh. Next to the shop computer were three parcels of books, securely wrapped in brown paper and addressed in her boss's trademark hand. Sophie leaned over for them. Her fingers brushed the mouse. With a tick and a whir, the computer screen burst into life – bright, blank, expectant. She fled down the narrow staircase and double-locked the door.

After the post office Sophie wandered up Little Bourke. As she waited to cross Swanston Street, a woman jostled and thrust past her to the very front of the crowd. Sophie stared at her thick brown ponytail. There was a very fine icing-sugar dusting of dandruff on the collar of her expensive black coat. The woman glanced up the street to gauge whether it was safe to cross. A smooth cheek, a strong nose. Sophie's insides corroded with instant knowledge. The lights changed and Tessa Notaras strode towards Chinatown. Without a second thought, Sophie fell in behind her.

No need to practise any spycraft, or even stealth. Single-minded Tessa stormed past restaurant windows, languid grey fish listing in their silt-filled tanks. Before Russell Street she took a left into an alley. No other pedestrians were picking their way past anonymous door grilles, milk crates and stacked garbage. Even so, Sophie didn't worry about being seen. Actually, she thought – walking more confidently, narrowing the distance between them – maybe it would be good if Tessa *did* see her. Life-ruining Tessa Notaras, acting as though nothing had happened! For the first time in a year Sophie felt the ghost of an old longing, an addict's craving for a showdown, a bust-up, to place herself in front of Tessa's focused frown and demand she be acknowledged, to challenge her, take her on, and – then what? Tessa emerged on Lonsdale Street and took a chance on a break in traffic. On the other side of the road Tessa disappeared into the tallest, shiniest corporate building on Lonsdale Street. Sophie was left trembling on the kerb. The revolving doors turned. The former mistress of Sophie's dead dad was gone.

Back at the shop Sophie sat behind the desk and reached for the mouse. She drove it like a toy car until the computer screen came alive. A year since she'd been online – now she clicked on the browser and watched the little icon bounce. She typed in her dad's name. 'John Clare death', Google autocompleted. 'John Clare suicide'. There it was, the third result: 'John Clare Tessa Notaras'. The photo came up. Her hair had been longer back then; it tumbled loose over her shoulder. Sophie's dad was standing behind her, his chin resting on the crown of her head. Tessa was pressing one of his hands high on her chest. Sophie had a horrible thought and raised her palm to her own chest to check. Yes, his hand was on Tessa's heart. Sophie clicked the link underneath and was taken to the *Herald Sun*'s article. 'WE FOUND HIM. Dummy-spit union boss fled to love nest,' the headline read. 'CLARE PACKAGE,' the photograph was captioned. 'John Clare, 57, relaxes in the arms of his mistress, Tessa Notaras. The Labor candidate for Melbourne went to ground after an historic election loss.' The publication date was Saturday, 28 August 2010.

A year ago, almost to the day. The garden of her childhood home. Sam's fury, her mother shoving the newspaper in her face and shaking it. The smell of warm keys and copper coins. Something had clicked; she stumbled across the grass. She found her father's body, his head on a pike like a warning. She screamed and screamed, not knowing what she screamed. Her mother opened her arms, but it was a helpless gesture, not a comforting one. Instead of falling into them, Sophie pushed her away. 'You did this,' she shouted, until Sam dragged her back. 'You did this!' Now she wanted to scream it at Tessa, to Melbourne at large, to the whole of Australia and *the world*. Sophie's dad was dead. Someone would have to fucking pay. Her chest was a wall of ice; she was trembling. She reached for the shop phone and dialled Sam's mobile. 'Possum Magic,' Sam crooned in a soft voice. He must be alone.

'Ahh!' She let her exclamation draw on and on to cover the sound of her erasing the search history. She closed the browser and put the computer to sleep.

'Ahh!' Sam made the same cosy warm noise back.

'I don't suppose you'd like a cup of tea with me in the shop?'

'Poss, I can't.' His voice changed. 'I'm just popping back up to the office.'

'What have you been doing?'

'What do you mean?'

She knew it was annoying but she couldn't help it. 'You said you'd just come back. Where had you been?'

'I was doing a coffee run.'

'Lucky for some.'

'Soph! You have the same amount of money to spend as me.'

'I know, I know,' she said. 'Sorry, Sammy.'

'That's all right, Possy.'

She smiled at his concession, the warmth that risked being overheard. She chanced a favour. 'I could walk up and get a lift with you later?'

'It might be a late one tonight, Poss. Sorry.'

The evening stretched ahead of her, terrifying in its freedom and lack of supervision. 'So do you want me to bring you something? After work?'

Sam gave a cheery laugh. 'Imagine how bad that would look! My girlfriend drops round with my dinner!' (It was fine for his girlfriend to cook dinner at home.) 'Anyway, work will pay for something.'

There was nothing more to say. In the year since her father died, she'd been down every avenue with Sam. They all ended with a giant red stop sign. The silence dragged on. 'It's just that I keep wondering,' Sophie began.

'*Sophie*,' Sam said. 'You can't solve something that isn't a crime.'

'But why can't I still wonder why?'

'I love you.' Sam's tone was kind and final. 'I'll see you later on.'

'I love you,' she said, but he'd hung up.

Sophie stood up from the desk, her eyes closed, and backed out into the safety of the stacks. It had taken her ages but she'd learnt to read again – to immerse herself in a Sherlock Holmes or a P.D. James, to follow precisely drawn characters through their bewilderment, grief and lust for revenge, their fictional worlds a tidy matchbox diorama of her own, less manageable, life. The mysteries that lined the walls took her all around the world, whisking her along the sturdy railway tracks of plot – always in the known, safe, mapped universe of genre. Detective fiction brought clarity to confusion and order to chaos. Sophie longed for clarity and order so badly she could cry. But she'd ruined everything. She'd let the internet into the shop. Her thoughts twitched and scattered. She couldn't read. She couldn't stay there. If only she could live her life as characters in crime novels did. When confronted by a mystery, they didn't lie down and give up. Their minds weren't clouded by apprehension; their bodies weren't rigid with fear.

Instead – was this the key? – they *did things*. Struck out, investigated, asked questions. That was the difference between books and real life. Detectives took action.

Sophie flipped the Closed sign and locked up the shop. She'd never done anything like this with Patrick, never left early or fucked him over. Despite all her hard work, maybe she was still that girl of a year ago. Maybe she'd never be good. But as she strode back to the headquarters of Australia's largest mining company, it was with a new sense of purpose. Fears and worries emptied out of her mind, leaving her only calmly certain. Compared with stalking her online, waiting for Tessa on the street was like nothing.

Through the revolving doors was the lobby, shining and cavernous. A neon logo glowed, two dynamic squiggles and the name of the company: TRAVALLION. Across the marble chasm was a long reception desk. Next to it were turnstiles, unlocked by swipe cards. Two uniformed guards stood watch as businesspeople flowed constantly in and out of a bank of lifts. There was no sign of her quarry. Sophie leaned against the glass shopfront of a bank as the afternoon grew colder and darker. Suddenly she was accosted by a penguin.

'Ocean sanctuaries now,' the man in the costume cried. 'Leave fossil fuels in the ground!' Commuters zigzagged to avoid him. 'Extreme weather will change everything!' A small girl approached and stared. 'Save my home? The Antarctic!' The girl's mother hustled her on. The man sprang towards Sophie, beaming. 'You care about all this, don't you?' He waved his literature. 'Global warming?'

Sophie smiled politely. 'Of course.'

'And did you see the video on YouTube? From earlier this year?'

Just hearing the word YouTube sent her heart racing. 'I don't watch YouTube.'

'Millions of views.' His hands emerged from slits in his wings. He swiped his thumb across the screen of his iPhone. Sophie made Sam keep his phone on silent. The sound of this one unlocking made her shiver. 'Here, look.' The video was filmed from the third or fourth floor of a building. A roiling brown river surged powerfully up to and suddenly across a line of parked cars. 'Guys,' someone said offscreen. 'Should we shift our cars?' The person filming didn't move. 'It's too late,' came their slightly louder reply. First a single four-wheel drive and then another rushed past, bobbing like rubber ducks. One by one the parked cars were sucked into the khaki torrent. 'My fucking *car*,' someone screamed.

'Toowoomba, January 2011,' the penguin said. 'Flash flooding, four people died.' His hands disappeared back into his wings. How long since Sophie had last held an iPhone? The YouTube interface looked different. The penguin misunderstood her frown. 'Yes, very crazy, very scary. More and more common. Is this the kind of world you want? The kind of future for your kids?'

'I'm twenty-five,' she scoffed. 'I don't have kids.' The revolving doors spun. Would Tessa recognise Sophie if she saw her?

Sensing her distraction, the penguin spoke urgently. 'It won't just be your kids' problem. It'll be yours. We're looking at life-altering changes to the environment in your generation. More flash floods, extreme weather, bushfires, drought. The biggest burden placed on the people who can least afford it – the poor, the global south.' Sophie had no money, but she wasn't poor. Forest Hill was remote, but it wasn't the global south. As for Toowoomba, she'd never been there in her life. 'With a small regular monthly donation you could make an enormous difference,' the penguin said. 'Imagine knowing you didn't have to think about any of this. Your money hard at work fighting climate change, while you just go about your life –'

'Oh, yes,' Sophie said gratefully. 'How much?'

She crouched and filled in the form with one eye on the exit. The penguin's attention wandered, looking for his next mark. The revolving doors turned and Tessa emerged. Sophie ducked her head and let her hair fall across her face like a curtain. 'Where are you headed?' the penguin called. Tessa ignored him. 'You care about global warming, don't you? Hey!'

Tessa wheeled around, her eyes bright with fury. 'Get a job!' Her expensive coat billowed as she headed for the top end of town.

6.

JOHN, JOHN'S DEATH, the past – Tessa Notaras had *no* time for it. The whole point of being a strategist was to get paid to think about the future. The whole point of work was to fill up the time she would otherwise spend on feelings. But as she rushed home from Travallion, Tessa plummeted deep into the sinkhole of her memory.

In 2004 she and her best friend Yasmin had embarked on what she'd thought would be a 'road trip around the US'. They'd saved four thousand dollars each from their graduate jobs in the Victorian public service. On their first night in Vermont, Yasmin met a guy. Rental car returned, Tessa moved onto Yasmin's new boyfriend's couch and Yas moved into his room. The guy reserved every sleeping hour for Yas. Every waking hour he worked for Democratic presidential hopeful Howard Dean. If Yas wanted to see him in daylight, she had to volunteer too. After a while, Tessa joined them. Soon she found herself engrossed in the pioneering online campaign. Driven young Americans rushed between meetings with open laptops balanced on their fingertips. They spoke in full sentences that ended not in question marks, but *periods*. Dean's inspiring presidential bid ended and so did Yasmin's relationship. Tessa's burgeoning new ambitions did not.

Back home John Howard had been Prime Minister for so long he seemed like part of the furniture. 'Liberal' elsewhere in the world meant 'bleeding-heart leftie'. In the 'Liberal Party of Australia' it meant the exact opposite: small government, big business, nuclear families. The economy had grown every year since Howard came into office. He promised to keep interest rates low and the country free from refugees and terrorists (in his eyes, one and the same). He'd won a fourth straight term in office as well as a surprise victory in the Senate. Unhampered by checks and balances, Howard brought in WorkChoices, a package of sweeping, revolutionary industrial relations changes. Suddenly bosses could undercut all the old rules about hours and pay simply by employing workers on individual contracts. They could just as easily un-employ them, sack them, without warning. Everyone in Australia suddenly learnt the word 'draconian' and they used it about WorkChoices. Not just unionists, bludgers, deadshits and slackers – everyone. The Labor opposition swore that if they won the election, due in 2007, they'd rip WorkChoices up. If Labor lost, Australia would be changed forever: its historically fair and reasonable workplace culture transformed into an American-style, winner-takes-all, dog-eat-dog dystopia. Over the Pacific Ocean, as Yasmin dozed in the plane seat next to her, Tessa made a vow. In some form or another, she would dedicate the next two years of her life to effecting John Howard's downfall.

It proved harder than she expected to find a job in party politics. After a few months pursuing false leads she saw an ad for the online director job at the Australian Council of Trade Unions. She'd heard of the ACTU before, obviously, but had to google it to make sure. Like the AFL-CIO the Dean guys went on about, it was the umbrella organisation for all the different trade unions in Australia. Although not formally part of Labor, it was affiliated to it – good enough. In her interview with Assistant Secretary Michael Hancock, Tessa finessed her time *around* the Dean campaign into a few months *on* it. Aged twenty-seven in 2005, Tessa was far too old to be 'social networking' on the internet, where anyone over the age of twenty-four was notably ancient and pathetic. Still, she showed Michael her Flickr and MySpace, carefully scrubbed of any wilder travel photos. 'This is what the ACTU should do,' she said fervently. 'Set one up for . . . um? God, sorry.' She'd forgotten John Clare's name. It was a miracle she got the job at all.

Tessa's new office was on the largely deserted top floor of the old ACTU headquarters in Swanston Street. A crack in the dirty window had been stabilised with duct tape. A giant grubby off-white PC took up most of the desk, keyboard discoloured from the previous user's hands. A mouse lay ball-up on a stained mousepad. Gingerly opening the desk drawer, she found dozens of boxes of medicated throat lozenges. She dumped them, shuddering, into the bin. After a second she pinched the edge of the mousepad and dropped it in too. What if the previous occupant had died in the office? At that point, halfway through 2005, the unions themselves appeared moribund. As she pondered her next move there came a discreet knock high up on the doorframe. In peered John Clare, eyebrows raised. In the four weeks between interviewing for the online director job and starting it, Tessa had paid more attention to him in the news. It was weird how he was called the ACTU 'Secretary', like he was Stalin, or in the Politburo. In photographs he appeared distracted or quizzical. He wasn't there to be *looked at*, he seemed to say. In interviews, his tone was invariably stern and courteous, unless he was presented with a silly point or invited to self-aggrandise. Then a lopsided smile crept onto his face, like Joey Potter from *Dawson's Creek*. And here he was, smiling at her in real life. 'Hello!'

Tessa did a stupid wave at waist height. 'Hi!'

'Yes, welcome, welcome.' John's gaze fixed briefly on the bin. Was he cross about the mouse mat?

'Thank you so much,' she gushed, to distract him. She stepped forward, though he hadn't initiated a handshake. 'I'm Tessa?'

'Yes, yes!' Their hands met and she made sure her grip was strong. 'Well,' he said, 'do you know where I can find more photocopy paper? I usually use the one downstairs, but . . .'

'Sorry! I'm new.'

'Of course! Well, welcome.'

He loped off like a Kings Cross ibis. All thoughts of changing her mind and running for the exits disappeared. In the weeks and months afterwards, she found herself mulling over their first encounter. How could she erase the ambiguous feelings generated by it and replace them in his mind, and hers, with something else? Something more positive, even enticing? The need to make a fresh impression became a craving. Of course, she should have realised. It was the first sign that she was falling in love.

The ACTU became her second home. Months passed, a year. John asked her about her holiday plans for Easter (she didn't have any). In the tea room, he consulted her opinion about *Australian Idol* (she didn't have one). Each time they spoke Tessa had the feeling of a spotlight being on her. When the spotlight turned off, her world went dark. Still, she was late to make the connection between her passion for work and her feelings for John Clare. Her job kept her *very* busy. From the moment the industrial relations reforms became law, the union movement astonished its enemies and itself by running a warm, slick, well-researched and well-resourced national campaign. Called 'Your Rights at Work', the campaign included paid advertising for the first time in the union movement's history. They set up on-the-ground activist groups in twenty-five targeted seats, and people actually *joined them*! John fronted huge rallies, his speeches carried live to marches in every major city and town. Thousands of supporters signed online petitions, donated online, fundraised. It was exactly the work Tessa had wanted for herself when she vowed, on the plane home from America, to make a difference.

In 2006 Labor discarded its loveable old leader, a jolly giant who'd lost twice, and installed in his place a duo of giggling young guns. The new top dog was Kevin Rudd, a moon-faced Christian nerd from rural Queensland. With his regular spot on breakfast television, he sidestepped Labor's factions and appealed directly to the public. His equally mould-breaking deputy was Julia Gillard, a red-haired, pointy-nosed, football-loving left-wing atheist former solicitor with a hairdresser boyfriend and no kids. Climate change was the greatest moral challenge of our time, Rudd said. A 'fork in the road' had been reached, and Australians had to choose between the future with him and more of the past with the man he respectfully called 'Mr Howard'. Rudd would ratify the Kyoto Protocol, apologise to the nation's ceaselessly fucked-over Indigenous people, get rid of WorkChoices and roll out a high-speed broadband network. Boom, the polls shot way up. All Labor and the unions had to do was keep their shit together till the election. Victory was within their grasp.

One weekend in late August 2007, Tessa was a guest speaker at a national activist training camp in Canberra. Her task was to teach trade unionists how to communicate with members of the public by email. She'd planned a detailed presentation about message framing, based on the George Lakoff book *Don't Think of an Elephant*, but was obliged to discard it and begin at the beginning. It was not advisable to start every missive 'Dear Comrade', she had to spell out. It was not a civilised contribution to the discourse to call the Prime Minister 'Little Johnnie'. 'But *arsehole's* fine, right?' some guy said, sparking round after round of complacent male laughter. By the last day the natural layer that separated her 'self' from the world had been destroyed. Her insides were empty and her self, if she even had one, floated on the outside like a ghost.

It was as Tessa waited in the long queue for the last flight to Melbourne that John Clare strode out of the airline lounge. He looked annoyed by the mass of travellers snaking through the terminal and then, when he saw Tessa, troubled. She summoned up the last vestige of her personality to greet him. A brief, startling current of understanding passed between them: the ugliness of the terminal, the frustration of the delay, the depletion of their spirits and how tiresome it was to travel for work on a Saturday. They shuffled up to the plane together and presented their boarding passes.

'Down the back on the right, thanks,' the flight attendant said briskly to Tessa. 'Welcome, Mr Clare,' he said to John. 'Can I take your jacket?'

Tessa waited for John to keep walking.

'Oh, this is me.' John gestured diffidently to a business class seat. 'Frequent Flyer points,' he explained.

Tessa raised her hand in farewell and trudged down the aisle to economy. 'Water?' she heard the flight attendant offer John. 'Or orange juice?' But as soon as she took her seat there was an announcement. 'Ladies and gentlemen, the captain speaking. Breach in security, I'm afraid. If we could ask you please to calmly disembark . . .' The rest was drowned by indignant moans. All the checked-in bags had been taken off and dumped. Everyone had to be rescanned and return to board again. It had been fine, exciting even, when 'breach in security' could mean a terror attack. Soon the word spread that someone had opened an airport emergency exit trying to have a smoke.

John digested this silently and ushered Tessa into the Chairman's Lounge, where the nation's largely male business and political leaders could be observed magnanimously chatting with rivals. Tessa swung her heavy backpack down and hung her parka on the back of a chair. Was it her imagination, or were people staring at her? As with all union merch, her t-shirt had only been available in men's size extra large. It was black, and emblazoned UNITED WE BARGAIN, DIVIDED WE BEG. John received a call and stalked off to answer it. Tessa went in search of the red wine she'd been craving all afternoon. What should she get John, pacing up and down on his phone? She guessed a gin and tonic. John swept over and snatched up the wine. Between calls, he returned to the table. 'What's that you've got there?'

'Gin and tonic?' She'd forced half of it down. Gin always made her want to cry.

'I'll have one of those next.' John's phone rang again and once more he wandered off.

Two years' worth of close observations swirled and coalesced into a new impression. Was it possible John Clare was a dick? Once, at the ACTU's new Queen Street office, Tessa had been lured into the tea room by the repeated chime of a spoon. She thought a speech was about to take place. Instead she found John's middle-aged personal assistant, alone, furiously stirring a cup of Lemsip. 'John likes the powder fully dissolved,' Ingrid explained. Fully dissolved! No one was worth pandering to like that. John Clare was a tall man with good politics, a nice voice, a full head of hair and some structure to his face. *Not* some kind of God.

Finally it became clear they wouldn't be flying that night. John didn't wait for the official announcement. 'Right! If we go now we can at least get a cab.' Tessa looked up at him, too tired to ask the question. 'There's no point hanging around,' he said gently. 'Come on, the union's paying.'

Half an hour later, keys in hand, they stood for a moment in the lobby of a modest hotel in Barton. 'What will you get up to, then?' John inquired, making it clear their evenings would diverge.

'I thought, get a burger from room service? Do some work? Play on the internet?'

'That's right. Web whizz.' John always referred to the internet as the web. 'Anyway,' he added, 'don't work too much, it's a Saturday night. Or if I *am* overworking you that much, please don't tell the media.' Tessa smiled. 'And if I don't see you, have a safe flight tomorrow.' Their obligations to each other were officially discharged.

The next morning Tessa woke to a pounding on her door. She grabbed the towel she'd laid over the accusing glow of the clock radio. Just after six. More knocking. 'Tessa?'

'Yes,' she said crossly, dragging on her jeans. 'I can hear you!'

John's face was haggard in the hallway's artificial light. 'I'm so sorry. It's not an emergency really.'

'What is it, then?' She felt like an idiot, with her messy hair and no make-up, swamped by her big union t-shirt in the stifling hotel.

'It's just that there's a . . . political situation.' She didn't move. 'That I was hoping you could help us with. I've got a suite, so we can talk in my work area.' His decisiveness made it more professional. They crossed into his room. It was a 'suite' in that there was a desk and a sofa at one end – but at the other end was his bed. The covers were pulled up, but more rumpled on the left side. Unused to sharing a bed, Tessa's had been rumpled in the middle. 'It seems *our candidate*,' John said bitterly, 'has got himself in some difficulties.' He went over to the desk and pulled the chair out for her to sit down. She moved the mouse and the swirling screensaver on his laptop disappeared, revealing an online news story. The headline read 'Kevin Rudd hits a strip club'. There was a photograph of the Labor leader underneath, baby-smooth face wincing in persnickety spectacles.

Kevin Rudd's hopes of becoming Prime Minister have been rocked by a visit to a New York strip club where he was warned against inappropriate behaviour during a drunken night while representing Australia at the United Nations. Mr Rudd yesterday issued a statement to *The Sunday Telegraph*, confirming he went to the club. But he said he could not recall what happened at the night spot because he had 'had too much to drink'.

'Oh, shit,' Tessa said. 'Oh, gross. That's a bit yuck. Hang on, this all happened four years ago – come on!'

John was looking over her shoulder. 'What do you think?'

'About what he did or how his chances will be affected?'

'Both.'

'It would be different if his wife didn't know. But we know from this article that she does. If she doesn't care, it's only bad if he touched up the dancers, wasted.'

'Okay. Andrew called me.' Tessa knew which Andrew he meant: Andrew, the Secretary of the Labor Party, in charge of the federal election campaign. 'He's organising some focus groups. But we wanted someone who could give us a more immediate sense of how it's playing. I thought of you.'

'You want me to monitor the reaction online.'

'Exactly.'

'That's no problem.' She scrolled down. The story had been published for six hours. Already there were a hundred and fifty-two comments. '*What a hypocrite,*' she read out. '*Preaches he's a Christian, and now this. How can you trust a man like that?*'

'Our whole campaign . . .' John muttered.

It was a relief for once to be calmer than someone else. 'Don't worry,' Tessa said. 'No one normal is up before dawn writing online comments.'

John appeared convinced. 'I'm going to find us some coffee,' he said. 'And I'll tell our friends' – he meant Labor – 'you're on the case.'

A few hours later they were in a cab to the airport. 'I saw your report.' John patted the bag between them on the car seat, presumably to indicate his laptop. 'Terrific. Concise. Strategic. So valuable.'

'And such great news,' Tessa said. 'About the strip club thing? It won't be a problem, and it might even be good!'

Should she tell him about her strictly apolitical brothers on Facebook? '*Krudd's got my vote, legend,*' Craig had written. Her other brother's status read: '*Cameron is . . . touching the dancers at Scores.*' No, maybe she wouldn't.

'Oh Tessa, I should have said – I hope this wasn't the wrong decision. You probably hate the thought of it. Well, anyhow.' She waited, intrigued by this new John, halting and stumbling. 'I've got more Frequent Flyer points than I could use in one lifetime. When I moved our flights, I put you up next to me. I hope that's okay, and – not an imposition.'

John's phone rang before she could reply. 'Hi, beautiful,' he answered warmly. Tessa turned away, her heart thumping. 'Have you spoken to Mum about it?' She turned back, hopeful. '*Sophie,*' John frowned. Thank God, his daughter. 'Sweetheart, if you knew Mum would be cross, why ask me? Do you think I'm some kind of pushover?' After a long pause, a smile spread over his face. 'These tricks don't work!' He rolled his eyes at Tessa. (Clearly whatever Sophie's tricks were, they were effective.) 'Sweetheart,' John concluded. 'I'm working. We'll have to talk about it later. In the meantime, just focus on your uni work, your thesis. I know! Just concentrate. Love you, bye-bye.' He hung up and drifted off into silence.

Later, strapped in side by side on the plane, John gazed at Tessa. 'How old are you?'

'Twenty-nine.'

'When do you think you became a woman?' Her surprise must have shown on her face. 'When did you feel grown up, like an adult?' he quickly clarified.

'Wow, well – I left home at eighteen, for uni,' she began.

'So did Sophie! But I just don't think – she just doesn't seem mature to me. If anything, she seems less mature now than at school.' John frowned past Tessa and out the window.

'Oh, I'm sure it's . . . Maybe the main difference is that I don't have a nice dad I could call for help,' Tessa said. 'Even when he was alive, we just didn't have that kind of relationship. Not like you and – your daughter.'

'Where was this, where did you grow up? Queensland, wasn't it?'

If she'd told him that, it must have been ages ago. 'I grew up in a place called Lota.'

'That's why I remembered. I've been there! The Police and Citizens' Youth Club or something – could that be it?'

'How funny, I used to do trampoline lessons there.'

'Me too!' After a second they both laughed. 'No,' John said, 'I went to some kind of campaign launch there, ages ago. Still registered to vote there? No, that's a pity. We'll need Bonner.'

'There's no way we could ever win Bonner,' Tessa said.

'No way, that would be landslide territory.' John tapped the armrest between them.

The seatbelt sign went off and everyone unbuckled. It was Tessa's turn to look out the window. Already she was lacerating herself for her needless personal disclosure. Her dad had been basically *fine*. If anything, her mum had been the really difficult one –

'You know,' John said quietly next to her. 'I didn't have a great relationship with my dad either. He *might* have been a good guy – I just wouldn't know. He left us after my little brother was born. So it was just my mum, my brother and me for a long time. My brother had a few difficulties. She looked after him, and I looked after her. So sometimes when Sophie calls me, I can't help thinking . . .'

'John!' Tessa and John leapt apart, startled. The flight attendant was clearly someone John saw regularly. They instantly fell into a friendly chat. Tessa resisted joining in, choosing instead to watch. She took in every detail of the parts of John's face available to her. John, she was thinking. *John.*

Back in Melbourne that afternoon he insisted on dropping her home to Northcote. 'I'm actually being selfish,' he smiled. 'If you get a separate taxi, you'll charge it to the union anyway. Look after the pennies . . .' he murmured, and held the car door open for her.

They were still chatting when the taxi drew up to her 1970s block and the unit she shared with Yasmin and Christian. 'That's my door,' she said.

'Well, go and open it then, so I know you're home safe.'

'Are you testing to see if it's really my house?'

'Would you lie to me about your house?'

The taxi driver spoke from the front. 'Are you getting out or not?'

Tessa tore her gaze away. 'Thank you! Yep, I am.' She opened the door and jumped out. 'Could you pop the boot?' She walked round the back and waited. With a clunk, the boot's catch released.

From inside the car she heard John, talking to the driver. 'Hold on, mate, I'll move round to the front with you.' After a second, he was next to her in the street. Backpack on, Tessa reached up. 'Just wait,' John said. 'Got everything?' She nodded. 'Okay, then.' She slammed the boot. 'Well, goodbye.'

Her gaze dropped down to his chest. Something she saw there sent a spark through her. So close had they been for hours, their heads together and voices low, that a strand of her own long hair snaked and curved gently down the lapel of his blue jacket. He saw it too, and moved his hand towards it, but instead of plucking it off, he pressed it closer momentarily, right over his heart. She could leave then. It was enough. A playful voice called after her. 'I said goodbye!'

She turned around. Seriousness dropped on her like a cloak. 'Well, I didn't.'

Back at the car he was serious too. 'What, say goodbye?'

Their journey together had taken them out of their normal lives and into a different world. Their closeness could be over then, but she didn't want it to be, and neither did he, she *knew*, she could just tell. It might never be acted on, or even discussed, but she refused to wave it all away. She *could not* betray herself in that way. She *would not* say goodbye. He was still staring up at her as she unlocked the door of her flat, opened it and went inside. That night she was in bed by eight. She pulled the covers up and rendezvoused with him in her mind. John's hands on her face, John's voice in her ear. As a child, she'd seen an ad for over-the-counter pain relief where parts of the body flashed red. A switch had been flicked and she was brilliant with desire. Night after night John filled her thoughts and dreams, and her body lit up, tingled and glowed.

After that weekend Tessa lost her grip on the ordinary rhythms of life. Her infatuation was ferocious, even violent. At least twice a day she leaned on Ingrid's desk to ask about John's diary. Mostly he was out, appointments in Sydney or Canberra, high-vis-vest photo ops touring work sites in marginal seats. When he was in, she hardly saw him. He rarely called on her in meetings. If she came into the tea room, he left it. It was as though the weekend never happened, that they'd never spoken, that she didn't exist. It was torture. She felt insane. When she was alone, she felt him with her. When she was near him, she felt alone.

One Sunday, journalists feverishly live-crossed from outside the Governor-General's residence as white fluff from the capital's poplar trees drifted like fairies in the sun. Howard emerged; he'd set the date of the election for 24 November 2007. It would be the fight of their lives, Kevin Rudd told the assembled media. The obstacles were immense. 'Labor's only won twice from Opposition since World War II, we have sixteen seats to win, and we're up against a really clever politician. This will go down to the wire.' The stakes were so high, they really couldn't be higher. Watching it on her share-house couch, Tessa turned her face to hide her tears. *The future*, Rudd kept saying. He said it more than thirty times. His energy was palpable. He was so charismatic, his delivery so polished, he could be a politician from some other (better) country like America or the UK, or an actor playing a politician on TV. 'This dweeb might actually win it,' her housemate Christian said. Too choked to speak, Tessa could only nod. Cometh the hour, cometh the Kevin. If anyone could do it, it was Rudd.

Six weeks later John stood in front of the whiteboard and worked through the final plans for election day. He called on Tessa last. 'Tessa,' he sort of coughed. 'Win or lose, do we have an email ready for the supporters' list?'

They'd barely exchanged a word in three months, yet there he was, pretending to care about her work? 'Yes,' she said. 'Well, *you* don't. I do.'

'Sorry,' John said. 'I meant – among your long list of things to do! – do you have some text prepared?'

She had; she'd shared all the drafts with John's adviser, Callum Worboys. Callum looked up from his phone and grunted. 'Yeah, she has.'

Satisfied, John capped his squeaky marker. 'Unless anyone has anything else?'

'Stop!' Pat Benison poked her head round the door of the meeting room. Pat was the President of the ACTU, a role theoretically more senior than John's, but in practice less political, lower profile and more ceremonial. Or maybe it was the fact of kind-hearted Pat being in the role that made it a soft and maternal one. 'You're not getting out of here that easily, John Clare!' John's mouth twitched in a tentative half-smile. 'First of all, win or lose, you've performed miracles.' Pat turned to the assembled staff. 'Hasn't he?' Next to Pat, Ingrid applauded, a pen in her mouth and a notebook under her arm. 'I said win or lose just then, but you know what?' Pat stared around like a children's entertainer. 'I think we're gunna win! I think we're gunna win by twenty seats!'

Over the sound of wild cheering, John held up his hands. 'Whoa, whoa, whoa.'

'And you know what seat I think we're gunna win? Bennelong!'

Finally John caught the hang of their double act. 'Pat, no! Impossible! Not Bennelong!' He gasped like an actor in a pantomime. 'Not John Howard's seat!'

As the ACTU staff cheered, Pat became sly. 'Would you like to make a bet?'

Tessa couldn't handle any more then. She slipped out and ran down the fire stairs to Queen Street.

7.

BATHED IN WARMTH and certainty, Sophie wasn't feeling the cold. Boundaries separate humans. We wind ourselves up in the morning and set off on our predictable paths. But what if one person diverts from their path and disrupts another's? There was nothing to stop her. Nothing! She stalked Tessa across rush-hour intersections, the *tung!* and *ding!* of rattling trams and the *ticker-ticker-ticker* of the green man. She stalked her past the landscaped calm of Parliament Gardens and the water-featured courtyards and cream-carpeted doctors' surgeries of genteel East Melbourne. Finally Tessa stopped at a block of four large Art Deco apartments opposite Powlett Reserve. She opened her handbag and stirred the contents until she found her keys, unlocked the front door of a ground-floor flat and went inside.

Sophie crossed the street and jogged up the grassy verge that separated the curved dark-brick flats from the road. She crept along the side path dividing Tessa's block from her neighbours' and emerged in a courtyard ringed with small trees and shrubs. Tessa's bins: boring. Tessa's back door: now we're talking. A panel of glass ran up the side. Sophie stood on tiptoe and pressed her face close. Across a dark hallway, about a metre to the left, a section of the kitchen was visible, bathed in overhead light. There was an open bottle of red wine on the counter, cork impaled on the corkscrew. The door to the right of the kitchen was closed but a glimpse of tile told her it was the bathroom. Beyond it she had the sense of a bedroom. With her hands up to keep her balance, Sophie peered the other way down the hall. The living room: the corner of a white sofa. Tessa was in there, she just knew.

Soon Tessa emerged, shoes and coat off, a wine glass in her hand. The flimsy grey silk of her blouse flattened against her torso as she walked. Twin ledges were revealed – the top of a balconette bra. What if Sophie's eyes glittered in the dark? She closed them. Irresistibly they reopened. In the kitchen, Tessa lit the gas burner closest to Sophie, set a frying pan on it and tipped in oil from a tall bottle. Out of sight for a while, she returned with a chopping board. Slabs of something white tumbled into the pan. Tessa leapt away – the oil must have spat. She unzipped her black pencil skirt and flung it into the hall, then pulled her silk top over her head and tossed that away too. It landed so close to Sophie, frozen in the dark, that if the glass wasn't there she could have touched it. Craning away from the stove, Tessa switched the pan to a back burner. She took a long swig from her glass and leaned with her elbows on the counter.

Sophie stared at her bare white back, the thin straps of her black bra. She was as graceful as a dancer with her long legs in black tights. Who was this woman, knocking back wine in her fancy flat? This *Boss*-magazine business bitch was the opposite of everything Sophie's dad had stood for, everything he'd cared about. She was cooking halloumi, Sophie could suddenly smell it. Tessa snatched the pan off the burner but it was too late – the kitchen was wreathed in smoke. An alarm sounded, piercing. She burst from the kitchen and ran towards the back door. The locks turned, the door opened. Sophie waited for the scream. It didn't come. Tessa had walked back inside, leaving an unseen Sophie crouching behind the door in the dirt. Entire body shaking, she crawled backwards into the shadows and scrambled to her feet.

From the neutral ground of Powlett Reserve she took one last look at the apartment. To her shock, the kitchen window was wide open. In her underwear, her arms sexily raised, Tessa was silhouetted against the light. Was this display for her? But no, Tessa was drawing down the frosted window, shutting out the night.

For the first time in more than a year Sophie had escaped the prison of her own leaden body and thoughts. She'd stepped out of her boring existence and visited the set of someone else's. For a moment she laughed, actually laughed out loud at the thrill. But it was also dark, and late, and she was arid with exhaustion. A year's good behaviour down the drain. What would Sam think if he knew? The funny thing was – Sophie wasn't smiling as she thought this – he probably wouldn't be surprised.

Sophie had been in a shit place in her life when she first met Sam. She'd started honours for her English degree but didn't attend classes. Somehow she missed the deadline to pull out and they charged her the full year's fees. There was this guy, Ed, a *photographer*. They'd been 'seeing each other', which she'd thought meant they were dating. Once he'd taken a picture of her sleeping naked and she only realised when she saw it on his laptop: 'I'd never show anyone, don't worry about it. I'd have to retouch the thighs first.' That got her started on the laxatives. Still she caught the tram to St Kilda whenever he texted her

Hey . . . Her housemates staged multiple interventions about her alleged 'disordered eating', her so-called 'depression', the fact she was months behind on rent and bills – even the way she hung her towel. 'It shouldn't touch *our* towels,' Eliza and Caitlin said, and Sophie pushed her chair away from the table so violently it fell over. Before the 2007 election, the understanding had been that the household would walk down to vote together, followed by their usual house brunch on Rathdowne Street. But Sophie woke late on the Saturday morning and found she'd been left behind.

Posters lined the fence at the local primary school. Labor had two, both of Kevin Rudd. One showed his moon face cracked open in a smile. KEVIN07, it said underneath. The other was more sober, Rudd's mouth in a tight line: NEW LEADERSHIP, it was captioned. The seat of Melbourne was so reliably Labor that the other side hardly bothered. An androgenic teen wore a Liberal logo tee over a full suit. 'Go for growth?' He offered her a leaflet, certain she wouldn't accept, and flushed when she took it with a smile. Your Rights at Work signs were everywhere and eager volunteers in orange shirts swarmed her as she approached – good. Having so long abandoned her for his work, the least her dad could do was win.

Afterwards, she walked past their usual cafe, but if Eliza and Caitlin had brunched there, they were long gone. It was time to GTFO of that stupid share house and leave those two dumb babies behind. She had no savings and substantial debt. She would have to repair to her parents' home and regroup.

That night Sophie arrived at Greeves Street a few minutes after six. Toby took a long time getting to the door. When he opened it, she could hear shouting. 'Dad froze the lobster thingies,' Toby said.

'Dad?' Sophie called down the hall. When she got to the kitchen she saw he was wearing a signed campaign t-shirt. Sophie craned up to kiss him. 'Have you signed your own t-shirt?'

'It was spare . . .' He shrugged. 'I'll get changed for the TV later.'

'So!' Her mother shouted from the utility. 'No special election party, Sophie! John's seen to that!'

'Ruined, ruined, it's all ruined,' Sophie joked. She and Toby were so familiar with their mother's rages they could almost follow along. 'It's all ruined' was one common refrain. 'Why do I even bother' was another. And, inspired by Doctor Seuss, they'd made up a rhyme about the last one, chanted throughout their childhoods: 'One fish, two fish, red fish, blue fish – selfish, selfish, selfish, SELFISH!'

The Balmain bugs were lying heavily in a fogged-up plastic bag. 'Maybe they can be defrosted,' her dad said hopefully. Her mother picked up the bags by the ties and swung them against the side of the kitchen island. 'Shit!' He leapt back. The bugs hit the wood like a brick.

Toby put his head down and escaped through the French doors. Sophie held up her hands. 'Take it easy, Grace.'

'I asked him to do one thing, one thing. And now the whole election party is ruined because he's lazy, careless –'

'One fish, two fish –' Sophie started, still sort of hoping it was a joke.

But her mother was glaring and her dad's face had gone pale and stiff. 'Sorry, Grace,' he almost begged. 'Grace, I'm sorry!'

Why did he just shut down like that? Sophie gave up and followed Toby out into the garden. He was sitting in the hammock, pushing his legs to make it swing. 'Toby? Why are you laughing? What's wrong with you?'

Embarrassed, Toby tipped himself onto his feet. 'Dad gave me a glass of Prosecco when the polls closed.'

'Ha.' Sophie was filled with affection. 'You're wasted.'

'I'm not! I feel bad, though.'

'Why?'

'Mum brought those things home from Vic Market. They were making all these scratching sounds? I made Dad put them in the freezer.' Toby's nervous teen voice buzzed and cracked. 'It's supposed to be a, like, quote unquote humane way to kill them.'

'And now Mum is going to kill Dad.' They looked in through the glass doors to the large living room and kitchen. Dad was leaning tiredly on the kitchen worktop, staring at his hands. It was so crazy to think of Toby at home with those two: Toby going to school every day and coming home to his parents, Mum and Dad, Grace and John. Sophie had been out of the house for so long she'd felt like 'the Clare family' had ceased to exist. It would be very strange to join it again.

'Well, we better head back,' Toby said. 'They fight less when I'm around.'

'Who else is coming?' Sophie asked as they went in.

'Forget about it,' their mum snapped. 'I've cancelled it.'

'What? The whole election party?'

'Yes, Sophie! It was supposed to be a supper. No supper, no point.' Their mum stalked out of the kitchen and slammed the door.

On the TV, excited voices predicted the first Labor Government in eleven years. Shoulders bowed, her dad began to assemble some leftovers from the fridge. 'Do you want some, love? Or come to the Workers Club with me afterwards, if you feel like it?' Sophie pulled a face and made her way upstairs. On the landing she paused to peer into the big front bedroom that had been hers as a child. Within a few months of her starting university it had been transformed into a tasteful hotel twin suite with two virginal guest beds. Her stuff, culled without consultation, had been stored under the stairs. Did anyone even stay in this pointless magazine-ready room? She'd never seen the quilts rumpled. Sophie had a flash of Grace every Christmas: the last to sit down, the first to jump up, confiscating the plates while the family were still chewing. Her mother couldn't enjoy a meal, or a room, or even a *moment* without desperately trying to clear it all away. 'Mum?' Sophie tapped on the door to her parents' room. She heard a gruff sound that might have been *come in*. Inside, her mother sat on the edge of the bed, her head in her hands. 'Mum? Are you okay?'

'I'm perfectly fine,' she snapped. 'And I said *not now*.'

'I thought you said come in.'

'I said the exact opposite of that.'

'I was wondering –' Sophie began.

'Is this about your share house? Because, Sophie, if you think you're moving back here, the answer's no. Toby starts grade eleven in two months, the most important years in his school life. Your father and I drove ourselves into the ground giving you the best possible head start at school. Now it's Toby's turn. I don't think he needs a new season of the Sophie Clare Show right when he's trying to concentrate – every day a new scene, a new drama, a new conflict – do you?' It was like Sophie was a stranger, or like her mother was. It was like they didn't know each other at all.

'Um,' Sophie said. 'I wasn't the one bashing up Dad downstairs and screaming. As far as I recall, that was you.'

'You have no idea about anything,' her mum muttered.

'I saw you with my own eyes!'

'You may think you're a grown-up, Sophie.' Her mum jumped up and strode towards her. 'But there's a lot you'll never know.'

Sophie found herself on the outside of the closed door. She could hammer on it and howl, but her mother had repeatedly shown herself to be immovable. If she was grown-up enough to fend for herself, why couldn't her mother be honest with her? And if she was still too young to understand – why couldn't she come home? Despair welled within her, abandonment and despair. She stormed down the hall to Toby's room. On his bookcase stood the battered green and gold Commonwealth Bank moneybox he had cultivated since childhood. She knelt on the thick pile of the rug and tipped the contents into her lap. Gold coins and fifty-cent pieces; a couple of fifty-dollar notes and some twenties had been folded small and wedged in. She swept up two fifties, two twenties, a stray five and a small handful of weighty and satisfying two-dollar coins and distributed them between the pockets of her jeans.

'Bye guys!' Sophie called from downstairs.

'Oh?' Her dad stepped into the hallway, tongs in his hand. 'You're off?'

'That's nice, Sophie,' came a bitter voice.

Sophie looked up to where her mother stood on the landing. 'Mum? Have I gone mad? Didn't you say the party was cancelled? I thought you didn't want me here?'

'No, please – don't let me hold you back.' Her mother turned on her heel and retreated to the bedroom.

'Sorry,' Sophie called to Toby, meaning the money. But since he didn't know about that, he took the apology to be about their family. He gestured wide and shrugged.

Sophie was still rolling her eyes as she opened the front door. A strange girl was picking her way up the path. She moved with an infuriatingly alert delicacy, like a Pevensie or a faun from Narnia. She had the exquisitely detailed features of someone small for their age, and the expressive and subtle countenance of an 'old soul'. Sophie wanted to shove her. 'Hi, Sophie,' the girl said.

'Hi, whoever you are.'

'It's me, Geraldine from next door?'

'Geraldine?'

'Geraldine – Girl?'

'Girl?'

'When I was young I used to write it like . . .' Geraldine mimed the letters in the air and spelled G-E-R-L.

'What a *touching* glimpse of your childhood,' Sophie said.

'Sophie!' Grace shouted from upstairs. 'You're leaving, Girl is staying!'

'Fine,' Sophie shouted back. 'BYE!'

She'd stolen the money to pay idiotic Eliza and Caitlin's idiotic bills, but over the next few nights she was drawn again and again to visit Cookie, the bar where she'd first met Ed. 'You're too beautiful to look so sad' was the first thing Sam said to her, lining up for a drink at the bar. He bought her a vodka soda and then another. He worked at *The Age*, or so he said. It surprised her; he didn't look like a broadsheet reporter. Dizzy from not eating all day, she leaned towards him and rested on his chest. 'So, what's your name?'

'Whoa.' He recoiled, laughing. 'We've been through all that, Sophie-Clare-aged-twenty-one.'

'Oh my God, sorry.'

'Sam Nugent, remember!' He shook her hand. 'I'm twenty-four.' He leaned forward and opened his eyes wide. 'I still live with my parents!'

'Let's get out of here,' Sophie said. Sadness stalked her, but she thought she could outrun it. 'We'll get a cab.' Sam looked at her to see if she was serious. She was. 'You can pay.'

Sophie and her housemates lived in a minuscule rented terrace on Pigdon Street. Rather touchingly, Sam took his shoes off at the door. In her bedroom, the glow of the fairy lights enhanced the pleasing architecture of his face. He was shivering slightly as he undid his own shirt buttons. When she pulled his hips towards her he flinched. A skittish man was no use to anyone. To put him at ease and get things moving she took off her own clothes, all of them. She indicated, with her eyes, that he should hop into her unmade bed. Sam did as her eyes asked, still with his jeans on. In bed he pulled her close. She yelped as her stomach touched the metal of his belt. He wriggled off the rest of his clothes. She pulled back the blanket. His dick was pointing towards her like the long hand of a clock. His behaviour was respectful, his ejaculation spectacular and his gratitude almost poignant. For her part, she didn't break down crying about Ed. The encounter was a success.

When Sophie returned from the bathroom afterwards, her bed was neatly made. Sam was in it, propped on his elbow, surveying her room with frank curiosity. He evidently expected to be there when she woke up. When he started lightly snoring she detached herself and lay next to him, her mind and stomach churning. She checked her phone for messages from Ed but found nothing. She typed, *I have a new boyfriend now. So, see ya.* When he did not reply, she wrote, with tears streaming down her face, *Just so you know, you really hurt me. You need some help before you're middle-aged, brain dead from drugs and totally alone.* Again, no reply. Crying very, very silently so Sam couldn't hear, she texted, *I think we could have had something beautiful.* When she realised he was not going to reply to this either, it was time to regain some control. She typed, *Please do not contact me again. Goodbye Ed.* Shaking, she put her phone down next to Sam's. Sam did work at *The Age*, as it happened, but in ad sales. By the time she had clarified, they were already a couple.

It was fair to say she had not been the ideal girlfriend over the first three years of their relationship. But for the last year, until tonight, she'd tried to be. She'd ruthlessly policed herself since her father's death. She'd maintained the highest possible standards. She'd switched off the internet to avoid the judgment of the crowd. She'd atoned for crimes Sam knew she'd committed and for the ones he did not. But tonight she'd broken all her own rules. In stalking her father's mistress, she'd also broken the law. Worst of all, she felt it: the energy. When her pulse and thoughts began to race; when something inside her threw off its shackles and ranged freely, and she lived not in her body and the world but in her mind and imagination. Last time she'd emerged from that state it was to find her father hanging on a fence. If Sophie Clare lived, truly lived – other people died.

It was a long train ride to the outer suburbs that night and a long walk from Nunawading Station. How Sophie missed Fitzroy, and Brunswick Street in particular. Giant terraces and tiny restaurants, laundromats and internet cafes, Asian grocers and St Mary's House of Welcome, all watched over by the vast bulwarks of the housing commission flats. It was a mixture of old and new and rich and poor, and it was the mixture itself, not any element on its own, that was civilised. The residents of Forest Hill were from backgrounds as diverse as those in Fitzroy, but the outer suburbs were where differences went to die. Big houses on big blocks, two cars in the garage or carport, Whiskas in the cat bowl, two-litre Diet Cokes in the American-style fridge. Through window after window Sophie saw largely identical families lounging in identical living rooms in front of identically huge TVs. She didn't look down on them. On the contrary, she experienced a painful longing to be doing the same, though not necessarily with her own family. *I want to go home*, she was thinking, even as she walked up her own short drive and slipped a key into the flyscreen door of the modern two-bedroom grey box they rented from Sam's parents. She'd almost feared Sam would be waiting, half-worried and half-cross. But the little house was empty, the tap dripping loudly in the stainless steel sink.

8.

LABOR HAD WON the 2007 election – it was clear as soon as the polls closed at six. The only question was by how much. On the screen of Tessa's share-house TV, deputy leader Julia Gillard grew pink with delight and her efforts to conceal it. At eight-thirty, Yasmin called from the bathroom, her mouth full of bobby pins: 'Last chance to come to the pub!' But Tessa stared at the TV, magnetised, as Kerry O'Brien crossed from the tally room in Canberra to a function space in Melbourne. Beer-holding unionists whooped and cheered. 'You don't think it's a bit early?' O'Brien asked.

John was on the screen, one leg crossed over the other like a woman, long fingers entwined on a square knee. Behind him stood his colleague Pat Benison. With one hand she ruffled John's lovely thick hair. In her other hand she held cordless hair clippers. 'I don't, Kerry!' Pat said. 'I'm feeling very lucky tonight!'

'What about the man in question?'

'I'm not the one with the weapon,' John said wryly. 'It's out of my hands at this point.' A cheer went up from the room behind him.

'I'm making the call, Kerry!' Pat cried. 'John Howard won't just lose the election! He'll lose Bennelong as well!' Pat flipped a switch and buzzed the clippers. Was it Tessa's excessively

66

sympathetic imagination or did John flinch? 'My friend John
Clare here is not a man to go back on his word!'

Yasmin appeared next to Tessa as Pat sheared John like a
sheep. She tucked one more pin into her bun. 'What's that
madwoman doing?'

'John made a bet or something. If John Howard lost his
seat, he'd shave his head. I think it was meant to be a joke.'

'But has Howard even lost yet?' The clippers were set on a
length that made John almost bald. He looked quite unlike
himself. 'He looks hot,' Yasmin said.

'Cheating on me, Yazzy?' Christian was in the living room,
ready to head out.

Was he wearing Yasmin's denim jacket? Nope, Yasmin had
hers on too. They were dressed exactly the same. 'Have a lovely
time, guys,' Tessa said.

She had a ten-minute shower with the plug in so the water
didn't go to waste. She lay in the cooling bath until it gave her
goosebumps. Her heart had expanded so much – she couldn't
breathe, she was choking on it. Loving him would kill her.
She had to quit her job, give it up and give him up. But who
would she be without him? Who would keep her company
when she was alone? The thought of John was better than
nothing. Drying her hair, Tessa heard a loud knock. With a
sigh, she wrapped herself in the towel. When she opened the
door, she saw John.

How weird that she could recall with perfect clarity the pain
of longing, ambiguity, rejection. Yet John turning up to her
door, a physical manifestation of what she most wanted in the
world – nearly four years on she could barely remember it,

could revisit it only in snippets. It seemed not to register with John that he'd turned up out of nowhere and she was dressed only in a towel. She stood back and opened the door of the share house wide. Before they could speak, Kerry O'Brien's voice could be heard from the television. 'Our next prime minister, Kevin Rudd.' They walked to the living room and stood next to each other. On screen, Rudd pushed through throngs of cheering people. The crowd was jubilant, ecstatic. 'He asked me to run, you know,' John said.

So the rumours had been true. 'You didn't want to?'

John's eyes were shut, and he looked so drained she wondered if he was falling asleep. 'I had unfinished business.'

Rudd had made it to the lectern. He shuffled his papers and gritted his lolly teeth in a smile. He put his hands out in a calming gesture like a principal waiting for silence in assembly. 'Settle down, guys,' he said. A bucket of cold water tipped over the room. The crowd was chastened, silent. The goofy and charming nerd was gone. His speech was a tense recitation of his huge to-do list. The party was over, Rudd concluded. 'You can have a strong cup of tea if you want – even an Iced VoVo on the way through – but the celebrations should stop there.'

John rubbed his hands over his new short hair with a moan. 'What have we done?'

In the tally room, they cut to the electoral map. 'Oh, look,' Tessa said.

John saw it immediately. 'We won Bonner.'

'I thought you'd forgotten.'

'Tessa –' he reached for her.

She turned away and led him to her dark, freezing room. 'Get undressed,' she said; she needed a show of good faith. She hadn't thought it would be like this, in her own house, completely sober, the mood almost sombre. His haircut made him alien. This John wasn't the John of work, of politics, of rallies and TV. She closed her eyes and had a sudden strong longing to get into bed by herself, to pull the covers up and summon the dominant, satirical John of her imagination, of fantasy. She opened her eyes to find he was shirtless. Strands of hair dusted his strong shoulders, offcuts from Pat's butchery. He was there with her. He was real. 'What was your unfinished business?'

John pulled her to him. The towel dropped to the floor. 'You.'

John had been in her house on the night of the election, inside her bedroom, inside her. The evidence was incontrovertible: his semen lay pooled in a condom, wrapped in a tissue in her bin. Still, when he neither called nor emailed on the Sunday, Tessa plunged straight back into uncertainty. On Monday, John didn't come into work. She printed out the end-of-campaign report she'd been working on sporadically for weeks: all the stats and achievements and data, the evidence that, as an employee at least, she was special. She banged a staple in the corner and wrote on it with a trembling hand: JOHN. Upstairs, on Level Six, John's stalwart PA was running a pencil slowly down one document to cross-reference it with another, concentration in every line of her soft, careworn face. 'Um – Ingrid?'

Ingrid carefully held her place on the page. 'Just one second.' Trays were labelled JOHN IN and JOHN OUT and INGRID IN and INGRID OUT. On her desk there was a big studio portrait of Ajax, her blue heeler. Stuck to her monitor were school photos of four little boys, or maybe two little boys but at different ages? A Blu Tacked tableau of a dozen native Australian animal figurines took pride of place on top of her computer. Ingrid ticked the bottom of the page and looked up with a smile. 'I like your wombats and stuff,' Tessa said.

'Thanks.' Ingrid sounded satisfied. 'John often brings them back for me when he travels.'

That was an interesting tidbit Tessa would think about later. She cleared her throat. 'Do you know –'

'Tessa.' Ingrid put down her pencil. 'I have wonderful news. Wonderful news. I've been on the phone to the Leader's office. They think the Prime Minister can come.'

'To what?'

'The victory barbecue! The Christmas party!' Ingrid sounded accusing.

'Gosh, amazing.' Was Tessa supposed to have known about that? Unless workplace intel was formally communicated by email, it often seemed to pass her by. 'Is John in today?'

'Oh no,' Ingrid said sternly. 'Grace has taken him to Bali. He'll be gone for – goodness – two weeks at least.'

'A very well-deserved holiday,' Tessa said.

'He'll be back for the barbecue.'

'Okay! Bye now!' Tessa's voice was high, like a meow. She rushed for the emergency exit and sat on the cold concrete of the stairs.

A clanking sound – someone had opened the stairwell door. It was ancient Terry, the policy officer, heading downstairs for a smoke. Terry clicked his tongue: 'Havin' a cry, are ya?' The tears Tessa could do nothing about, but she wiped her nose on the back of her hand. 'Yeah, big changes ahead.' He looked at her closely. 'You'll want to get out of here, go corporate.'

Tessa stared at him, baffled. 'Why would I do that?'

'Peacetime very different to wartime,' Terry said. 'The fight's over.'

Waxed, blow-dried, make-up applied so carefully as to be invisible, Tessa had planned her entrance to the Your Rights at Work victory barbecue slash Christmas party for the full two and a half weeks John was away. The second she set foot into Flagstaff Gardens, Ingrid ran up in a panic. 'The tomato sauce, Tessa, for the barbecue? The ketchup! Next to my desk, Tessa, my desk?'

Tessa sighed and trudged back to the office. There were four enormous catering bottles, each carefully double-bagged. How was she supposed to manage them on her own? She began the arduous trek back to the park with two in each hand, stopping every hundred metres for a rest. In front of her, suddenly, John appeared. In shorts, ridiculously: navy chinos; she could see his *knees*. He stopped dead in the yawning entrance of the underground carpark. He watched her take in the fact of his presence and the absurdity of his shorts. His face, which had been downcast, even morose, instantly flushed and enlivened. Voices sounded from the carpark. He glanced back and signalled somehow his connection with the two figures who joined him, blinking, in the light. She put down her bags and got her phone out of her pocket, half-turning and acting engrossed.

'If we have to do it, let's do it,' John's wife said. Wide-legged black linen trousers flapped at her elegant ankles. Her perfectly white loose cotton top nipped in artfully at the waist. She set off up the street without a momentary glance at Tessa. Left in Grace Clare's wake, Tessa felt sweaty, red, unstylish, confused, rejected and a mess. When enough space had opened up between them, Tessa picked up the bags and trailed along behind. The boy was John in miniature, the same tanned calves in ironed shorts. Though he couldn't know anyone was watching, his walk was tense and self-conscious. The family paused for traffic at William Street. John stared resolutely ahead. Suddenly Tessa was furious. He'd *knocked on her door*. He'd consumed her like a starving man. Ordinarily it would have been highly unnatural for her to impose herself. Now, with a confidence born of anger, she joined them at the main road.

'Hi!'

John's face couldn't settle on an expression. He looked away to check the traffic.

'Toby,' Grace said. 'Why don't you help with those bags?'

The son blushed and took two. John reached for the others, but – she hadn't even noticed – they'd twisted around her hand and her fingers were marked with painful red and white lines. John saw them and looked distressed. Tessa's heart filled with love. To disrupt the current between them, she forced herself to speak flippantly. 'Ingrid was freaking out. No tomato sauce for Kevin Rudd's sausage – imagine.'

'Yes, we mustn't let down the leader,' Grace said. 'I doubt he'll even come.'

Tessa felt defensive, on John's behalf, but pretended it was for Ingrid. 'Oh, but Ingrid organised it, and his office said . . .'

Grace stepped out into the road. 'I think we have a lot of disappointment ahead of us with that man.'

Tessa looked up at John. He looked back, sad and serious. 'But we won the election for him,' Tessa said. 'Our whole campaign . . .'

'He'll dance with the one that brung him,' John said. Grace tutted at 'brung' but even Tessa could have told her it was a trade union thing, a common trade union phrase! Safely across the road, John remembered his son. 'Tessa does the web stuff, Tobes.'

Toby gave her a polite smile. 'That's cool.'

'Congratulations on all your work,' Grace said.

'Thanks!' Tessa said, adding awkwardly, 'You too.'

Grace looked down her nose. 'You didn't bring your own bags for the sauce? Instead of using plastic?'

The bulk of ACTU staff were standing around the barbecue with stubbies. A satellite group were kicking a soccer ball. 'That barbie looks nice and fired up!' John said. Tessa shuddered to hear him sound so false. As he approached the edge of the crowd it swarmed him. To be with him was awful, to be away from him was worse. Tessa turned to reply to Grace, belatedly, about the plastic bags, but John's wife had made a beeline for Liz Eccles. The legal officer could have been one of Melbourne's arts workers in her complicated wrap top like half a kimono, her short grey hair expensively cut. Of course Grace would be friends with her. They greeted each other with a sophisticated kiss on each cheek.

Ingrid ventured anxiously into Tessa's blind spot and clutched her upper arm. 'The sauce, though: where's the sauce?'

'John has it,' Tessa said. 'And . . . his son.'

'Toby!' Ingrid ran to give him a hug. Tessa was assaulted by years of imagined Clare family history, a montage of milestones and anecdotes and confidences, private moments behind closed doors and closed ranks. This was a mistake, this was all a mistake. Ingrid's phone was ringing; she fumbled with the little neoprene pouch she wore clipped to her belt and held her phone at arm's length to read the display. 'It's the Leader's office,' she gasped. 'Hello-this-is-Ingrid.' She squinted into the sky as the caller spoke, then frowned down at the ground. 'No, I understand.' Tessa and Toby looked at each other with terrible clarity. Ingrid shut her phone. 'Rudd can't come. His meeting in Sydney ran late. He's not even on the plane.'

'Fuckwit,' Tessa swore.

'Sorry, Ingrid,' Toby said.

'Tessa.' Ingrid took her arm to speak to her privately. 'Don't tell John.'

Tessa stared at her, astonished. 'You don't have a beer,' someone said, and thrust one into her hands. It was Manny, the most junior of the three men on the media team, the only one who wasn't terrible. He dragged her over to a vacant patch of grass. 'Are you okay?'

'Doesn't it all feel pointless now John Howard has gone?'

'Yes,' Manny emphatically said.

She remembered Terry on the stairwell, his assumption that she would move on. What made him think she didn't belong? 'Maybe I should get a real job.'

'Ugh.' Manny gulped his beer and tapped it gently against her bottle. 'We both should.'

'No, really.' Half her beer was gone already, a mistake in the raging sun. She gestured into the crowd. 'That guy from Union Aid Abroad doesn't even know my name. I've been here nearly three years!'

'Do you know his name?'

Tessa pushed him. 'Manny!'

He straightened up, laughing. 'What are you trying to say? Are you saying *you* feel out of place?'

'Okay, Manny, okay!'

'Telling *Mansif Rahman* you feel like you don't fit in!'

Tessa tapped the neck of his bottle with hers. 'Okay, I'm a tool. Finish that last bit, we'll get some more.'

As she tipped her head backwards to drink she made sudden and accidental eye contact with John, visible on the other side of the crowd. He looked away, unreadable. Manny hadn't noticed; he was looking at his watch. 'Eye on the time, mate?' It was Callum, John's number two. In John's absence he'd been riding high on the glowing post-election coverage. The media seemed to have decided it was all his idea – *The Age* had used Tessa's least favourite phrase in its feature about him, that the campaign had been his 'brainchild'. Callum's shirt was undone an extra button for the party. In the tangle of his almost pubic black chest hair Tessa was astonished to see the glint of a delicate golden cross.

'Just going to do it now.' Manny pulled out his phone and walked away.

'Got any plans for Christmas?' she asked Callum, her face deliberately blank.

'Down the coast,' Callum said. 'You'll be heading off soon, then.'

'For Christmas?' She'd be having Christmas in Lota as usual; she was dreading it.

'Leaving the ACTU, I meant,' Callum said. Tessa stared at him. 'You've never really been at home here.'

Before she could reply, Manny returned. 'Yep, so just checking we're on for Rudd in Flagstaff Gardens. He'll be here in about twenty. Right mate. See you soon.' Manny hung up and turned to Callum. 'ABC are on, *The Age*. The others I confirmed this morning.'

'Oh, shit.' Tessa darted deep into the crowd, not sure who she was looking for – not John, not John. Ingrid – but John's PA was nowhere to be found. She saw Michael Hancock, the Assistant Secretary, resting a beer on the gentle curve of his pot belly. 'Michael,' she gasped.

'Hang about, hang about.' Michael was relaxed. He was with a group of old guys, bosses from other unions maybe, standing in a circle with their legs wide apart. 'I'll be back,' Michael told them, not necessarily displeased to be dragged away by a woman. They found a quiet spot on the outer edge of the group. 'What's up?'

'Rudd's cancelled but I think the media's still coming, thinking that Rudd's coming.' It was hard to explain. 'I thought Ingrid was going to tell John but . . .' Tessa still couldn't see her anywhere. 'I just think it's going to look a bit awful if all the cameras turn up and Rudd's not here. Like the unions have been snubbed.'

'Yeah, right. Leave it with me.' Michael strolled off.

Tessa watched John check his phone, frown and gaze towards the road. Her heart broke as Michael approached with the news. She also wanted to hit him. Avoiding the moment of impact, she found her way back to Manny. 'Beer time,' he said, and passed her a fresh one.

'Shh.' She could see Callum sense danger and join John and Michael, his hand already reaching for his mobile. Despite his grievous catalogue of personality disorders, he was very good at his job. Tessa saw Callum's eyes find Manny. He beckoned him with a peremptory gesture. Manny scrambled to receive his bollocking.

It was so hot, but a hat would destroy her outfit and sunscreen would ruin her make-up. Tessa drained half her new beer and wondered what she would do for a wee. She caught sight of a distant brick box that might be a toilet block. Her speculative musing became a more urgent need. One stall was already occupied inside so she darted into the other. She was buttoning her jeans when she heard the sound of someone crying. As she washed her hands, the other door opened. Ingrid was dabbing first one eye and then the other with a rosette of toilet paper. 'Ingrid,' Tessa ventured. 'Are you okay?'

Since Tessa valued discretion and privacy above all, she thought Ingrid might feel the same. But Ingrid rushed closer with relief. 'Oh, I'm such an idiot.'

'You're not, you're not.'

'John didn't even want to invite Rudd, I just thought it would be nice?'

'You don't have to worry,' Tessa said. 'Callum's cancelling the media.'

'What media?'

'The camera crews.'

'But it was never supposed to be for media,' Ingrid panicked. 'It was a social thing, a private thing, a goodwill thing, John said no media, the Leader's office said no media –'

'Don't worry, there's no media! And John knows Rudd's not coming, so there's nothing to worry about.'

'Of course John knows. Rudd would have called him.'

'Oh. I don't think Rudd called him, but –' Ingrid started out of the toilet block. 'Ingrid!' Tessa jogged after her. 'I don't think Rudd called him but it's all fine! He knows!' As they got closer to the party both women noticed the camera guys at the same time, two men lugging equipment from William Street. Beside them trotted a smooth-haired TV reporter, jacket over her arm to keep it fresh.

'Oh *no*.' Ingrid started to cry again.

'Hey.' Tessa put her hand on Ingrid's shoulder. In the distance, Callum strode towards the news team, looking matey and conciliatory. Manny followed behind, staring at the grass. 'Look, Callum's sorting it out. It's all fine.' The camera guys had put down their equipment to listen. They hoisted it back up to walk off. The reporter was already making a call. 'See, it's fine.'

Back at the barbecue, John was clapping his hands to get the attention of the group. 'I'm so embarrassed,' Ingrid said, holding back. 'John's going to hate me.'

'Ingrid, I can guarantee John would never hate you.' It wasn't an exaggeration; John's respect for his PA was legendary. Ingrid gave a reluctant smile. Desperate to hear his speech, Tessa hooked her arm in Ingrid's and led her back to the buzzing crowd.

'But that's enough bragging,' John was saying.

People groaned in joke dismay. Someone shouted 'More!'

'We won the battle, but the war is not over. A strong labour movement needs not just a powerful party, but powerful workers. Powerful workers need powerful unions. I want everyone to have a relaxing break over Christmas. And when we start back in 2008, the real and difficult work begins.'

The applause was warm and instant, but John seemed depleted, scattered. Tessa felt a painful urge to put her arms around him. Instead she fished out two new beers and found Manny. 'Strips torn off me,' Manny managed to gasp. 'About checking all the facts before I call the media.'

'Um – Callum told you to call?'

'Shh.' Manny put his hand on her arm. 'I'm just the fall guy. Look, there's John's wife. Grace! This is Tessa.' Tessa lurched forward and – why? – held out her hand.

John's wife looked at it coolly. 'We've met.' Grace turned back to Manny. 'Liz and I were just talking about global warming. You know, eleven of the past twelve years have been the warmest since reliable records began.'

'Well, hopefully –' Tessa began.

'Since 1850!'

'Maybe,' Tessa tried again, adopting a bit of Grace's tone, brisk and up herself, 'it will be like nuclear war, you know, something a generation worries about but just . . . doesn't happen.' This was something she had thought about quite deeply. You couldn't scare people to death and expect them to change the world; you needed optimism, and at least a tiny bit was warranted – think about mankind's ability to pull together in crisis: spray deodorants and the ozone layer, that sort of stuff. Anyway, Kevin Rudd was in charge now, and he called climate change the 'greatest moral challenge of our time'. But Grace and Liz were frowning at her, and Manny looked concerned. Tessa receded, tucking herself behind Manny at an angle, leaning into his shoulder blade and trying to disappear. 'There's still hope, that's what I meant,' she mumbled, but the conversation had moved on.

'Yes, she's having a very tough time,' Grace was telling Liz now, as if Manny and Tessa weren't even there. 'I feel like saying: "Sophie, grow up! You're *twenty-one*!" During the election campaign, she . . .' Grace lowered her voice. Tessa craned to eavesdrop, astounded. Sophie, the luminous centrepiece of the family photo on John's desk? How could a girl that beautiful experience pain? Liz murmured something. 'Mmm,' Grace said, 'it was hard for John obviously, the biggest fight of his career . . .' Those words – *hard for John. John likes his Lemsip fully dissolved.* Everyone was always thinking of John!

Tessa raised her head from Manny's back. To her surprise, John was visible through a gap in the crowd, staring at her from the edge of a cluster of excited young people. *I hate you, I love you, help me. FUCK. YOU*, she silently telegraphed. He was drawn back into the group for a photo.

'Why are you being so weird?' Manny dragged her away, leading her deeper into a circle of exotic trees and spiky bushes. 'I don't want Ingrid to see me smoking,' he explained. 'Oh, Tessa, God, sorry.'

'What?'

'Your dad – didn't he have lung cancer?'

Tessa hadn't even considered that Manny would remember that piece of information or seek to protect her feelings about it. She gave him a grateful smile. 'That's so nice of you, but actually he never even smoked – don't worry about it.' Manny dug around in his trouser pockets. 'Hang on,' she said.

He froze. 'What?'

'Do you pluck your eyebrows?'

He began to laugh and covered his face. 'Stop it, I don't.'

'You look like you do, look at those perfect arches, and what's that little hole?'

'Ugh! My shameful past. I used to have an eyebrow ring. At uni, hey.'

'Manny, no! Was this when you sold *Socialist Worker*?'

'*Green Left Weekly*? No, that was at school. Uni was when I wore wide-legged jeans and girls' t-shirts? And listened to Asian Dub Foundation on MiniDisc.'

'MiniDisc players, I remember them!'

'Yeah, so I got it pierced with one of those barbells, with little balls on either end? This was in second year, to impress a girl – but pus just *oozed* out of it for six entire weeks. So it didn't work. My mum made me take it out to visit the London cousins. It just closed up, so – fuck!' Manny tripped over a calf-height fence protecting an ancient tree. 'Ow.' He stared down at his forearms. 'Ow,' he said again.

'Ow,' Tessa agreed. When he scrambled to his feet, she gently flicked the tan bark off his palms. 'Are you okay? God, you're not, look!' Already one of his wrists had swollen so much it met the edge of his shirt cuff.

'Shit a brick, this kills. Ah!' One nice thing about Manny was that he never wore any hair product. His thick dark hair flapped back off his face as he blinked up at the sky. He screwed his eyes shut and a tear slid down his cheek. 'Not very tough, am I? Sorry, Tess – embarrassing.'

'*Manny*. Nothing embarrassing about it.'

'Stacking while I talk about my romantic failures – not embarrassing at all.' His laugh turned into a cry of pain.

Her plan to get John alone. Their reunion. If she didn't talk to him today she wouldn't see him till after Christmas. She hooked her arm through Manny's good one. 'Come on,' she said. 'I'm taking you to hospital.'

His face a mask of pain, Manny allowed her to lead him to the edge of Flagstaff Gardens and in the direction of Royal Melbourne. To keep his mind off his wrist she chatted endlessly and mindlessly about work: what it would be like now the Liberals were gone, what John would do all day, what John thought about Rudd, what Ingrid thought about John and what Manny thought about Grace Clare. By the time they got to Vic Markets tram stop Manny looked a bit more like himself again. 'Hey, Tess.' He turned to her shyly. 'Thanks so much, but you don't have to come.'

'No, I'll come, seriously!'

'No, really. I think I was just in shock or something back then. You go back to the party. You don't have to miss it for me.' In the twilight, the tram was approaching, lit up and almost full. Manny let go of his sore wrist and gave the driver a wave.

'But how will you get home afterwards?'

'I'll just call my brother, he'll meet me there and sort me out. Thank you, though. Seriously.' He held out his good hand and for a second she awkwardly clasped it. 'You're the best.'

Loneliness engulfed her as soon as the tram doors crashed shut. Tessa had no one to see and nowhere to be. Yasmin and Christian weren't exactly waiting for her back home. If John remembered election night at all it was with regret. She'd acted like a freak, accosting him and his family. His horror as he watched her talk to Grace – like Tessa was a suicide bomber fiddling with her vest. She tipped her head back to sob. No, she wouldn't go back to the party to be ignored. Fuck that!

At the office, she swiped her security card and got in the lift. It opened onto a completely deserted fifth floor. Mountains of paper were stacked by the photocopier. She dumped the reams of A4 and took the empty boxes with her. In her small office she tore nearly three years' worth of memorabilia off the corkboard above her desk. Fliers for rallies, the Obama badge a colleague had brought back from the US, a KEVIN07 sticker. What did any of it matter? Why had she tried so hard for abstract men who didn't care about her, and abstract ideas the men themselves didn't care about? Fuck politics and fuck them. When the computer whirred to life she highlighted every single file and deleted it in a rage. Suddenly she gave a cry of distress – her results! She needed her stats and numbers and so on, the concrete proof of her achievements, for her CV – for her next job. Then she remembered her end-of-campaign report, lying unread in John's in-tray for two weeks while he *rekindled his marriage* in Bali.

Upstairs, Level Six was dark and silent. She tiptoed to Ingrid's desk. Straight away she noticed a new figurine sitting by the keyboard. She leaned over the partition to inspect it. A little monkey. John must have brought it back from holidays. Something moved in the corner of her eye. It was in John's office – it was John. By the light of a reading lamp, he was flipping through a document. 'Ah.' He raised her campaign report. 'Tessa, come in.' Consumed by hideous out-of-control emotions, she couldn't bear to face their real-life source: mild, handsome, pleasant and courteous where she was furious, overcome, hateful and inflamed. Inside his office, the door closed behind her. Still she didn't want to look up at him – there was something imploring in that pose, a woman looking up at a tall man. She frowned at the carpet and tried not to cry. 'I didn't book the trip,' he said. Her heart leapt. 'It was a surprise.' This, with its undertone of romance, made her scowl. He seemed to read each flicker of her mood. 'A not entirely welcome one. I was hoping to see you – at the barbecue. But you were with Mansif . . . Of course, I can't complain.' No, he couldn't – his fucking wife had been there. He read her thoughts again. 'I hope it wasn't uncomfortable for you.'

Tessa made a sound like 'ha'. He hadn't taken another step towards her but the way he was leaning brought him closer. He took her hand and led her to the very centre of the room. She looked up into his face, into his eyes, and read there everything she'd ever dreamt of reading. 'I missed you.'

'I missed you too,' he almost groaned. He rushed to the door and locked it. When he came back they sank to the floor.

It felt teen and inexperienced to basically hump and grab each other, the bulge in his ridiculous shorts, the underwire of her bra uncomfortably pulled up. Finally every part of his body was touching her body, his hands on her hands, his forehead on her forehead, his elbows by her elbows, the soft skin of his inner arms on the soft skin of hers. She felt smothered by him, crushed by him, utterly subsumed in him, her night-time imaginings made real. It was perfect.

Get out of there, Tessa wanted to scream to her younger self. Don't go into John's office. Run away, just run away. Standing in her kitchen in her East Melbourne flat, Tessa was so deep inside her old memory she raised a hand to her hot cheek and expected to find it sunburnt. The face she touched was the same, yet she found herself unrecognisable. No more union t-shirts for her, no more share houses. No more fighting the good fight. Was *she* the stranger, or was that woman from the past? She scraped the charred halloumi off the pan with a spatula and peeled and salted a cucumber. She spooned some olives onto the side of her plate and chopped a wedge of lemon. Dinner could still be salvaged. She was used to making the best out of ruins. She sat with her plate and her wine on the floor in front of the fire. She should rehearse her presentation for Wednesday, but she was too tired. She should sleep, but she was too crazed.

Next to her, her phone beeped. A text from Manny Rahman: *Hi Tess, just realised it's been a year since John died. If you ever want to hang out, get a coffee and have a chat, I'd –.* The message went on. She cancelled out of it. Droplets of sweat sprang up around her eyes. Her heart pounded. How dare he get in touch with her, to assume he knew what she was feeling? Sure, the worst thing that ever happened to her had been front-page news *twice*. But that didn't make it public property.

9.

FROM HER SIDEBOARD Tessa slid out her giant battered shoebox of memories and dragged it across the white fluffy rug. On her knees in her tights and underwear she sifted through the detritus of her snatched moments with John. The first thing she looked at was the photo. It seemed ludicrously risky now, but had seemed perfectly sensible then. They'd met up in Flagstaff Gardens the day after the barbecue. They'd walked – Tessa had *skipped* – she'd done most of the talking, nearly all of it nonsense. In the densest, most private part of the park, John laid out his light jacket for her under a tree. Coins came loose from the pocket and slid onto the grass. She handed them back up to him. 'Look after the pennies,' she said. He stared at her, entranced. 'Remember?' Tessa said. 'When we were coming back from Canberra? You said it when we shared a cab.'

'I remember everything about that cab ride,' John said.

Soon they were half-sitting, half-lying down and kissing, right there in the park, less than a kilometre from where they'd spent the previous two and a half years working together. He had his hand down her jeans. She reached up for his face. He sucked her fingers in his mouth. That did it, for some reason – she came. After a moment, they both took their hands out and laughed, Tessa almost crying, hysterical in the aftermath of lust. John leaned against a tree and she leaned against him. They recapped every time they'd ever spoken and said what they'd really wanted to say.

Later Tessa pulled her treasured Cybershot from her bag, stretched out her arm and took a picture of them together. She looked at the photo now. She'd held up the camera to capture the beginning of a new life, as blithely as if it were Yasmin she was snapping on a night out, not an adulterer caught in the act. John looked keen, alert and – with his election night buzzcut nowhere near grown out – still slightly alien. Tessa could see evidence that he'd already been old: in the open neck of his shirt his collarbone created a slack hollow of wrinkled skin. He'd been fifty-four then. He'd be fifty-eight now, if he were alive. Maybe he'd been right to make such a big deal of their age difference: 1978 minus 1953 (she ran the old maths). Twenty-five years. A quarter of a century. She couldn't imagine ever again possessing the optimism and naivety required to take that photograph and print it out at Kmart.

Against her better judgment Tessa had remained working at the ACTU after she and John 'became intimate', his stiff, old-timey euphemism for the elation and frustration of their affair. Her role changed, but in an ill-defined and informal way, and she couldn't be sure it was a promotion: she was John's 'new Callum' after Callum departed to work for Kevin Rudd. John overcompensated in front of colleagues, avoiding eye contact and speaking to her with a neutrality that registered as disdain. She left meetings hiding tears of fury and shame. 'I know I'm not always perfect,' he pleaded. 'I'm trying to get the balance right!'

Once John's wife came to the office to take him out for lunch, the sleeves of her dark green silk shirt rolled up, her eyelashes as thick as a child's. Ingrid and Tessa were sitting at their desks. 'Look at you two, sitting there like John's guard dogs,' Grace said. Later John apologised over and over again as Tessa cried. He consistently refused to be drawn on the topic of his wife or his marriage. Yet Grace had an amazing way of *popping up* in conversation. Grace hated it when she came out of a shop and couldn't find him, John said. Grace thought he walked too fast. 'He's a nightmare, socially,' John said about a politician, and Tessa just knew he was quoting Grace. Once John had his hand on Tessa's stomach: 'You know, when you're pregnant, your diaphragm relaxes, so you moan like a ghost in your sleep.' She rolled away, because she didn't know, and at the rate they were going she never would. Nosing about in a Braidwood antique shop, pretending to be a couple, John had leapt upon some kind of fireplace tool. 'It exactly matches the one I broke at home!' He was with Tessa, but shopping for his *real life*. Resting her cheek on the seatbelt of the rental car, Tessa had sobbed and sobbed as John struggled to console her. Stiffly, he revealed there was 'nothing to be jealous of'. He and Grace had not been 'man and wife' in 'a long time'. But Grace still got to wake up next to him, to hold his hand in the street. Grace got to say 'my husband', to walk through the world with the knowledge she'd been chosen.

Finally one day they went to Sydney for a conference. As usual they stayed in the cheapest and most horrible hotel room – John felt bad about charging the union for two when one would remain empty. 'Send me an email,' he said the next morning. He was sitting up in bed with his glasses on, newspapers scattered around him like a homeless man, staring at his Blackberry. He realised he sounded like her boss;

toggling from intimate to professional was a constant source of tension. 'Please,' he added.

Tessa reached for her laptop under the bed and sent him an email: *Madman* was the subject line. '*Just relax.*' She heard the whoosh as her laptop sent it and the Blackberry's answering beep.

'Oh, it worked,' John said, disconsolate. His electoral success had put the unions – and him – out of business.

At a dingy two-star conference space near Paddy's Market, John managed a rousing speech about transitioning activists into members, took some questions, mingled good-naturedly, posed for what he called 'selfos' and was done and dusted by midday. A clear chunk of time opened up before them: half a day with no work commitments, eight hours till Grace would expect John home. But, instead of sneaking off to a bar or the beach, John insisted on staying. Afternoon tea was served on the unsightly concrete rooftop courtyard; the delegates smoked and networked. John and Tessa escaped briefly to the far side of a ventilation shaft.

'Tess.' John grasped the balcony railing. 'I feel like that guy.' He shielded his eyes with his hand and gazed over the singularly unbeautiful panorama of grimy Haymarket roofs and dripping air-conditioning units. 'You know the guy?' John put on his anecdote voice. 'He's stuck on a cliff and a boat comes by. "Mate, mate, jump in the water and we'll pull you in," the boat men say. "No, mate, I'm waiting for God to save me." A helicopter hovers and a man gets ready to throw him a rope. "No, mate," the guy says, "I'm waiting for God to save me." What happens next? He falls in the water and drowns. "God," he says to God, when he gets to Heaven. "I was waiting for you." "You deadshit," God says, "who do you think sent you the boat and that chopper?"'

That was exactly what Tessa was offering – a new life, a chance to be rescued. Was he finally taking the plunge? She spoke warmly but with caution. 'What are you thinking?'

'Labor kept begging me to run,' he said. 'I could be in government now. I've fucked it up, I've really fucked it up. I didn't realise it would be my last chance.'

The Sydney conference had been the beginning of the end. One day John didn't come into work, and didn't answer any calls or texts. Tessa overheard a worried Ingrid. 'Take care of yourself. John? Take care of yourself.' Tessa couldn't even pretend to play it cool. She rushed in and demanded to know what happened. 'It's John's daughter, Sophie,' Ingrid explained. 'She had a fall, cut her hand pretty badly, she had to have surgery, she'll need physio, oh, the poor girl.' The poor girl – the poor *girl*? Sophie by then was *twenty-two*. When Tessa was that age, her father had been dead, she'd moved alone to Melbourne, where she knew no one, she'd paid all her own bills and occasionally some of her mother's. Nobody ever called *her* a poor girl!

When John got into work that afternoon he went straight to Tessa's desk. 'Come for a walk,' he said, and they went down to Flagstaff Gardens, past where the victory barbecue had been, back to the location of the hope-filled first photograph. When he took her in his arms and kissed her, as passionately as the first time they'd kissed, she wondered for a wild moment if he'd somehow thought of a way to make it work. But his face was white and his grip on her shoulders so tight. She started crying, because she knew what was coming. It was a farewell.

'Why?' she sobbed.

'I thought my children were grown-up, but they're not,' John said. 'You'll find, when you have children . . .' She cried out at the outrage and pain of this, but he didn't seem to notice. It was like he was talking to himself. 'Your responsibilities last forever. They still need me. Sophie – she's having a hard time. Well, you know what it's like to be a young woman. You're only young yourself.' *John had come to Tessa's door.* He'd been the first to say 'I love you'. Why enter her life just to ruin it? She could hardly talk she was sobbing so much. 'You're the last love of my life,' he said, and he was crying. 'I'll never love anyone the way I love you.' She stumbled back across the park, alone. They'd been together for less than a year.

When he chose Sophie and his family instead of her, Tessa spoke to no one and ate nothing. After a week Yasmin dragged her to a Vietnamese restaurant and made her eat the broth part of a chicken pho. Tessa bought a candle, one of the big ones in a jar, lit it every night and uttered an incantation: 'By the time this candle burns down, I'll be okay.' After four weeks, she emailed the Labor HQ boss to say she was looking for work. *Aha!* Andrew wrote back. *Tessa the web guru. If you're in Sydney, Falcon Hellier might be just the thing.*

I can be in Sydney, she replied.

Falcon Hellier was a government relations and lobbying firm founded by former Labor powerbrokers. Asked if she'd prefer corporate or political campaigns, she said, unhesitatingly, corporate. She wanted to be as far away as possible from trade unions and the Labor Party, from factionalism and the charade of democracy, the pretence that there was no hierarchy and that women were valued, even as grey faceless men carved up the world between them on gruff phone calls and over Chinese meals. She yearned to manage and be managed, for metrics and KPIs, Frequent Flyer points and the *Harvard Business Review* blog, annual reviews and excellence, things that could be controlled, things *she* could control. She emailed Ingrid to say the company might call John for a reference. They did, and John's feedback was *glowing*, David Hellier said, when he called to offer two and a half times her ACTU salary. Tessa requested and immediately received a two-thousand-dollar signing bonus to cover the cost of moving.

When she was packing, she heard a knock. There was a John-sized shadow in the pebbled glass next to the front door. She stood silent and completely still. After a while, he left. The last thing she wrapped was the sadness candle, quarter-burnt and stained with black.

Tessa's new clients were uniformly objectionable, the people and their businesses. Fizzy drinks, coal, an international chain of cancer-causing solariums, a building materials firm that had lied about asbestos: all received the benefits of Tessa's ruthless focus and unrelenting twelve-hour days. She was on permanent alert for John's infrequent texts, the horror that she'd receive one *and* the horror they would stop. Barack Obama's Inauguration took place on a freezing January morning in Washington, DC. In sweltering midsummer Sydney, Tessa watched the ceremony over breakfast. When she picked up her phone to head out, she saw she'd missed a text. *Hope and change. I wish I was watching this with you. I miss you every day and wish we could still be in touch, but I'll stop writing. I can see you don't want to hear from me. John xxx* She *did* want to hear from him. But these were the words she'd wanted him to say: 'Tessa. I made a mistake and I'm sorry. I've left Grace. I love you.' True to his word, he never texted her again.

She threw away the sadness candle. Not because she felt better, just because it was dumb. She started working Saturdays in the office, and sometimes Sundays too. Her career grew and grew, and when bad people and bad companies wanted someone bad to fight the bad fight and win, they knew exactly who to call: Tessa Notaras, a lonely, unloved, unlovable workaholic with nothing to distract her from what she did best: think about the future, strategise, fight and win. When would John discover what she was doing and reach out, to take her to dinner and beg her to stop, to please, *please* use her powers for good? (*Tessa. I made a mistake and I'm sorry. I've left Grace. I love you.*) But he either didn't find out or didn't care, and she became the bad person she'd been pretending to be. The only thing she had to take her mind off her terrible memories was her terrible work. The only person taking care of Tessa was herself.

Oh God, she hated herself for ever loving him. No one was as unhappy as she was. No one had been fucked over as badly by one man. She should toss the photo in the fire, toss all this shit in, the whole box of memories and pain. She should get in herself and burn too. She let the photo fall to the rug. She reached around for her knife and snatched it up. Savagely, she stabbed the picture – once, twice – and it seemed to her they were actually bleeding, the old in-love Tessa and the old in-love John; blood was splashing back and spattering her and it was on her hands and her bare chest and her bra and her stomach and her tights and her lap – but it was just the bottle of red wine, tipped on its side and soaking the expensive rug.

10.

Out in the suburbs, Sophie was still awake and crying. Sam's side of the bed was empty. Her mind surged with different relationship-ending scenarios. He'd found out about her visit to Tessa's flat. He'd found out about Matthew, and what she'd done the year before. She imagined Sam kissing someone else in an alleyway, his hand snaking up a tight skirt; Sam on the ground outside the pub, his skull caved in from a titanic king hit; the Pajero flipped and crumpled on the M1, topsy-turvy Sam hanging unconscious from his seatbelt. Those were the options, the only two explanations for his absence after midnight on a Monday: either he'd left her or he was dead. In the olden days she would have soothed her anxiety by bombarding him with calls and texts. Phoneless now, all she could do was wait. If this was what happened when she tried to find answers, she'd never take action again.

It was nearly 1 am when she heard the Pajero scrape the driveway. She ran into the small laundry where Sam entered through the garage. He crushed her in a hug. 'Possum Magic! You're still up!'

She could smell smoke on his jacket and the ghost of alcohol on his breath. She gathered up his lapels and shook them. 'Sam!'

'I had *one* drink, and one cigarette. We worked till eleven – we deserved it!'

'Who's we?'

'The whole team. Yeah, Adam, other Adam, Costa, Shalini.' Sophie rolled her eyes at the mention of his prettiest colleague. 'Even Marek graced us with his presence.'

'That sounds fun,' she said sadly.

He was sensitive to her key change. 'Possy-wossy, what's up?'

'I just –'

'Soph,' Sam spoke with gentle admonishment.

'No, it's not about Dad –'

'Because, Soph – it's not helpful.'

'I know! I'm not talking about him. I'm talking about us! All I want is dinner and telly. Normal life. Being together! I can't have another night alone. It's not good for me.'

'Well, the pitch is tomorrow,' Sam said gently. 'So I'll have pitch drinks afterwards.'

'Sam!'

'Okay,' he said. 'When I find out where we're going tomorrow, I'll call you in the shop. You can join us after work. You don't have to be alone. Okay?'

Sophie allowed herself to be led back to bed. 'Okay.'

So Sam was alive. After a shower, he took up position on his side of the bed, dropped off quickly and started snoring. Sophie, on the other hand, was filled with a terrible regret. At first she'd taken it fast with Sam because fast was all she knew. She'd go out, text him and extravagantly ignore him when he turned up. She'd spit a mouthful of vodka soda in his face just to see what he would do. She'd throw her glass in a bin, just to hear it shatter. 'Sorry, sorry, sorry': she could hear Sam apologising for her as she marched out of the club. She would be pacing out the front, desperate to fight. 'Why are you apologising for me? Why don't you support me? Whose side are you on?' He'd drop her home to make sure she was safe; she'd cry when he tried to leave. 'Stay with me, stay, stay.' She would wake in the morning and sob into his chest; he'd roll on the condom, brow furrowed in concentration. That was what the whole furious dance was leading towards, the fighting, the fleeing, the pleas: Sam's urgent thrusts, even as her tears were still drying. 'You're too beautiful to be so sad.'

After what he called his 'stint' in ad sales at the paper, Sam had joined a new digital advertising firm, Cataclysm. It was based near Domain Interchange, and every Friday night his tight-knit team went for drinks in a pub on Dorcas Street. Sophie's breakup with Ed the photographer had splintered one friendship group and her ongoing enmity with her housemates had ruined the other. With no Friday-night plans of her own she'd bitterly complained about Sam's. Eventually, he invited her along. It was a big moment, meeting the colleagues. She'd taken the afternoon off from the bookshop to relax with some pre-drinks and get ready. Just as she was putting on her make-up, Eliza and Caitlin knocked on her door. There was no easy way to say this, they said easily, but they wanted Sophie gone. She was no longer welcome in the Pigdon Street share house.

'But it's a *share house*,' she sobbed. 'I *share* the house. You can't kick me out.'

'There's something very wrong with you,' one of them said; . she couldn't remember if it was Eliza or Caitlin. 'Why do you want to be around us – when we don't want to be around you?'

Sophie had to redo her whole face, ruined from crying. She did not consider cancelling her plans with Sam. Early to the bar, she got talking to a pensioner named Clancy; when

Sam showed up she was perched on his lap, charming his pensioner friends and getting all her drinks for free. Sam was embarrassed, and his embarrassment made her furious. 'Fine, if you don't want to be seen with me, don't fucking be seen with me!' She stormed out the back of the pub, turning to check he was following her. Something went badly wrong in that moment: she tripped down a step, staggered and fell. Her outstretched hand landed on a beer glass. The blood, it was insane. Knocked out for surgery, she came to with her mum, dad, brother and Sam in a semicircle around her bed, all facing off in a solemnity competition, all taking turns to tell her she could've *died*.

When she was out of hospital, her dad paid the overdue bills and the three months' rent on Pigdon Street, pleading with her to not tell her mum. He drove her to St Kilda Beach and bought her a soft serve with a Flake. Sophie ate it with one hand, the other strapped to her chest in a sling. The waves lapped at the shore, a mild tang of pollution in the air. Beside her on the sea wall, his face twisted in actual anguish, her father begged her to take her future seriously. 'What's next for you? Come on, sweetheart, what are your dreams? Journalism, isn't that what you wanted?'

'Yeah, but I had to finish my honours to do the masters, and . . .' Sophie shrugged with her good arm.

'Don't worry about studying it!' John said. 'Lots of reporters got cadetships when they were fifteen, sixteen – they didn't even finish high school. Learn on the job! Get your shorthand, study your beat. You're a curious person, a charming girl; you love to write – you could do the writing part standing on your ear. You've just got to find the opportunities, and when you find them, make sure you're ready!'

Sophie made a grumpy sound. 'That's not how it works anymore. Anyway, I've got a job. I love Patrick, I love the shop.'

'Where will you live?'

Sam had said they should move out together to his parents' investment property in Forest Hill. She expected her dad to laugh. Forest Hill? Sophie Clare in the suburbs, really? But instead he said it was a 'very sound idea' and she was a 'very lucky girl'. Sophie snorted again.

'Hey.' He put his arm around her. 'Sam's a lovely young man. Polite, confident, a go-getter.'

'But he's nothing like what I imagined.' She groaned. 'I know I sound awful, I *am* awful, but this isn't how I thought I'd live my life. This isn't what I dreamt.' She'd just assumed she'd be *discovered* by now, spotlit, whisked away. Actually making her way in the world hadn't really been part of her plan.

'Does Sam make you laugh?' her dad said gently. 'Is he kind to you?'

'He's so kind,' Sophie said. 'No one is kinder.'

'Sweetheart, that's what you need. That's all I could ask for, and all *you* should. Kindness is everything. Everything.'

'How would you know?' Sophie burst out. 'Mum's horrible to you. She's horrible to me!'

On the wind, the sounds of Luna Park wafted over to them, the rattle of the roller-coaster and shrieks of people having fun. After a while, her dad spoke carefully. 'We've been married for a long time.'

'She's a bitch to me and a bitch to you. The only person she's ever nice to is Toby. She's not even that nice to him.'

'You've got to remember – when she was your age she was all alone in the world.'

'*I'm* all alone in the world. Soon I won't even be in the world! I'll be in the suburbs!'

'You'll never be alone. You have me.' Sophie did a sceptical *hmph*. 'Sweetheart.' He swivelled his whole body and put his hands on both her shoulders. 'Wherever you are, whatever you do, while I'm alive and you're alive, I'm looking after you and loving you.'

'But what if you leave me, what if you die?'

'Oh, love,' her father said. 'First of all, I'm ten feet tall and as strong as an ox.' Sophie laughed. 'Really, you must know this.' His voice became so hollow, so reverberating, it was as though he was speaking from a black hole: 'I know I wasn't around a lot. But everything I've done – every big decision in my life – maybe one day I'll tell you all about it. But I've always tried my best for you.'

Now, years later, Sophie lay in bed, eyes wide open in the dark, replaying the scene like CCTV footage. What was *that* supposed to have meant? Every big decision in his life? Did he mean not running as an MP in 2007? But that made no difference to her. Perhaps he'd been thinking of sundry alleged sacrifices he'd made in her childhood. But coming to 20 per cent of Sophie's parent–teacher meetings and speech days hadn't been a sacrifice made by her dad. Only having a part-time father had been a sacrifice made by Sophie!

Next to her, Sam snored gently. Sophie carefully arranged her body around his and breathed in time with his breaths. What would she do without him? Sam had done all of Sophie's packing so she didn't have to see Eliza and Caitlin again. He carried everything for her, and continued to do so, even when her hand was better. They set up the Forest Hill unit as nicely as they could, though Sam's parents, Rosemary and Dennis, forbade any painting or nails for pictures or Blu Tack. Sam wanted to buy his own home before he turned thirty, so all Sophie's earnings from the bookshop and all of Sam's from Cataclysm went into a central pot. From there they both withdrew fifty dollars a week 'pocket money', not nearly enough for any clothes or outings or fun. The only real joy in Sophie's life became cooking, not least because groceries came out of the shared account. When she got home from the bookshop she'd walk through Forest Hill Chase and buy the supplies for a two-, sometimes three-course meal. She'd prepare it watching *ABC News* and *7.30 Report*, and when Sam came home they'd watch a show and eat together. She put on seven kilos in a year and never wanted to have sex. Sam didn't seem to mind, in fact the more fat and imprisoned and domesticated she became, the happier he seemed to grow, sleek and groomed and bolstered. Daily she'd googled Irritable Bowel Syndrome and 'symptoms of depression', but the thought of actually doing anything or changing in any way was impossible.

By the time *MasterChef* burst onto the nation's screens, midway through 2009, the gap between Sophie's real life and how she'd imagined her life would be was cavernous. Televised every bleak midwinter night except Saturdays, the new cooking show became her star by which to navigate. Ten minutes into the second episode, she created a Twitter account, @mastersoph, to track what people were saying about it. Sam watched with a benign smile as she set up a BlogSpot with a homemade MasterSoph logo. Over the course of twenty weeks she amassed seven hundred Twitter followers and her witty episode recaps got thousands of views. Sam's colleague Adam designed her a fancy new blog header. At the shop, Patrick gave her a talking-to because she spent so much of her work day online. But a great momentum had been building inside her, a feeling that soon the world would see and get to know the real her. And, sure enough, the week after office manager Julie Goodwin was crowned Australia's first MasterChef, Sophie Clare was formally summoned to Victoria's newspaper of record.

The *Age* Deputy Chief of Staff Gavin Purves had a grey face, a neckbeard and a checked shirt flaked with scurf. He selected a cardboard file labelled WEB from a towering pile on his desk and sifted through a pile of hideously unformatted print-outs of Sophie's most popular posts. 'They look a bit better on the screen,' she said.

'I'll take your word for it.'

'Shall I bring up my blog on my laptop? Do you have wi-fi?'

'The guest wi-fi doesn't work. Interested in journalism?'

'Oh yes,' Sophie said fervently.

'No shorthand?'

She allowed her face to show this was ridiculous. 'No.'

His tone softened. 'We're starting a new section on the website. Current title . . .' (Sophie just knew it was going to be 'Your Say') '. . . is Your Say.' She nodded. 'We're going to need columns, or, as they'd be called on this web property, blogs. Four a week, about Melbourne, pop culture and the web.'

'Starting when?'

'Starting now.'

Fuck all you journalism students! Sophie Clare was twenty-three and worked for *The Age*! Life was beginning! Her *real life*, life in the spotlight, life as a drama, played out upon the stage.

Within a year, it would all be over, and nothing would be the same again.

11.

SOPHIE HAD ONLY been freelance for a few months by the time of the newspaper's 2009 Christmas party, working on her four posts a week from the bookshop or home, communicating with no one except Gavin Purves, who was a pussycat, really, actually a really sweet guy. Freelancers were third-class citizens, rarely invited to the newsroom and never to Friday-night drinks. Freelance writers for 'the web' were fourth-class. But Sam used to work at *The Age* too, albeit in ad sales (second-class), and he was always so good at real-life networking, or, as Sophie called it, keeping pointless low-stakes connections alive for long periods of time. He insisted they go, and piloted her smoothly around the excited figures of the ad sales department: the men all gussied up in their best going-out shirts; the slinky tops of the women held in place with Hollywood tape.

It was always that first hour that was hard at parties, when Sophie, being introduced, heard names without actually hearing them, so focused was she on herself, her face, her body, her voice and how she was coming across. But soon the walls between people dissolved: strangers could talk to strangers, everything she said seemed warm and intimate, and everyone was in on the joke. But right as she was feeling her *most* outgoing and expansive, Sam's ad sales gang retreated to the balcony of the Docklands function space for a smoke. Sophie was plotting a reckless solo cruise around the main party when Sam saw a figure skulking in the dark corner of the deck. 'There he is, the deviant,' he said.

'Hey, *Matthew*,' someone shouted approvingly. Everyone laughed and raised their drinks to the tall man hunched and murmuring into his phone. He hung up and came over, grinning wryly at being over forty when everyone else was in their twenties. 'Just saying goodnight to my kid.'

There was a grubby smear on his black suit jacket. Sophie found herself reaching out to touch it. 'Did your child wipe something on you?'

'No.' He looked down at her hand, still holding his lapel, and said gravely, 'I think a woman must have cried on me.'

Matthew sloped off and Sophie found herself staring at the rippling black water of the Yarra, stunned. Later, she slipped away from Sam and found Gavin Purves alone at the bar with one large buttock perched on a stool. 'Gavvy,' Sophie said. 'Has anyone ever told you who you look like?' Gavin stared into her shining face. Only in manipulation did Sophie feel sincere. She pronounced her verdict: 'Russell Crowe.' (*In a fat suit*, she kindly forbore to add.) 'Now, Matthew Straughan. What's his story?'

'Yeah,' Gavin said regretfully. 'Probably confidential, hey.'

'Oh my God, Gavin!' Sophie gave his arm a little push. 'You don't have to tell me any secret stuff, just the goss.'

'He was always doing politics, right. State politics. Then he got the plum job – Canberra. Moved up with his wife and she was either pregnant or just had a kid or something like that. Did his first week up at Parliament. Then there were all these fires, right, in Victoria. So for some reason he comes back, offers himself to Don' – Don was the *Age* editor – 'and just gets a hire car and drives into the bush.'

'Okay . . .' Sophie's listening face was one of her best faces. She could tell Gavin loved it. 'That's weird. Why, do you think?'

'Some people reckoned he was from one of the towns, or his parents were there, or he might have a woman in one of the towns, something like that. He was always pretty messed up. Once, Michelle was in his car, she opened the glovebox and inside, she reckoned, there was a gun.'

'Who's Michelle?' But Matthew was weaving through the party towards them. He raised his eyebrows to see them in conference. 'Gavin was just telling me a ghost story about you.' Sophie ignored her boss's panicked look. She put her hand under her chin as if she was holding a torch: '. . . and then he *disappeared* into the bush.'

'Ahh, but as you can see' – Matthew extended his arms like Jesus resurrected, though still a bit sore, from the cross – 'I made it.'

After the party, Sam was next to her in the back seat of the cab home to Forest Hill, but she felt the strong physical sensation of having left him behind. She was speeding into the future. Tiny, inconsequential, Sam was receding into the past, smaller and smaller until he almost disappeared. In front of her, vast, larger than life, like a light show projected on the side of the Sydney Opera House, shimmered the louche and spectral figure of her lord and saviour, Matthew Straughan.

How terrible it was to be obsessed with someone over forty. Matthew didn't even have Twitter. Or rather, he had

@straughanmatt, but it lay dormant, without even a tentative 'My first post . . .' Having exhausted Google mere days after they first met, Sophie was forced out onto the streets. By January she'd broken one of the *Age*'s key unwritten rules about freelancers versus full-time staff and shown up to newsroom drinks in a pub near the corner of Collins and King Streets. The first person she saw at the Black Bream was Gavin. 'Gavvy!' Sophie gasped. 'I was just on my way to the train station . . .' But she didn't need an excuse. She was drawn into his little group by two men she immediately recognised. Beautiful Matthew's perfect face was slightly marred by an alcohol flush, his eyebrows raised in a pissed leer. The second man wasn't a journalist at all but Callum Worboys, her dad's closest offsider and friend, his unelected, unofficial ACTU number two, a trade union hard-man and so-called campaign mastermind. She hadn't seen him since – when? Well, obviously 2007; that's when the election had been.

'Oh my God, Callum Worboys! I literally haven't seen you since the election,' Sophie said.

'*Literally.*' Callum used a dumb voice to imitate her. He gave her a one-armed hug so that her face was briefly crushed against his chest.

'I didn't think men were allowed to have hairy chests anymore.' She wrinkled her nose at the open collar of his shirt. 'I thought I read it in a magazine – that men are supposed to wax.'

'That's back, crack and sack,' Callum said.

'And it's only for fags,' Matthew added.

Sophie looked at him with a horror that was genuine, not feigned for flirting purposes. 'Are you *homophobic*?'

He was briefly chastened. 'Quite the opposite.'

'He means he's gay,' Callum said.

'I don't think so,' Sophie said with certainty.

'No, I *love* men,' Matthew said, and he did seem very solemn and heartfelt.

Callum looked suspicious. 'But how do you know Matt?'

The casualness and unsexiness of 'Matt', 'Matt's' obvious and unsexy drunkenness, the mild confusion of seeing Callum at all and now the very slight aggressiveness of Callum's question all undermined the glee and satisfaction of Sophie's perfectly executed ambush.

'Sophie's a very promising young journalist I'm taking under my wing,' Matthew said.

Callum gave a snort. 'I see.'

'Drinks,' Sophie said. 'I'll get this round. Matthew, come up with me! I won't know what to get otherwise.' Matthew ordered, and as the bartender busied herself, Sophie reached into his inside jacket pocket to slip out his wallet, warm as a body part. She removed two twenties and, by accident, a folded photograph that was caught between the notes. It showed a tiny boy in poignant car-patterned pyjamas. 'Is that your boyfriend?'

'It's my son.' Matthew took the wallet and gently slid the picture back inside.

'He's very sweet.'

'What about *your* boyfriend?'

It was unsporting of him to have brought up Sam. Sophie frowned. 'He's fine.'

'Won't he mind when I take you home with me?'

'I don't think he'll find out.'

'And what about your other boyfriend?'

She followed his glance back to the table. Gavin was staring at her, his thumb holding down the ice cubes as he drained his rum and coke. She gazed up at Matthew. 'You could take him in a fight.'

'I'm actually very weak, you know,' Matthew said. 'Fragile.'

Sophie put on a concerned face. 'Do you think you'll be able to make it to a cab?' He fell forward a little, a miniature collapse. 'Come on,' she coaxed. 'Drink your drink and I'll help you home.'

Later, as Matthew paid the driver, Sophie stared at the doorbells outside his apartment building in Collingwood. 'Which is yours?'

'That one.' He seemed almost annoyed. The button said FLAT E.

'Why does it say *flate*?' She giggled so much he had to grab her elbow and hustle her into the lift. Matthew's flat was compact but plush, with floorboards polished to a high shine. His small kitchen was part of the living room. On the open shelving Sophie saw a stack of six white dinner plates and five white side plates, six white wine glasses and five red wine glasses. She had a hunch and went over to his dishwasher. Inside was one wine glass and one plate, clean. A single fork lay in the top tray. 'Did you run the dishwasher just for this?'

'I did.' Matthew was so tall that in order to be closer to her level he crumpled his midsection and leaned sideways like an accordion. It was not a good posture, and through the gaps between his shirt buttons she could see some of his hairy tummy. Sophie brushed past him to better explore the living room. A big television was sitting on a black TV stand. There was a single black leather couch. 'I love your divorced-man aesthetic. Is this a *throw*?' She pointed at a grey blanket folded prison-like into a tight rectangle.

Matthew seemed pleased. 'It is.'

Even the loneliness of the flat was appealing; after his split he obviously got to start again. Sophie wanted to be with him, of course, but she also wanted vaguely to *be* him. To be alone like this to do whatever she wanted. Oddly enough then her last thought before sex was of Sam – and how she'd never be able to make her own choices and live her own life for as long as he was in it.

The Friday after that, Sophie lay in wait in a corner of the pub. At nine she could wait no longer and texted the number she'd copied from the paper's internal directory. *Will I see you at the Black Bream?* She ended it with three kisses. She was home in bed, alone and seething, when he graced her with his baldly factual reply: *In Canberra with my boy.* No kisses. The week after that, Sophie sat on his doorstep in Little Oxford Street and watched as his cab pulled up half an hour later than they arranged to meet. She ignored him until they were in the lift. Then she shoved him hard into the reflective walls. 'There's a security camera,' he said. They exited sedately and he opened the door to his flat. She pushed him again, towards the bedroom. He stopped, and she kept going, but he yanked her arm to stop her. She was furious. 'It's hard to have an affair, you know. It takes a lot of organising.'

'I know.'

'I don't have to *play* hard to get,' she snapped. 'I *am* hard to get.'

'I know.' He kissed her. After they'd had sex, when he thought she wouldn't notice, he buried his nose in her hair and breathed it in. She *had* noticed. It was what made her think she would almost certainly leave Sam.

The next time she came to his flat she saw he was already very drunk. She kissed him. 'Yuck,' she said. 'You had a kebab for lunch.' In the bedroom, the bed was sheetless, just a yellowing mattress protector and the puffy cloud of a coverless duvet. 'Ugh! You knew I was coming!'

Matthew stood there like a little boy getting in trouble. She shoved him once towards the bed and he caught her arm before she could push him again. They kissed and she bit his lip, hard. 'That hurt,' he said.

'If it hurts, you should cry out. So I know to stop. Why are you so fucking silent all the time?'

They stared at each other until Matthew opened his arms and she fell into them. Later she scraped his nipple hard with her fingernails. 'Fuck!' Matthew shouted.

'That's better,' she said.

Their covert relationship proceeded with the utmost seriousness and an almost nauseating sense of increasing momentum. One night, as she rose from his bed to get dressed, he buried his face in the pillow and mumbled something. 'What?'

He repeated: 'Imagine if you could just . . . stay.'

She kissed him pristinely and perfectly on the lips. 'I can't stay until I'm invited.'

'Stay.' He grasped her by the shoulders. 'Stay, stay, stay.' Smiling, she got up to leave.

He even texted her a few times. Coming from him, famously a non-texter, the 'X' at the end felt like a marriage proposal.

One Friday night she rang his buzzer as planned and received no response. She called him, impatience mounting, because although she could edit her call log, the number would show up on her phone bill, and who knew when Sam might take it into his head to have a look? No answer. She rang the buzzer again. This time the front door clicked. Upstairs Matthew was slumped on the doorframe. 'Why are you here?' he mumbled at the floor.

'Matthew? What's wrong? You said to come, remember?'

'I didn't.' He seemed to be genuinely in pain, his face almost green. 'Oh God.'

'What's wrong?' She was panicking. 'What's wrong?'

He ran towards his bedroom. Was he crying? After a moment, Sophie tiptoed after him. Through the open door to his ensuite she watched him vomit copiously into the toilet. She crept away unseen to wait on the black leather couch. When he joined her, his hairline was wet and she could smell toothpaste. He sat on the couch as far away from her as possible. 'Sorry,' he said. 'I had a big one.'

'A big one?'

'Last night,' he said. 'I was out with the guys. Gav, Callum. You know.' Suddenly he moaned again.

'Matthew! No one forced you to get wasted.'

'My little boy,' he said almost inaudibly.

She knelt on the floor in front of him. 'What about him?'

'It was his birthday last night.'

'And . . .? You didn't get to be with him? Why didn't you tell me?'

Matthew didn't answer. His hands were covering his face and he said, from under them, 'I can't do this anymore.'

Sophie thought he meant drink. 'You'll feel better when you've had a sleep.' She guided him gently to his room and tucked him into bed. She got in next to him and stroked his hair till he was almost asleep.

'This is what a normal relationship is like,' he murmured. 'You can just relax together.'

They had sex then but she wasn't even sure if Matthew came,

or even if, for a lot of the time, he was actually inside her. Sam had a lot of problems: he screamed and covered his Coke if a wasp came near it, when he wore sunglasses he looked like a blind person, he literally thought the word 'misled', as in 'deceived', was pronounced 'my-zeld', like, 'she myzeld him', his weird uptight parents looked like the twits out of the Roald Dahl book *The Twits*, he was a try-hard with a girl's laugh. But getting an erection was not a problem. All Sophie wanted was a man she could fantasise about sexually without being appalled by the gap between her fantasies and the reality, a fuckable man who would dote on her without rendering himself contemptible. Why was it so hard?

That night, after the botched root, Sophie retreated alone to the ensuite. She brushed her hair with Matthew's round plastic currycomb and reapplied her lipstick. Back in the bedroom, Matthew turned away from her brisk kiss. She wished him a cold and disappointed goodnight.

Later, home before Sam, Sophie was freshly showered and reading in bed. 'Ugh,' she said when he came in. 'You absolutely reek of smoke.'

'Hey now.' Sam emptied his pockets onto his bedside table and his car keys dropped to the floor. 'Whoops!'

'Did you even drive home or were you too drunk?'

'Possum Magic? Are you okay?'

'This life.' Sophie tossed her book aside. 'It's not what I wanted.'

'Well, it's not exactly what *I* wanted,' Sam said mildly.

Stung, Sophie cried, '*You're* not what I wanted.'

'Do you know anyone who'd stick with you as long as I have?' He stared at her, hard and serious.

'What's that supposed to mean?'

Sam took off his jeans and folded them. His voice was cold. 'You spend half your life lying around or freaking out. Then the other half being insane and embarrassing. I don't even know who you are anymore.'

When he turned off the light she cried softly, alone. He reached over and put his arms around her. It was a huge relief to be close to him. 'You have to promise we're breaking up,' she said, muffled against his t-shirt.

'What did you say?'

'You have to promise we're breaking up.'

'I promise,' he said, and they fell asleep.

More than a year later, in the very same bed, a very different Sophie sobbed and sobbed until Sam turned and pulled her to his chest. 'You have to promise you'll never leave me,' she said.

'I promise,' Sam said. 'I'll never leave you.'

12.

'Mrs Clare? Mrs Clare?' Grace blinked until her eyes alighted on the crotch of a man's beige chinos. She moaned and struggled to sit up. She was in hospital, a blue curtain drawn around her bed. She pulled her gown higher over her uncomfortably unsupported chest. 'You're awake, good.' The man spoke gently. 'I'm Doctor Nguyen. We've pumped your stomach and sewn up your noggin. You've been in the wars, love. You've given yourself a big fright, haven't you?'

Grace nodded, a tear sliding down her cheek. 'How did you find me?'

'Ambos brought you in. Neighbours called them. You're a very lucky lady.' Darkness in the vast empty hangar of Grace's mind. A flashbulb of memory in the very back corner. Blood on the tiles. Girl and her mum Belinda covering her in a towel. Underneath – she almost couldn't bear it – she'd been wearing just her nightie. 'Look.' Dr Nguyen moved a plastic chair from the corner of the cubicle to within Grace's reach. On it was a bulging Johnston Street Pottery bag. 'There's your stuff, clothes and all that, the girl from next door brought it.'

She was struggling to come to grips with the real world. 'What time is it?'

'Tuesday morning. Time for me to head home! You too, whenever you feel up to it. Bloods are fine, skull x-ray fine.

No rush, okay? Rest, rest. Time for you to take care of yourself. Now look, all right? Don't be scared when you look in the mirror. You'll heal up fine, and when the hair grows back you won't even see the scar. Oh, hey!'

Grace couldn't help it, she was sobbing.

13.

In *MEN'S HEALTH* magazine they always said to shop from the perimeter aisles: vegetables, the fresh stuff. Shopping for the Jolly Trolley took Toby straight to the heart of the supermarket. He gathered up all the usuals, plus anything he'd heard the patients or families mention: Twisties, Smith's chicken chips, musk sticks, Allen's raspberry lollies, Fantales, Tim Tams original flavour, Violet Crumbles, milk bottles, Cadbury Snack with different coloured fillings, Light and Tangy Thins, Burger Rings, Pizza Shapes, the orange box Shapes – was he going overboard?

That afternoon the hospice sitting room was crammed. The word had spread about Toby's trip to Dickson Woolies. Every visitor had been lured out for a drink. Lots came in especially. Someone put Katy Perry on their iPhone and all the children started to dance. Soon the dancing was just running and skidding. Helen came out of her office and whistled like an umpire. 'Now now, everyone. People are trying to rest.'

'There's time for that when we die!' cried Mrs Zhang from Magpie. Everyone laughed and clapped her, including Helen. The patients and their families trickled back to their rooms, smiling.

In his bed in Lorikeet, Lawrence gave the musk stick a big sniff. He broke off a bit and put it on his tongue. Bald and liver-spotted, he looked like a goanna on a rock. 'Mate, I love these bloody musk sticks,' he moaned. 'You keep pumping me full of sugar, I'll never die.'

'Sorry, Lawrence,' Toby said.

'Oh, you bloody duffer. Hey, come here. I got a message for ya.' Lawrence patted the expanse of bed beside him. His hand was like a crocodile-claw backscratcher from a tourist shop.

'Oh cool, thanks.' Toby perched on the side of the bed.

'No fucking worries,' Lawrence said. Toby looked encouraging and gently squeezed the claw. 'That *was* the message, you clown.' Lawrence gave a fond laugh. '*No fucking worries.*'

But Toby did have worries. Lots of them. He mulled them over in the hospice kitchenette as he loaded the plates and cups into the dishwasher. Every single problem in his life could be traced back to a specific moment in a specific day a year and a half earlier in the communal showers at college. Toby had a *thing* about them. Beyond the hygiene concerns, he was so tall he worried people could see his head over the dividers, tantamount to seeing him naked. A further unusual feature of the communal showers was that the water didn't drain into an individual plughole. Rather, it ran down towards the back of the stall into a trough shared by all three showers in a row. One day, early in first year, he was carefully soaping his entire body when he saw something that made him gasp – blood, everywhere, eddies of blood in the shared trough.

'Toby, just chill out,' came the voice from the next stall.

It was Astrid, a girl who didn't shave her armpits. He remembered her name with a mnemonic – *Astrid*: *strid*ent feminist. He hadn't realised she knew his. But the way she drawled it – Tow-beeeee – he knew at once it was her. 'How did you know it was me?'

'First of all, I can see the top of your head. And I saw you walking to the shower with your lame little caddy.'

'Oh.' Should he ask if she was okay? 'Are you okay?'

'It was period blood. I'm perfectly fine.'

He spoke in a dumb high voice. 'Yeah, no worries!' He ran his hands over his whole lanky, unsatisfactory body to get the suds off and escape.

'You know that mint and tea tree body wash doesn't actually make your balls tingle?' Astrid said. 'That's an urban myth.'

'Oh, ha-ha!' Toby had never heard about the tingles. He'd hoped the tea tree would be good for the three to five pimples that routinely plagued his back. He wrapped his large towel around himself so it covered him nipple-to-knee, picked up his 'lame little caddy' and fled. Despite living on the same floor, he rarely encountered Astrid during his first two terms at uni. He studied his law and modern Chinese. He attended toga parties and played mixed doubles tennis on the university team. Just as he had at school, he hitched his wagon to that of a slightly more popular guy. Wherever James Cranshaw was invited, Toby was invited too. It was chill.

One night in May, Cranshaw got it into his head he should try to pick up a MILF in Kingston. 'I support you,' Toby said. 'But you won't be allowed anywhere in Kingston dressed like that.' He waited in the almost-empty common room while Cranshaw went to change out of his rugby shorts.

On the big TV an ashen Kevin Rudd was fending off criticism of his environmental policies. As part of his campaign he'd promised an emissions trading scheme to reduce carbon pollution. He dumped it in April 2010. A month later, seemingly out of the blue, he announced a vast new tax on the mining industry. Toby was all for it. You break it, you buy it, that's what he thought about mining companies and the environment. But Travallion, Allaman, XLT Civet, a bunch of weird cowboy outfits from Western Australia, every mining worker, every right winger and even some normal people were shocked by the new tax. It was clear Rudd had not anticipated the backlash. 'Well, um, as I said before, Kerry, um, some of the large mining companies and some other companies are going to say *all sorts of things* as we sort out the detail of this . . .'

'Wow.' Next to Toby, Astrid was staring up at the screen. 'He looks like a Christmas ham.' She held out a black can. 'Guinness?'

Toby had never tasted it before. 'Gosh,' he said. 'It's like eating a second dinner.'

Gratifyingly, Astrid laughed. 'Here, you have it.' She slipped another one for herself out of the pocket in her cargo pants.

On TV, the questioning had moved on. The Prime Minister had promised to tackle global warming by putting a price on carbon. So why had he dumped his emissions trading scheme? Rudd responded hotly: Liberal leader Tony Abbott thought climate change was 'absolute crap'. The Greens opposed it because it didn't go far enough. How was he, Rudd, supposed to deal with those numbers in the Senate? He wasn't a miracle worker. 'Call an election on it,' Astrid shouted at the screen.

Then Rudd bemoaned the lack of global action. 'There was no government in the world like the Australian Government, which threw its every energy at bringing about a deal, a global deal, on climate change!' At the 2009 Copenhagen climate talks, he and his team 'sat for three days and three nights with twenty leaders from around the world to try and frame a global agreement'. O'Brien broke in with a question. Rudd lashed out, his voice brittle with bitterness and regret: 'Now it might be easy for you to sit in *7.30 Report* Land and say that was easy to do. Let me tell you, mate, it wasn't!'

'Oh my God,' Toby said. 'He's losing his shit.'

'We are fundamentally committed on climate change.' Rudd's teeth were gritted. 'We need to do further work on the global front, further work on the national front, because I am absolutely passionate about acting on climate change. We've been frustrated domestically politically, frustrated internationally by the lack of progress there, but we will not be deterred, we will progress this matter, and we will achieve the best possible means of bringing down our greenhouse gas reductions, our greenhouse gas levels, in the future! And the bottom line is this, the bottom line is this,' Rudd repeated desperately, 'there is no way you can stare in the mirror in the future and say that you have passed up the core opportunity to act on climate change. I will not do that. The Government that I lead will not do that, but I cannot wish away the two realities I've just referred to.'

'Okay, okay,' Kerry O'Brien said.

'Okay, wow,' Astrid said. 'We're all going to die.'

'I'm sure it'll all be okay,' Toby said lightly.

'Toby,' Astrid said. 'Copenhagen was *it*. The chance. Barack Obama was there. Wen Jiabao was there. All the leaders of those islands that will be under water in like, fifteen years. They went there to get a deal. They didn't get one. Do you want to play the Degrees of Warming game? So, one degree. Fires sweeping across Australia for the entire summer pretty much every year. The Great Barrier Reef will be bleached. Two degrees. The oceans turn to acid. Agriculture doesn't work properly anymore, half a billion people starve. Sea levels rise seven metres, a third of the world's species become extinct.

Limiting global warming to two degrees was the point of the Copenhagen Summit, by the way.'

'But didn't they do that?'

'Commit to it? No, they *recognised* it. Recognised that ideally, somehow, it should just happen. A two-degree limit isn't binding, and they didn't agree on how to achieve it.'

Toby's mouth dried up. Astrid was sitting with her leg tucked under her, cradling her Guinness. He found himself staring at the ring-pull on the can. The world around him had gone quiet. 'But what if it's more than two degrees?'

'Once you get there, the game ends. It's not predictable after that. New York and London under water. No more polar bears, obviously – no more ice.'

'What about Australia?'

'We would have burnt down already. A totally barren desert. No wonder Kevin Rudd's lost his shit. He knows how badly they've all fucked up.'

'Clare Bear?' Cranshaw was wearing a suit. He blew some smoke out of an imaginary gun. 'The name's Cranshaw.'

'Oh dear. Um?' Toby turned to Astrid. Without looking away from the TV, she raised her hand in farewell.

At the end of semester one, after exams, the college emptied out. There were four or five weeks of holidays till uni started again. Most people went home, wherever that was. On the phone to his parents, Toby had hung back, keen to be guided by them about whether to return. No guidance had been issued, and no invitation. One day in late June 2010 he found the dining room even emptier than usual. With his giant serving of macaroni and cheese he gingerly took a seat next to the only other first year: Astrid. In the summer, her look had made more sense: tanned skin, brown freckles, long unbrushed brown hair, floaty, patterned sleeveless tops that showed off her controversial underarms. By winter break, her vibe had become more weird. She sat huddled in a promotional fleece branded by the accounting firm Deloitte. Her Birkenstock sandals were paired with men's football socks. Toby turned to her politely. 'So why are you still around?'

Astrid lifted the thick lid of melted cheddar off her pasta and balanced it on the side of her plate. She licked her fingers like a cat. 'I come from a broken home and my parents are both cunts.'

'My parents are still together –'

'But they're cunts.'

He laughed. Were they? He'd never assessed them from the outside before. 'Funny you mention it,' he found himself saying. 'They were in the paper the other day looking like a pair of dickheads.'

'Show me the article,' Astrid said. 'I want to read it.' He searched on his phone for 'John Clare The Two of Us'. His mum and dad regarded him complacently from the photo on the screen.

As Secretary of the Australian Council of Trade Unions, John Clare, 57, led the most successful campaign in the labour movement's history and helped put Labor's Kevin Rudd in the Lodge. John's wife, Grace Clare, 54, is a former lawyer and now amateur potter. They live together in Melbourne's Fitzroy and have two children.

Grace. I was living in my aunt's terrace in Fitzroy when she died suddenly. Just out of school I found myself alone, the owner of this crumbling white elephant. When I started law at Melbourne Uni I put an ad up for housemates and

John applied. He was twenty-one, studying history. He had a hippy beard and hair to his shoulders. Halfway through the interview he excused himself. I found him flat on the floor in the outdoor toilet fixing the plumbing. Of course, I let him move in.

I was so studious, so ambitious. He was like a reptile, basking in the sun doing nothing. We got together in 1975 just after Gough [Whitlam's government] was dismissed. Hard to believe it now, but John didn't really care! He was a dreamer back then. He didn't get political until he started to work on building sites. Now he's like a man possessed. He can't stop until everyone in Australia is safe and fairly treated at work.

Our relationship changed when we had Sophie in 1986. I expected to complete my family the year after and return to my career. But I wasn't able to have Toby until much later. You can't go back to work after a break like that. It was a big comedown for me, from running big cases to running a home. But I like to think I applied the same rigour to both jobs.

With both children launched it's like I have a second chance at life. Now the Your Rights at Work campaign is over I see John more often. But I wouldn't mind if he kept working till he was eighty. I love him dearly but I certainly don't need him under my feet.

John. I turned up to this big old house in Fitzroy and there she was. She'd only just left school but she had the poise and articulacy of a QC. I was intimidated by her, but I needed somewhere to live. The room was dirt cheap because the place was falling apart. I kept telling Grace she should complain to the landlord. It wasn't until I proposed years later that she told me she owned the house herself. She thought if I knew I wouldn't have got a job. She was right, I was a lazy bastard.

Grace was an incredible dynamo in the workplace. By the time she left she was the youngest female senior associate in the firm. I was a slow developer, travelling, trying different jobs. I thought I might be a landscaper, something to do with my hands. I took some work on building sites while I sorted myself out. I was a very average chippie, but being active on the sites was when I realised my purpose in life. Union member, then union rep – when I was thirty I joined the ACTU as an industrial officer. It was like coming home.

Grace was always a fantastic mother. Politics is not nine to five and she had to shoulder a lot by herself. It can't be easy living with someone like me. During the [Your Rights at Work] campaign, I was lucky to stay two nights a week under my own roof. There's a Labor Government now but you can't be complacent. Nowhere in the world is as fair and equal as Australia but injustice still remains. I can't stop while I still have more to give.

'Toby!' Astrid said. He gave her the phone. 'Mmm, your dad's a hotty.' Toby groaned. Astrid scrolled, munching. 'Ugh, your mum: *I like to think I applied the same rigour to both jobs.*'

'I know.' Toby winced and took his phone back. 'What do you study, anyway?'

'Commerce,' Astrid said. 'Yeah.'

Afterwards, Toby said it was his turn to provide refreshments. As Astrid waited in the hall, puzzled, he darted into his room and selected two little bottles of red wine from the bottom of his doorless storage cupboard. Back in the common room he handed her one and twisted the lid off the other. 'Do you want me to try and wash some cups?'

Astrid shook her head. 'Why do you have these little aeroplane catering bottles?'

'They're for pre-game? When I'm going out? Like, I want to have a drink to loosen up. But opening a whole bottle would be a waste?'

For some reason she found this funny. They had another one, and another. Soon Toby felt emboldened to ask Astrid why she didn't shave under her arms. She shot him a sharp look and said, 'Political reasons.' He mused on this. 'And,' she added after a bit, 'it acts as a fuckwit repellent.'

When they walked back to their block she waved towards her door. 'Want to come in?' She laughed at his surprised face. 'Don't freak out about it,' she said. 'Women have sex drives, you know. And it's my curse to be heterosexual.'

Back in his room, Toby searched the directory for her email address. *Sorry*, his email subject said. In the body of the message he typed: *I don't know why, but whenever anyone suggests anything spontaneously I say no. Someone could offer me a free car or an all-expenses paid holiday to Japan and if I was surprised, I'd still say no. I just wanted to make sure you knew that the surprise (and my personality) was at issue tonight. Not you. Best, Toby.* If he was being honest he would have added: *Besides, if you want me, awful flawed me, there must be something wrong with you, and why would I want to lose my (proper, fully naked, penis-in-vagina) virginity to someone defective?*

A new email popped into his inbox. Toby's pulse raced. But it wasn't from Astrid. It was from his dad. He stared at it, his hand wavering over the trackpad. Once, at the height of the union movement's Your Rights at Work campaign, a satirical current affairs show had conducted a Q Score popularity test for some big names in Australian public life. Prime Minister John Howard had been at Net Negative; the words chosen for him were tough, clever, dull, stubborn. Then Opposition Leader Kevin Rudd's favourables (+41) had been out of control: smart, warm, funny, strong. Watching at home with his mum, Toby was shocked to see a picture of his own father flash up on the screen. John Clare, ACTU Secretary: 63 favourable, 18 negative, 14 don't know. His words were: leader, intelligent, friendly, calm. Toby's mum rested her glass of wine on the arm of the kitchen sofa. 'Chummy, self-absorbed, passive, absent,' she said. This had the rhythm of a joke, and Toby liked being treated like an adult, so he laughed. But the great Australian public had been right about his dad in 2007, and their assessment was just as true in mid-June 2010: '63 favourable, 18 negative, 14 don't know' was exactly how Toby felt about his calm, intelligent, friendly leader of a father. He clicked on the email.

Hi mate, his dad had written. *Coming to Canberra on 23 June. Last sitting day up at Parly so I'll be racing round pressing the flesh and militating on behalf of the working man. Then I can do the fun stuff with you. Probably there at nine. I've got a rental car so I'll buzz you when I'm in the carpark. Love you mate. Love Dad.*

On Wednesday his father pulled up to the carpark right on time. From his window in college, Toby watched as he stayed on his phone for ages, first texting then making calls. Finally, at 9.26, Toby just went out and got in.

His dad hung up. 'Just a sec, mate.' He checked his texts again. 'I'll just get rid of this,' he muttered. Eight minutes later, he tossed his phone in the cup holder. 'Toby!' He gripped Toby's knee. 'I wanted to come in and see your room!'

'After, maybe,' Toby said.

'You're the boss!' His dad pulled out of the carpark. 'Now, I've got a lot of boring stuff on, but it will be much better and much less boring doing it with you.' His phone rang as they drove across Commonwealth Bridge. 'Bugger, put me on speaker, will you, Tobes,' he said. 'Yes, mate,' he called into the phone.

'Mate,' a man's voice replied, 'he's headed for the loony bin and he'll drag the whole gumment with him.'

'Hang on, mate,' his dad said. 'Take me off speaker, would you, Toby-mate? But hold it up to my ear, I've been done by the cops on these roads before.' Toby rested his elbow between the seats as he held up the phone. Oh! He finally realised: *gumment*! Trade union–speak for government. But the conversation was over and, frowning, his dad was chewing the inside of his cheek.

'Now,' he said. They'd cleared Parliament House security and 'faffed around' (his dad's words) with passes. 'We'll set you up in Aussies with a cappuccino and a giant muffin. I'll get my meetings done, then we'll make our escape, okay? My flight's not until seven-thirty or something. Ages.' He sat Toby down, tossed some papers at him, and went off to join the coffee line. Toby listlessly surveyed the front pages. 'Rudd's secret polling on his leadership,' read the headline in the *Sydney Morning Herald*. 'The *Herald* has learnt from a number of MPs that the Prime Minister's most trusted lieutenant, his chief of staff, Alister Jordan, has been talking privately to almost half the caucus to gauge whether Mr Rudd has the support of his party.' Toby looked around at chatting staffers and their alert, flustered guests, all perked up and staring in the hope of seeing someone 'famous'. Here Toby was, in the so-called heart of Australian democracy – literally nothing was going on. The breathless story in the newspaper could have been about a different planet.

His dad brought back two coffees, one in a china cup and one to take away. 'I'll be off, Tobes – half an hour at most.' But he was waylaid before he'd even left the cafe. 'That's my young fella over there,' Toby heard him saying proudly. Two women peered curiously at him and beamed. Nine minutes passed as he chatted. He threw his now-empty takeaway cup in the bin and gave Toby a second wave goodbye. The clock for his 'half an hour at most' started again. He didn't return till after four. 'I shouldn't have got this bloody rental car,' Dad said, giving a wave to the booth man in the carpark.

'Sorry,' Toby said.

'What?' His dad looked at him quickly.

'Well, you only got it so you could pick me up. You would've got a taxi otherwise.'

'Toby! I still want to see your room at college, come on, let's go there now. Tell me everything about uni. Go on, turn my phone off. Work is over for the day.' The iPhone lay inert and threatening in the cup holder. Screen smeared, it was thick as a brick with a backup battery clicked on. Toby reached for it. 'Plug it in first, and then we'll just leave it on charge. Sound off, no interruptions.' Something inside Toby decided to follow the first, more generous instruction. After plugging it in to charge he turned it off.

Approaching college he became fearful that his dad would be spotted by an adult in charge and treated like a visiting dignitary. Instead of showing him the dining hall and the common room, Toby led him straight through the ground-floor entrance of the first-year block. He heard the sound of the Coke machine and subliminally registered a threat before an actual real-life threat could be seen leaning against the staircase, fingering the ring pull on her Sprite.

'Hi, Astrid,' Toby said. 'This is my dad.'

'Hi, Toby's dad,' Astrid said. 'How can Kevin Rudd live with himself?'

'Oh, you mean . . .?'

'Dropping the emissions trading scheme!'

'You've got me there,' he said, and did something so fucking annoying, something Toby had forgotten in his time away from home. Whenever his dad was trying to charm someone he raised his hand to the back of his head and briefly ruffled his own hair.

'I'm just showing Dad my cell,' Toby said, and ushered him quickly down the dark corridor.

In the car afterwards Toby braced himself for questions. Instead, his dad chatted about politics. 'Yeah, usual first-term government teething problems,' he said, 'a jumpy time.' Toby saw him glance at the dashboard clock, then his silent phone. 'Look,' his dad said. 'I know I said I'd take you for Vietnamese. But would you just indulge me? I want to look up an old friend.'

They zoomed through Anzac Parade in the absurdly powerful rented Commodore. 'Getting every bloody red light,' his father said, agitated and even a bit sick. They circled slowly around Campbell until they found a long curving street heading up to a patch of bushland. Peering at the house numbers, he brought the car to a stop outside a small house of yellowy-grey brick. 'Well, this is it.' Toby unbuckled his seatbelt to get out too. 'Just hang on, mate.' Crushed, Toby slumped back into his seat. His dad leapt up the stairs and hammered on the flyscreen door.

Toby felt a tear in his eye and brushed it furiously away. Why the fuck was he crying? His dad was a good guy! He'd done nothing wrong, unless it was a crime to be a really busy and successful public figure? Or to secure rights at work for millions of Australians far less lucky than Toby? And Toby hadn't done anything wrong either! So why did he feel so fucking sad? He gazed up at his dad. A slim older woman was standing at the open front door. He hadn't known it back then, but of course it was Helen. His dad seemed to be pleading with her. Finally, he turned away. His face was ghastly. No longer a leader, calm, intelligent, friendly; he seemed tortured, bewildered, devastated, torn. When Toby dared to look back up, his dad was wearing his sunnies. He got into the car and said, 'Right! Airport!'

The rental car wasn't due back till seven, so they had some time to sit in the parking lot. 'Dad?'

'Yes, mate?'

'Are you okay?'

'Oh, mate.' He ruffled the back of Toby's hair with the same gesture he'd used on his own in front of Astrid. 'You might be cleverer than your old man and two centimetres taller. But it'll be many years before you have to worry about me. That's my job – to worry about you.'

In a way it was Toby's dream to have his dad's attention, his loving concern. But the idea of causing worry suddenly distressed him. His eyes filled with tears. 'Sorry.'

'Hey, hey. There's no need to say sorry. Keep your eye on that, do you promise? If you're about to say sorry, make sure it's really your fault. Now, let's just chat for a sec, okay?' Toby nodded.

'What I see when I look at you is a handsome and intelligent young man with a big heart.' Toby could sense a 'but' coming. His dad seemed to read his mind. 'There's no but!'

'Okay.' Toby smiled.

'In a way, I'm envious of your potential. I've always tried to be hands off with you kids. Let you live your own lives, make your own mistakes.' (What mistakes?) 'But if you don't mind – I just want to make a little speech to you.'

'Yeah, sure, please.'

But having been given permission, his dad seemed to stall. 'When I was your age . . . I felt like a boy. But then soon, maybe too soon, I felt like a man. People were looking to me to look after them. To do it I had to – well, there's nothing worse than that phrase, *man up*. But other people . . . society . . . I was forced into making life-long choices, choices that would affect me forever, before I was ready.'

Toby was absolutely baffled. His dad's entire *bit*, most recently encapsulated in his interview for *Good Weekend*, was that he was basically a larrikin surfer who didn't have a proper job till he was thirty. 'You mean . . . don't choose my career too early? Like, do lots of work experience?'

'Your mother –' But his dad stopped. He changed tack. 'Yes, certainly, there's no need to settle on a career too soon.'

'Is that what you were going to say?'

'It's not just Sophie who's the sensitive one. Okay. What I wanted to say – I've just been thinking, I must tell Toby.'

'Tell me what?'

'Just – don't feel you have to settle down. It's lovely to be in a relationship. But it's lovely to meet lots of people. Life is long. I myself could easily live to be eighty or ninety. That's a quarter of a century at least still to go. What I'm saying is – be a good man. A kind man. But don't settle down till you're ready. And if you're in a relationship, and it's not quite right, don't just grit your teeth and stick it out. You matter too. Right!' He reached suddenly for his phone. 'What's going on in the real world?' He clicked the home button but nothing happened. 'Is the phone off? Shit!' Once that emergency was sorted they handed over the keys to the rental car and strolled towards the terminal. 'I wish we'd made it to Hoang Hau,' his dad said. 'Oh God!'

'What?' Toby's nerves revved and twitched. 'What?'

'I forgot to drop you back at bloody college.' Dad shook his head with a disbelieving laugh. 'Let's have a look.' He reached into his back pocket and took out a twenty from his wallet. 'That's for dinner.' Toby started to demur. 'No, take it, and here's one for the taxi.'

'Your phone's ringing,' Toby said.

Dad looked down at his flashing screen. 'I better just get rid of this. John Clare? What,' he was saying, 'mate, what? But how does Mark Simkin know? I'm just getting on the bloody plane. Why didn't anyone say?'

'Um, Dad?' They'd reached the front of the cab rank.

'Look, hold on, I'm coming back,' Dad said into the phone. 'Put a lid on this madness.' He hung up. 'Labor wants to replace Rudd, it's on the bloody *ABC News*. He's been the Prime Minister for how long? Less than three years into a ten-year Labor-bloody-epoch. What a fucking disaster.'

'The cab's waiting.' He meant that he, Toby, was hopping into it.

'Thanks mate. Thanks for keeping me company today. See you soon.' He jumped into Toby's taxi. 'Parliament House!' The cab accelerated away.

Back at college that night, Toby was light-headed with hunger when he entered the common room. Astrid was shouting at people trying to change the channel. 'Political history is being made, you dumbshits! Hello. You're back.'

'Yeah. I missed dinner.'

She looked at him sharply. 'What do you expect me to do about it?'

'Oh God.' He was horrified. 'Nothing!'

But she invited him to her room to see what she had in her bar fridge. Desperate, as well as curious, he accepted. Her floor was covered in clothes, long necklaces were draped on doorhandles and a purple scarf lay over the lamp. 'I don't have anything special,' Astrid said, all the while assembling the nicest meal he'd had in about six months: hummus and two types of cheese, crackers, olives and a thinly sliced green apple. She filled two glasses, clearly stolen from the dining hall, from a cask of red wine on her desk. Next to the cask was a pile of commerce books, neatly tabbed with sticky notes. She relaxed into her chair with one leg folded under her. Behind her, an A4 photocopy of a poster listed THE ADVANTAGES OF BEING A WOMAN ARTIST.

'You're so interesting,' Toby said, his mouth full. 'You really seem like an adult.'

'It's probably just the child-of-divorce thing.'

'Sometimes I wish I was a child of divorce.' He looked at her quickly to make sure she wasn't offended.

She wasn't, she was laughing. 'Maybe you will be! There's still time.'

'I don't think my parents even like each other.' Toby's mind went back to the 2007 election party. The frozen Balmain bugs. His mum hitting his dad, literally pushing him in the chest. 'I don't know why they're married.' Toby drained his wine like it was water. 'Sorry.'

'About the wine? Honestly? It's about sixty cents a glass. So don't worry about that.' She gave him another one.

'A cask's a great idea actually.' He studied his glass. 'I do this other weird thing?' For some reason he was confessing to her. 'Every night since I was about fourteen I've had to listen to Harry Potter audiobooks to get to sleep.' Unsmiling, Astrid waited for him to go on. 'And I know it's dumb, and childish. But I've always been jealous of Harry Potter. Like, envious. Not because he's a hero. But because he's an orphan.'

'Yeah,' Astrid said. It was a very accepting sound. 'I have a thing to get to sleep too. I have to wank.' They both burst out laughing. Astrid pulled her laptop towards her. 'Let's see what's happening with this mess.' She clicked around until she found a news clip. On screen Kevin Rudd stalked up to the lectern like a dad sick of the noise at a sleepover. The Parliamentary Labor Party would hold a leadership ballot in the morning. The winner would be the prime minister. 'I was elected to do a job,' Rudd said. 'I intend to continue doing that job.'

'Okay,' Astrid exhaled. She shut the laptop. 'My speciality is male anger. I can sense it coming from miles away. I'm a male anger connoisseur. And I can tell you that man was furious.' She brought the cask over to where Toby was sitting on the bed and refilled his glass. 'What were we talking about?'

Toby waited till she was sitting back down to address the poster next to her head. 'When you invited me in a few weeks ago – you made it sound as if you were willing to' – he corrected himself quickly – 'or wanted to, even, have sex.' She nodded. 'Would you still? Even if I've never done it before – like, I've done *stuff*, but not like . . . properly?'

He'd finished his plate and she got up to put it in her sink. 'Yes, I would. But if you haven't done it before, we'd just have to treat it as a fun learning opportunity. We'd have to skill you up on the basics, bring you up to a level of competence before we could engage in what *you* would probably call having sex.'

'Foreplay and so on,' he said, trying to mimic her tone.

'Oral sex is still sex.' A switch flicked inside him. He whirred and shivered. Astrid took off her fleece. 'Go and swish some water around your hummus mouth first.'

At the crack of dawn he padded down the hall from Astrid's room and collapsed, exhausted, in his own bed. When he woke up after lunch, Australia had its first female prime minister: 24 June 2010, a day for the history books. Toby Clare was officially, by anyone's standards, no longer a virgin.

It became their habit to snuggle on the couch together after dinner. But people had started to trickle back from holidays and the common room was getting pretty full. One night Astrid had to reach quite a long distance to show him her phone and ask, 'What's the deal with your sister?'

On the screen, Sophie's headshot stared up at him from the *Age* website. Toby scrolled for a bit. There were four hundred and fifty comments on her blog post about which local non-entities could be called the Charlotte, Miranda, Samantha and Carrie of Melbourne. He shrugged. Astrid took her phone back. 'She's either really clever or really dumb.'

'Yeah,' Toby admitted. 'I can't work it out either.'

'Was she always like this? When you were young?'

Toby thought back. 'She was always so much older than me,' he stalled. 'Mainly I remember this thing she does.

She's always like . . .' He angled his face to catch the light. 'She makes a thousand little expressions for any one expression a normal person would make. People would come up to her at the shops and ask if she was famous. Once my dad saw a guy taking photos of her at Fitzroy pool. She was like, ten. Dad grabbed the camera and threw the film in the bin.'

'So she's a massive show-off, then,' Astrid said.

'No, it's hard to explain. In grade eleven there was some massive scandal at her school –'

'Campion,' Astrid said.

'Yeah, Campion.' Astrid had gone to Billings, the equivalent school in Sydney. 'Every year my school, the boys' school, did a play with the Campion girls,' Toby said. 'Normally a grade twelve would get the main part, but Sophie got Lady Macbeth. It was a massive deal, there was a photo of her and Guy Wells in *The Age* – Guy Wells was in grade twelve then but he's actually a real actor now? He played the son on *McLeod's Daughters*?' Astrid nodded, impressed. 'The buzz was so crazy, actual members of the public were trying to get tickets. I'll always remember this because I was home when Mum got the phone call. It was the drama teacher telling her to pick Sophie up from dress rehearsal. "She's done it again," Mum was saying in the car. "She's embarrassed herself and she's embarrassed me." Sophie ran into the car, just absolutely sobbing. Mum was like, "You're a disgrace. You've disgraced yourself." She always said that. You know her name's Grace? Sophie used to call her Disgrace Clare as a joke.'

'But what happened?'

'So I got to school the next day and everyone was talking about her. Sophie Clare, the insane root.'

'Have we eaten on the insane root,' Astrid said. 'That takes the reason prisoner?'

Toby looked at her admiringly. 'But what's that a quote from?'

'*Macbeth*!'

'Apparently Sophie had done it with Guy Wells at some point. He thought it was just a casual thing. She didn't. And he told everyone about it, in detail, and there was a picture people had on their phones, but obviously I never looked at it – I can't believe that's a quote from *Macbeth*! I never realised.'

'Did Sophie do the play?'

'No, no. She was totally depressed, just like . . .' Toby put his hands up and made his face a dead mask. 'We thought she was going to drop out of school. But Dad sorted it out and made her go back. Got her special consideration for exams. He always solved Sophie's problems. She's the favourite.'

'Okay, say something else as a bridging remark,' Astrid ordered. 'I want to talk about sex but I can't do it right after the sibling stuff.'

'Okay.' Toby sat up straight. 'Why do you study commerce? Your whole vibe just screams art, politics and social change.'

'Money is everything,' Astrid said darkly. 'Now, I want you to get more comfortable with advanced fingering. Trim your nails and meet me in the showers.'

In the biggest of the three cubicles Astrid leaned against the wall. 'Now what,' Toby whispered.

'Ugh, I don't know,' Astrid said. 'Just go down on me.' Toby carefully knelt on the small square tiles of the shower floor. They cut into his knees, though of course he wouldn't have dreamt of complaining. He performed oral sex on Astrid, repeating her guidelines in his mind: kiss the lips, tongue the lips, kiss the clit, tongue the clit. It had only been after he mastered each step that she encouraged him to freestyle.

She surprised him by turning around and presenting her arse. Fuck it, they were in the shower. He opened her cheeks and lapped at her arsehole for a bit. 'You're a great sport, Toby.' He jumped to his feet, pleased.

'Okay, thank you for the arse thing, but I called this meeting to test if I can squirt. Now, turn your hand palm up.' Toby did it. 'Then, like, beckon to me. No, with two fingers. Start like that, see what you can find up there.' She leaned her back against the side wall of the shower stall, opened her legs and braced herself. A good foot taller than her, Toby rested his left elbow on the wall above her shoulder. He reached his right hand down to what the tags on XVideos would call her 'full bush' and slipped his two longest fingers in as far as they would go. The inside of the vagina was smooth and warm, like a tongue. 'Now . . .' Astrid said.

'Come here,' Toby murmured into her ear, concentrating on making the beckoning gesture. To his surprise, her knees buckled a little. She looked up at him, shocked. 'Oh, sorry,' he said. She stared at him. 'Oh, I can feel something. Like a little shelf? I don't know.' Something about the way he was angling his hand and arm made him feel as if he might have a pectoral muscle. Or at least a bicep? 'Are you cold, do you want to get under the shower for a bit?' She shook her head slowly. He wondered if she was a bit drunk. Gazing up at him, her pupils were suddenly enormous. 'Shall I keep going?' She nodded yes. There was definitely a sort of zone up there. 'I'll just keep, kind of, moving them around.' He was talking close to her ear in case anyone came in. She raised her arms above her head and tilted her pelvis into his hands. Her arms were getting in the way, he clamped his left hand around her wrists and pushed them up against the wall. She thrust her hips forward.

Maybe it was all the steam – her back began to slide down the wall. 'Would you like to lie on the floor?' She nodded dumbly. With his hand still inside her they took a few steps towards the cubicle door. Connected, they sank to the ground.

The soles of Astrid's feet were touching so her bent legs were open. Their previous encounters (lessons?) had taken place in her room, where the purple scarf draped on the lamp had drawn a literal veil on the proceedings. Now he surveyed her in the bright light of the showers, mentally labelling the anus, labia and so on. Truthfully he didn't watch heaps of porn – it had made him feel bad about his body, because the men's bodies were so good; if the men's bodies were not good, he felt bad for the women. His bicep and shoulder were burning from his sort of swivelling, rowing motion. (A brief vision of his mother screwing half a lemon into a chicken's cavity – no, don't go there.) This was hard physical labour in a very tender internal region. Surely it couldn't be that good for Astrid? But her eyes were beatifically shut, and her mouth hung lax and open. She started to move her hips, which made it difficult for him. He sat on his haunches and used his left hand to press her pelvis gently. Hang on – what if he just swept his hand across what she called her 'clit'?

'Ugh,' she mumbled. What did that noise mean? In his scientist mindset, he needed to collect more data. He did it one more time. Suddenly his palm filled with liquid – liquid from her. There was more – it splashed up his wrist. He slid his hand out gently and stared at it.

'Toby,' she said. Tow-beeee.

'Whoa,' he started to say. But Astrid had sat up. She put both hands on his cheeks. For the first time, after fourteen occasions of intercourse, Astrid was kissing him.

'Clare Bear, you fucken Lothario,' a voice hooted from outside the stalls. 'Sex on the beach, you fucken ho!'

'He means me,' Toby said to Astrid, but she was scrambling onto her knees and away from the door. 'Cranshaw,' he said politely, 'can we catch up afterwards?'

Astrid jumped to her feet. 'Just leave me my towel,' she said, 'and get out.'

'Shall we?' Helen came out of her office with her backpack on. 'I thought we'd get Old Saigon for dinner again, if you're not too bored of it.' Toby blinked. The dishwasher cycle was almost complete. Outside the little kitchenette, the hospice sitting room was silent. What was the time? He slipped his phone out of his pocket. 'Um, yeah, for sure.'

'What's wrong?' Helen said. Toby was staring down at the screen. There was a text there from Geraldine, the girl next door from back home. Helen seemed to intuit his need for privacy. 'I'll just pop my head round Mrs Zhang's door.'

Toby steadied himself and looked again at the text, sent hours ago during the party. *Hi Toby, your mum took an overdose of sleeping pills, fell over in the bathroom and knocked herself out. I'm going to visit her in the hospital and get her out this afternoon if they let me. She's fine, but she was crying for you when they put her in the ambulance. I think you'd better come home.*

14.

On 23 June 2010, Sophie had been lazily engaged in a fight on Twitter and wondering why Matthew Straughan hadn't answered her previous seventeen texts. Suddenly her attention was wrested from her screen by the dramatic sting of ABC's seven o'clock news. 'The rumblings within the Labor Party are getting louder tonight,' the host ponderously declaimed. 'Several government sources have told the ABC that MPs are being sounded out about a possible move against the Prime Minister.'

Holy shit! Sophie went on Twitter, where everyone reckoned it was for real. On *7.30 Report*, Labor's most senior statesman was in the studio for an interview about his portfolio of Defence. Kerry O'Brien asked him about the rumour. 'All I know,' John Faulkner said, 'is I've been sitting here talking to you. And so it might be on the *ABC News* – well, it's also news to me.'

It was thrilling, almost *insane*. She recalled a strange episode from her high school. In grade nine maths Mrs Maher had been off sick and was replaced with a substitute who, eschewing 'Mrs' or 'Ms', introduced herself confidently as 'Kate Wayne'. Daily the girls teased her, talked to her in silly voices, giggled constantly and called her Weight Gain. One day Annabel Evans snuck up and snipped just the tiniest bit of hair from the substitute's ponytail. Abruptly Weight Gain burst into tears. Sobbing, she fled the classroom. Sophie experienced the same flood of excitement as she watched *Lateline*, where a gruesome union heavy pronounced Kevin Rudd politically dead. Twitter was *abuzz*. Deputy Prime Minister Julia Gillard was at that *exact* moment holed up in the Prime Minister's office issuing a leadership challenge. The scent of blood was in the air, and Sophie loved it!

The toppling of a sitting prime minister, or the 'coup', as right-wingers instantly began to refer to it, had an interesting little coda. As soon as Gillard was sworn in, she was handed a note by the Member for Sophie's old home electorate of Melbourne, the most inner-city, most progressive electorate in Victoria. The Member was retiring – not, he hastened to clarify, in protest against the former prime minister's removal; he'd been trying to resign for months. Immediately, people began to guess who would be handed the safest of safe seats, held by Labor for more than a hundred years. One name rose to the top of the list, a candidate who had lived in the elec-torate for nearly four decades: ACTU Secretary John Clare. Keen for a mandate of her own, Gillard called the election less than a month into her term. Sure enough, John Clare was on the team and tipped for a Cabinet role when Labor inevitably romped home. Soon after that, Gavin Purves's boss, Marilyn Coutts, scheduled what she called 'a little catch-up'. Sophie put on a push-up bra and caught the train into *The Age*.

Sophie stared out at the newsroom, where shabbily dressed men and frowning women toggled between mobiles and landlines, the ringers on both set to top volume. They were all too old to work in an open plan office – it was sad. The chief of staff was twenty-six minutes late to their meeting. Sophie wouldn't have minded if she'd been an hour late, or three, or *five*. She would do anything for a glimpse of Matthew. But she still hadn't seen a hint of him by the time Marilyn plonked a giant diary on the breakout room table, isolated the ribbon bookmark and flipped it open to the day's page. She took her glasses off to rub her bloodshot eyes. Her newsroom nickname was the Sinister Spinster. Actually, she looked more exhausted than scary. 'Your blogs,' Marilyn said.

Blog *posts*, Sophie thought. 'Yes?'

'You're doing pretty well with them. You would've seen Julia Gillard called an election?'

It was a bit unfeminist of Marilyn to treat Sophie like a total dick. 'Obviously,' she said. 'My dad's running?'

'Why don't you mix the two things up then. The pop culture and the politics. Blog about the election. What young people think. What people are twittering about. The buzz on the street. That kind of bullshit.'

'Is this a new job, or . . .'

'It's the same,' Marilyn said. 'How are you paid now?'

'Per blog post.'

'Well, just add in an extra one each week for the five-week campaign. I'll tell Gavin you're authorised.' She scrawled a ballpoint note in her diary, slammed it shut and stood up.

'Um, Marilyn,' Sophie scrambled to her feet. 'Have you seen Matthew Straughan around?' Marilyn was frowning at her. 'I want to run a few things by him.'

'He's gone. He's not in a good way. As for you – I'd advise you to move on.'

Did Marilyn know about them? Did everyone? And what did she mean 'gone'? Sophie poked her head into Gavin's office, but it was empty. She strolled to the tea room, feeling self-conscious. Gavin was eating a food-court stir-fry with a plastic fork. Sophie leaned against the doorframe. 'Hi, Gavvy.'

'Sophie. How've you been?'

'Where's Matthew?'

'Yeah, look.' Gavin sighed. 'He might've rushed coming back to work after the fire. He's had a hard time. I think he wants to see more of his boy, hey. Anyway, the big boss had a chat. Gave him a leave of absence. It's not forever, just till he feels better.'

'Is he having some kind of breakdown?'

'Oh, nah, yeah, just a hard time.'

Sophie was filled with joy. It wasn't her at all. He was just battling his demons! A laugh rose in her chest.

'What,' Gavin said coyly.

'Oh my God, Gavin.' Sophie caught sight of something odd. 'You've bitten off half the prongs on your fork.'

The title of her first election blog post was 'Weird-eared PM ignites Twitter'. It began with a JPEG of a horrified cat, eyes bulging in shock. Sophie wrote:

What has been seen cannot be unseen, as the meme has it.

A debate during an election campaign is always high stakes. Often, it marks the first time undecided voters pay attention to the candidates for Australia's highest office. Last night, we were introduced to Julia Gillard's ears. Obviously, she's always had them. But last night was the first time we noticed.

Was it the earrings that caught Twitter's attention? Two large pearls dangling from delicate hooks. They trembled as our first female Prime Minister stated her case for Labor's second term. And the lobes they trembled from? Let's just say, they were bigger than average.

'Mum just rang me to make sure I saw Gillard's ears,' wrote @lindsaaaaaaay. 'Hoooooooly sh*t, Gillard's ears,' tweeted another. Like a 'wizard's sleeve', said @bandicootbill.

By the end of the debate, nearly a thousand people had joined a fan page dedicated to 'Julia Gillard's insane earlobes' on Facebook.

Tony Abbott didn't get off lightly either. 'Watching the inaugural meeting of the Huge Ear Club. Maybe in politics it's your ears that grow when you lie, not your nose,' theorised @aiden26099.

Commentators have called the debate a tie: Julia had the better arguments, but for the first time since becoming Opposition Leader, Tony Abbott looked like a prime minister. But were all-important swing voters even listening to Gillard?

Dismissing a leader just because she's got Dumbo ears – that's a lobe blow.

Whenever she set up a blog post in *The Age*'s system, she left it in Draft. The subs gave it a once-over to make sure she hadn't said 'pubic' instead of 'public', then they'd switch it live by midnight. The system allowed her to see the URL for the post in advance. She always scheduled a tweet for about seven-thirty in the morning so that, no matter what time she woke up, her followers (all three thousand–plus of them by then) could read her post on their commutes. She did it for the ear post and went to bed.

The reaction on Monday morning was immediate, and appalling. 'Not cool' was the first reply she saw. 'Fucked up' was the second. Then: 'Are you serious?' She did a search for her name and the article URL and found the most intense and horrible shit: 'Umm, @theage what is this trash?' 'So Tony Abbott is going to bring back WorkChoices but John Clare's daughter cares about Gillard's ears.' 'Your daily reminder that no one is more sexist than other women.' (This one was tweeted by a man! Fuck *him*!) The worst were the people who crawled out of the woodwork to agree with her: 'LOL gillard is a bitchfreak' and 'if you think her ears are stretched lol you should see her pussy'. Reading those, fear sliced through her – the raw, dark horror of men's hatred for women.

But no, Sophie Clare would not be accepting any criticism at that time. 'Excuse me, I didn't start the conversation about Gillard's ears, I reported on it. Don't hate the player, hate the game,' she tweeted.

'Stop digging,' some bitch wrote back. Sophie knew her from her avatar, this dumb skank who worked for the 'pop culture' website Hoops. A capital letter–free zone, her bio read: 'i kissed a girl and i liked it . . . works at @hoooops . . . opinions are mine and not of my employer.' Dumb! Dumb dumb dumb!

'Thanks for your input,' Sophie bitterly wrote back. Her phone chimed and she scrambled to snatch it up. It was a text from her dad. *Not helpful to reduce Julia to her looks, darling. Be mindful when you write. Love daddy.*

By the start of week three, the Liberals had pulled ahead in the polls, and Sophie saw something that made her blood boil. A commentator – male – tweeted: 'Polls bad, but will females allow the first female PM to be voted out after a few months in the job?' Sophie snorted and clicked to reply. Instead she cut and pasted the tweet into a Word document, waved her hands over the keyboard like it was a ouija board, and when the spirit of outrage moved her, typed, 'THE SEXIST TEST'. As Sophie explained, the Sexist Test was very simple. It was if you say 'female' instead of 'woman'. Only sexists used 'female' as a noun. Bang! Huge views, basically viral, because lots of people agreed and lots of people really didn't. Shortly after publication, Sophie found herself on Yep FM for her first ever radio interview.

'Yeah but why is that sexist, though?' asked Fitzy (or perhaps it was Kipper, or Sando). 'Julia Gillard *is* a female.'

'Or that's what we've been told, hey,' said another one.

'Yeah,' sniggered another, or maybe the first one. 'What if she's just a bloke pretending to be a lady to play the gender card?'

'She's not a lady or a female or a bloke, she's a woman,' Sophie said tartly. 'Anyway, it's not sexist to say "female prime minister". But it *is* sexist to call the Prime Minister *a female*.'

'Too-shay, Sophie Clare,' Kipper said. 'Too-bloody-shay! Well, I for one welcome our new female overlords. And this is Lady Gaga, "Bad Romance"!'

Julia Gillard was in serious danger of losing but Sophie Clare was starting to feel omnipotent. The whole of Australia's political and intellectual life, such as it was, was being played out by a hundred or so avatars communicating in 140 characters on Sophie's Twitter home feed. And there *she* was, Sophie Clare, sending out volleys and watching these people scurry for them. Alone, she stood on the edge of a vast sea, an *ocean* of others' dumb little opinions – she raised her arms in the air – she marshalled great forces – she unleashed *her* opinion, the one true opinion, and it crashed down on her enemies and engulfed them. It was powerful. And very comforting to occasionally make others feel as she did most of the time: like shit.

15.

ONE DAY DEEP into the 2010 election campaign Sam called her and spoke in a fake voice. 'Soph, hi! What are you doing?'

Sophie was repeatedly walking the length of Smith Street attempting to casually bump into a tall, weird, possibly impotent substance abuser with whom she was unaccountably sexually obsessed. 'Nothing,' she said. 'Why?'

'Actually, I've got your dad here?'

'She's too busy to see her old dad,' Sophie could hear in the background.

'John's been kind enough to give us some of his time,' Sam said carefully.

Sophie frowned at her reflection in a record shop window. 'Why are you talking in that weird way?'

'I'm with Marek too. We're just grabbing a drink in the city? At Becco? So come by!'

Australians didn't really say 'come by', it was an American thing, and it was annoying that Sam said it – like when he said 'my bad'. What's next, butt instead of bum? The nation's unique culture must be preserved! Outside Becco she saw her dad's long legs stretched across half of Crossley Street. Sam was perched on the edge of the seat next to him, stressing.

'Why am I here?' Sophie demanded.

'Got to go, mate, my little girl's arrived.' Her dad hung up his phone and enveloped Sophie in a hug. 'We're having a bit of an issue. Marek's view is that we *must* have a glass of wine at Becco. But they won't serve us till six.'

'Where is he? Why are you even meeting with Sam's boss? What does Cataclysm have to do with you?'

Sam cast her an injured look. 'The pitch? Our pitch? We're pitching the industry super funds?'

'Victory!' Out walked a squat man in an expensive shiny suit, sunglasses pushed up his forehead like swimming goggles. From the restaurant behind scurried a minuscule young woman. Carrying a bottle of white wine in a bucket full of ice, she balanced easily and weightlessly on her high heels.

'Soph,' Sam prompted. 'You remember Shalini?'

'Hi again, Sophie.'

'Shalini? I don't. But hi.'

'Let me take that.' John grabbed the ice bucket.

'Glasses, Shalini,' Marek said. She trotted back inside. 'They gave me the wine early cos money talks. But the waiters aren't serving till six.'

'Yes, good on them,' John said.

Marek laughed, abashed. He was Sophie's height, and maybe forty. He looked like the sort of guy who had three children under three at home, looked after by his wife who didn't work. 'Marek,' Sophie said in a fascinated voice. 'Do you have kids?'

'He's got two boys,' Sam leapt in. Sophie glared at him.

'Yeah, I've got two little fellas at home,' Marek said. 'Another one on the way, a little girl.'

'I knew it,' she muttered. Sam shot her a quelling glance.

'Watch out for the girls, Marek,' John said. 'One day they're riding on your shoulders. The next day they're hanging you out to dry on the *Age* website.' Sophie was relieved when he gave her a little wink. He looked tired and, though he was not strictly balding, she could see more of his scalp than she was used to. 'Let me take those,' he said – Shalini had come out with five glasses on a tray. 'Wine for everyone?'

'So, Marek.' Sophie turned to Sam's boss. 'Why are you such a slave driver?'

Marek glanced nervously at John. 'Ha-ha.'

'Just kidding,' Sophie said. 'But Sam does work so hard, doesn't he?'

'They both work hard, these guys.' Marek jutted his elbow at Sam and Shalini. 'A great team.'

Shalini was holding her wine glass by the stem like a hand model. 'Sophie, your dad was *so* helpful today.'

'I'll talk about communicating labour values with anyone, that's not a problem. So, Shalini' – her dad turned the full beam of his attention on Sam's colleague – 'when I said "labour values" then, it's labour with a "U". If I said "the values of the Labor Party" it's . . .'

Shalini raised her eyebrows. 'Yes, I can see this is very important to you. Labor with no "U".'

'Very good.' Sophie felt a stab of pure jealousy.

Soon a keen young man in a cheap black suit hurried towards them. 'Aha, Jason!' her dad said. 'My glamorous assistant. I'm off, got an event in Chinatown. The epicentre, the beating heart, of Melbourne's vibrant Chinese community.'

'No need to make a speech,' Sophie said. 'You're not an MP yet.'

The two men rushed off in lockstep. Marek put down his empty wine glass and lit up a cigarette. He looked at his giant watch. 'Finally.' He peered into the restaurant until someone saw him clicking his fingers. A waiter came out, expressionless.

'Another bottle, and the bill mate, and a receipt mate, thanks. And get us some clean glasses.'

Marek's shirt was made of very thick, slightly shiny cotton. Underneath, his defined chicken-breast pecs looked like a child's Batman costume. 'So, Marek,' Sophie said. 'Why do you have such *bulging* muscles?'

Marek's face illuminated with delight. He tensed his biceps and chest until a vein stood out on his forehead. 'Why do you ask?'

'I'm just not used to seeing male muscles in my daily life,' she said.

'Gee, that's nice.' Sam pretended to be offended. Sophie had always felt able to tease him in this way; it was one of the nicest things about him. But Shalini said, 'Aww,' and laid her head on Sam's shoulder. The wine arrived, in a fresh ice bucket, and Sam said, 'New glasses!' to jog the waiter's memory.

'But you *do* work out,' Sophie said.

'Yeah, I've got a trainer.' Marek waved his ciggie airily. 'And sometimes I run to work? From Prahran?'

'But how do you bring your stuff? Your laptop and stuff.'

'My wife puts it in a cab.'

Sophie nodded. 'And do you have a shower at work?'

'Sorry, Marek,' Sam said.

Marek poured more wine into a fresh glass for her. 'Yeah, oh yeah, for sure.'

Over his boss's bowed head, Sam frowned his warning frown. Sophie was suddenly furious. If somewhere life existed, if somewhere people were having sex, feeling excitement, tapping into genuine emotions, sharing the truth about themselves or others, living as characters in movies do – well, it was happening without her, and the person holding her back from it was Sam. Soon it would be time for them to leave. With no audience, and no need to keep up appearances, Sam would get cross at her for her perfectly normal behaviour. They would walk to the station and wait for the train that would take her from the city – the one by two kilometre grid wherein she was alive – to the suburbs, where she fell off the radar and went dark. There would be no chance of seeing Matthew.

'Gaylords!' she exclaimed.

Sam and Shalini turned to face her with identically strained smiles. Only Marek looked intrigued.

'Marek,' Sophie cried. 'Are you telling me you don't know Melbourne's premier Indian restaurant?'

'Oh, it's actually Gaylord, with no "S", not Gaylords,' Sophie said, after she'd led her band of unlikely conspirators down Little Bourke Street, into a seedy laneway and a different world. 'My apologies.' The dark red and gold carpets were just as she remembered, the white tablecloths and starched white napkins. 'I know what I'm having. Sit next to me, Marek.' She patted the brocade banquette. Sophie put the stiff peaked napkin on her head and raised her right hand to make a backwards 'L'. 'The Lord bless you and keep you; the Lord make his face to shine upon you and be gracious to you,' she murmured like the chaplain at her old school. She opened one eye to see how this was going down. Marek was watching. She took a selfie as she finished it off. 'The Lord lift up his countenance upon you . . . And give you peace.' The selfies looked, actually, really funny and quite hot. She quickly posted one to Twitter with the caption 'Bless you, Gaylords'. Sam and Shalini were boringly and factually discussing the menu. Sophie turned back to Marek. 'How many Twitter followers do you have?'

'Eighteen hundred, yeah. I run a series of networking mornings, called Short Blacks? So I have a pretty large personal following?'

'I have four thousand,' Sophie said. 'Sorry to lay that on you!'

Marek pursed his mouth. 'It's so easy being a pretty girl on the internet.'

Sophie checked her phone and found people had assumed her tweet was a homophobic remark. 'GUYS, I'M ACTUALLY IN GAYLORD, THE INDIAN RESTAURANT,' she responded in all caps. The food arrived. She picked at a poppadom. Shalini was eating tidily and methodically.

'You know all about curry, Shalini,' Marek said, raising his eyebrows and then his chin to show he was 'making a joke'. 'What do you reckon?'

'It's nice, Marek, thank you. Sophie, it must be so exciting that your father will be an MP.'

'It doesn't mean anything to me.' Sophie slid out of the banquette. 'My dad's job is just my dad's job, who cares.'

'You need to update the deck first thing tomorrow, Shalini, okay,' Marek was saying. 'Then we'll run through the pitch with no notes.'

She went to the bathroom whenever a social event bored her, but this time, once she was away from the table, she had the impulse to keep walking. She'd cruise up towards the heart of Chinatown, see if her dad was around – she needed certainty that he wasn't cross with her about her election blog posts. Ideally he'd go beyond reassuring her. Maybe he'd say he was proud?

153

Sophie made her way up Little Bourke and lingered for a moment at the window of Maxim's Chinese bakery. Fanny Chen had kicked off a craze for their fresh fruit cream cakes at school, literally no Campion student could turn thirteen without one. Were all those Old Girl bitches aware that she, Sophie Clare, was now famous? Or were they too busy with their pointless work for Doctors Without Borders? Halfway across Russell Street the traffic started moving. She pulled up short and took refuge on the traffic island. One of the Chinatown arches spanned the next bit of Little Bourke. Its red legs ran down to a carved stone plinth. Sitting on the plinth with his head in his hands was her dad. A taxi was approaching and Sophie watched as he lunged too late to signal it. He resumed his tired posture, face rigid with despair. Another taxi appeared on Russell Street. She saw him swell with the energy he needed to hail the driver and slide into the passenger seat. He leaned away from her to put on his seatbelt. The cab drove off.

In a daze, Sophie wandered back towards Gaylord. She heard her phone buzzing and had the mad thought it was her dad. But it was just Sam, telling her Marek wanted to leave. 'Just go then,' she snapped. When she returned to the dark, narrow laneway a few minutes later, she was met with an incredible sight. There was Matthew Straughan, leaning against the brick wall with his hand above Sam's head, looking for all the world as if he was putting the moves on him. He detached himself as she approached and leaned back, smirking. 'Give Sam his space, Matthew,' Sophie said. 'No means no.'

A woman was standing separately from and a little behind Matthew. She was old, a mother's age, like thirty-five. Seeing Sophie notice her, she adjusted her messenger bag and said, 'I'm Fleur, hi everyone.'

Shalini held out her hand and said, 'Shalini.'

'What are you guys up to?' Sam said. 'On a date, ooh!'

Fleur blushed and laughed a confirmation. She had a short haircut and for sure cycled to work. Sophie could imagine her meeting Matthew's boy, Ryan; after a while, when she'd been dating Matthew for ages, Fleur would call Ryan her 'little man'. Sick, betrayed, Sophie zoned out and leaned against the wall. Sam nattered away – he was good in situations like this: sensitive enough to catch that the vibe was awkward, not suspicious enough to work out why.

Suddenly Matthew was beside her.

'Are you really on a date?' Sophie asked. 'Does she know you have erectile dysfunction?'

Matthew laughed, and his whole face transformed, and when he stopped laughing his horse's eyes were soft and loving instead of sad. Sophie stared up at him. She loved him.

'But wouldn't you prefer to have sex with *me*? She looks like a public servant.'

He was relaxed, playful. 'Come over, then.'

'What, to flate?'

'Yes, come to *Flat E*.'

'Sophie?' Sam and Fleur and Shalini were waiting. Marek was still on the phone, standing with one leg up on a high step, doing a ridiculous stretch.

Sophie waited, face shining, till Marek hung up. She gave him a little goodbye cuddle. 'My dad's right, Marek – you *are* a game-changing genius like Steve Jobs.' He was ecstatic. 'So wonderful to see you,' she said courteously to Shalini, then, with a pitying smile, 'Bye, *Fleur*.' She hooked her arm through Sam's and half-dragged him, half-skipped towards their train.

'I feel bad leaving Shalini to get home alone,' Sam said.

'Oh please.'

'Did your dad really say that about Marek?'

'Ha,' Sophie shouted with laughter. 'As if, Sam. Marek's a dick who doesn't respect you, and my dad only helped you because you're my boyfriend. But you know what they say: leave 'em laughing.'

Back home Sam set the alarm, fussing about needing his sleep before the pitch, trying to make her feel like it was her fault they'd stayed out late. 'Gee, that's weird,' she said thoughtfully as they lay in their customary attitudes on either side of the bed. 'I don't remember drugging you with Rohypnol and dragging you to Gaylord in a wheelie bin.'

Sam turned his pillow over. 'You always take things too far.'

'I was just minding my own business in Collingwood,' Sophie said. '*You* rang *me*.'

It was not until Sam was asleep, with frighteningly long pauses between his congested breaths, that Sophie was hit with a revelation so astonishing she became faint. *Matthew had read her Twitter while he was on a date. He had seen she was at Gaylord. He had sought her out.* It was on, and this time it was for real.

16.

SOPHIE WOKE THE next day before six with a blog post fully formed. She filed it and was asleep again before Sam's alarm sounded at seven.

> Finally, the end of a long campaign and it's time to take stock. I want to thank everyone who has come on this journey with me as *The Age*'s newest and most popular political writer. Thank you for giving me and my posts twice as many hits per day as the full circulation of *The Age*. You'd think I would be on a contract, wouldn't you? But I'm not.
>
> You'd think people would be asking me: 'Sophie, where's your groundbreaking work of long-form nonfiction?' But they're not. My boyfriend's boss told me it's easy to be a pretty girl on the internet. But it's not. The abuse I get daily on multiple platforms – just for existing and having an opinion!
>
> But if you think the casual sexism I get every day is bad, there is someone out there copping it a lot worse. Let's take a moment to look at the mountain of shit Julia Gillard had to plough through every day of this gruelling campaign, just to do her job.

(Here Sophie rounded up some of the most egregious of the many sexisms Julia endured, carefully leaving out her own post about the ear stuff.)

> Sure, she's not perfect, but being imperfect never stopped a man from being prime minister. Strong, smart, qualified, funny – and not Tony Abbott. With one day left, it's time to unite behind Gillard and join #teamjulia.

At ten, when Sophie woke up properly, she found shirts and ties littering the floor. How had she slept through Sam's anxious pre-pitch fashion parade? She reached for her phone to ensure the subs had received her copy. She was shocked to see forty-seven Twitter notifications waiting for her. Since she hadn't posted anything since the Gaylord tweet, she was scared to open the app. When she managed to, though, she was happily surprised.

'She's not perfect, but not being perfect never stopped a male candidate for prime minister, writes @mastersoph #teamjulia' read the first tweet, by the female half of a brother–sister indie duo – that was cool. Then there were more, all with links to her post, all . . . positive? Or at least not hating her? She clicked on the hashtag and scrolled down a row of Twitpics with smiling women declaring themselves Team Julia. She checked what her post looked like on the site. 'Julia's not perfect, but she's ours. It's time for women to get on board.' Wow, the headline was actually okay. She scrolled down and saw a sub had changed 'mountain of shit' to 'mountain of doggy doo'. 'Are you fucking serious,' Sophie howled. But it was mainly a howl of relief, that she'd found a way of getting attention that didn't result in death threats.

She positively *glided* through her invasive bikini wax at Cindy's in Forest Hill Chase. Afterwards, Sam called. Cataclysm's presentation pitch to the industry super funds had gone perfectly. They'd all talked about Sophie's Team Julia article in the pitch? It had prompted a 'big riff' from Sam about the value of word-of-mouth marketing and influencer endorsements, and how any digital campaign should incorporate real people and 'amplify supporters' voices across all channels'?

'Yeah, cool,' Sophie said. 'Did Marek like the post?'

'I don't think he'd read it. Me either, actually, ha-ha, but we were able to riff.'

'Riff.' Sophie clicked her tongue, but she was so elevated, so full of thoughts of Matthew, that she did it without disgust.

'Yes, come to Flat E,' Matthew had said. Sophie assumed he meant the next day, the Friday. When she rang his bell at seven there was no response. She was deeply ashamed about her text message history with him, at its dashed hopes and gaping asymmetry; she seemed to be disadvantaged in that medium in ways she couldn't understand. On text, like in life, No Reply was his default setting. Yet in person, she could always coax an interaction out of him. She couldn't write, but neither could she let her dream of the evening go. She decided to walk instead through the city, down to King Street and the last-chance saloon.

There in the Black Bream was Gavin Purves, chunky white-shirted back puffing out over his khaki slacks. 'Hello, Gavvy.' Sophie gave him a little kiss on his whiskery cheek. 'You look like a soft serve. Where is everyone?'

'Well . . .' There was a long pause. He could barely speak either. What was it with men? 'It's the election tomorrow, isn't it? But these guys are here.' He waved around at the dregs of the newsroom and the ad sales department, too unimportant to be working the night before the election and too unloved to have to rush home. Unless Matthew was hiding in the toilets, she was not going to get lucky. All at once Sophie felt tears prick at the top of her nose. 'Saw your piece went well today,' Gavin said gently.

'I *know*. I was on Mamamia, loads of blogs, everyone wants a bit of the Sophie! Hang on, I'll get us a drink.'

'No, it's okay, hold on.' He looked towards the bar. 'Here she is!' He waved at a plain woman.

As she came nearer, carefully balancing a jug of beer and some glasses, Sophie realised who it was. 'Oh, it's you, it's –'

'Sophie from Gaylord,' Fleur said, 'nice to see you again.' She held up a glass and Sophie nodded. Fleur poured her a beer, topped Gavin up, poured herself one and shifted the jug slightly towards the rest of the group.

'You've met Fleur then,' Gavin said.

'Yes, lucky me.' Sophie couldn't bring herself to look at her. 'Isn't she going out with Matthew?'

'We've been seeing each other for a little while,' Fleur said. 'But I don't think either of us are after anything serious. I'm only just back from Timor.' Fleur sat back on her bar stool with a smug look on her ruddy, healthy, boyish face.

Sophie ignored her little conversational crumb. If Fleur thought she was going to ask about Timor, Fleur was very mistaken. 'So where's Matthew tonight?' Sophie felt Gavin shift uncomfortably next to her.

'In Canberra with Jo and Ryan,' Fleur said easily.

'Hang on a sec.' Sophie's phone was ringing. She took her beer over to the quietest bit of the pub, where a few tables were set up for people who dared to eat the food. 'Sam?'

'Sophie,' Sam said. 'Holy shit.'

'What?'

'Did you have to put that bit in your piece about Marek? For fuck's sake.'

'I didn't know he could read.'

'You don't even care, do you?'

'Care about what?'

'My *job*.'

'What about *my* job? As a writer and commentator?'

Sam made a contemptuous sound.

Sophie was conscious of the mood she needed to maintain to be able to get through the evening. She could just about manage the crushing disappointment of no Matthew. She couldn't also deal with Sam being a baby. 'Sammy, I'm so sorry.' Her voice rang with sincerity. 'Is Marek there? Put him on the phone.'

'I would *never* do that.' But the fight had gone out of him. 'Well, pitch drinks are ruined, pretty much, so I'll just meet you at home.'

'I'm out, but I'll meet you later.'

'Out where?'

It was literally a feminist issue that Sam demanded to know her location. She never bothered to ask him. '*Bye*, Sam.' She hung up. 'Wooo!' Back at the table she plunged into the conversation like a dog jumping into a dam.

'Whoa . . .' Gavin grasped her waist to stabilise her.

'So, Sophie,' Fleur said.

'Yes, Fleur.'

161

'I do sound like I'm interviewing you, don't I? But I'm wondering if you've got the inside scoop on your dad's campaign.'

'Oh, boring.' Sophie turned away.

'No, honestly,' Fleur said. 'I'm surprised you're out tonight. Doesn't he need you to hand out for him tomorrow?'

'He has minions for that. You know, he's very big in the minion movement.' Gavin chuckled, and Sophie leaned her shoulder into him. 'Thanks, Gavvy.'

'He'll need every vote he can get.' Fleur looked between Sophie and Gavin. 'Melbourne's going Green. Haven't you seen the polls? Jonas Banks is going to win.'

The chatter in the bar suddenly seemed very far away. 'What do you know about this, anyway?'

'Fleur's doing Environment now,' Gavin said. 'Now she's back from Timor.'

'I literally don't give a fuck about Timor,' Sophie said. 'Don't even say the word Timor to me again.' She reached for her phone, to speak to her dad, to warn him. But first there were emails waiting for her to check. Her eye was instantly drawn to one from Gavin's boss, Marilyn Coutts. 'Yo, yo, yo, here we go, Gavvy. Another fan letter from Marilyn.' But when she opened it – it was a punch to the chest.

Sophie – freelancers are not on staff but the same guidelines that apply to staff apply to you. Any media appearances, for example, Mamamia and others, must be run by me. We pay you for your 'written content', you are not to become 'content' which earns other websites clicks. This is a warning. Furthermore it is not right to make your employment as a freelancer a political issue. If you would like to achieve some qualifications and apply for a staff job, be my guest. MC.

'Gavvy, what the hell.'

He rubbed her arm reassuringly. 'You know what they call Marilyn, don't you?'

'Hey, Gavin,' Fleur chided.

'Everyone finds her scary, don't worry about it,' he said.

'She can't even write, that email was illiterate,' Sophie sniffed. 'I'm going to blow my nose.'

In the bathroom she googled Jonas Banks. For fuck's sake. This Green was going to win? He was *thirty-one*. Sophie screenshotted a picture of him. 'Guys,' she tweeted, along with the pic, 'are you seriously going to vote for this fucking sneaker designer?'

She stared at herself in the mirror as she listened to her dad's phone ring out. 'Um, Dad! It's me . . . Sophie? Your *daughter*,' she said to his voicemail. 'I've just noticed this weird Green who's supposedly going so well? Do you want me to hand out for you tomorrow?'

Back at the table, Sophie picked up her bag and slung it over her shoulder. It seemed for a second like Gavin would try to step between her and the door. She held up her hand. 'I'm off.'

She stormed down to Southern Cross Station. A text came from her dad on the train: *I'd love you to hand out, sweetheart, here's Jason's number, he'll set it all up for you, love daddy*. A second later another text appeared from him, but aside from a full stop it was blank. A third one came through. It was a phone number. Finally a fourth one arrived: *Third time's a charm ha ha love daddy*.

Sophie opened Twitter, where her notifications had changed from upbeat solidarity from low-status Labor-voting beta femmes to a stream of vicious invective from every enviro-Nazi in the electorate of Melbourne and beyond. Mainly they seemed to have taken her sneaker-designer joke as a deadly serious claim about Jonas Banks's background and suitability. *Actually* (they all started their tweets by saying) he was the 'longtime CEO' of Carlton Legal Service, which (Sophie did a quick google) appeared to provide free legal advice for poor people. 'Oh my god, guys,' she tweeted everyone, 'sorry I insulted your Greens boyfriend by saying he looked like a sneaker designer. Go back to fellating your vegan sausages.' Soon she was getting an aggro new tweet every thirty seconds. People were now completely *insane* at her that Rudd had dropped the emissions trading scheme, and that Gillard had said there would be no carbon tax under a government she led – as if either of these things was Sophie's fault. Conscious that her station was coming up she stopped replying to individuals and started turbo-tweeting to her feed at large.

I see all you people have forgotten the emissions trading scheme was blocked in the Senate by your best friend the Greens.

Shout out to all you Greens, who'd be cap and trading ye olde carbon as we speak if you hadn't voted down Labor's ETS.

Shout out to all you dumbshits who say you're voting for a third party in a two party system! You're the conscience of a nation!

Newsflash! When Greens heap shit on Labor, they're doing the Liberals' work for them.

Fucking Sam started calling her repeatedly, just as she was about to bash out another zinger. She cancelled him, again and again, as her fury rose and rose.

So Tony Abbott will be PM, ban abortion and bring back WorkChoices but don't worry, Jonas Banks has sexy glasses and a reusable coffee cup!

Everyone started replying that Australia had preferential voting, you dumb bitch. Sam phoned again. Sophie answered. 'Stop fucking calling me!' The train wasn't moving. They were at Nunawading Station for God's sake. She leapt at the closing doors. Her body got through but her bag didn't. She pulled at it. With a clunking sound the doors opened again. Sophie stumbled on the platform and fell on her arse. Some lady asked if she was okay. Sophie was staring down at her phone. The screen was cracked. She sighed. The woman asked again. Sophie shouted: 'I'm fucking fine!'

17.

SATURDAY THE TWENTY-FIRST. Election day. Sophie felt her side of the bed move. She kept her eyes shut until she heard a sound near her plugged-in phone. She reached out and grasped Sam's wrist.

'Fuck, Soph!' He wiped his wet hand on the back of his jeans. 'Well, if you don't want a tea . . .'

Laughing, Sophie sat up to take the mug. 'I'm a ridiculous person, sorry.'

'Oh my God,' Sam said. 'Your screen!' The spiderweb of cracks seemed to have expanded overnight.

'Just sit next to me while I see what mean things people are saying to me. Please, Sammy, I'm so sorry about last night.'

Sam sighed and squidged a little closer to her on the bed. As she suspected, her notifications were a shitshow. Should she just delete her tweets, get them out of her timeline and her life? But quite a few people had liked them. The one about the Greens doing the Liberals' work for them had been retweeted twelve times. It wasn't great, but it was something.

There was only a small queue to vote in the primary school at the end of their street. 'When will we get *out* of this hellhole,' Sophie quietly moaned.

'But this is democracy,' Sam said.

'No, I mean *Forest Hill*. It's all *so* average.' She frowned at the taped-up collages children had made of their own smiling faces. 'Even the art is shit.'

'Look, we're saving money, aren't we? As soon as we get a house deposit I promise you we're out of here.'

'Out of here to *where?*'

'I suppose it depends where we can afford to buy.'

She stepped back. 'So it could be somewhere worse?'

'*No*, it won't be worse, I promise. Come on, don't lose our place in the line.' He looked down at the ALP how-to-vote. 'Mary-Anne King needs us, whoever that is.'

'That reminds me.' Sophie took her phone out and gingerly unlocked the shattered screen. 'Dad wants me to hand out for him. I'll just send a text to whoever this guy is, hold on.' She quickly typed: *Hi Jason, it's Sophie Clare, Daddy said you'd know how best to utilise my star power handing out today. We'll be in town from midday.*

'Why do you do that?' Sam was looking over her shoulder.

'Do *what?*'

'*Utilise my star power.*'

'You know what they say,' she said. 'ABG!'

'Nobody says whatever that is.'

'Always be grandiose, baby!'

'How about just being normal? Other people seem to manage.'

'Okaaay,' she began, but they'd reached the front of the queue. They announced themselves and their addresses together then stood separately in the cardboard booths. 'Sam!' she called afterwards. 'Take a photo of me voting. No, use my phone.' She posted her ballot paper half into the box and did a Marilyn Monroe sexy pose.

'Do you want me to take another one, for public consumption?'

'What's wrong with that one?'

'Okay.' Sam handed back the phone.

'Ugh. Let's just get in the car and go.'

'Haters gonna hate,' Sophie captioned her sexy voting pic. '#teamjulia!' She stared out of the window at the nothingness of the Eastern Freeway, her mind full of Matthew. Was he back? Could she somehow give Sam the slip, knock on the door of Flat E? 'Why is your suit in the car?' she suddenly asked.

Sam looked down at the steering wheel and got pink in the face. 'For the party? The election party? There'll be a live-cross, and we'll be on TV shaking your dad's hand and stuff?' How weird; she'd never thought of Sam as having fantasies. When she used to ask him what he was thinking, he'd always say 'work' or 'footy', or, if it was the summer, 'cricket'. When she'd tried to ask him about *sexual* fantasies (ages ago obviously) he'd said, 'Just any sex.'

'Cool, okay.' She checked on the fortunes of her voting selfie tweet. Many early responses and faves. As she refreshed, she saw she was mentioned by someone. The tweet said: 'Don't show @mastersoph.' Don't show her what? Sophie clicked. Her mind took in all the salient bits. The person who'd posted had a 'twibbon' in his profile picture signalling his support for the Greens. The account he was tweeting to was that of @hoooops, the pop culture website that Sophie hated. She clicked to see what Twibbon guy's reply was about. The original @hoooops tweet read: 'Awkward! Even the Labor guy's wife is voting Green.' There was a link to the Hoops website, which Sophie clicked.

'What?' Sam said. 'What?'

'Shut *up*, something bad's happened.' The article loaded. There was a photo of Sophie's parents earlier that morning voting in a Carlton polling station. Her dad's arm was around her mum. He was smiling happily as he slotted his ballot paper into the box. Sophie's mum was leaning slightly away from the hug, hands awkwardly at her sides. Her giant ballot for the Senate was folded but the other, smaller piece of paper dangled open. On it, there was a clear number one in the box next to Jonas Banks's name. Next to John Clare there was a two.

'What?' Sam said again.

'Nice breach of privacy photographing my mum's vote,' Sophie quickly typed in reply. 'Excited to see what electoral laws you've broken.' She sent the link in an email to her dad, in case he hadn't seen it. And she sent it to Toby. *Un-fucking-believable*, she wrote, and returned to searching Twitter. 'Oh no.' She sighed deeply. 'It's on Jeepers.' Jeepers was an email newsletter for so-called political insiders. They also had a website where you could get a line or two of an article before you had to pay. The photo was up already. Poor old Dad. It was fine for Sophie to have opinions, as a journalist and commentator! But a man should be able to count on a vote from his own *wife*. Sophie realised she hadn't bothered to send the link to her mother. *Hi Mum*. She pasted the link in a text and ended with the words she remembered so well from her childhood. *Try not to disgrace yourself!*

Sophie was saying 'Oh no' and sighing and groaning but she didn't really think any of this *mattered*. She didn't *care*. In fact it was nice for once to feel blameless. 'Go and park near Greeves Street, I reckon,' she told Sam cheerfully. 'We'll pop in and see what those weirdos are up to.'

They sat on the front steps of ninety-nine for ages. 'Can we at least go inside?' he said.

'Why, do you have a key?'

'No,' Sam said, as if to a child. 'But I thought you might?'

'You're mistaking me for someone whose parents love her.' Sophie jumped up. At the side of the house was a wooden gate. She slipped her hand through the semicircular hole. No padlock protected the bolt and she was able to unlock the gate and push it open. An iron-railing fence, as tall as two Sophies, rigidly demarcated ninety-nine's narrow side passage from the flats next door. For as long as Sophie had been alive, a wall of cascading winter jasmine had suffocated the fence so completely that it was almost impossible to see the pointed spear tips on top of each picket. Now it was so wild and over-grown that, when pushed, the gate could only open two-thirds of the way. She hurried through the long dark passage, tendrils reaching out for her hair and clothes, and emerged with relief into the back garden. She hopped up onto the patio and tried the back door. It was locked, obviously – pointless. She jumped off the patio and walked backwards on the lush green lawn until she was almost at the back fence. Leaning back on the sturdy rope hammock strung between the gum trees, she stared up at the windows of her parents' bedroom and Toby's room. Nothing. On the top floor was her mother's ridiculous 'studio': 'architect-designed' and clad in corrugated iron like a spaceship or a chicken coop. No movement there either. She shivered as she ran through the long side passage again, feeling the legs of a thousand imagined spiders in her hair and on her face. 'Yuck.'

'This is such a waste of manpower. We're ready and willing to volunteer.' Sam moved from buttock to buttock, trying to warm up. 'It's not exactly the Obama campaign, is it? Why don't you give that Labor guy a ring, instead of waiting for a text?'

Sophie shuddered. 'Now you're mistaking me for someone who makes calls.'

'Well, we could definitely be door-knocking right now, getting out the vote. GOTV,' he abbreviated carefully.

'God, Sam, we don't GOTV here. Voting's compulsory. Fuck it.' Sophie leapt to her feet. 'Let's have lunch.'

'Where, though?'

'Don't complain, but Cocoro.'

The tiny Japanese cafe was the closest possible eatery to Matthew's flat. Sophie drank her miso, furious and stymied. 'Is this chicken okay, do you reckon?' Sam was eating with the serving spoon instead of chopsticks. He levered open the crevice of a ponzu-smothered chicken thigh. Inside it was a terrifyingly labial dark pink.

'God.' Sophie pushed her chair back from the table. She walked out past the kitchen, through the painfully neat rock-garden courtyard and into the outside toilets. Her mind was clear. Her eyes were bright. She felt like a beast in a cage. When she returned to the table it was to encounter something unexpected and horrifying. Sam was holding her phone and trying different passcodes! She raced up behind him and grabbed it out of his hand. 'Sam!'

'Fuck, ow.' Sam was cradling his right hand in the palm of his left. Blood bubbled and dripped. 'My fucking fingerprint is cut off!' Sam lifted up his right thumb. The pad was hanging off like a piece of bitten grape. Sophie looked down at her phone, where her screen, still lit, was missing a long isosceles shard. 'Fucking hell,' Sam said, bewildered.

But Sophie was staring at her phone. Matthew Straughan had just texted her. That exact second. There was the notification: Matthew Straughan. But she couldn't swipe the broken phone to unlock it. The message was trapped.

Sophie kindly held Sam's arm all the way down Gertrude Street and dropped him in the emergency department. Then she *ran* to the State Library end of Russell Street, where she knew there was a phone repair place. But the man couldn't do it immediately. She'd have to come back. When, *when?* Tomorrow, he said. She collapsed against the counter. 'Okay, six,' he said. 'Not before six, because that is too early. Not after six, because then I close.' She ran back to St Vincent's, where Sam was still slumped in the waiting room, the tea towel from Cocoro soaked in his blood. No harm no foul, Sophie thought. But *no.*

'That was fucked behaviour.' There were two lines between Sam's eyebrows and his bottom lip stuck out.

Tears welled up pre-emptively in Sophie's eyes. 'What's that supposed to mean?'

'You *ripped* the phone out of my hand.'

'Why did you even have it? And I didn't rip it. Why are you always so horrible to me? All I ever do is try my best.'

'Sam Nugent?' A nurse beckoned them to the desk. They hurried into a curtained-off cubicle, where a muscled doctor with a triathlete's waxed arms laughed joyously at Sam's thumb. 'On the run, mate?' he said. 'There are better ways to hide your identity. I could give you a local for this – but you're not a baby, are you, matey?'

'Actually, he *is* a baby.' Sophie put her arm around Sam.

Sam looked at her gratefully. 'Okay, okay,' the doctor said. 'Your beautiful girlfriend's taking care of you.' Sam closed his eyes as the doctor put some stitches in his thumb. 'All done. So brave, big boy, would you like a sticker?'

Sam had lost the masculinity contest. 'No thanks.'

They emerged to find it basically dark. Sophie tried to sound relaxed. 'What's the time, Sammy?'

He made a big deal of using his left hand to dig around in his pocket for his phone. 'Five-fifteen.'

'You look so tired.' He really did. 'Let's get you home, shall we?'

Back at the car, Sam struggled with his seatbelt. 'If you'd booked your test you'd be able to drive me home.'

'If we lived in civilisation we wouldn't need a car.' But she leaned over to help him out. 'And now just cruise down to near the State Library, so I can pick up my phone.'

'But we could easily just get on the Eastern Freeway.'

'Sam!'

He looked over his shoulder to reverse. Sophie felt him catch sight of his suit in the back seat, and waver between his old plans for the night and the new.

'Sammy.' She ran her hand up his leg and rested it briefly where the zip of his fly curved like the handle of a jug. 'I really think you need to rest at home.' He took his foot off the brake and drove.

The dashboard clock read 17:55 when Sam pulled up on the corner of La Trobe Street. 'Okay!' Sophie hauled her bag up onto her lap. 'Thank you so much!' The light changed and the cars behind them started beeping. 'I'll see you back at home, okay? I'll come back as soon as the . . .' She didn't want to say *as soon as the election party is over*, because the word 'party' would make Sam think of what he was missing. 'As soon as my dad knows the result!' The light turned orange and the beeps were furious. So was Sam's face. She leapt out of the car. 'I love you!' Sam accelerated off.

She ran down the road and burst into the phone repair place. The man didn't look up. 'Not good, what you have done to this screen.'

Sophie groaned. 'I *know*.'

'You need a phone case for this one, a screen protector.' He turned the phone round and round in his hands, inspecting every bit of it.

'But it's fixed?' She tried to keep her voice sweet.

'Yes, but –'

Sophie snatched it from his hands and turned it on. 'Just tell me how much it was,' she said, desperately waiting for the screen to come alive.

'For you, three hundred dollars.'

'What?' Sophie looked at him. Tears welled in her eyes.

'Oh-ho, now you look at me? Sixty dollars.' This also seemed too much, but she reached over the counter with three twenties in her hand. The man removed his glasses and folded them. Her extended hand wavered, unacknowledged. Finally he took the money. 'Remember, princess,' he said. 'Other people exist.'

Outside, Sophie's battery was only at one per cent. But Matthew's text was there unread. She clicked it. *Around tonight if you're free x*. Sophie howled at the moon. 'YES!' She collapsed against the wall, her legs trembling. He'd sent that message at lunchtime and now it was *dark*. Her broken screen had allowed her to do something she'd never have had the discipline to do otherwise: play it cool. Five whole hours!

She'd shown that bitch who's boss. She texted back, *I'm on my way xxxxx*. The message sent. Her phone battery died and the screen went black.

They had sex, love-sex. Matthew said: 'Imagine if we could do this anytime we wanted. Stay, stay, stay. Imagine if you were free.'

But afterwards, he turned onto his back and looked at the ceiling. 'You know why the kangaroos died on Black Saturday, don't you?' he said. 'Why they burned off their paws and died?'

'No?' Sophie propped herself up on her elbow and looked deep into Matthew's sad, dark eyes.

'They saw the fire coming and they ran away.' The kangaroos, he meant.

Sophie stroked his cheek. 'That's good, isn't it?'

'But then they couldn't help it. They came back.'

Who was Matthew talking about? Him, or her? Who was the kangaroo, and who was the fire?

18.

THE NATION WOKE that Sunday to a hung parliament for the first time since World War II. Labor had lost so many seats in Queensland and New South Wales that Gillard could not form a majority. But neither could Abbott and the Liberal–Nationals, and so, until it could be sorted out, Australia was without a government. In Melbourne, Sophie's dad had lost the seat to Jonas Banks, who became the first Greens MP ever elected to the House of Representatives.

In the little house in Forest Hill, Sam's side of the bed was empty. Beside her, Sophie's newly charged phone was pulsing with texts, notifications, emails and missed calls about what the papers were already calling her father's 'dramatic breakdown'. She went out to pick up *The Sunday Age* from the neighbour's driveway. There, on page three, her dad was shown pushing away a camera, his hand looming massively in the foreground of the photograph. Her mum stood to one side, her mouth an O. Sophie scrolled back on Twitter until she saw her timeline bloom with astonishment about her dad's behaviour. She brought her laptop into bed with her and watched the ABC election coverage from the night before. She didn't have long to wait. At 6 pm, Kerry O'Brien announced that exit polling showed the race would be close. At five past six, they'd crossed from the Canberra tally room to the seat of Melbourne, where 'Labor's John Clare' was facing a 'tough battle' and a 'long night'.

Kerry O'Brien (*more weary than pugnacious*): One hundred and six years the seat of Melbourne's been a Labor stronghold. Now you've lost it, if these exit polls are to be believed.

John Clare (*sighs*): Gee, thanks, Kerry. Well, we'll have to wait and see, won't we.

Kerry O'Brien: So who lost it – Kevin Rudd, Julia Gillard, or you?

John Clare (*staring at the floor*): Ha.

Kerry O'Brien: Serious question, what was the community telling you?

John Clare: Well, Rudd called climate change the greatest moral challenge of our generation and then did nothing. That didn't help.

Kerry O'Brien: His fault, then, and Julia was brought in to clean up his mess.

John Clare: She wasn't *brought in*, she won the leadership fair and square.

Kerry O'Brien: Not a very good campaigner, though, was she?

John Clare (*sighs again, exhausted*): Bloody hell, Kerry. When we won the election, back in 2007, that was it, our chance to tackle the big stuff. But we didn't, we couldn't. The old ways aren't working, the things that brought us all together, the way politics worked, the way community opinion was formed and led, the old ways we made change. With all the will in the world we couldn't get a price on carbon sorted.

Kerry O'Brien: You were offered a safe seat in 2007, weren't you? Wondering if you made a mistake?

John Clare: You're not hearing what I'm telling you. Politics is not a game. Look around you. Look outside. Look at what the science is telling us. We've all got to stop blocking our ears, stop turning on each other. We've got to make sacrifices now that won't pay dividends for decades. Best case scenario, we act now, and future generations can say, 'Gee those buggers went a bit overboard. Everything's fine!' But it's going to take a level of maturity that none of us seem to have.

Kerry O'Brien: You're a Green, then? If you said all this during the campaign, you might be in with a chance.

John Clare (*staring at the ceiling*): What's the bloody point?

Kerry O'Brien: Is that Mrs Clare there? Does she want to say why she voted for the other guy?

John Clare (*muttering*): I don't have to stand here chatting to you, Kerry, my work on this campaign finished at six, when the polls closed. You'll have to find someone else to wank you off as you speculate. Okay, mate? Thanks.

Her dad groped awkwardly in the back of his trousers for the little box connected to his mic. He threw them both on the ground. The camera momentarily focused on the tangle of wires before bouncing back up to capture the Trades Hall crowd parting silently to let him through. They all stared at the camera as if it might know what to do.

Back on Twitter, Sophie could see there were about sixty tweets tagged #wankyouoffasyouspeculate. Hashtag jokes were the lowest form of humour. Sophie tried to call her dad but the phone went straight to voicemail. It was almost dark when she heard the rattle of the screen door. Sam had spent election night with his parents, who'd 'taken care' of him and his 'injury', unlike Sophie, who'd 'used him' as a chauffeur and then 'pissed off' to 'God knows where'. 'Don't say "pissed off" to mean *went somewhere*, Sam, it sounds gross.'

'How should I use it, then?'

'To mean annoyed? You could say you were pissed off with me?'

'I don't think I have the energy to be pissed off with you anymore.'

Sophie rolled her eyes. 'What's that supposed to mean?'

But Sam's expression was blank and his voice cold. 'It means exactly what I said.'

On Monday morning, after Sam had gone to work, Sophie packed her suitcase to leave him. But she was still refreshing Twitter when she heard the Pajero in the drive. It was four-thirty, three or four hours earlier than she usually expected him home. 'We didn't get it,' he said.

'Get what?'

Sam looked disbelieving. 'Don't fucking worry about it.'

'What? What?'

'We didn't win the pitch okay? The industry super fund one? The one you and your fucking dad ruined for me? Okay?'

The brutality in his voice was almost exhilarating, Sophie thought. 'Okay!'

The packed suitcase remained in the bottom of her cupboard as she considered her next move. An email from the Sinister Spinster appeared in Sophie's inbox with the subject line *Thank you*. Sophie didn't even think to feel scared as she clicked it. *Now the election is over we'll be looking for a roster of new voices for The Age online*, the email said. *Please submit your final invoice to Gavin Purves. Regards, Marilyn.*

Sophie went to bed before dinner. She woke the next day to see Sam picking up her phone from the bedside table. She was not quick enough to snatch it back. 'Weird,' he said. 'Matthew Straughan's texted. What does he want?'

Her mind was churning. She'd erased her text history with him, she was sure of that. She would have to say he was stalking her. He'd developed an obsession with her. Matthew was mad; Sam knew he was mad, everyone did. As Sam watched, she put in her passcode and opened the message. The text read – stupefyingly, absurdly, incredibly – *With my reporting hat on . . . any truth to this rumour? Inquiring minds at The Age would like to know.* The text ended with a link to Jeepers. She was so relieved she could hardly speak. The Jeepers post faded away into a padlock symbol, but the subject line and summary gave her the flavour.

Where's John Clare?
Labor's candidate for Melbourne has gone underground since Saturday's historic defeat and televised dummy spit. Asked whether the former ACTU Secretary would receive a talking-to from the Leader's office, a Labor source said, 'He would, if we could find him' . . .

Sam reached for Sophie's phone. 'I'll tell this guy Matthew to piss off, will I?'

'No!'

'Whoa,' Sam said, affronted. 'Glad to see you're more energetic. Probably time to get back to work.'

'Yeah, I don't think I told you.' Sophie turned over in bed and spoke into the pillow. 'I quit.'

After Sam stalked out, she reached once again for her phone. She was in darkness, but here at least was light. *I'll tell you everything when I see you. Remember when you said imagine if I was free? I am now, and I'm all yours.*

Miraculously, Matthew replied. His text said, blissfully, declaratively, lovingly, *Thursday 8 pm. Flat E.*

On Thursday Sophie caught the train in early to wander around the city and practise being a free woman. But although men vied to help her lug it up from Parliament Station, her running-away suitcase was heavy and literally a bit of a drag. Sophie dumped it in the small downstairs lobby of the Unique Crime and burst into the shop with a dramatic spin on the carpet. Patrick, dusting the Melbourne section, regarded her with a slightly puzzled expression. She'd worked fewer and fewer shifts as her freelancing took off. She remembered, then, that she hadn't turned up to her last two or three shifts at all. Never mind: 'The most insane stuff is happening to me, seriously. I swear, Patrick! Everyone's looking at me! I can't walk a metre down the street.'

'I'll put the kettle on,' Patrick said. Sophie chattered away about this and that. The Sinister Spinster, sacking her like that for no reason! Fuck her, though, Sophie would get another job, she'd work in TV, or not work at all, do yoga and have Matthew's baby. 'Sam's baby?' Patrick asked, but Sophie just laughed. 'You know you can always come back to the shop full-time,' he said carefully.

'Fuck the shop!' Sophie screeched, but he didn't mind, he loved it!

'Why don't we call Sam?' he said gently after a bit. 'Or your mum and dad?'

Sophie focused on him for the first time, properly. Her gaze narrowed, and all she could see was his pinched and concerned face. He was trying to bring her down! 'You're bringing me down!' she shouted. 'Whose side are you on?' She slammed out of the shop, ran down the stairs and yanked up the handle of her suitcase. She was storming up Little Collins when she heard a shout from behind her.

'Sophie!' It was Patrick, leaning out of the downstairs door. 'Please come back!'

Just like a movie! Most gratifying. But when she rolled up Little Oxford Street and pressed the buzzer for Flat E, she was greeted only with silence.

19.

Nothing like a brush with death to make one appreciate the routine and mundane! Back at the big table in the Greeves Street kitchen, Grace was filled with gratitude for her beautiful home, glowing in the afternoon sun. Or perhaps the drugs had not yet worn off: the local for her head wound, the codeine she'd been sent home with. Before hospital, her bed had been a locus of sleeplessness and pain. Now her entire body longed for it. Girl fussed in the corner of the kitchen while the kettle, overfilled, jiggled in its electric base. 'Do you want sugar?' Girl said. 'Or milk?'

'Thank you, sweetheart.' Did Grace's don't-fuss, brush-off smile still work with half her head covered in bandages? Was Grace not being grateful enough? She wouldn't have made it to hospital at all if Girl hadn't shown up.

Girl put the tea close to Grace. 'I hope it's okay.'

She'd made it in John's mug. Well, she wasn't to know. 'Wonderful!' Grace's voice bounced loudly in her own head. 'Probably time for you to head home, sweetheart.'

Girl's mouth turned down at the corners. 'But who's taking care of you?'

Grace was much reduced: she was tired and she was compromised. She couldn't be around another living creature, not in her state. 'Heavens!' Grace held Girl an arm's length away. 'Oh, sweetheart, don't be silly! You've done enough! I couldn't have done it without you!' She led her to the door. 'Thank you so much. Thank you! See you anon! Bye-bye now!'

When the door closed she collapsed against it, trembling from the effort of seeming strong. Who was taking care of Grace? Please! It had been the same throughout her whole life: no one. That's who. She made her way carefully up to the bathroom. Remembering the flashbulb glimpse of her own blood, she was expecting and braced for a mess. The bathroom, however, was pristine. *Girl,* Grace thought. She really was very kind.

In the mirrored door of the medicine cabinet she studied herself for the first time since her accident. How mad she looked, how stricken. The bandage didn't fully cover the shaved patch on her head. She patted it with her fingertips. Something seemed to have seeped through. She eyed it with disgust: was it blood or antiseptic? She gave her body a careful sponge down, put on clean, soft clothes and got into bed with her phone, her iPad and her newest Ottolenghi. Relaxation, however, eluded her. She'd spent twenty-five years, a quarter of a century, building a home for her husband and children. Yet here she was, broken and alone. Where had it all gone wrong?

She dialled Toby again, and was unhappy but not surprised when her call once more went unanswered. This time she opened up her iPad and searched for Hawker Langton. Toby had started off in the nicest, most expensive college at the Australian National University. At the end of his first year he'd inexplicably transferred out of it. Even from the depths of her own fury and depression after John's death, something had struck her as fishy. 'Toby, why? You don't even get meals!'

'That's fine, Mum,' he replied. 'I'll do all the admin, it won't be a bother.' Now she peered down her nose at the drab institutional architecture on the college website. This new place was very obviously suboptimal. So why had he wanted to change? She called the number for Reception. 'Yeah?' It was a young woman, probably a student. 'Hawker Langton?'

'Yes, hello,' Grace put on The Voice That Got Things Done. 'Perhaps you can help me. I'm a bit worried about my son.'

The girl seemed to be eating, or chewing gum. 'Who's your son?'

'Yes, his name is' – Grace enunciated clearly, expecting the girl to type his name into a computer – 'Toby – Clare.' The girl exhaled. 'Do you know him?'

'Um, yeah! I know him!'

'Do you think you could put me through to his room?'

'Someone else is in the room, obviously. There's a waiting list?'

'Why would someone else be in his room?'

'Are you really his mum? Cos it could be a privacy thing.'

'I'm his mother, and I pay the fees.'

'What, still?'

'He's only nineteen!'

The girl let out a mirthless little 'ha'. 'No, I mean, are you seriously still paying? Check your bank – I think it's all stopped at our end. Cos he got expelled in semester one, before exams.' Grace's head was spinning. When was the last time she'd seen him? A flash of Toby at John's funeral, his arm protectively around Ingrid, John's old PA. But, of course, she'd seen him at that awful lonely Christmas. So sometime between the New Year and what, June? July? He'd dropped off the face of the earth. 'Are you a lesbian, though?'

This dragged Grace out of the hell of her private calculations. 'Why,' Grace said nastily, 'are you? Because if you are – sorry, I'm not interested.'

'Um, I've got a boyfriend, thanks,' the girl said. 'But I saw Toby when he was expelled. His mum came to pick him up, I met her. And I don't think it was you.'

'Put me through to the Head's office.'

'I don't know how to do transfers on this phone.'

'I've got an idea,' Grace said. 'Walk into his office and get him.'

The handset was plonked onto a tabletop. After a minute it was picked up again. 'Mrs Clare?' It was a man's courteous voice.

'You've expelled my son,' she said. 'You've expelled him without the opportunity to be heard.'

'Ah! That is not the case, my good lady, I can assure you!'

'Are you laughing?'

'No, no! I can assure you! Well, I am – but it's merely a stress reaction! You see, I find this conversation, and conversations like it, very, *very* difficult. The future of a young person. But sexual harassment – no, it is not acceptable. Students have the right to live safely.'

'Sexual harassment!'

'Regretfully! Regretfully! I told him I wanted to see him, gave him the right of reply. He admitted – admitted! – what the young lady said was true. I was left with no choice.'

'When was all this?'

'We asked him to leave before semester two started – last week of July.'

'He's been missing for a *month.*'

'You can't reach him on his phone?'

'He's not answering.'

'Not answering is not the same as being lost. Perhaps your son does not wish to be found.'

20.

THE SHOP WAS her favourite place in the world. Yet without customers, or Patrick, or a simple courteous phone call from Sam, the comforting surrounds dematerialised and the only true Sophie became the Sophie from the past. She'd spent all night, the entire train ride into town, and her entire morning behind the counter raking over the events leading up to her father's death. Sam had been right as always: it was pointless. Nothing good could come of it, and no answers could be found. Sophie recalled something she'd read in the Dolly Doctor advice column as a tween. Find an elastic band and wear it on your wrist, Dolly Doctor said. Every time you sense yourself spiralling, flick it against your skin. Sophie shook her long hair out of its bun and recalled herself to reality: I'm in the shop, at the top of Little Collins Street. I'm not in danger and I haven't done anything wrong . . . *today*. Her mind slid to Matthew's buzzer, the sign for Flat E. She flicked the elastic band painfully against her wrist. *Stop*. She only had to last until six. Then she'd be out of her own inadequate safekeeping and into the much more competent care of Sam.

But by six she'd dusted every shelf and reconciled the till without hearing from him. Her fourteen missed calls from the shop phone had gone unreturned. She called one last time. He didn't pick up. He'd promised she wouldn't have to spend another night alone. Now the day was over. She had nowhere else to go. He'd abandoned her.

Downstairs, Sophie flipped the Closed sign and locked the door. Every day she reported for duty at work. Every night she reported for duty at home in their boring, soulless box in Forest Hill. Every cent she earned went into their joint bank account, saving for a far-off future that never came. For a whole year she'd kept to the conditions of her self-imposed parole: no internet, no insanity. She never went out. She never had fun. Just who was she bothering to be good for?

She left work and stormed on autopilot towards Parliament Station and home. She found herself veering up into the park and towards Tessa Notaras's flat instead. There she noticed, with a keenness of observation that felt natural and gifted, that when Tessa had lifted the kitchen window the night before she hadn't fully closed it. The gods were on her side. Tuesday was bin day, and the efficient denizens of Tessa's block had kindly left four out for her. Sophie wheeled one up the grassy verge and stomped on the flowerbed to make a nice stable surface for the bin, which she lay on its side. Mounting the bin without a wobble, she pushed up the window to create a Sophie-sized space. She sat on the ledge till she could swivel her legs in. She inched under the window, straight into Tessa's sink.

Her shoes were covered in dirt and wet leaves; she tramped it all into Tessa's cream bedroom carpet. The low bed had a plain wooden headboard and was neatly made with expensive white sheets. On either side was a small table. One had a lamp and nothing else. The other had a lamp, a silk sleep mask in a floral pattern, a little bottle of melatonin tablets from America, a box of tissues, an iPhone cord, and a baby pink porcelain tray the size of a deck of cards. The tray held a few items of delicate gold jewellery. The only other feature of the room was a wall of white cupboards. Inside were none of the cheap mistakes and failed experiments overflowing from Sophie's half of the IKEA wardrobe in Forest Hill. There must have been thirty silk shirts and blouses here, some still on the dry cleaner's hangers. Next door, Tessa's bathroom was almost painfully charming. It had tiny hexagonal black and white tiles, a small white bath on white lion paws and a tall enclosed shower with fluted glass doors. Sophie opened a cabinet to find a cornucopia of make-up, beauty treatments and maintenance tools. She glanced back companionably at her reflection and rolled her eyes. Of *course* Tessa had a Mason Pearson hairbrush. She opened the shower door and looked at the products on the stainless steel shelf. Ha! T/Gel. Flaky-scalp bitch!

The living room beckoned. As in the hall and kitchen, its floorboards were immaculate old pine. The room was large, large enough to be divided in two with a sofa, like the library back in Greeves Street. The sofa was large as well – white and comfortable and positioned in front of a wood-burning stove. 'I cost four thousand dollars!' the sofa screamed. 'Okay, I get it,' Sophie replied. In the middle of the sofa was a battered Scanlan & Theodore shoebox, so clearly the repository of private and personal treasures that it may as well have been labelled SECRET STUFF. She sat down, lifted it onto her lap and tossed away the lid.

The first thing she saw was a picture of her own parents, staring up at her from the pages of *Good Weekend* magazine. They'd been interviewed for The Two of Us a few months before her dad died. Sophie had only skimmed it at the time. She read it now with new eyes. 'I can't stop while I still have more to give.' Were those the words of a man who'd take his own life? Next there was the front page of the *Herald Sun*, her dad with his arms around Tessa. 'WE FOUND HIM: Dummy-spit union boss fled to love nest.' Yeah, yeah. None of that was news to Sophie. She tossed it on the floor. Then there was a document headed: FINDING INTO DEATH WITHOUT INQUEST: JOHN COURTENAY CLARE. She folded that one up and slipped it into her pocket for later. A boarding pass for a CBR–MEL flight in 2007, weird. More bits of newspaper and articles about her dad. Some of Sophie's own blog posts from 2009 that had been republished in *The Age* summer lift-out! Who was the stalker now?

Next she pulled out a photograph. It was crumpled, red-stained and damp, and peppered with narrow slits or cuts. Sophie smoothed it on her lap. Who *was* that man? He had the face of her father but an expression she'd never seen before. His hair was buzzed close like a tennis ball. The only time he'd looked like that was in 2007, his head shaved live on election-night TV – a full three years before his relationship with Tessa became front page news. Three years? Tessa stared up at her from the photograph. John belonged to her, Tessa's expression said. Her air of possession was total. It was too much. Sophie's vision blew out and a white mist clouded her head. She threw the box off the sofa and ran to the front door. She was halfway down the grass when the worst happened. 'Sophie Clare!'

Sophie turned.

Tessa was standing there, keys in her hand. 'You were in my house!'

'It's a flat,' Sophie said.

'You were in my home and I'm calling the police.' Tessa reached inside her coat pocket.

'*I* should call the police!' Sophie said. 'How long were you with my dad? When did your affair start?'

Tessa looked at her sharply. 'Election day.'

'Election day *when*? Which election day, 2010 or 2007?' Tessa was staring at her. 'You see' – Sophie pulled the battered photo out of her pocket – 'I've been doing some detective work.'

Tessa gave a cry of fury and lunged towards her. 'You've been looking through my stuff!'

'You're a cheat!' Sophie cried. 'You're a fucking cheat.'

'We loved each other,' Tessa said in a low voice. 'The night he died he was leaving her. He was leaving her for me.'

'I'm sorry to disappoint you there.' Sophie shrugged. Here at least she was on solid ground. 'I found the body, you see. The dead body of my dad. And I read the suicide note. The suicide note from his pocket. Do you know what it said?'

'I don't care.' Tessa started walking towards the door. 'I don't believe you anyway.'

'It *said*.' Sophie waited. Tessa stopped. 'Dear Grace,' Sophie quoted. She could see Tessa trembling. 'Dear Grace, I'm so, so sorry.'

Tessa turned. 'He had nothing to be sorry for.'

'The whole of Australia had been wondering where he was for a week. Imagine having to say: actually, guys, I was having an affair with a complete fucking nobody. Boffing some bitch from the office. Yeah, guys, this is Tessa, she's got dandruff and a LinkedIn. Yeah, hi guys, thanks for the page one story about me, I ruined my family for a six out of ten.'

'You were ruined before.' Tessa's words hung in the air, conclusive and true. 'And actually.' Tessa cocked her head thoughtfully. It was Sophie's turn to hold her breath. 'Two things. One, your mum. Who was she having sex with the night your dad died? This isn't a test. I don't know the answer. I saw her shagging someone on the couch in your house. A little corner of my mind is still wondering who.'

'You –' Sophie started.

Like a striking cobra, Tessa reached out cleanly and snatched the photograph out of Sophie's hand. 'Second,' she said. 'Just before he died, John received a video by email. I can remember it, every frame. You were in it, and some men. I'm sure your dad loved it. I mean, I loved it, but I'm a Sophie Clare fan from way back. All your insane blog posts, your crazy tweets! Amazing!'

Sophie was running away.

'He died of shame about *you*,' Tessa shouted after her. Sophie was halfway down the street. 'You killed him!' Tessa yelled. 'Your mum killed him! He died because of you!'

21.

He died of shame about you. *You killed him. He died because of you.* In the week after her dad's failed election campaign she'd lost her job, left Sam and profoundly let down Patrick at the shop. That night a year ago the door to her old life had closed behind her but the door to her new one remained locked. Flat E was empty. Matthew wasn't home. Alone on Little Oxford Street, she recalled the words of her father, spoken on the sea wall: 'Wherever you are, whatever you do, while I'm alive and you're alive, I'm looking after you and loving you.' She took her phone out of her coat pocket and dialled him. His phone was off. She was crying, and hid her face away as a pedestrian approached. But the tall figure came right up to her. She found herself grasped in strong arms. Matthew spoke in a gentle voice. 'Oh, love. Did you think I'd forgotten you?' She nodded into his chest. 'I could never forget you.' She stood back, wiping her cheeks, and turned her body in the direction of his flat. But he took the handle of her running-away suitcase and set off in the other direction. He saw her confusion. 'I'm just having a drink. Just a quick one. Please come.'

She slipped her hand into Matthew's and they walked together to the pub. In the corner, two men courteously made space for them in a small U-shaped booth. 'Here she is,' Gavin Purves said.

'You're back,' said Callum Worboys.

She turned away from the booth and looked up into Matthew's eyes. 'But you're the one always saying stay, stay, stay.' She gestured to her suitcase.

'Just have a drink.' He used his gentle voice. She remembered the first time she saw him, how he murmured softly into his phone to his boy. At the bar he slipped his hand around her lower back. 'What will you have?'

She pouted. 'The most expensive drink in the whole bar.'

'The most expensive drink in the whole bar, please,' Matthew ordered. 'And three double rum and Cokes.'

Sophie looked back at Gavin and her dad's old best friend. Matthew's gang. 'But why are they here?'

'Why, don't you like them?' Sophie made another little moue. 'They certainly like you.' Matthew slid his hand under her waistband. 'They think you're very beautiful.' She angled her pelvis so his hand could reach down further and craned her face up for a kiss. Matthew grabbed a tray to carry all the drinks back to the table. Conscious of having behaved badly earlier, Sophie said a shy hello.

'I see your drink has four straws.' Gavin raised his eyebrows jokily.

'I don't think so.' Sophie slid her enormous cocktail out of reach.

'Don't worry, Sophie,' Matthew said. 'You don't have to do anything you don't want to do.'

Callum said probingly, 'So Gavin tells me you're a journalist?'

Sophie darted a look at Gavin. He said stoutly, 'You're too clever to be a journalist.'

Matthew slid his hand around her waist. 'She's too beautiful.' Callum looked sceptical, though at her cleverness or her beauty she didn't know.

It was Gavin's turn to buy drinks, and he came back with the same expensive one for her, this time with one straw. 'You'll have to move,' Callum told her sternly. 'I need to get up.' It felt like a small rejection; she returned to the warmth of Matthew. He opened his legs, angling the space to her, and she reversed into it, lying back in his arms, which he wrapped around her, his hands loosely in her lap as she talked deeply and meaningfully to Gavin, about what she couldn't say. Callum returned with another Sophie Special, which was what they were calling her big drink, and she felt only warmth and gratitude when he slid it across the table till it almost touched her chest.

Soon she checked her phone under the table and found it popping with texts and missed calls from Sam. She opened Twitter. Someone she'd never met had tweeted her saying, 'Where's your dad, Sophie, finally got jack of you and left?' 'Piss off,' she replied. She posted another tweet, this time to her whole feed: 'Every single person on Twitter is a boring cunt. You and you and you.' Someone replied, 'What's your fucking problem?' She responded: 'You.' Just as she was about to tweet again, Sam phoned.

''Scuse me for a minute,' she said vaguely. Next time Sam called she answered from the bathroom. 'Mmm?'

'Sophie! Oh, thank God! Sophie. Are you okay? Where are you, Poss?'

'Stop calling me Poss. And stop calling me.'

'Poss –'

'I'm not,' she shouted, 'Poss!' And she smacked the phone against the sink. Oh shit, ha-ha, her screen had another lightning-bolt crack. Another sixty bucks for that phone man who hated her. Suddenly she felt a sick coming. She wouldn't make it to the toilet. She vomited into the sink, once, twice. She ran the tap and swished water around her mouth. She washed her phone, tragically splattered with the sick, and dried it with a paper towel. She opened her Twitter. She'd been mentioned by the girl who worked for Hoops: 'ignore @mastersoph guys, daddy's gone and the age sacked her so she's desperate for attention xx.' Sophie looked in the mirror but couldn't really see herself. Honestly, it was as if she wasn't there. It wasn't scary, it was good. If she wasn't with Sam, the only thing tethering her to her past was this – her phone, the internet. Bang! Sophie smashed her phone on the rim of the sink. There was a sore, red, phone-shaped rectangle on her palm from the banging, but no blood. She posted the phone remnants into the sanitary bin and shimmered back into the main bar, free. At the table she waited for Gavin to move so she could be next to Matthew. 'Pray, madam,' Sophie sniggered. 'Don't derange yourself.' Gavin cocked a bushy brow. 'You know, Hercule Poirot? Agatha Christie. He says stuff like that all the time.'

'I didn't know you liked reading,' Gavin said.

'Mysteries. Maybe I'll write one.'

'You could, baby,' Matthew said.

'What would she write about?' Callum said. 'She's just a girl.'

'It's my turn to go to the bathroom,' Matthew said, and she moaned, 'Nooo,' and Matthew gently handed her over to Callum, who said, 'Give her to Gavin. No, you need experience to be a writer. War. Politics. Poverty. Real life.' Of course, he was right.

Gavin rested his chin on the palm of his spare hand, and moved his fingers back and forth across his jaw so his whiskers made a sound like *shh, shh, shh*. She reached up from his lap and put her hands on his chin to make the sound too, but she couldn't. 'Your hands are too soft to make it,' he said.

Matthew came back, and Sophie worried he'd be cross to find her stroking Gavin – but he wasn't, their relationship wasn't a *police state*, not like the one she had with Sam. Matthew was a real man and she, Sophie Clare, age twenty-four, was a grown woman. Hey, that was what she could tell Callum – she wasn't a girl at all. But Callum wasn't there, and anyway, it was time to go to her new home. She looked at Matthew with a secret message in her eyes and he understood and reached out his hand for her.

Out on the footpath, Callum was talking to a pretty blonde and smoking. He saw Sophie and Matthew and threw his menthol on the ground. She realised she'd left her suitcase inside. She turned around to see Gavin wheeling it towards her. 'Time for a nightcap?' And together the four of them walked down Little Oxford Street to Matthew's flat. Why not? What was the hurry to begin her new life with Matthew? There was all the time in the world.

The next morning she awoke on top of Matthew's bed covers, the thin grey blanket from the sofa laid over her. She was wearing Matthew's white shirt, but Matthew wasn't with her. She buttoned the shirt and went out into the living room. The microwave clock said nearly five. Gavin, fully dressed again, was asleep against a wall, chin sunken and arms crossed like a businessman stranded at an airport. Matthew was sleeping too, stretched out on the black leather couch in just his underpants. Sophie got the grey blanket from the bedroom and laid it over him. His skin was like white marble, his face was like an angel's face. She bent over him once more and kissed his beautiful cheek. When she looked up, she saw a glowing tip move on the balcony. She collected her running-away suitcase and took it with her into the bedroom. She showered in the ensuite and got dressed. Her make-up was like a mask. When she came out, Callum Worboys was sliding the balcony door shut. A cloud of cigarette smoke came in with him. She recalled him looming over her, his delicate gold cross clinking her teeth. 'You're off?' he asked. 'Take care of yourself.'

Sophie knew somewhere she could go. The modest workers' cafe on the corner of Vic Market was still there and already open. It was the cafe she went to with her dad after they shopped at the markets every Saturday of her childhood. A heater glowed high on the wall and she sat under it. 'Just plain toast? Toast with butter?' She wished she could close her eyes and be seven years old again. Toy dogs for sale that walked three steps forward, yapped and flipped. Fruit guys slicing pieces of apple for her to try. Holding her dad's hand in the jostle at the deli counters. She'd been so frightened of the meat hall smell, Dad gave her a handkerchief to hold up to her nose. What would he think if he knew what happened the night before? God, she wanted to scrub her skin off. She was sitting out the front of the Therry Street soap shop when the owner arrived to open up. 'Never had someone waiting on my doorstep before,' the old guy cautiously said.

'I used to come here with my dad when I was young!' Sophie ran from table to table, picking up first one soap and then another. Shells, starfish, flowers! She remembered all this! 'I'm going to need one each of these, these, these.' She made a pile on the table. 'And bath salts, ah! What do you think is the most beautiful, most luscious bath salt?'

'The pink one, I suppose. It's rose.'

At the Hotel InterContinental she paid four hundred dollars for a room – every last cent she had in her account. She ran herself a bath and lay in it. She couldn't manage her room-service chips, but she drank quite a lot of white wine, crystalline and cleansing. She dozed, and when she woke it was the evening. The door was held open for her and she swept out into the night. What if she'd simply focused on her work at *The Age* and made a success of it? Was that still possible? And what if she had simply been kind to Matthew, and loved him, instead of berating and taunting and hurting him, would they be together now, happy and in love? Was *that* still possible? Yes, there was only one person to blame for all this: Sophie Elizabeth Clare. Something about her was bad, that was the fact of it. Throughout her life, a great many people had called her a dumb bitch. They'd all, every single one of them, been right.

She saw there was an unusual set-up in the Black Bream. People she recognised from the newspaper were not standing in clumps like normal but were sitting around a group of tables pushed together. Cutlery placed at an angle on plates, balled up napkins in remnants of gravy. They'd been *eating*? At the head of the table was Chief of Staff Marilyn Coutts. Sophie gave her a genial nod. 'Hi, Gavvy,' she said, not that she cared about Gavin Purves, but people, among them Fleur, were looking at her as though she didn't belong. She wanted to show her close and relevant personal ties to the gathering, to stay a bit longer in the hope that Matthew would magically appear. There were a few empty seats. One of them could be for him.

From her position halfway up the table, Fleur said, 'Sophie? Have you found your dad?'

'What do you mean, *found*? He's not a lost dog.'

Fleur looked around. 'Her dad's John Clare,' she told people who looked confused.

'I'm an important journalist in my own right,' Sophie said tartly. Despite her long sleep in the InterCon, she briefly buckled from tiredness. She lifted herself over the armrest of Gavin's chair to sit in his lap. Marilyn pushed back her chair. 'Here we go,' Sophie joked. 'The Sinister Spinster!'

'I don't want to interrupt anything,' Marilyn said sardonically.

'You're not,' Gavin said.

'Gavin?' Sophie put on the voice of her chaplain from school. 'Do you deny Jesus?'

'There's something in the papers tomorrow,' Fleur said. 'Sophie, you should be at home with your family.'

Sophie had a wild thought they'd interviewed Sam about her leaving him. Gavin was trying to raise himself to his feet. 'You have twice denied Jesus,' she warned, but in a funny way.

'Come on, Sophie.' Fleur stood and extended her hand.

Gavin tried again to lift his pelvis and tip her off his lap. Sophie screamed and jumped up, shoving his meaty shoulder. 'Don't fucking touch me, you pervert! I can feel you have a stiffie! You're fucking disgusting, Gavin! If you ever speak to me again I'll call the police!'

'Sophie!' Fleur said.

But Sophie was gone.

Sophie, you should be at home with your family. Fuck you, Fleur, as if you knew anything about anything. Sophie walked and walked. She made it all the way to Greeves Street but found herself unable to take the last step. Knocking on the door in the dead of night, rejected, a wreck – impossible. She couldn't be that person in front of her parents. She'd tried so hard her whole life to not be that person, even in front of herself. She would wait until it was morning, fresh and new.

Shivering, she went round to the side gate. She slipped her hand inside the semicircle and drew back the bolt. She pushed it open three-quarters of the way. Not a sliver of light penetrated the canopy of trailing, clutching tendrils. She used the side wall of her childhood home to guide her along the dark path. It seemed to go on forever. She rested her cheek tenderly on the rough brick. She remembered suddenly the meat hall at Vic Markets, the tiles that could be hosed down, blood pushed by the force of the water, down into the drain. Fear filled her. She ran the last few steps into the garden, lay cradled in the hammock and hugged herself tightly until she passed out.

She was woken on the Saturday morning by the *clunk-clunk* of the French doors being opened, and the flapping and squawking of the two people in the world she least wanted to see after sleeping off a deranged bender. Her mother was wearing a long patterned gown. It was cotton and block-printed, but cinched at the smallest part of her waist. It somehow carried with it the flavour of the boudoir. Sam was clutching a newspaper. Less cross than she would have expected, he seemed focused, energised, even powerful. 'Good morning,' Sophie said humorously. 'I'm afraid you find me at a disadvantage.'

It was the type of thing that usually would have annoyed him, but Sam's glance was conspicuously compassionate. 'Your lips are blue,' he said.

Grace snatched the paper out of his hand and shook it at Sophie. 'If you're looking for your father you're at the wrong place.' Of course, that was it. She'd been looking for her dad. Her mother brandished the front page of the *Herald Sun*. Grace read out the caption of the photo. 'CLARE PACKAGE: John Clare, 57, relaxes in the arms of his mistress, Tessa Notaras. The Labor candidate for Melbourne went to ground after an historic election loss.'

Why were they wearing the same jumper, Dad and this woman? 'They look like the photo on a knitting pattern,' Sophie said.

Her mother was staring at the front page. 'It would be more accurate, surely, judging by the picture, to say his mistress was relaxing in *his* arms.'

For a brief second, mother and daughter shared a wry glance. Suddenly Sophie remembered something. She looked over to the passage between the side of the house and the tall iron-spiked fence. Many things had happened in the previous days and weeks; she was not precisely certain what was real and what was not. But when she'd remembered the Vic Market meat hall, inching in the dark – the carcass smell had not been imagined. Sophie jumped off the hammock and began her long march across the grass to validate what she already knew.

The surprise was how it was perfectly upright, hung on the railing like a wet towel on a hook. The spike was in the base of the skull so his head hung, it seemed, in shame. That was where the blood had come from, lots of it. His feet dangled half a metre from the ground. A centimetre of vulnerable white stomach was exposed between the belt and the cable-knit jumper. What a ridiculous, awful jumper. It was horrible. She would take it off him. He was her dad, and that jumper was not right. But before she could pull it off, strong hands grabbed hers. Dragged, bundled away, all she could do was scream.

22.

NEARLY AN HOUR after their confrontation, every nerve in Sophie's body still jangled. 'He died of shame about *you*,' Tessa had shouted, and plunged her into a nightmare, the worst kind of nightmare because it was real. Sophie ran to Parliament Station but couldn't face going home. She blindly strode down Collins Street and did the stations of the cross: the Black Bream, the forecourt of *The Age*. But in each place there were new faces, strangers in strange places. What happened was in the past, a past that felt like the present, a past that couldn't be altered, only horrifyingly re-experienced, over and over again. She'd reached the end of the road. A shop was lit up and open on the top level of Southern Cross Station, a bubble tea stall called PopPop. Behind the counter, a guy in a paper hat was doing his uni homework. 'Just a Classic Milk, please,' Sophie said. 'With the pearls.'

She wandered over to the balcony and stared down the enormous escalators. Up so high, she could almost touch the vast undulated metal canopy of the roof. Far below, trains pulled in and out like clockwork toys. The noises sounded so detailed and specific in the huge empty space; normally they were muffled by people. She collected her drink and sat at a table. From her pocket she brought out the folded coroner's report she'd stolen from Tessa's shoebox. She sought solace in its blunt facts.

IN THE CORONERS COURT
OF VICTORIA
AT MELBOURNE
AUSTRALIA

I, JUDGE ANDREW J. McGREGOR, state coroner, having investigated the death of JOHN COURTENAY CLARE without holding an inquest:
find that the identity of the deceased was JOHN COURTENAY CLARE
born on 22 May 1953
and the death occurred on 27 August 2010
at 99 Greeves Street Fitzroy 3065

From: INJURIES SUSTAINED IN FALL
FROM HEIGHT

Pursuant to section 67(2) of the *Coroners Act 2008*, I make findings with respect to the following:

INTRODUCTION AND PERSONAL
CIRCUMSTANCES

1. Mr John Courtenay Clare was 57 years of age at the time of his death. He lived in the family home in Fitzroy with his wife of nearly three decades, Grace Clare. He is survived by two children, Sophie and Toby. Mr Clare, a graduate of Melbourne University, was a well-liked and respected trade union leader. His medical history was without psychological issues save for the prescription of Temazepam for short-term sleeping disturbance.

2. In July 2010 Mr Clare resigned his role as Secretary of the Australian Council of Trade Unions to run as the Labor candidate for Melbourne in the 2010 Federal Election. His bid was unsuccessful. Following the election, without his wife's knowledge as to his whereabouts, Mr Clare drove to the East Melbourne home of a female acquaintance. There he invited her to holiday with him in the Mornington Peninsula beachside town of Flinders.

3. Mr Clare and his acquaintance holidayed for six nights, uncontactable by family, friends and work colleagues. During the trip he was observed by his companion to be 'emotional' but 'not disturbed'. On the final day in Flinders, an embrace between himself and the acquaintance was photographed without their knowledge by a photographer from the tabloid *Herald Sun*.

4. On the evening of Friday, 27 August 2010 at approximately 7 pm, Mr Clare returned to the family home in Greeves Street. His bag packed with personal items remained in the vehicle. His companion stated his intention was to speak with Mrs Clare prior to moving out of the family home. I find I cannot come to a conclusion as to his motives for returning to the residence.

5. Simultaneously, the newspaper was attempting by phone and email to contact Mr Clare for a comment regarding his week-long 'disappearance'. They sought his comment with a view to publishing the photograph along with a story on the front page.

6. Mr Clare's personal laptop was closed but 'on standby' in the room he used as his study. I find I cannot come to a conclusion as to whether Mr Clare became or was made aware of these enquiries before his death.

7. Mrs Clare returned from yoga at approximately 8.20 pm to find the house 'empty'.

8. Mr Clare's companion waited around the corner in the vehicle for 'more than one hour' before returning alone to her home in East Melbourne.

9. On the morning of Saturday, 28 August 2010, the daughter of the deceased discovered Mr Clare's body in the unpaved walkway between 99 Greeves Street and the adjacent block of flats.

10. The unusual upright position of the body on a tall spiked railing prompted the death to be reported to the police as a murder.

INVESTIGATIONS

1. 99 Greeves Street is a large, two-storey Victorian terrace house with a modern third-floor 'studio' extension. Police discovered a tall stool had been placed on a table in the studio allowing Mr Clare access to the roof via a skylight. It was apparent that Mr Clare climbed through this skylight to access the roof. Standing at the edge of the roof, Mr Clare fell or jumped backwards onto the pointed railings below.

2. Mr Clare sustained fatal injuries from this fall.

3. A short 'suicide note' was discovered in the pocket of his denim jeans.

4. Dr Stacy Mantzaris, Forensic Pathologist at the Victorian Institute of Forensic Medicine, performed an external examination on the body of Mr Clare, reviewed a post-mortem CT scan and the Victorian Police Report of Death, Form 83. Anatomical findings were consistent with the mechanism of injury.

5. Post-mortem toxicology testing did not reveal the presence of ethanol (alcohol) or any other common drugs or poisons.

6. Dr Mantzaris attributed the cause of Mr Clare's death to injuries sustained in a fall from height.

7. Mr Clare was formally identified by ante-mortem and post-mortem fingerprint comparison.

COMMENTS
Pursuant to section 67(3) of the *Coroners Act 2008*, I make the following comment(s) connected with the death:

1. There is a strong inference arising from the death that imminent publication of details relating to Mr Clare's private life may have driven him to take his own life. It is incumbent upon the media to avoid intruding on a person's reasonable expectations of privacy, unless doing so is sufficiently in the public interest.

2. Within a short period on Saturday, 28 August 2010, Mr Clare's death was reported in the media first as a murder, thereafter as a roof maintenance accident, and finally as an unexplained death (accompanied by information about appropriate 24-hour crisis support services). It behoves the media to ensure that factual material in news reports and elsewhere is accurate and not misleading.

3. Due to the haste with which the first reports were published online, Mr Clare's son found out about the death of his father on the website 'Facebook'.

4. These findings should be brought to the attention of the Australian Press Council.

(Signed)
ANDREW J. McGREGOR
Coroner

Sophie went back to the PopPop counter. 'Do you think I could borrow a piece of paper?'

'Is it really borrowing, though? Are you going to give it back?' The guy tore a ruled page out of his yellow notebook.

'And a pen?' He sighed and handed it over.

Back at her table, Sophie wrote 'Dad' and underlined it. After a bit, she wrote: Saturday, 21 August 2010: lost the election. Left party alone. Flinders with Tessa. Friday, 27 August 2010: told Tessa he'd leave Mum. Went home; Tessa was in the car with him. His bag was already packed from Flinders trip. The newspaper story. Did he know about it? My video. Did he see it? Did he see Mum, talk to her?

(A memory flashed in Sophie's mind: her mother banging the frozen Balmain bugs on the kitchen worktop. Then her dad had only ruined dinner. What if he told her he'd ruined their marriage?) The suicide note. Falling or jumping off the roof: why backwards?

Sophie pressed her palms into her eyes and rested her face in her hands. Her thoughts slid sideways like she was about to fall asleep. Had he felt the spike enter his skull? She shook her head and wrote 'Tessa: the photograph'. She'd been with him since 2007. Thought he was leaving Mum for her. If not, motive for murder. At 99 Greeves the night Dad died. She saw Mum having sex.

It was impossible to think of her mother having sex, impossible beyond most people's inability to imagine a parent doing it. Grace never laughed. Or cried. Sophie had never seen her dance. She didn't even listen to music. 'Mum', Sophie wrote, underlining it. Did she see Dad that night? Did he tell her about Tessa, about leaving her? The newspaper story: when did she find out? That was a motive too. After a bit, Sophie added an extra person: 'Me', she wrote and underlined. Thursday night: Matthew's flat. The video. Friday: Vic Market, bath at the hotel, Black Bream after dinner, walk home, Dad already dead – the blood smell. Saturday morning: the newspaper, found the body.

Sophie scrunched up the piece of paper and stuffed it in her empty cup. At least *she* was in the clear. But in the clear of what? If her dad wasn't murdered, he topped himself. If he topped himself, it was because, in the classic phrase, 'the balance of his mind was disturbed'. What could be more disturbing than being sent a video of your mad daughter in some kind of . . . *scenario* with your one-time closest work colleague?

Sophie wasn't a detective, she was a criminal; she had disgraced herself in public, in her workplace and on the internet, and she'd disgraced herself in private, in Matthew's flat.

The problem was – and, as the scale of the horror made itself clear, she jumped to her feet and scuttled like a caged rat – she'd thought the Matthew's-flat mistake was a secret. It had been excised from her internal narrative; only the memory of Callum's necklace tap-tap-tapping her teeth told her it had really happened. She knew logically that the incident existed in the minds of the men who'd been there, the men who'd participated. Matthew, Callum, Gavin. But in all the time she'd spent in their company, singly and as a collective, they'd hardly strung two sentences together. She'd been sure, as sure as she could be, that the events of that night were locked away inside them, never discussed or shared.

But someone – who? – had recorded it. And the recording had been disseminated, sent to her father's email. Where else might it have gone? Who else might have seen it? Had it been uploaded to a website or websites? Were people watching it right now? Sophie gazed up at the Southern Cross ceiling, a vast wave and a small miracle of design, lines linked up like a grid, each grid a starburst, nodes joining to nodes connecting to nodes, forever. So too were her personal shames, the worst things she'd done and had done to her, connected, networked, beamed around the world. She tore her gaze away, steadied herself at the balcony railing and focused on the trains down below. It was nice how they just kept going, to and fro, to and fro. 'Excuse me,' someone was saying. 'Excuse me.' Someone had seen her. Someone was coming to get her. Everyone in the whole world knew what she had done. What she'd done was ineradicable but she herself wasn't – she was just flesh and blood. Dad, was this what it was like for you? She raised her knee to the barrier and lifted herself up. 'Dad,' she was calling. 'Dad.'

23.

A six out of ten with dandruff and a LinkedIn. That's what Sophie Clare had said. *Dear Grace, I'm so very, very sorry.* Her flat had been compromised on an almost cellular level. Moving very carefully, as though protecting another, more fragile, person from a shock, Tessa packed away her box of memories and vacuumed up the dirt from John's daughter's shoes. She got the last two slices of bread from the freezer and made herself toast and a tea with sugar. She washed her plate and cup, had a shower, put on her pyjamas and got into bed. Tomorrow she would be making one of the biggest presentations of her career. Monday night's orgy of memories and regrets had derailed her preparation enough. She had a full diary, a tight schedule, firm goals and a strategy to achieve them. Any mental breakdown would simply have to wait. But when it came time to switch off the light, she found she couldn't sleep.

Tessa's post-breakup exile in Sydney had lasted eighteen months. Yasmin and Christian had always sworn they wouldn't marry before their gay friends could exercise the same privilege. But by mid-2010, Yas had removed her coil, Chris had taken a proper job as a primary school teacher, and together they'd bought a small family house in Reservoir. They held a commitment ceremony at Collingwood Children's Farm. Tessa flew down for it and charged a client for her stay at the Hyatt.

'How are you, really?' Yas squeezed Tessa's hands on the dance floor. 'You still miss him, don't you? It makes sense other guys don't match up. But, Tess,' Yas said gently, 'isn't it time to come home?' When Tessa bought her East Melbourne flat, Yasmin took only a sip of the sparkling she'd popped to celebrate. She was pregnant.

At her 2010 election party, Yasmin had been scattered and frenetic in the manner of all hosts, and it was Chris who'd showed Tessa around. 'Thanks for making it this far out.' He waved away her praise of their house: 'not quite up to your standards.' Out in the backyard, many of the guests displayed the triangle insignia of the Australian Greens on t-shirts and lapels. Christian led her to the centre of the group, announced, 'Tessa works in corporate marketing for big business,' and left her to fend for herself. She took refuge in her phone and, when the polls closed, the TV. It was even harder than she'd expected to hear John's name. He'd been rejected by Grace, who voted for the Greens candidate. And he'd been rejected by his neighbours, who'd been happy to vote Labor for a century but didn't vote for him. Tessa only wanted John to feel bad in one specific way: missing her. Her phone lit up with a text from Manny: *Tess are you watching this? I feel like crying!*

God, me too, she wrote back.

Her phone beeped again almost immediately. *Let's grab a drink when you're settled in your new place.* Before she could reply, Kerry O'Brien had crossed to John. His face was weary, discomposed. 'You're not hearing what I'm telling you,' John's voice rose. '*Politics is not a game.*' Even before his microphone hit the ground, Tessa had apologised to Yas, ignored Chris, and rushed straight out for a taxi.

In the back seat she unlocked her phone to text him for the first time in two years. *Thinking of you,* she typed with a kiss. Then she felt scared. What if someone read it and found it suspicious? She erased the kiss. What if he'd deleted her number? She added at the end: *Tessa.* What if he'd forgotten her? She added, in brackets, *Notaras.* John did not reply. She asked the cabbie to pull into Dan Murphy's drive-through so she could drop some cash on a consoling shiraz. When she arrived home forty-five minutes later, she stepped out into a dream. John was there, leaning on the bonnet of his Saab.

Hadn't she secretly hoped he'd come? He'd chosen the last election to throw in his lot with hers. Why not again? She opened her door with shaking hands. He hung back shyly, accepted a glass of wine but took only a sip. Sitting on the very edge of her sofa, his hands holding hers, he said the words she'd longed for two years to hear. Somewhere along the line he'd made a mistake. His family *had* needed him – but they'd needed John the cardboard cut-out man, John the cardboard cut-out father. There was a *real* John, one they didn't care to see, and the real him wanted Tessa. Needed Tessa. 'I love you and I want you and I need you,' he said. 'Run away with me.' His phone rang, loud and insistent. He fumbled to turn it off – too late. Spectres haunted the room: the pain of their past, the work he needed as much as he needed her, the insatiable demands of his family. She asked him for a sacrifice, and he seemed to make it gladly: he handed over his phone. She turned it off and put it in her bag. The connection to his old life was cut.

It was dark when they set off and something strange and sweet happened in the car. Their time together had always been on the clock, bookended by meetings or snatched from an unknowing Grace. Every minute had to be squeezed from every hour, twisted and wrung out to not waste a second. But that night, as they drove in companionable almost-silence, Tessa leaned her head against the seatbelt. How rare it was to feel safe to rest. That evening, she slept happily, perfectly at peace, until she half-woke at the jolt of the handbrake in the long wooded driveway of a beach house. She woke further to find herself in John's arms – like a child, she thought at first, but 'Across the threshold,' he said, carrying her into the house, and she'd suddenly become a bride. The next day she woke properly to find him asleep next to her. She kissed him and kissed him but his eyes stayed closed; it became a game – what could she get away with? She draped herself half over him and kissed him. She climbed on top of him and manoeuvred him inside her. Suddenly he gasped and she saw tears leak out from under his eyelashes. At last, he looked at her. 'Sorry,' he said. 'It's just that I'm so happy. I thought I'd never get to touch you again.'

But sex came back faster than security. She was touchy at first, edgy and shitty and tense. It wasn't that she *purposefully* wanted to punish him for leaving her the first time. Used to her solitude, she was also experiencing small domestic discomforts. Could he hear her in the bathroom? She had turned off her phone too and hidden it away in her bag alongside his. But what if Anders Nielson's office was trying to get in touch? She couldn't spend months cultivating the CEO of Australia's biggest mining company for lucrative consulting work only to drop everything for John. What if he left her again? As John lit the logs in the wood burner, Tessa wandered the house in a daze of panic. It was tall and triangular, with wooden beams crisscrossing the roof space. Her explorations took her down the hall. She ran out of the third bedroom in tears. John caught up with her at the front door as she fumbled for her coat.

'What's wrong?' he said. 'What's wrong?'

'You've brought me to your family's house,' she cried. 'I saw the two beds, the toys, the books.' Even as she said it she realised she was being silly – John's kids were in their late teens and twenties, not little children at all. He wrapped his arms around her and held her until she stopped crying.

'It's my friend Wally's house,' he said. 'I helped him build it years ago. The toys are for his grandkids, when they come to stay. But *we're* staying here now, you and me, and no one else. Tessa?' She looked at him. He repeated: 'It's just you and me and no one else.'

They drove into Flinders for supplies. On a cloud of happiness, Tessa reached for John's hand outside the small local shop. At first, out of an adulterers' habit, he flinched with guilt and looked around. She found herself spiralling, because of the flinch and the Sunday papers, their headlines on boards outside the front window: HUNG PARLIAMENT, they read, ABBOTT AND GILLARD COURT INDEPENDENT KINGMAKERS. 'Work is calling! Real life is here!' the papers seemed to yell. 'You're living on borrowed time!' But up on the deck, under the verandah of the shop, John took her in his arms, swivelled her sideways and dipped her for a kiss. 'We're together now,' he said, as she laughed with embarrassment and love. 'Inside, outside, in front of everyone, everywhere.'

An icy wind whipped up from the sea and she shivered as they packed their groceries in the car, each item more indulgent and sensuous and expensive than anything she'd have bought on her own. John took her hand and rushed her down the street to where, in the shelter of some gum trees, a small shop stood back from the road. The sign on the front read WENDY'S WOOL.

'You'll like this,' John said. Inside, rows of jumpers hung off coathangers hooked up on the walls. Different sizes were available but all were the same pattern and all were the same off-white. Wendy sized them up with glittering marsupial eyes: not just which jumper they needed, but the nature of their relationship and what they'd been doing all night and morning. John paid, and Wendy studied his credit card.

'You two aren't local,' she said. 'Where are you staying?' (There was no doubt in Tessa's mind that Wendy from Wendy's Wool had alerted the *Herald Sun* about John's whereabouts. No doubt at all.)

They put the jumpers straight on. At the fish and chip shop they ordered a minimum portion to take away. Outside, John tore a hole in the side of the butcher's paper. Steam ballooned into the winter air. 'Are you trying to make the chips go cold?' Tessa pretended to be appalled.

'I'm letting them breathe!' He was stung, colour flooding to his face.

'*Hey*,' she said. 'It's me, not Grace. I was joking, not criticising. Nothing you can do is wrong. Nothing will make me not love you. Hang on . . . nothing will make me not love you,' she repeated, puzzling over the double negatives.

John looked down at her, held her face gently in his hands. 'Everything makes me love you.'

There had always been problems when they were together, bumps and imperfections. What was different was how they were *fixing* them. They were using proper nouns with each other: 'my friend Wally,' John had said; 'Grace,' Tessa chanced. That was new: the concrete engagement in John's past and personal life, the openness of their discussions. Was it because, with his election loss, he no longer had a job? The last vestiges of their old, unequal power arrangement were dismantled, bit by bit. The podium John used to stand on as a winner, a leader of men, a national figure, and Tessa's boss. If she dug deep and was honest with herself, there was also the pedestal on which Tessa had allowed John to place her, to gaze up hungrily at from time to time – her youth, her potential, the freshness she brought to his life, her relative lack of complications, of history, pain and scar tissue. The photograph with shaved-head John had captured Tessa, aged twenty-nine, at the very peak of her beauty. She was only thirty-two when he came back for her, but heartbreak, loneliness, hard work and disillusionment had all taken their toll. It wasn't that her face and body had undergone significant change. *She* had, deep inside. The ability to turn heads was a fleeting feminine privilege, unfairly distributed, unequally bestowed. Tessa would never have it again, and truthfully she didn't care. The podium and pedestal were dismantled and packed away. John was still taller than her, but they faced each other eye to eye. Everything seemed possible.

Days passed in bed, by the fire, walking on the beach. She stopped worrying about her phone. Working for Anders Nielson became unthinkable, foreign and absurd. On the Friday they drove to Cape Schanck blowhole, where waves smashed against the rocks and were forced up in a plume of spray. But the tide was out and they descended a rough wooden staircase, down to a small hidden beach. It was freezing, and rain was in the air. They collected stuff: shells and sticks. They pushed each other around, teasing. Tessa's ponytail whipped into John's eyes from the wind. She said sorry, but he grabbed her and turned her around and buried his face in her hair, breathing it in and kissing her neck. 'John.' She turned around. 'Have a baby with me.'

A wave splashed their feet, soaking their shoes and jeans. The tide was coming in; they'd be trapped forever on the beach. They joined hands and ran to the stairs. Up in the carpark, John got a blanket from the boot, tartan and woolly with moth holes and stains. He draped it around her shoulders and pulled her in tight. The blanket was so clearly a relic of his old life, so obviously used for family picnics – she felt like crying, but this time from relief, because now all that was over. 'Let's go and pack,' he said. 'Grace goes to yoga at seven every Friday. I want to be there when she gets back. I'll tell her. I'll tell her about us.'

They parked outside the primary school around the corner from Greeves Street. John repeated the plan for the fourth or fifth time. He'd go into the empty house, pack some more stuff, be ready and waiting for Grace's return. He'd tell her his decision and meet Tessa back in the car. 'Okay?' he said each time. 'Okay?' Was he making a promise to her, and comforting her, or did he want her sympathy for how hard it would be?

'*Okay.*' She turned her face away so he'd finally just have to go. In the side mirror she watched the tall figure in a funny jumper get smaller and smaller as he made his way across the street. Suddenly she wished she'd been kinder. By then John was out of sight.

How long had she stayed there, waiting in the car? The time without him stretched on and on. It was dark, it was freezing, she wished she could turn the heater on. Half an hour passed, an hour, perhaps. Abruptly she twisted around and reached into the back seat for her weekend bag. Guilty, but also defiant, she turned on both their phones. Hers started up more quickly and an ordinary week's messages filled her screen.

John's phone must have taken longer to start because it was massing its energy to explode. Notifications pinged and buzzed. Texts first. Labor people, journalists, not Grace. Emails: Labor people, journalists, not Grace. REQUEST FOR COMMENT, someone emailed over and over again. REQUEST FOR COMMENT. Suddenly one arrived from someone whose name she didn't recognise. She wouldn't have clicked if not for the subject line: YOUR DAUGHTER SOPHIE. She opened it with a dark foreboding. *Just thought you might like to see what she was up to*, the message read. A video was attached. Tessa tapped on the file to open it.

The video filled the screen. The action took place indoors at night. Figures, maybe two or three of them, passed in front of a lamp, and the *lamplight – no lamplight – lamplight again* made the film grainy and hard to parse. There was a tall figure stable in the centre. A slight figure seemed to be attached to him. Another tall figure drew close. The slight figure was sandwiched in between. The camera was held by a shaking hand. Finally it settled on its subject. The slight figure was Sophie, wearing just her underwear, her head wilted forward so she seemed to collapse into one of the men. The two men were so much taller than her their heads didn't fit in the frame. The first man bent to kiss her. Tessa saw a square jaw and a cruel mouth. The second man turned towards the camera. He unbuttoned his shirt halfway. She saw one leg tuck behind the other. Lazily he stepped on the heels of his shoes to slip them off. As he bent down, light flashed on something dangling from his open shirt. He stood up and thrust his pelvis forward to unbuckle his belt. 'Are you coming or not?' he said to the person holding the camera. 'Come on, then,' another voice said. The video shook and ended.

Heart on fire, she clicked around John's phone a little longer. Then she grabbed her overnight bag and stumbled out of the car. She slammed the door behind her and stood shaking on the footpath. Who was she more angry with? Grace and Sophie for having him in their clutches? Or John, for being clutched? She pushed open the gate of ninety-nine. In one of the two big front windows, a curtain was folded back on itself and open a crack. She peered in and, in the glow of a single lamp, made out the contours of a grand sitting room. A giant sofa faced away from Tessa and towards the back of the room. Butted up against it was a narrow table covered in framed photographic proof that the Clares were the perfect family. She should never have allowed him back to Greeves Street. That room – that home! – was as seductive as a living thing. She wanted to run but was rooted to the spot. She heard a guttural cry. All at once a figure reared up, kneeling on the seat of the sofa, head thrust back and throat exposed. It was Grace Clare, petite in normal life, looming then, strong, almost Amazonian, glinting and scintillating, powerful with sex. She shook back her hair, her eyes gliding past Tessa paralysed at the window. Someone was sitting on the sofa in front of her, Tessa could see the back of his head. Grace loosened the belt holding her linen robe and pulled it open. She straddled the shadowy figure. Chin raised and eyes shut, her face was expressionless as she rose and fell, until suddenly, with a sigh, she stopped. She leaned forward, and Tessa could see her white shoulders move with her deep breaths. She touched her forehead to the dark figure's forehead. Who was it? Was it John? Pain annihilated her until she ceased being Tessa and became only pain.

She must have walked or run back to East Melbourne. She had no memory of the journey. When she woke in her own bedroom on Saturday, 28 August 2010, she'd known even before she'd *known* that she was once again alone. It was Yasmin who'd brought the *Herald Sun* to her attention, hammering on her door until Tessa forced herself up and out blinking into the morning. Obviously she was shocked by the front page – and what was CLARE PACKAGE supposed to mean? But she'd have been lying if she didn't admit that, however briefly, she'd burned with a ruthless happiness. At *last,* at *least* the whole world knew that she and John had been together. She pictured Grace reading it, and felt poisonous and glad and vengeful. She pictured Ingrid reading it, and Manny, and felt some pangs of worry. She pictured Anders Nielson reading it in his level-forty executive suite – shit, she needed to check her work email; she needed to set up the meeting with him! In love, she couldn't possibly do the work. Without love, work was all she had. Before she could scramble for her phone she heard another knock at the front door. Yasmin burst past Tessa to protect her. 'Are you the media? Because she's not talking.'

'Sorry.' A calm voice. 'Yes, I am, I'm Fleur Franks, from *The Age*? But – Tessa, if you can hear me? I'm not asking you about the love nest or whatever. I've got some news I think you should hear from me, if you can. Before you find out online.' Yasmin started to shut the door but Tessa wrenched it open. A pleasant professional woman stood on the threshold. 'I'm really sorry, Tessa. I think you should sit down.'

John Clare was dead, Fleur Franks said. Yasmin screamed, but Tessa only stared. 'He was discovered at home this morning. His body was in a strange position, and for a while they thought he might have been murdered. But a note has been discovered – he took his own life. I'm really, really sorry.' Tessa truly believed this stranger; she really *was* sorry.

'Obviously, with my reporting hat on, I should ask for your reaction . . .' Fleur said.

'But I don't have a reaction,' Tessa replied. And she didn't. She unpacked and washed the clothes she'd worn all week by the sea. She put on the woolly jumper John bought her. She got into bed and stayed there. John's funeral was attended by labour movement VIPs and was covered in all the national papers. Guests to the funeral were invited to make donations to Beyond Blue, the depression charity. No one mentioned the word suicide, but the stories all ended with an italicised note that 'anyone affected by the issues in this story' should call Lifeline. In the days following the funeral, which she obviously wasn't invited to and anyway could never attend, Tessa was so maddened and bereft she considered calling the number herself.

On the day they'd got caught on the freezing beach, lashed by the rising tide, John had wrapped her in the blanket and turned the car's heater on full blast. When they got back to the tall wooden house, John had gone straight to the pine-panelled bathroom and run her a bath. He got down on his knees with his sleeves rolled up to mix the cold into the hot. He undressed her and helped her over the side. He knelt back on the bathmat and they held hands over the side of the bath. 'Tess,' John said. 'I'm old and I'm a fuck-up, I've messed up a lot in my life and I've messed you around. But I'm here now and I love you and if you wanted to have a baby with me –'

Tessa had sobbed with happiness in the bath. She sobbed in her bed now. Just one night later he'd written an apology to his wife and thrown himself from the roof of his family home.

A few weeks after John died, Tessa was invited up to Anders Nielson's level-forty executive suite. The Travallion CEO showed her to a white leather armchair. He unbuttoned his immaculate grey jacket and arranged himself in the armchair opposite. 'Green tea, water?' Tessa declined. Nielson leaned forward. 'I'm worried about the unions. They have a lot of power on the sites. The union guys can speak to my guys. My guys can't speak to my guys.'

'What about human resources, about email,' Tessa started to say.

Nielson anticipated her: 'We can't email them. They're underground, they're driving multi-million-dollar machines that could flip over and kill them. This' – he mimed frantic texting – 'it's not how they work. The unions can make their case to them but we can't.'

Tessa felt a laugh bubble up inside her. Unions thought big business was all powerful, but the boss of Australia's richest company was moaning that unions had the upper hand. How she longed to tell John. 'I understand,' she gravely replied. 'Of course, organising is the movement's great strength.'

'A proposal,' the Travallion boss said. 'Spend a week, if you would. Blue-sky thinking. What can I do to make sure something like Rudd's mining tax never happens again? No brief, no restrictions. Just your advice.'

Was it a strength or a curse, her ability to intuit what was being asked of her before someone, usually a man, was forced to make his needs clear? It had certainly made her childhood easier, navigating her father's moods. Her brothers couldn't, and they dashed themselves against him like flies on a windscreen. Her post-John life was a wasteland of grief. It had been a relief to step out of it and into Anders Nielson's shoes, taking on his worries and justifying his choices. His corporation extracted resources from the ground, resources that belonged abstractly to 'the earth' and more concretely to the people whose land they lay beneath. The resources had no value in situ. They only became valuable through the process of extraction. Extraction was something only the vast international mining companies could plausibly undertake. If the community wanted money from the resources, it was to the miners they had to turn. They should be glad for what royalties and taxes they could get. The alternative was nothing, dead minerals in the ground, useless; big bills and the air-con flicking on and off. Every new mine created the need for settlements and towns, conjured from scratch on bare dirt. All required retail and commerce to support them, which in turn created jobs. When the resources were exhausted, the company packed up and disappeared. They left behind deformed land and ghost towns – but wasn't it better to have profited and lost than never to have profited at all? Once extracted, the resources stopped being something solid of the earth and became something exciting and more valuable: energy, possibility, growth. Once sold, the profit became the company's. The pass-the-parcel of ownership ended when the resources were used. The pollution and carbon emissions were nobody's responsibility and the future's problem. No wonder Anders Nielson lay awake at night. All his money and power rested on the most fragile and fickle of mechanisms that could be withdrawn at any stage: community consent.

Tessa had written her proposal, a two-page document titled simply 'Miners' Wives'. Nielson had given a brief, dry chuckle at her confidence. 'Okay. So you think women, the women you want to target, will come?'

'Definitely.'

'And then how will you scale up?'

'I won't be able to tell you until I see what they get up to.'

'And what will I get out of this?'

'At best,' Tessa said, 'you'd have a mouthpiece from this room directly to thousands of women whose towns, families, relationships, entire lives depend on mining. Their fervent advocacy to their personal networks and beyond. Data. Reams and reams of data, the largest focus group of regional and rural women in Australia.'

'At worst?'

'At worst . . . well, nothing. At worst you get nothing.'

'Speculative.' Anders gazed out at the empty sky. No other building in his vista came close to the height of his office. 'Well, speculation is what I do here.' He finally deigned to read the Costs sheet she'd attached to the proposal. 'You shall have your budget and your staff. The project and your contract will be renewable annually, as you suggest. And as for your compensation.' Tessa waited. If he only agreed to half of it, she'd be mortgage-free in just a few years. 'That seems more than reasonable.'

That was who she was now. That was how she lived her life. Her work had become everything to her, the only thing she had. Tessa lay in her bed, motionless and alone. She had no breath left. It would be easier in some ways if she just never breathed again. But her body took over and air roared back into her lungs. She leapt to her feet and went to the living room for her laptop. Back in bed she adjusted the screen so the glow was less intense. Instead of opening Firefox as usual, Tessa typed the Miners' Wives URL into Safari. She clicked Sign Up and entered an old Hotmail address she used at university. Prompted to choose a username she paused for a moment before typing 'lookafteryourpennies'. She navigated to the Relationships section and clicked to start a new thread.

'I got six days of happiness before the love of my life died,' she wrote. In the body of the post she typed:

Hi ladies, I'm a regular user but made an anonymous account to share this. The love of my life and I were on-again and off-again for a few years before we finally got together properly. We had six perfect days and nights together and planned to be together forever and have a baby. Then he died suddenly and left me alone. Sometimes I wonder if I can keep going on.

She closed her laptop and slid it under her bed. She turned off her lamp and took up her iPhone. She turned the brightness down low and lay with it close to her face. She navigated to her own thread. Replies had started rolling in:

'You have my deepest sympathy.' Heartbreak emoticon.

'It's okay to have bad days, because they remind you that you loved them. It's okay to have good days because it means they're right there with you.'

'One day you will think of him and a smile will come to your face before a tear.'

Hug emoticon. 'He is watching you from heaven.'

'As long as he is in your heart, he will never truly die.'

The screen went blank and so did Tessa's mind. She was asleep.

24.

A TEXT LIT up Girl's phone in her top-floor bedroom in Unit Seven, 93–97 Greeves Street. It was Millie: *Go on chat!*

Girl dragged her ancient, humming laptop onto the bed, but carefully, because it turned off if the plug fell out. The fan whirred and vibrated so much it felt like a live animal. It was so unfair – Millie had an iPhone on her family's plan *and* a MacBook Pro. Her best friend started typing the instant Girl logged on: *Have you done oral?* She ended the message with a sad face.

OMG don't bully me, Girl typed back. *You know I'm a pathetic virgin.*

Your Latin oral, you psycho!!!! Millie replied.

Hello? Girl got 95 per cent in first-semester Latin; she would probably take it for VCE – of course she'd memorised her bit from Virgil's *Aeneid*. It was in English, not even Latin – almost *too* easy. The point of the assessment was to 'perform text to entertain others', as the Romans had. They'd be marked on their 'phrasing, voice inflection and metrical effects to convey meaning and emotion'.

I know, psycho, Girl typed now. *Haven't learnt it yet, ego sum valde stressed outttt.* She could imagine Millie in her family's massive home in Drummond Street. She and her older brother had the whole top floor, including a bathroom and a TV room.

The 'teen retreat', their parents called it. It was almost eleven. Millie would never learn it in time for tomorrow. Smiling, Girl shut the laptop, packed up her homework and undressed. Her mother was not due back for half an hour and the flat was empty. Even so, she wrapped herself in her towel to go one door down the short hall.

Standing close to the bathroom mirror, Girl could see her face, her shoulders, her – she never said 'breasts', her mind just passed by the word without saying it – and her diaphragm. When she hopped over the edge of the bath, the extra height let her see the smooth curve of her narrow waist. The mole which had been next to her bellybutton throughout childhood and primary school was now closer to her right hip. She was nearly fifteen – hopefully her hips had stopped growing? She liked them as they were, larger than her waist but still narrow. She thought of the hideous female bodies she'd seen on the weekend during her freezing plunge in Fitzroy Pool. What had been more gruesome: the fact of the flesh – puckered, sagging, bloated, stretch-marked? Or the awful confidence with which it was paraded round? If Millie had been there, they could have laughed. But without her best friend, the pool change room was like a freakshow or a haunted house: you could be this hideous kind of woman! Or this! Or this gruesome woman! Or this! No, thanks. Girl would never be like that. Grace was elegant and reserved and sophisticated and clever. That's what Girl would be like too.

'But the queen – too long she has suffered the pain of love,' Girl orated in the shower. 'Hour by hour nursing the wound with her lifeblood, consumed by the fire buried in her heart.' Only the Accelerated Learning students were allowed to take Latin at Parkville High. There were just ten grade tens doing it. What a waste! She wished she could perform to the whole school – the whole world! She dried herself and wiped a circle into the fogged-up mirror. Her skin was always clear but it looked its absolute best when she'd just got out of the shower. This meant it was dehydrated – she'd read that in Millie's mum's *Vogue*. She crouched and opened the laminex vanity. Her washbag was hidden right at the back behind a phalanx of bulk-bought discount shampoo. Girl always wore tampons at school when it was that time of the month – pads were absolutely unacceptable, as sexless and babyish as a nappy. But when she was at home, she used pads. Now she dug through the Libra wrappers in the washbag until she located her most precious possession: Grace's expensive face cream. Breathing it in, she dabbed it onto her cheeks. She felt simultaneously that she was near Grace and that she *was* Grace. But what was the time? Her mother could be home any minute. She screwed the lid back on, swaddled the pot in its decoy wrapper, and tucked the washbag away.

In the hall, tiptoeing in her towel, Girl was terrified by a noise from the front door. A bump and slide like someone being pushed against it and collapsing. Then, worse – a key turning in the lock, the handle twisting. She stood paralysed as a black boot was shoved through the crack. The door swung wide to reveal her mother, keys in her mouth, hauling two armfuls of unfolded removal boxes. 'You're early,' Girl accused.

'You're up late.' Her mother pushed the boxes up and leaned them against the wall. Girl escaped to her bedroom and put on the tracksuit bottoms, crop top and long sleeve t-shirt she wore as pyjamas in winter. 'It's a bloody sauna in here, Geraldine, electricity costs money,' her mother called. Girl could hear her flicking the flat's two heaters off at the wall. Finally her mum knocked at the bedroom door. She'd taken her heavy boots off. Her blue Victoria Police shirt was tucked into the world's most horrific 'slacks', made out of the same charmless, hardy material as Girl's school backpack. Girl frowned to show she didn't approve. Her mother rolled her eyes. 'So you're not going to ask me about the boxes?'

'What's with the boxes?'

'I wasn't planning on telling you tonight.' Her mother looked simultaneously tired and pumped, like she'd spent her whole shift gunning coffee from her travel mug. 'I think you should sit down.' She was using a different, more professional tone. In spite of herself, Girl's heart beat faster. She sat on the edge of the bed and clutched Big Ted to her stomach. Maybe her dad was getting remarried. Imagine if it was to someone famous. Imagine if it was to like, Cate Blanchett or Nicole Kidman, and Girl would have Christmases in LA. 'Your dad hasn't been much use, money-wise,' her mother began. 'He does the bare minimum, put it this way, about two months out of every six. Same time, I've been training in my new career, putting in the hours. I know it's been hard on you, not having your mum around at nights –'

'What? Are you quitting?' Girl was outraged. Did she go through all that just to give up?

'What?' Her mum was startled. 'No, I've got a promotion. It's a good one. And I'll be working days.'

'Oh my God,' Girl muttered, trying to work out how she felt. 'Promotion' sounded good. Maybe there'd be more cash coming in. But if her mum wasn't working nights, she'd be *around*. Girl had come to rely on her privacy in the evenings.

'I think you'll really like Wodonga. Actually,' her mum said, 'I had a boyfriend from there once, before I met your father.'

Girl frowned automatically at this needless personal disclosure. Then her voice seemed to be on delay. 'What do you mean, Wodonga?'

'You'll do term four in Wodonga – it's actually earlier than they wanted me to start, but I knew it would be better for you to spend the last term of grade ten getting the hang of the new school, I told them you start VCE in –'

'NO.' Girl got to her feet. 'NO.'

Her mum stood up. 'Geraldine, I know it's –'

'Get out, get out, get the fuck out, I'm never leaving, I'm never moving, I'm not going with you, never, never, never.' Her face was contorted and ugly as she screamed. Her thighs were shaking. When her mother left, she collapsed straight onto the floor. Millie. *Millie.* Nicholas Farrelly knew her name now; he'd asked to share her Bunsen burner. How would she survive? Her school, all her subjects, felafel in the canteen, Mrs Taylor, her life, number ninety-nine, *Grace.*

An hour later she was still crying when she heard a tap at the bedroom door. Her mother poked her head in, illuminated by the light from the kitchen. Girl couldn't stop herself. She let out a sob. 'Oh, Girl. Just wait till life gives you something worth crying about.' Girl wailed. Her mother sighed. 'This is for you.'

'It's not, you're doing it for you. You're ruining my life. I hate you, I hate you.'

'Okay.' The crack of light started to narrow. Suddenly it grew wide again. 'Work's paying for the unit in Wodonga for the first month. I'm going up there on the weekend to find a new place.' Girl let out a strangled cry. 'I'm not paying rent here if I don't have to,' her mother said. 'We've got to clear our stuff out and get moving.'

'I wish you weren't my mother.'

Girl was sure her mother was going to say she wished the same. Finally, she said, 'I'm the only mother you've got. Actually, the only parent. So it's me, or no one.' She pulled the door shut and left.

Girl sobbed, but sobbed thoughtfully. Because that wasn't quite true, was it?

25.

It had been a bit mean but largely fine when Cranshaw only used Astrid's nickname with him. But then Toby heard it everywhere: whispers and points in the queue at the dining hall, shouts over the cubicles in the bathroom, and scrawled in black marker on her door: *Shower Floor Whore*. With Astrid ignoring him, he had no choice but to hang with Cranshaw. Hanging with Cranshaw meant getting wasted, so that was how he spent his time. It had been easy to just pretend the 2010 election didn't exist. His mum offered to fly him down for polling day but Toby declined. 'I'll do a postal vote,' he'd said, but with his packed schedule of doing fuck-all, he hadn't got around to organising it.

On the Saturday night Toby briefly caught the exit polls after dinner. It wasn't looking good, for his dad *or* Gillard, to be honest. He went off to run an iron over his going-out shirt. He popped back into the common room on his way out.

'Mate, did you see your dad chuck a wobbly?' someone asked.

'No, mate, didn't catch it,' Toby said.

'Workies time, Clare Bear,' Cranshaw called. Toby shrugged and let himself be dragged to the Workers Club. They danced at Academy and Cranny picked up a Radford chick. They got home at five and slept through breakfast. Toby checked the news on his phone. His dad had lost. Toby texted him. His dad didn't reply. On the Sunday morning, Toby struggled to the dining hall for lunch. Astrid was scraping her plate at the bins. 'I see you come from a long line of losers,' she said.

'Astrid, please.'

She waited for a second. He was unable to marshal his thoughts. Her plate clattered onto the counter. She whirled on her heel and marched off.

A week later, he stumbled out of ICBM, another club where Cranshaw knew the bouncers from rugby. Cranshaw was trying to get some girl to come home with him. It was so embarrassing to hear his best friend wheedling and bargaining that Toby wandered off alone. Lined up in front of the big Northbourne Avenue newsagent were stacks of all the Saturday papers. On the front page of the *Herald Sun* was a picture of Toby's dad wrapped around a woman half his age. 'WE FOUND HIM,' the headline said. 'Dummy-spit union boss fled to love nest.'

'Cranny!' Toby called.

The girl took her chance to say goodbye. Cranshaw staggered over and punched Toby gently in the stomach. 'Either help or stay out of it.' Toby pointed at the paper. 'Who's the chick?' Cranshaw asked.

Toby laughed bitterly. 'Who's that stranger she's with?'

He was asleep later that morning when his mum called him. He didn't feel like calling her back. There was a knock at his door. He didn't feel like answering. As low, worried voices conferenced in the hall, he cracked open his laptop and navigated to Facebook. He saw then he'd been tagged in heaps of comments ending 'RIP'.

Yep, safe to say his dad's death fucked him in the head.

Toby longed, when he returned to college after the funeral, to act as if nothing had changed. But Cranshaw was distanced, respectful. He stood two rounds at the Workies before slapping Toby's back and issuing a weird statement about grief. Stunned into acting out of character, Toby called him a fucking faggot. 'My mum's a counsellor, man,' Cranshaw said. Toby gave him a little push to the chest. Cranshaw simply crossed his arms. 'Sorry, mate,' he said. 'I care about you.'

Drinking helped. It didn't stop the emotions, but it disinhibited him enough to express them. He cried to some old woman in the Phoenix, literally sobbed into her bosom. Some nightclubs had hospitality nights on Mondays, and some on Tuesdays. Toby went to both. He'd started uni with nearly three thousand dollars saved up from tutoring and birthday presents. Soon he was down to half that. One night he was given – he wasn't exactly sure how – the gift of quite a painful black eye. Annoyed into breaking her silence, Astrid came up to him at breakfast. 'Look after yourself, Toby,' she snapped. 'Idiot.'

Behind her a guy whooped, 'Shower! Floor! Whore!'

'Shut the fuck up,' Toby screamed at him.

Astrid turned away. 'As if you even care.'

His dad had been absent for so much of his childhood, physically away for work, mentally away when present. In a sense, it had always felt like the Mum and Toby Show, with occasional appearances from guests who acted like stars. Sophie spent the first post-suicide Christmas with Sam and the Nugents in Forest Hill. Only Toby and his mum pulled a cracker before lunch at Viet Rose. On Boxing Day he lay in front of the cricket on TV and lost himself in the rhythm of the match: *tock* of the ball – crowd roar – expectant hum – *tock* of the ball – crowd roar – suddenly Toby had a brainwave. Why not move out of his expensive college for second year and simply *never see Astrid again*?

He managed to switch to Hawker Langton before uni returned. Losing his deposit cost his mother nine hundred dollars. Paying his new deposit cost him almost the same amount. Still, it felt great to disappear into a new place where no one gave a single shit about him.

Once invisible, it was difficult to act like a real person. His life was like something the old him used to have anxiety dreams about: not just skipped lectures, but skipped tutorials too; probing emails from his Modern Chinese tutor; a formal warning from the Dean of the Law School; acid reflux from eating Kingsley's Chicken every night; total friendlessness, with even Cranshaw ruefully dumping him. After a night on the rum and Cokes he found himself heading to the actual casino. He withdrew a chunk from his depleted savings and ran it through the pokies. The next morning, early, he was prodded awake by a stranger. 'Do I need to phone your mum? Or the police?'

Toby stared around him. He was under a tree in Glebe Park. He blinked up at the woman: blondish-grey hair to her shoulders, slim and athletic in her trouser suit. An image popped into his mind: the woman at the flyscreen door in Campbell, his dad's despairing face as she turned away. 'No, I'm okay.' He scrambled to his feet.

'You've got somewhere to go?'

'I do!'

He followed the exact route his father had driven that day almost a year earlier, climbing to the top of a winding street in Campbell and locating the plain little house. He bounded up the stairs to the front door and hammered on it.

'Toby Clare!' She seemed to know him immediately. She hustled him in, gave him a towel and a dressing-gown and pointed him towards the shower. 'Throw your shirt out,' she called after him. When he emerged there was a fried egg sand-wich waiting for him and coffee in a giant mug. Helen Macklin was her name. She knew 'Johnnie', as she called his dad, from 'many moons ago', back in the days when number ninety-nine had been a Melbourne Uni share house. She kindly and skilfully turned the tables and spent the rest of the morning interrogating him. He left the house with a plastic container of flapjacks, a freshly washed and dried shirt, an invitation to return at any time, and not a single piece of usable intel about his father or what had made him cry.

Still, it was with a lighter heart that he cruised through campus on the way back to Hawker Langton. Outside a cylin-drical lecture theatre known as the Tank, he'd stumbled upon what cops would have called a fracas. About twenty female students were marching around with signs saying 'No Means No'. A guy was watching nearby, holding his mountain bike. 'What's happening?' Toby asked.

'It's a protest.' They both laughed. 'Yeah, you probably guessed that,' the guy said. 'It's Susie Jacobs, the sex woman.'

'The sex woman?'

'She's speaking tonight about what men want.'

What *did* men want? Toby hovered near a pillar and googled Susie Jacobs. 'Why have sex when you could scrub a floor instead?' read the title of the top result. It was from a month-old profile in *The Australian*. According to veteran therapist Susie Jacobs' interviews with a hundred men, their wives would literally prefer to do anything other than have sex with them. The photograph accompanying the article showed a tiny, birdlike woman of about sixty-five, surrounded by a group of eight stolid and mournful middle-aged men. Six were overweight. Four had moustaches. All regarded the camera balefully. Nope, Toby was Team Wife on that one. There would be no answers for him inside the Tank.

'Is that Toby Clare?' someone cried suddenly – a woman's voice.

'Shame, shame, shame,' someone began chanting.

'Shame, shame, shame,' others joined in. In the centre of the group was Astrid. There was something a bit 'Britney Spears shaving her own hair off' in her eyes. She appeared very angry indeed.

'Astrid?' he ventured.

'Oh, here we go!' she said furiously. 'You should be giving the speech in there, not just watching it. You always get what you want!'

'Wait a sec,' Toby said.

'And you're a slut-shamer,' someone shouted.

Toby held up his hands. 'Whoa, hang on.'

'Men like you just use women and walk away,' someone said.

'Exactly like your dad,' Astrid said.

'Pardon me,' Toby clarified. 'My *dead* dad?'

Astrid was defiant. 'We all saw the paper! What he did to your mother, and that woman he had an affair with!'

'So wait a second,' Toby said. 'Are you a slut, and did I shame you? Or were you not a slut, and I used you? Did you like me, and want me around, or did you hate me, and want me gone? Which is it? And how would you know what I wanted? You never even bothered to ask.'

Astrid burst into tears. The women encircled her. Toby waited for a moment on the outside. No one spoke to him. He walked away.

The next day he woke to find a letter under his door. It requested that he present himself at the Head's office. He did so.

An accusation had been made, he was told by Dr Bhatt. The activities outlined in the detailed complaint had taken place a year earlier and in another college. An incident in the communal showers had been 'particularly unfortunate'. Any sexual assault, past or present, would not be tolerated in Hawker Langton. He would not be expelled from university, not to worry about that. But he could not return to on-campus accommodation for semester two. 'Righty-ho!' the Head concluded. 'Clear your stuff and be out by July.'

Well, thank God for Helen, that was all Toby could say. One phone call was all it had taken, no questions asked. A ride back to her house, a place to stay, and – with the Jolly Trolley – something of value to do with himself all day. Now just a few months later his place of safety had been compromised. His mother had called him repeatedly and then hurt herself, possibly on purpose. To lose one parent might be regarded as misfortune. What did it say about Toby if both his parents topped themselves?

The door to the hospice kitchenette was pushed open and Toby scrambled up from the floor. Helen tutted when she saw him wiping away tears. 'If the dishwasher's going to make you cry every night I'll get someone else to do it.' She led him out through the sitting room to her little office by the front door. 'I don't need to know the ins and outs of your life,' Helen said. 'You're a grown man and you need your privacy. But if something's upsetting you, you know I'm here.'

'I've fucked up, Helen.' Toby's eyes prickled again. 'Everyone hates me at uni. Astrid hates me. That's why I was kicked out, for making Astrid feel like shit. Dad said not to get married too young!' Toby suddenly sobbed. 'But as if I'd ever have that problem! No one loves me or will ever love me.'

'Oh, you poor boy,' Helen said. 'What does your mum say, have you told her?'

'As if I could ever tell her! And Helen.' He was properly crying now. 'She was ringing me all weekend, then she had an accident or something, something's wrong with her, she had to go in an *ambulance*. But I can't see her. I can't tell her what's happened at uni.'

'What about your sister? What would Sophie say?'

What *would* Sophie say? Sexual harassment. Leaving aside the harassment part, he shivered with shame thinking of his sister knowing that he'd had sex. But he was nineteen now, it would be more shameful if he hadn't. He checked his phone. She'd still be at the shop. 'I could call her,' he said. 'I suppose.'

'Toby, I've loved having you here. The residents love you. At one time, maybe twice in my life, I loved your dad. But I'm not your mum. I think you owe it to her to let her *be* your mum. To tell her you're in trouble and see if she can help. Don't do it on your own if you don't have to. They're the only family you have left. Go home and give them a chance.'

26.

AFTER GREETING TESSA gravely, Christine James showed her to a lift marked PRIVATE. 'Anders is so pleased you could brief the Resources Council,' Christine said, her eyes fixed heavenward as they zoomed to level thirty-nine, folded reading glasses on a chain around her neck. 'It's so important to have buy-in from the other companies.' Tessa put on her most serious face and murmured her agreement.

The lift opened almost silently to reveal a sumptuous marble vestibule and a pair of double doors marked TRAVALLION BOARDROOM 1. The table that ran down the centre of the room was polished honey-coloured wood, long and gently ovoid like a surfboard. At its head sat hatchet-faced Australian Resources Council CEO Malcolm Blackman. Around him a dozen board members were arranged, eleven men and one woman, high-ranking individuals drawn from a selection of the nation's biggest mining companies. In a second-tier horseshoe around the edge of the room sat other members of the ARC secretariat: a policy guy, the coal guy, Joey Nikolić the comms guy she'd already met, and – with a little table of her own, and a laptop to take notes – a pretty and well-groomed graduate Joey had employed to assist him.

Christine stepped forward. The room fell respectfully silent. Christine controlled access not just to the CEO's level-forty executive suite, but to his phone, inbox, calendar and good graces. 'It's Travallion's pleasure today to play host to the regular meeting of the Resources Council,' she said. 'Anders has asked Tessa Notaras to bring you up to speed on a pilot project she's been trialling for a year. Soon Tessa will be meeting with Anders to discuss the extension of her contract and her ideas for phase two. Any thoughts should be shared directly with Tessa so she can feed them into her plan.' With a nod, Christine withdrew. The meeting participants exhaled and returned to their phones.

'Hello everyone,' Tessa said loudly. 'Lovely Melbourne weather for you!' A few people grunted to acknowledge the charcoal sky. She knew, from experience, that unless a woman entered a room with a voice that demanded to be heard, she could wait patiently for hours and never be granted the chance to speak. Even when she was booked, as now, to make a formal presentation, she always spoke as soon as she entered the room, just to gently habituate the men to the reality of a woman's voice. Still her hand trembled as she hooked her laptop up to the projector. She rocked to her toes and cleared her throat, a louder sound than she'd intended. 'Um,' Tessa croaked. 'In 2010?' With superhuman effort, she brought her heart rate under control. 'Last year.' Deep and confident, just as she'd rehearsed. 'The industry's campaign against the Rudd Government's mining tax was an unmitigated success.' The room, which had been tense, slightly relaxed. 'Two reasons why. The first: it quantified, with facts and figures and hard data, the disastrous financial impact the so-called Resources Super Profits Tax would have on mineral resources, and on Australia.'

In the beta seats, the policy boffin nodded convulsively. 'The super tax on mining,' someone said.

'A very successful reframing!' Everyone smirked. 'The second reason for its success was that it humanised the mining industry and gave it a face. It said: if you attack mining, you attack real workers, families and communities.' She flicked her presentation onto the first slide, a screenshot of an ad that had run online only during the mining industry's multi-million-dollar special interest campaign. 'I don't know if you remember these ladies.' There was a quiet murmur of recognition from the room. 'A lot of *our guys*' – she used Nielson's term from their first meeting – 'were hampered when it came to speaking out against the tax. In many cases their own contracts prevented them from advocating for the industry.'

'There's a reason for that,' a man said. He was from one of the smaller companies that rotated in and out of the board every few years. 'Can't have everyone speaking to the media.'

'Of course.' Tessa smiled encouragingly. 'Exactly. But their wives weren't restricted. And they were formidable advocates for the role resources companies played in their lives and the lives of their towns.' She clicked the screenshot and it animated into a clip.

'Don't know what we'd do without mining,' one woman said, her big friendly face crinkled in concern.

'This place would be a shithole without it,' her friend said. 'Don't know if I'm allowed to say that, ha-ha!'

An older lady spoke up, her mum, perhaps. 'Our whole family relies on mining. It's what we do.' The other two nodded respectfully. They all gave the camera a hard stare.

'Many urbanites, many commentators, feel comfortable saying mining should be shut down or taxed out of existence,' Tessa said. 'It's easy for them to say because they don't person-ally know anyone who'd be affected.'

Another board member piped up. 'They'd be affected soon enough. Where does their electricity come from?'

Someone always felt the need to toss out this simplistic shit. 'Very true,' Tessa agreed. 'So by mid-2010, the industry found itself faced with both an opportunity and a threat. The opportunity was there to carry on the good work of the campaign. To personalise the contribution mining makes to our communities, and tell the stories of the men and women who make it happen.'

The board woman spoke up. 'Haven't we just been listening to this from the ad guy?'

One of the younger board members raised his gaze from his iPad. 'Jennifer is correct. We're paying the ad guy through the nose to do this for us.'

'The threat,' Tessa said. 'The *threat* was that if we didn't do the hard work of connecting with members of our own industry, the unions would do it instead.' A ripple of interest passed through the room. 'To inoculate against the next mining tax, or a punitive new carbon tax, we have to build up real support within our own community . . .' She slowed down and glanced around. 'And empower them to be the industry's best advocates.'

'Tessa's really qualified for this, actually,' Joey Nikolić broke in. 'She worked for the trade union movement.' There were uncomfortable sniggers from the miners, and one from Tessa herself.

'So here we are.' Tessa called up the site on her browser. 'Very simple: it's just a web forum. Organic, woman-powered: a true online community, just like the internet's good old days. Miners' Wives is the name of the site. Self-explanatory. Here's our tagline.' She highlighted some text under the logo.

'I'd like to tell you where it came from. A few weeks after the forum launched, a user created an account under the name of KathyCat. It took half a year before she wrote her first post. She asked if there was anyone in Port Hedland who could help her open a jar. She'd promised to take a Victoria sponge to her daughter's school cake sale – the sponge she could manage, but she couldn't open the jam. Neuropathy in her hands,' Tessa explained. 'She'd been commuting back and forth to Rockingham General Hospital to get chemotherapy for her breast cancer.'

The room was totally silent.

'Normally her husband dropped everything to help, but he was on shift. KathyCat posted the message at 10 am. By midday the thread was updated.' She swapped back to her slides. There was a picture of three women. The one in the middle, wearing a headscarf, was holding a perfect Victoria sponge. 'The caption says: *With thanks to Kelly, Fran and Mel (behind the camera). Mia will be very happy with her sponge. I can't thank you girls enough.* And then she wrote what became our tagline: *A strong woman stands up for herself. A stronger woman stands up for everybody else.*'

Malcolm Blackman cleared his throat. 'Very nice.' A few board members glanced up from their phones and nodded.

Tessa switched back to Miners' Wives. 'You can see down here, it says about three hundred signed-in users are online as we speak, and two hundred just browsing. The forum's divided into five sections: Life, Children, Relationships, Home and Work. Each category expands into sub-forums – there's a place for everything.' She clicked on Relationships. Naturally, she'd deleted her own thread the instant she'd woken up. 'Just Not On is one of our most popular sub-forums. It's a space where the women come to ask if they're being unreasonable. Here are some titles of the currently active threads: *Husband won't let me shower twice a day. My vego daughter turns my other kids off meat. A teacher at my son's school called him thick. Sister-in-law wants me to babysit so she can do personal training.* "Am I wrong," all the posts conclude, "or is this JNO?" The best JNOs bring in hundreds of replies. We've got a real community here, wonderful mining women, all connecting and helping each other.'

Next Tessa flicked to an impressive chart. It showed the twelve months since the site's launch, the growth from absolute zero to nearly thirty thousand users. ('Nearly thirty thousand' was actually twenty-seven thousand. Thank God it was more than twenty-six thousand, or she would have had to have said 'over 25k'.) But, she pointed out, the number of registered users was not the important metric. Consider also the number of non-signed-in users who visited every day ('lurkers', in forum speak), and the length of time people spent on the site: literally hours. Some sessions were seven or eight hours long. Like Tessa herself, many women appeared to spend all day at work with the forum opened companionably in a tab.

The next slide showed the members' locations: Western Australia, the Hunter Valley, the Bowen Basin, Latrobe Valley, and a weird but welcome ancillary presence in all the major capitals. They were aged between twenty-five and fifty, and they themselves or at least one close relative worked in mining. When surveyed about how many Facebook friends they had, the majority ticked 150–200. 'Here they are!' Tessa said. 'The best advocates for mining in Australia!' No one smiled. Whatever, fuck them.

'Now, meet FIFO Fi.' She flicked to her carefully selected case studies. A photo filled the screen of a smiling pony-tailed blonde with thin eyebrows. 'Her real name's Fiona. Her husband's a fly-in fly-out diesel fitter in a copper, silver and zinc mine north of Kalgoorlie. She's in Perth with their two little kids. The husband flies out to work for seven days followed by seven nights, fourteen straight twelve-hour shifts. Then back to the family for seven days. Then he hops on the plane to do it all again. Fi's an amazing woman, a stay-at-home mum who studied psychology at uni.' Tessa flicked to the next slide, a screenshot. 'Her blog's an incredible resource for women whose partners are rostered away. She talks about the divided self. To cope with the long hours away, the men have to shut down caring about their family. Then, when they come home, it's hard to unseal the place they've put all their feelings.'

'Boo hoo, suck it up, princess.' It was one of the board members.

Malcolm looked over his glasses. 'Yes, what's the husband on – one fifty? One sixty a year? All for two years' training and a driver's licence. If she's writing anything about mining it should be' – he put his hands together in prayer – 'thank you, thank you, thank you!'

Tessa had to pretend he hadn't spoken. 'Many mining workers find it hard to talk about the mental-health impacts of FIFO work,' she said. 'For their partners to be so clued-up like this, taking advice from someone in the same boat – it's invaluable. We set her up with her own blog under the Miners' Wives masthead. She was profiled in *Women's Weekly*. Off the back of that she was offered a book deal.'

'So is Anders getting a cut of the book deal?'

'Yeah, what's in this for us?'

Tessa decided to skip the next slide. A Perth-based stay-at-home mum had leveraged her connections on the forum to create a flourishing side business. 'Miss You Dolls' printed a high-res image of the absent parent on the face of a stuffed cotton doll. 'Ideal for cuddling, spray with aftershave or parent's scent.' The photo showed a little girl snuggling a doll with the face of a man in a hard hat. No, these people didn't deserve to hear about it.

The slide she found instead prompted a glad, approving noise from every single person in the room. 'I can tell you all remember this woman and her question on *Q&A*.' She clicked the image to animate it. Voice shaking, a middle-aged woman addressed the Prime Minister: 'Julia. *Mizz Gillard*. Before the last election you said there'd be no carbon tax under a government you led. Now you have this idea.' The woman ducked her head to stumble over a note. 'A market-based mechanism to price carbon.' She looked back up. 'No matter what, it's going to make my cost of living go way up. Can you at least be straight with us and admit it's a tax?' The Prime Minister had giggled in her light-hearted way. 'Oh look, Lynne! Thanks for your question. All this argy-bargy about what it's called is slightly ridiculous. I'm happy to call it a tax. As for your cost of living . . .'

'Game-changer,' one of the board members said.

'Total, bloody, game-changer!' Malcolm bellowed.

'There's a backstory to all this.' Tessa brought up the forum on the laptop browser. 'The thread is called "Help me be brave enough to ask this question". And you can see, the woman, Lynne, posted that she'd got into the audience for *Q&A*. Sixty-three people encouraged her to speak up.'

None of the board members were on their phones anymore. 'Another interesting thing,' Tessa said. 'Here's a thread about the Alexander Stones expansion.'

'What's a thread?'

She couldn't tell who'd asked. The entire audience was on the edge of their seats.

'Oh, every time I say thread, it just means discussion. Alexander Stones,' she went on. 'Vast mine, Australia's biggest, one of the world's biggest. Travallion has an expansion on the table. This thread is called "How can we get this approved?" It's women from the Alexander Stones site itself, and women who live in Golby Cut, the big town centre out there. Completely self-organised. One found the details of all the decision-makers, state and federal. They emailed them with their stories, advocating for the expansion. Look, you can see the MP has written back, and this user has scanned the reply she received.' There was a glorious engaged *mmm* sound from the room. 'We started to get so many journalists coming to the site looking for people to quote, we had to start a new sub-forum called Journo Requests. Our members have been quoted in national, state and local papers.'

'Hang on a sec,' one board member said.

Everyone turned towards the man who spoke. 'Um,' Tessa said. 'Shall we do questions now, or –'

'Look, I just typed in XLT Civet,' the man said.

Of course, Jeremy Horn from XLT Civet. Famously the company had sent in a private militia to brutally repress South American environmental protesters. Twenty people had been killed. But for all their global profit and profile, they were a small player on the Australian scene, dwarfed by Travallion and Allaman. It was always the lower status or damaged players you had to look out for in meetings – so much aggression. Tessa was cautious: 'Yes?'

'People here are complaining about our travel policy. How you don't get Frequent Flyer points doing FIFO anymore.'

'Just a minute,' someone else said. 'I've gone into the bit about our Pilbara operations and there's a . . . thing, thread, whatever, here from the union delegate. He's answering questions, he's getting them to join. To join the union!'

The board members stared at her, their eyes accusing and their expressions sour. She'd hoodwinked them into engaging with something new – and now look what happened! They'd been fucked over! Well, she didn't answer to these guys; they had no say over her or her work. Tessa played her trump card: '*Anders*,' she began. The board members perceptibly quietened. 'When Anders commissioned this strategy a year ago, as an experiment, he was very keen that the mining companies be hands-off – at least in the eyes of the public,' she said. 'It's so important for the companies to not be seen to be involved . . .'

The comms guy piped up again. 'Can I suggest we table more questions now, and Tessa can report back in future? It's time for a quick break.' Everyone picked up their phones and trooped out. Joey turned to Tessa. 'That was great, wasn't it?'

'Oh, I don't know.' Cravenly she fished for reassurance: 'It went a bit hostile at the end.'

He clapped his hand on her shoulder. 'Mate, you did so well.'

Keen to avoid any board members lingering in the foyer, Tessa crossed to the window to gaze out. Melbourne had been born rich, or close enough. Gold was found in Victorian goldfields in 1851, and the wide streets of Hoddle's city grid were studded with sumptuous and ornate public and private buildings, cut and pasted from England to the colony. Waves of immigrants brought amazing coffee and different types of food. The beach was shit and it got cold enough in winter that you had to wear a coat. All this combined to give the city a stately, cosmopolitan, intellectual vibe. When Tessa had first visited, age fifteen, she'd known she'd make her home here, that she could be an entirely different person in the city's beautiful streets, her family and Lota left far behind. But from up this high, all she could see was glass and steel. Everything that made Melbourne special was lost. Her eyes unfocused in a blur of grey. When she blinked, she saw her own reflection, two new lines between her eyebrows.

What was she doing? Scenes from the presentation flashed through her mind. Their idiotic questions. Malcolm Blackman with his hands together in prayer: 'Thank you, thank you, thank you.' He was imagining FIFO Fi's diesel fitter husband, but clearly he felt all Australians owed the miners a debt of gratitude. Truthfully the Resources Super Profits Tax had offended Tessa just as John Howard's WorkChoices had offended her: both were too extreme, 'draconian', an overwhelming, almost personal misuse of political power. Perhaps she hated overt shows of dominance because of her dad, her childhood blighted by his bullying and fits of pique. Well, as politicians always stolidly replied when asked to reflect on their reasoning, Tessa was not a psychologist. And whose side had the community been on both times? Not the government of the day's – Tessa's.

There had always been a lovely ebb and flow of national opinion, as reliable as the tide, always around fixed points like the fair go. These things always balanced out over time.

The arc of Australian history was long and it bent towards being chillaxed. But something had tipped the scales, something was going wrong. Rudd had come to power saying climate change was the great moral challenge of our time. He'd ratified the Kyoto Protocol, but he'd dropped his flagship emissions trading scheme. Out of nowhere, with the soil of public opinion obstinately untilled, he'd introduced a giant tax on Australia's biggest industry. He'd messed that up too, lost the confidence of his party, lost the leadership. Up stepped Julia Eileen Gillard, made for the job of prime minister. But she didn't win it fair and square and she never for a second got a clear run at it. Rudd poisonously leaked against Gillard throughout the 2010 election campaign – allegedly! Labor had been lucky to squeak back in. Gillard had promised 'no carbon tax under a government I lead'. Then she'd changed her mind.

In March 2011 a crowd of climate sceptics rallied in front of Parliament House. In a way, the participants weren't so different from the average trade union rally – old white guys with work boots and basal cell carcinomas. But the signs they carried were terrifying in their naked hatred and misogyny: DITCH THE WITCH, said one. Gruesome effigies of Gillard and the Greens leader Bob Brown twitched and danced above the crowd. One of the signs about Gillard read JU-LIAR: BOB BROWN'S BITCH. Still Gillard ploughed on, one day at a time. Now a slimmed-down Rudd lurked in the wings, doing the numbers to get the leadership back. More than a century the nation had waited for its first female prime minister. She'd be lucky to be in the job for two years.

It was the waste that hurt, the criminal waste. Not just of Gillard, as a woman and a leader, but of political capital too, and the calm consensus that had developed on climate change. Instead of a rational argument about how to fix it, it was now a fight to the death about whether it was real. Opposition Leader Tony Abbott was on the record as calling climate science 'complete crap'. He'd addressed the protesters at the rally in March: 'As I look out on this crowd of fine Australians, I want to say that I do not see scientific heretics,' Abbott barked, next to a sign that read CARBON DIOXIDE IS A HARMLESS TRACE GAS. 'I do not see environmental vandals,' he continued, next to a sign that said THE POLAR BEARS ARE FINE. This was the clown the miners wanted to win the next election – and Tessa was working for the miners. Public opinion no longer ebbed and flowed. Instead, there was a line in the sand. Up on level thirty-nine of the Travallion offices, Tessa was standing on the wrong side.

There was no doubt in her mind that she would present her new plan to Anders and he would love it. Her website had performed beyond her wildest dreams. In phase one she'd helped the women join together as a group: Miners' Wives. In phase two, she wanted to help them develop and communicate their own unique perspectives. Workshops to help the women blog, to teach them digital photography, video, podcasting. Thrust the promising voices onto the stage in front of a built-in audience keen to hear from them; work with producers on a reality show or documentary project. All this would cost money, half a million dollars more than phase one, but Tessa was confident she could make it worth it, for Anders' bottom line and her own.

So was it right to be on Team Fossil Fuels? Clearly not – but should she sacrifice the best work of her life just because politicians were incompetent? The miners she'd presented to were idiots. Tony Abbott was an idiot and a thug. The Labor Party seethed with idiot backstabbers. The Greens were idiotic and naive. There were no adults in the room. It was frankly terrifying to be the only person in the country, the world, who could strategise themselves out of a paper bag. Amid this carnival of chaos, being good at her job was a moral act.

The truth was, she was tired and she was lonely. She would do anything, give anything, to believe in someone or something good the way she'd believed in John Clare and their work together in 2007. But she had loved him, and he'd left her – not once but twice. No one was looking after Tessa except Tessa. When Anders Nielson gave her a new contract, she would sign it.

'Ahh, Tessa.' She turned. 'Still here – good.' Anders appeared as if summoned by her thoughts. 'You don't mind if we speak for a moment?'

'No problem.' Tessa sat in the chair he'd indicated. 'I've just made my Miners' Wives presentation, actually, to the Resources Council.'

'I heard,' he said. 'I'm afraid I have some news you may find disappointing.' Due to his own 'misgivings' and some 'significant concerns' from colleagues, Miners' Wives would no longer proceed as an 'experiment operating outside the law'. It was insupportable to be badmouthed on 'an online presence' for which they themselves had paid. At first Tessa could hardly understand what he was saying. Then she felt something wash over her: injustice. It was a feeling she remembered strongly from childhood, the times when she, the good child, was swept up in her father's brief authoritarian crackdowns. The key, in those cases, had been to not make a fuss. A fuss would make her father double down. Rather, she just left her brothers to it and melted invisibly away. When her dad's anger wore off, she went about her business as usual. Would this be the same?

She found herself strangely unwilling to melt. She thought of all the women she'd come to know through Miners' Wives over the previous twelve months. One opposed a carbon tax while spending hours collecting and composting her own, and her neighbours', food waste. A die-hard Liberal voter had said she'd 'definitely' be friends with Julia Gillard if she met her at the office. A lesbian working on an NT rare-earth project didn't believe in same-sex marriage. In a deeply conservative rural electorate, a group of women crowd-sourced a legal challenge to save a refugee family from being deported. 'They're human beings,' she said now. 'Complex, vibrant human beings. The bad parts are inextricable from the good parts.'

Anders appeared not to have heard. 'When Rudd came to power I think we all understood that changes would have to be made.' He waved his long white hands to indicate quote marks. '*Climate change is real* – that was the price of entry into the debate. You had to say it to be allowed to speak, to be allowed even to exist. We had an entire team of people prepping for the emissions trading scheme, doing the maths, making it work. All companies did. Licence to operate, you know – you factor it in.' Anders leaned back. 'But maybe you've noticed? Things have changed. Here's my problem. There's a conversation out there, and one side is getting increasingly angry and polarising.'

'Those protesters back in March,' Tessa agreed. 'Ditch the witch.'

'No, Tessa. The *progressives*. They're off the reservation. The other side, real people, the quiet Australians, they're furious. They don't have columns in the *Sydney Morning Herald*, they don't have' – he grimaced – '*Twitters*. They don't have a voice.

Miners' Wives is over, it's finished. But your expertise may still be of use. What if we take what we learnt from it and use it to . . .' He pinched his thumb and forefingers together and seesawed his pale hands up and down. 'Rebalance the conversation?' He jumped up. 'A proposal. Blue-sky thinking. Well, you know the drill. Christine has found some time for you next Monday. Midday. Schedule it in.'

27.

'I've been wanting to ask . . .' Girl trailed off. 'No, it's okay.'

Grace looked up from the Bunnings catalogue she got Ned and Brendan across the street to save for her. Obviously she didn't believe in cutting down trees for advertising, and had once threatened Chemist Warehouse with legal action for repeatedly defying her No Junk Mail sign. Still, she could not deny herself all earthly pleasures, and foremost among them was reading the Bunnings catalogue at her kitchen table. 'Say, darling, say,' she said. 'Out with it.'

Girl stared at her lap. 'I don't think this is a good time.'

Grace prided herself on not being susceptible to hints; picking up on subtext was a young woman's game. She'd dropped subtext entirely after having Toby, just like she'd stopped hiding in the cubicles after her shower at Fitzroy Pool. Young girls moved their towels around their bodies in a coy dance. Grace and the other grown women just dried themselves off and got dressed. She existed in the real world, where facts were exchanged and preferences communicated. Be straightforward! Life wasn't that hard! But Geraldine was still in that painful purgatory between wants needed and wants expressed. 'Cough it up,' Grace said sternly.

'Well, you know how my mum's in the police now. Like, a constable? She's been doing nights, remember? She's been posted – well, whatever, doesn't matter.' Tears started to slide down Girl's face. 'We have to move to Wodonga for two years. She's going up this weekend to look for flats! And then as soon as she's found one we're moving out!' Girl was sobbing. 'I'll be finishing school in the middle of nowhere.'

'Oh, love.' Grace waved Girl over and patted her little shoulder blade, as bony and fragile as a bird's wing. 'Poor love, the same thing happened to me with my father, almost the very same age.'

Girl sniffed. 'I remember.'

'Yes, my Auntie Manna rescued me, it's not an exaggeration to say. I moved into this very house.' Grace rapped her knuckle on the table's worn and knotty pine, though of course nothing about the now giant kitchen was the same anymore. 'Well, I'm terribly sorry to hear that, darling, what a disappointment for you. And you love your little school.'

'Leaving is my worst nightmare.' Girl's face was white and blank.

'I remember how awful I felt too. Of course, Campion was quite special – well! I mean, I was really at home there.'

'I was wondering if . . .'

'Mmm?'

'Well, I wondered if I could move in with you. I wouldn't get in your way, I promise. I would clean and tidy. I'd pay for my own food. And pay rent.'

Needs. Girl had them. She seemed almost desperate. In some ways, it felt good for the pendulum to swing back into place. Girl was too young and busy to remember how they met, but Grace knew. Girl had come into her life through an act of Grace's charity. She'd purchased twenty tickets to Parkville High's famously first-rate raffle. Their relationship had become neighbourly, with Grace drawing on Girl to provide such services as glass-washing after a party and watering the plants. When Anton turned Grace's whole life upside down, everything with Girl had been shaken up too. They became students of his, and studio mates. But since John's death the balance had shifted. Girl was the neighbourly one, performing acts of charity for Grace. She had found Grace when she was injured. She'd seen Grace hit rock bottom.

Grace recalled a *Women's Weekly* she'd read in her dentist's waiting room. In it the pop star Kylie Minogue talked about her breast cancer, diagnosed when she'd been very young and dating the handsome French actor Olivier Martinez. She'd seen off the cancer, but she and Martinez had broken up shortly afterwards. There'd been a public outcry at what had seemed like his betrayal. In the magazine article, Kylie or someone close to her set the record straight. Olivier did nothing wrong – it had been *she* who ended it when she got better, not him. Grace had felt an instant accord with the pop starlet. Martinez had observed Kylie at her lowest ebb, when her life hung in the balance and she could barely lift her head. Once the moment of weakness passed, you'd do anything to forget it. Why keep a witness around? Grace was in the grips of a strong housekeeping urge. She wanted to tidy her old weak self away. Truthfully, she wanted to tidy Girl away too. Her ambivalence must have been only too clear.

'Don't worry.' Girl stepped back towards her schoolbag. 'Pretend I didn't say anything.'

Grace half got up. 'Girl, you don't have to go.'

But Girl was already in the hall. After a moment, the front door banged shut.

*

For the second time in a few days, Grace climbed the open-tread oak staircase and entered her half-a-million-dollar shrine to the madness of love. At the sink, she dampened a linen cloth and ran it across every surface. She peeked into the reclaimed clay bin; it was a desert, dry and cracked. It was Anton's obsession that not a scrap of clay should go unrecycled. She'd found it hard to have the patience herself – but then, she wasn't a real potter. She wandered over to the back window and pressed her foot down on the pedal. Ignored for a year, her wheel whirred instantly into action. She checked the big metal clay cupboard. Multiple unopened bags of white stoneware. She dragged one out and peeled the plastic off, slicing a chunk away with wire and tossing it between her hands. 'Feel the connection to the earth,' Anton would say. Anton! She dropped the ball of clay onto the table and smashed it with her fist. She squashed it, patted it into a cube and rolled it towards her navel. The old movements came back to her, backwards and forwards. She wedged it into a ram's skull. She prepared first one ball, then another and another. She went over to the wheel and sat down.

When Grace was in her second-last year of high school, her mother had died after a long illness – so long it had stopped registering, so long that, despite always being terminal, it seemed like it would never end. The reality of the death was a nasty shock. So was what happened afterwards. Her father sat her down in the formal sitting room of their sepulchral Federation home in Malvern. He had an announcement to make: they were moving back to England. Back to England? Grace had been born there, but she wasn't from England! 'Well, I am,' her father said. He picked up his briefcase and went into the office. There were to be no arguments.

For the first time in her life, Grace wagged school. A couple of tram rides later she pitched up on the doorstep of her Auntie Manna. Even if she hadn't copied the address from her mother's book, Grace would have known 99 Greeves Street was her aunt's house. Wind chimes hung tinkling in two sturdy olive trees. Every trim on the tall and crumbling terrace was painted lilac, even the intricate cast-iron lacework. Three windows ran along the top-floor balcony, one cracked and one boarded up. Grace picked her way through unlocked bikes, weatherbeaten chairs and stolen milk crates to knock on the orange front door. Her future hung in the balance. Auntie Manna had answered and saved her life. Grace would move in with her, complete her schooling at her beautiful, ordered, academic haven of a school, and then, Grace had promised, more to herself than to Manna, she'd be out of her aunt's hair.

She'd picked her way round the house, overrun with people who had nothing to do on a work day, and who, though all comfortably in middle age, could sit cross-legged with more ease than she could. 'This is where I do my classes,' Auntie Manna said, pointing round at a pile of colourful cotton cushions shot through with spidery silver and gold thread. 'And this is where I do my treatments.' Manna stood in the doorway to the tiniest room, an almost-cupboard with a single narrow bed. 'But I don't do them at night. You can sleep there.' The classes, it turned out, were yoga and meditation. The treatments were 'healing'. 'Your mother found them very helpful. Particularly towards the end.'

Grace had caught the tram home in a haze of relief and confusion. There had been no desk in the room – how would she work? There appeared to be no bathroom – was that even possible? The house's one toilet was in the back garden.

The bath was in the kitchen, behind a tablecloth draped on a stick! Most baffling and unsettling: Grace's mother, dying of cancer, had defied her husband's wishes and seen her 'mad sister' once a week, in secret, for years. 'Your mother was always so proud of you and your achievements,' Auntie Manna had said. Surely that couldn't be true. When Grace and her father talked law or politics, her mother excused herself with a bitter smile and always the same parting words: 'I'll leave this to the brains trust.' When teenage Grace had leaned into the rattling tram's leather seats and closed her eyes, one image of her mother's difficult final days rose above all others: her nose, thin and pointed like a bird's beak; her face turning away from Grace on the pillow. She'd never asked Manna if her mother really loved her. Manna was so kind she'd only have said yes.

Grace usually retreated to her room before her father got back from work. But the night she'd visited Greeves Street she took her books to the sitting room and stayed up late to wait. She presented her case in the measured and factual way he'd enjoyed teaching her before her mother committed the crime of getting sick and Grace committed the crime of growing up. 'You're aware I don't approve of Anna,' her father said, using the name her aunt was born with. 'Nor do I approve of you living in the shadow of Fitzroy's slums.' Grace drew breath to continue arguing. 'But you're almost eighteen' – she was sixteen – 'and I consent.' He would leave her behind. It was the only argument with her father she'd ever won.

Grace's mother's terminal diagnosis had cast a shadow over a large proportion of her childhood. Less than a year after Grace moved in, Manna went to hospital with a 'bit of a chest' after the flu. She either had pneumonia or caught it while she was there. The adults in the house were shocked and immobilised by her death. Not Grace. It only surprised her that more people didn't keel over daily in her home and on the street. She dealt with the calls of people wanting healing and yoga, turned away petitioners on the doorstep, organised the cremation, ordered her aunt's affairs and cleared the house of hangers-on, all while taking her final exams. Grace started her first day at Melbourne University in 1974, the dux of her year at Campion and the new owner and sole occupier of a crumbling, unsellable nineteenth-century white elephant. Well, a lilac elephant, but she'd had the more vibrant trimmings repainted as soon as she could hire some help.

Nothing about university was as Grace imagined. None of the few girls she'd been close to at Campion went on to do law at Melbourne. She spoke up in tutorials as she had all through school: confident, dominating, knowledgeable. But she found the discussion centred not on facts but on the other less comforting and precise aspect of the law: fairness. 'Of course, Grace would have you think . . .' a tutor had said in week two, and some sort of joke followed; its premise was her persona, already established, of conservative black-letter judge. The tutorial group had all tittered. It was a bit rich to talk to her about 'social justice'. Yes, Grace was a homeowner, and received an allowance, wired biannually, from her father. But she was all alone. Completely and utterly alone. Even poor people had families. Even poor people had love!

The weekend after the tutorial group had laughed at her, Grace took a study break at Readings. Back then her favourite bookshop was housed in a different, smaller shop on Lygon Street. Grace took a pen and a sheet of notebook paper out of her bag and wrote ROOMS AVAILABLE IN LARGE SHARE HOUSE IN FITZROY. She added her phone number and stuck it up with the other notices. Her huge empty house came alive with the sound of the phone ringing. It rang twice on Saturday, four times on Sunday, and at least three times a day for the rest of the week. By the following weekend she had five new housemates. The first people she interviewed were students like her: Chrissie, Robert and a guy named John Clare. A few nutters she turned away gently. Toàn she was glad to welcome. As a full-time social worker, he'd at least have a regular income. Helen Macklin phoned the day after Grace had taken the ad down. 'Please tell me there's a room left, please.' Desperation of all kinds horrified Grace, even then. But trying something new seemed to have worked for her: there was a giant vat of some kind of lentil mixture simmering on the stove, gentle music coming from the record player in Chrissie's room, and John, surprisingly good with his hands, had already knocked up a partition to make the bath more private. Grace agreed to show Helen her old room, the treatment room, still home to the jumble of pregnancy yoga cushions and mats she felt unable to throw away. Helen's eyes filled with tears. 'Please, I love it, it's perfect, oh, please.'

Helen finished school a year earlier than Grace and spent the time working in a sandwich shop. No one in her family had ever been to university. No one from her year in Wagga Wagga had even applied. Gough Whitlam and Labor had abolished university fees; still her family warned her not to go. Petrified she'd run out of savings, she'd spent the first three weeks of uni sleeping in her car. She couldn't tell her family; her dad would haul her back home in heartbeat. 'Then you have to take the room,' Grace said. 'If you don't mind how small it is.' Helen gasped with happiness. Her crooked front teeth looked like they were doing a curtsy. They were charming – for a second Grace regretted her own straight and disciplined smile. 'Oh, but I have to check with the landlord,' she added quickly. The mocking laughter of her tutorial group still burning in her ears, there was no way she'd tell her new housemates that she, an eighteen-year-old, actually owned the house. Helen looked terrified. 'I'm sure it'll be fine,' Grace said. 'I'll square it with him.' Helen threw her arms around her in celebration.

Helen's mouth, her top lip as plump as the bottom. Chatting late into the night they'd fall asleep in Grace's bed only to wake up and start chatting again. They memorised each other's uni timetables and met up on campus two, three, four times a day before walking home together. Grace felt a physical feeling of lightness she'd never before experienced. That November, her father sent her non-refundable plane tickets to London, booked without consultation. She'd tossed them negligently in the kitchen junk drawer, the one with the bills and rubber bands and burgundy-tipped corks and little plastic tags to close the bread. Helen snatched them back up. 'Oh God,' Grace remembered her saying, 'I'm so jealous I could cry. You gotta go, Gracie, you gotta go.' If Grace had thought about Christmas at all it was to envision a group dinner with her housemates, pulling crackers around the table. But Helen was heading back to Wagga, John was going on a surfing trip along the coast, and Robert and Chrissie had plans. Only Toàn would be sticking round, and while he was perfectly nice, his wide circle of outside acquaintances meant he was less a main character in the share house and more part of the ensemble. (Grace had never told anyone about the Christmas she'd spent entirely alone before university started. She would have been very grateful for Toàn's company back then.)

Reluctantly then, in the gap between first and second year, Grace went to stay in her father's plush two-bedroom Kensington maisonette. He worked right up to Christmas Eve and her days were her lonely own. She fulfilled immediately her key mission of buying tights for Helen from Biba in every beautiful colour – electric blue, cyclamen, amethyst, jade, copper, mulberry and petrol. With that happy task completed she found herself at a loose end. It was a season of IRA bombs going off in places that Grace would otherwise have tried to visit, places like Harrods and Oxford Street. When combined with the biting cold, she found herself unwilling to leave the house. The sun disappeared, if it had appeared at all, by about three in the afternoon. Five more hours had to be filled before serving dinner to her father at eight. Once a week Mrs Fallon came to do some 'light housework' with her apron and slippers in her handbag. She talked with such pride about her adult son Ralph that Grace suspected a plot to fix them up. She started going out on Fridays, long walks on frigid streets, squirrelling away tidbits for Helen: a single pelican lived in St James's Park, she was known as the Lady of the Lake. There was a shop in the King's Road literally called SEX! These imaginary conversations took up so much of her mind and time that a thought slipped out one evening at dinner. 'If your surname was Fallon, why would you call your son Ralph,' Grace mused. 'Ralph Fallon, Ral Phallon, Ralfalon, it all merges together.' Her father stared at her coldly.

'I'd forgotten what a child you are,' he replied. 'And wipe off that awful lipstick. You look entirely like a clown.' Grace rolled her eyes, something she would never have dared to do in her youth, or even in the first week of the holiday. Her father laid down his cutlery. 'You're not the Grace I remember.'

What had driven the 'brains trust' apart? Her father's anxiety and grief over her mother's diagnosis when Grace was ten? Or the other notable change around that time: Grace's own tentative steps towards young womanhood? It was clear that for her father to love her, she would have to remain a child forever: enraptured by him, in awe of him, smaller than life-size and utterly obedient. It simply hadn't been possible. She spent the rest of the visit laundering all her clothes, getting her hair cut and planning her real life in her new 1975 diary from WH Smith. Taking advantage of London's cosmopolitanism, and its anonymity, she'd also secretly bought two scandalous books. They lay waiting for her in the bottom of her suitcase, lurid covers concealed with brown paper. *The Female Eunuch* and *The Joy of Sex*: that was the type of woman Grace would be, a woman who owned and read those books, if not then, in her father's maisonette in Kensington, at least in her future, bolder life back in Fitzroy.

Grace humped her suitcase up to the front door of 99 Greeves Street just as the summer sun was rising. How odd to think she'd once tried to sell the house. She slotted in her key with a blissful sense of returning home. Her father had almost certainly booked her ticket because travelling over New Year's Eve was cheaper. Still there was a poetic rightness in returning on New Year's Day. Nearly four decades later Grace could still recall the toe-curling smell of clove cigarettes that greeted her when she opened the door. It didn't mask the dense, somehow moist fug of grass. The two large front reception rooms rented out to Robert and Chrissie were each filled with slumbering students. At the back of the house, every surface of the kitchen was covered in beer cans and bottles of wine, with cigarettes extinguished in the dregs. But there was no one around, at least no one awake, and she took advantage of the privacy to have a bath. Afterwards she put her big winter coat on and held it tight as she ran upstairs. Happiness? Jet lag? The cloud of marijuana? Whatever it was, she pondered for a moment slipping between her sheets and for the first time in her life sleeping naked.

Opening the door, she found her room had been taken over by three sleeping figures. Across the bottom of her neatly made bed lay a stranger, a golden-tanned, long-haired man. Next to each other, a head on each of Grace's two pillows, were Helen and John. Twenty-two, strapping and handsome, John Clare was hailed as a friend by everyone on campus. Clever too – one of his history essays had been published in a book. He didn't claim attention, he just got it, everywhere he went. Grace had been unwilling to play along, to gaze at him, make allowances for him, fall in behind him. She fully expected him to punish her for it. He never did. She saw how his striped collared t-shirt was rucked up to expose his smooth, tanned surfer's belly, a trail of hair leading down to his football shorts. Grace looked away. Next to him, Helen was wearing shorts too, one elegant leg drawn up balletically. Her lips were red without lipstick like they always were. She was drooling slightly in a way Grace recognised; it meant she'd soon wake up. Helen stirred and lifted the back of her hand to her mouth. Clutching her coat closed, Grace withdrew. Downstairs, she quietly got dressed from her suitcase. The Biba tights she hid away. By the time she remembered them, she and Helen were no longer friends.

Over the course of Grace's absence, a lot of bonding appeared to have taken place in Greeves Street. 'John's really smart, Gracie,' Helen said. 'Not just about uni stuff, about people too. As smart as a girl.' Grace felt begrudging, angry even. Already John had so much going for him; she had to credit him with interiority too? And when had he learnt carpentry? His plan over the holidays was to cruise along the coast with Wally, the blond guy who'd been asleep in Grace's bed, surfing and doing casual work until Wally's band 'needed' him back for practice.

'Sounds important,' Grace had said, giving Wally and John a raised eyebrow smile.

'Heard that song?' Wally asked. '"Living in the 70's"?' Everyone had heard that song, even Grace. 'My mate's band did it.'

'Oh, I thought you were going to say you did it,' Grace said.

'Yeah, nah,' Wally sadly replied.

The summer of 1975 was wet and cold and vile, hardly a summer at all. Every day Grace walked Helen to her job at Waltons department store and met her in the evening to walk home. The hours between were a blank. The image of Helen and John and Wally on her bed – it flashed into her mind as she was cooking, cleaning, getting ahead on her law reading and waiting for Helen's work day to finish. One night a couple of weeks into the new year John and Wally rolled back into town. From her own big room at the front of the house Grace could hear them stumbling into John's. The next day, she popped her head in and saw Wally's swag laid out next to John's mattress. Number ninety-nine was a residence, not a dosshouse. When she needed to communicate as 'the landlord', Grace went to the Law Library to use the Selectric. She'd stick the typed 'letter from the landlord' up on the fridge, fold marks included, like she'd received it in the mail. Might it be time to issue an edict about the sharing of rooms?

'And what are your plans for the weekend, John and Wally?' They were in the kitchen breakfasting together. Helen was yawning and combing out her long hair – she washed it every second morning so it could dry on the walk in to Waltons. John and Wally were drinking coffee in their ragged singlets, a full day's work ahead of them on a site in Coburg. Grace had spoken awkwardly because she didn't know if 'Wally' was short for a real name, like Walter, or if it was one of the nicknames men liked to call other men. She didn't want to unknowingly collude in calling him some awful new slang for poofter.

But Wally looked pleased to be addressed. 'Going to Sunbury, ay!'

Helen put down her comb. 'What! You're going to Sunbury?'

'Mate, they're playing, aren't they?' Wally said.

'Skyhooks?' Helen was excited. 'Can they get us in?'

'Well, me and Johnnie are going,' Wally said.

'John!' Helen gasped. 'Why didn't you tell me!'

'Sorry, Hel,' John said. 'You've got work on Saturday.'

Everyone around the circular pine table looked at Helen. 'Well, I *was* working on Saturday,' she said. 'But now I'm going to Sunbury with you!'

Grace had seen enough trains puffing away without her to know when one was leaving the station. 'Oh, me too,' she said. 'I love the Skyhooks. And did I read in *The Age* that Deep Purple was going to play?'

Wally looked delighted. 'You like Deep Purple?'

Grace had seen a piece in the paper about how Deep Purple would be paid sixty thousand dollars while local bands played for free. Beyond that, she knew nothing about Sunbury Rock Festival. It was a nasty shock to realise they'd be camping for two nights on a farm. 'But camping in what,' she said, 'cabins?'

Titters all round at silly old Grace. The girls went in Helen's car and the boys in John's van. Helen had packed the boot that morning, wearing jeans and a t-shirt. Blue-lipped with cold, she ran back inside for her fringed leather jacket. Out beyond the airport the buildings grew further and further apart until all they could see was scrub and mud and dams and trees and cows and power lines. It was so grey and rainy it was like driving through a storm cloud. Grace was filled with misgivings. Still, it was better to be filled with misgivings next to her best friend than to be safe and warm at home alone.

'Here we go!' Helen turned the car onto the bumpy dirt track at Duncan's Farm. 'Hold the wheel for a sec.' She took off her jacket to reveal her perfect pre-planned outfit. Grace stroked the leather fringing into neat lines and folded the jacket carefully on her lap. She saw that under Helen's thin red t-shirt her breasts bounced as the car jolted along – was it possible she could make out the shape of Helen's nipples? Not just the pointy tip – in the cold of the car she could definitely see each of those, like the eraser at the end of a pencil. No, it was like she could see the – she hadn't known the word for areola back then – diffuse pink bit, a delicate puffy cone. 'Shit, what,' Helen said, following Grace's gaze. She grabbed her armpit and pinched the fabric to inspect it. 'Sweat patches?'

'No, I was checking, but don't worry, you don't.'

They'd rounded a corner on the dirt road. 'Shit!' Helen said again. 'It's chockers.' Before them was a line of fifty cars. Hundreds of people were on foot, rolling their swags down the hill and running after them. In the far distance was a stage with a thick-striped awning, battered by the rain. A kombivan was edging back against the flow of traffic, half on the track and half in the scrub. Helen wound down the car window and honked. The passenger door of the van slammed and Wally ran round to Helen's window. His friendly face looked distraught. 'You sheilas are gunna kill me. That's what I said to Johnnie. The sheilas are gunna kill me.'

A car had pulled up behind them and the driver leaned on the horn. 'Just a sec,' Helen said. She let off the handbrake and crawled forward.

Wally jogged along and leaned in again. 'I've had a shocker,' he said. 'We have to pay. Graeme's fucked us over. He can't get us in. Yeah, I'm really sorry.'

'But can't you just pay?' Grace said.

Wally and Helen both looked at her. 'It's twenny bucks each, love,' Wally said.

'I've got the money, I'll pay,' Grace said.

'What,' Helen said, 'for all of us?'

'Yes,' Grace said, laughter bubbling up. 'For all of us!'

It was a weekend of firsts, the first time she'd been out in the rain and not worried about getting wet. The first time she'd drunk beer from a longneck. The first time she'd done a wee in the bushes since she was a child. Not the first time she'd seen a band – but definitely the first time she'd been one of those girls sitting on a man's shoulders to do it, lifting Wally's long hair up and fanning it out over her legs. Afterwards he swung her around to the front of his body and slowly brought her down against him. Dizzy from the longnecks and the triumph of fitting in, she turned her back to him and leaned into his chest. When she looked around again, John and Helen were gone.

At first, Wally was happy to look for them with her. Soon he drifted back to the music. They weren't in the tents, or cooking at the camp site. Finally she went to John's kombivan. If the van's a-rockin' don't come a-knockin', of course she was thinking, but the van didn't seem to be moving. She dragged a tartan esky over and stepped up onto the lid. She peeped into the window and waited for her eyes to adjust. This was what she'd seen by the light of the moon on the farm at Digger's Rest: Helen's arm on John's shirtless back. John's bare arse, banging away, his jeans halfway down his thighs. Helen's long white legs splayed open. After a little while John stopped what he was doing and propped himself up on his elbow. He used the hand that was closest to Grace to caress the side of Helen's face. He tucked a strand of hair behind her ear. Then he reached down the side of her body and squeezed where her thigh became her bum, squashing the soft white flesh. Grace stared and stared at John's fingers pressing into Helen's skin. I want that, her mind said, her heart said, her whole body said. I want that.

It was the Australia Day long weekend so they didn't get going till the Monday. Helen threw her swag into the boot. 'Aren't you . . .' Grace said from the passenger seat, then bit her tongue.

Helen ducked to look in at Grace. 'Aren't I what.'

'It's none of my business, but aren't you worried about not wearing a bra?'

'Should I be?'

'You don't worry about the muscles, about sagging? About the message you're sending?'

Helen laughed, a flash of her pigeon-toed teeth. Then she leaned into the car so one knee was kneeling on the driver's seat. She lifted her t-shirt slowly, tucked it under her chin, and squeezed her breasts together as if they were talking. 'Mind your own fucken business,' she made her breasts say. Just as Grace imagined, the nipples were puffy and light pink – Pascall raspberry marshmallows. Helen dropped her t-shirt back down and hooted with laughter. 'That's what they'd say!'

Grace said stiffly, 'Are you okay to drive?'

'Why, Gracie,' Helen said. 'Can you drive?'

Grace wanted to cry. 'No.'

'Then I'm okay!' Helen honked the horn three times and yelled, 'See ya, Sunbury!'

When they got home, Helen said, 'Thanks, Grace, I'll pay you back.'

That was Grace's cue to say 'Don't worry about it'. Instead she said, 'There's no rush.'

Sunbury Rock Festival 1975. The beginning of the end. Grace sensed that something had changed when she walked Helen into work on the Tuesday. That evening, as usual, she waited for her outside Waltons. Minutes ticked by. Half an hour. Grace found a payphone and rang Greeves Street – no answer. She ran into Menswear, Helen's department. Helen had been sacked at one minute past nine that morning. Nine hours earlier – where had she gone? Should she call the police?

Grace cried as she walked home. Helen was not in the kitchen, not in the treatment room. As she stood in the hall, wondering what to do, she heard the sound of laughter from behind John's closed door. They came down long after dinner, tender and grinning. Helen had been on a news clip about Sunbury after she'd called in sick to work. Fired as soon as she returned, she caught the tram to John's worksite in Coburg. Little glances at each other revealed how they'd spent the evening. 'Oh, bugger, Gracie, you didn't go into town for me, did you?'

'No, no,' Grace muttered. The next day a carefully typed 'letter from the landlord' appeared on the fridge. The small room known as the treatment room was needed to store the landlord's possessions. It would have to be vacated within the month.

It shouldn't have been a disaster: Helen had plenty of friends, far more than Grace; she'd easily find a room in a different house. But something else had happened, too, some sort of family emergency. Helen had to rush back to Wagga to help. By the time it resolved, it was a few weeks into the new semester. No job or place to live, no hope of catching up on classes. John drove Helen's stuff up to her one weekend. He returned to Melbourne with a pinched white face. Grace never saw Helen again.

Wonky pots, collapsed pots, blobs she couldn't even stick to the bat. Up in her top-floor studio, Grace was surrounded by mistakes. Just like her whole bloody life. Her pyjamas were covered in clay. It was in her hair, her eyelashes. She stood up with a cry of frustration. The stools around the worktable were tall, Anton- and Alexander Technique–approved, and had a two-level foot-support portion that folded up when not in use. Now she kicked it down, stepped up and placed her knee on the stool to climb onto the table. She knelt and pulled the stool up after her, flicked down the foot-support and mounted the second step. From this position her head was touching the skylight. She unlocked it and, with great difficulty, forced it to slide up and open. The August night was shockingly mild. Holding on to the rim of the skylight for balance, she climbed easily to the seat of the stool and crawled out onto the roof.

It was a special roof and, in concert with architects, she'd thought about it long and hard. It had a pitch of five degrees so, per council requirements, the extension was less visible from the street. The surface layer was crammed with little plants that looked after themselves and insulated the house. She'd put so much work into this bloody studio! Into creating a new self worthy of love! It hadn't worked. Now Grace picked her way over the sedum towards Girl's and Anton's flats. As she got close to the edge she felt a wave of vertigo. There was the fence, its tall pointed spikes. Her mind returned to its bleak inventory. Her mother had died and her father had moved continent rather than care for Grace. Her aunt had taken her in but abandoned her too, in death. She lost the best friend she'd ever had by kicking Helen out of her own home. Not a single acquaintance remained from her years in the law. Pregnancy yoga, mother and baby groups, two decades of Parent Teacher Association meetings, tuckshop duty and running the bric-a-brac at the Campion Bazaar; she knew the majority of her neighbours and the shopkeepers on Brunswick Street by name; there were the other potters from Johnston Street Pottery – yet could Grace really say she had friends? They'd have coffee if they saw each other, but they wouldn't see each other to have coffee. John had chosen to die rather than remain married to her. Anton had fled without a goodbye. Sophie was a law unto herself and always had been. YOU KNOW WHAT YOU DID YOU CUNT. Who else could have left the message but her daughter? But Toby – she'd always relied on her son. Sexual harassment? Could there be a worse indictment of her mothering? *She has no one now*, her cleaner's husband had said. He was right. Could she do it, kill herself? But, God, she couldn't. She dropped to her knees, shaking. She crawled backwards away, from the edge, until it was safe to turn around. Back in her studio she slammed the skylight shut and ran down the stairs to her room. *Girl,* she texted with shaking hands. *I apologise that I left you hanging. Why don't you stay with me this weekend while your mother's away? We can discuss a more permanent plan for you to move in then. Best wishes, Grace.*

28.

'HOW NICE TO meet another Clare,' Sophie's boss had greeted him formally. 'Your sister is a wonderful help to me in the shop.' Hard to think of a less apt description of Sophie than 'a wonderful help' – except maybe 'shy and retiring'? But as Toby watched his sister dust, tidy, indulge customers and answer the phone with a servile greeting, he realised Patrick was right. She had changed. When her shift ended they made their way to Parliament Station. Toby dithered about tickets and was deliberately monosyllabic and hopeless, just to make her shout at him. Instead she hustled him to the platform and offered him the only free seat in the carriage. 'You've got your backpack,' she said. 'How's uni?'

'Um . . .' He'd left the 'getting kicked out of uni' thing for when they were in person. Now he couldn't anticipate how this downcast and enervated new Sophie would react. 'I kind of hate uni,' he said. 'When we see Mum tomorrow I might ask if I can move in with her.'

Sophie laughed bitterly. 'Good luck. I tried that once and she said no.' Her gaze moved to the window and her face was still and strange. 'Of course, it might be different with you, perfect baby Toby.'

He hugged his backpack on his knees and pretended to be resting on it. He was shocked awake half an hour later by Sophie.

'Nunawading, wow,' he marvelled. Bumper-to-bumper traffic crawled both ways along a huge road. 'Didn't we drive through here once? On the way to Healesville Sanctuary? Where a kangaroo kicked Colin McWhatever's dad in the balls?'

'He wasn't just kicked in the balls,' his sister said. 'He was kicked in the balls and eviscerated.' Toby shuddered. 'Like you when you see Mum tomorrow,' she added, finally cracking a smile. Sophie led them off the main road and deep into suburbia. 'So Sam won't be home for hours,' she said after a bit. 'He has work drinks on a Friday. Do you want to take me out for dinner? To say thanks for staying over?'

'Do you want to take *me* out? I'm actually a bit skint.'

'What, you? What about all your tutoring money?' But at the takeaway she got them double chips, fish and two beers. They sat at the picnic table overlooking the children's play equipment. Now was the time. He'd tell her the story as it unfolded, start with Astrid, not with Dr Bhatt. Toby took a deep breath, but Sophie leaned forward before he could speak. 'I saw Tessa Notaras.'

Toby's eyebrows shot up. 'Did you ask her where they got those lame jumpers?'

'Ha!' Sophie banged the table with her palm. 'He was wearing his when he died, did you know? God, when I saw him – I wanted to rip it off, it looked so dumb, and fake, and not at all like him, like he wasn't my father at all.' Toby felt the old sting. Sophie saw his face and sighed. 'What?'

'Don't worry about it!' There was no point.

'Toby, *what?*'

'It's just – you said *your* father.'

'Our father,' Sophie intoned. 'Who art in heaven. Sorry, people hate it when I do that.' She jabbed her plastic fork into her fish. 'I don't even know why we're talking about his jumper.' Her voice rose. 'You brought it up!'

'It's just I hated it so much too, it was like a costume – his affair costume. Sorry, I actually don't have that many people I can talk to about this stuff.'

But his sister was still upset. 'As if I want to think about finding Dad's dead body!' Her breathing was fast and her cheeks were red.

'God, sorry, Soph. Hey.' He waited until she looked at him. 'I'm really sorry. It was really insensitive of me to forget about that, about finding him. I was thinking about them on the front page, that's all. I think about the newspaper all the time. More than I think about the funeral. More than I think about Dad. I couldn't believe that picture. It's like I didn't even know who he was.'

'I know what you mean. I'm sorry, too, by the way.' Sophie took a sip of her beer, so he did too. 'Ugh,' she burst out. '*Finding the body*. Normally I can't even say it – *the body*. If I even hear the word "body" it's like I'm running, or being attacked. It's horrible. But when you saw the picture – did you know who *she* was?'

'Tessa?' A flash of red marks on white hands, slim thighs in tight jeans, Ingrid's anxious face. 'I think I saw her once at Dad's work barbecue. I can't be sure. But where did you see her?'

'Just on the street in the city a few days ago. I stalked her, basically. Followed her home. Don't look shocked! She's so weird in person. Uptight, really corporate? I seriously don't understand it. They were together from 2007 – did you know that?' She didn't pause long enough for him to respond. 'I spoke to her!' she said. 'Well, she shouted at me. She thinks Dad was planning to leave Mum the night he died. He went home to tell her he was leaving. Toby! Don't you see how crazy this is? Tessa Notaras was there that night!'

'I know, it was in the coroner's report.'

'Oh.' Sophie looked disappointed. 'You've read the coroner's report?'

He shrugged. 'It's on the website.'

'But the coroner doesn't know this: Tessa went right up to the house to find him. She reckons she looked through the window and saw Mum. Shagging someone!'

A jolt of shock passed through Toby. 'What do you mean, someone?'

'That's what Tessa asked me. Like – was it Dad?'

'But who else could it be?' They both gave identical little horrified screams. 'I never thought about our parents like this.' Toby said. 'I'm serious. I don't just mean the sex thing – obviously it's a cliché to find that gross. I mainly mean the emotions. I always thought emotions were something people in movies had.'

'I know. And something I had because I'm crazy.'

'I thought how they were with us was how they were all the time.' Toby inspected the remaining chips. 'Should I chuck these or wrap up the rest for Sam?'

'Just chuck them. He stays out so late on Fridays there's literally no point. Come on, let's continue our tour of the most boring suburb in the world.'

'I quite like it.' At the outer edge of the park they stepped over a low log fence. Sophie's face looked alive again, and was making all its little movements. Toby squinted at her. 'Why are you so perky all of a sudden?'

'I don't know!' Sophie spread her arms to take in the curve of the cul-de-sac. 'Sam never lets me talk about Dad. I just feel better when I'm talking about this stuff – sex and death and love and betrayal. It's when everything's quiet that I freak out, I don't know why.'

Toby took another deep breath. But before he could tell her about Astrid, Sophie stopped and stared at him. 'Why did you get all silent back then?'

'Back when?'

'When I asked if you knew about Dad and Tessa in 2007? Your face went all weird.'

'Okay, Sherlock Holmes,' Toby said. 'Dad came to Canberra over mid-year break last year. On the way to the airport, he dropped round to visit some woman.' He glanced over to see if Sophie was listening for once. She was. 'I just sat in the car waiting. When Dad got back in, he looked really cut – he looked like he'd been crying. Something had happened at the doorstep but I didn't know what. Later, I went to see who lived there.'

'Toby, wow. I didn't know you did stuff like that.'

'Basically I was pretty low when I knocked on the door. The woman said I could come in. She told me she used to live in Greeves Street.'

'What, when it was a share house?'

'Apparently she'd been really close to Dad at uni.'

'Like dating?'

'She didn't tell it to me all at once, but basically she and Mum were best friends in first year. Then they started growing apart, and Helen started to date Johnnie, which is what she called Dad. Helen, that's the woman's name. I've actually,' Toby said carefully, 'been spending quite a bit of time with her.'

'What's she like? What's the house like?'

'Nice face, funny teeth, long grey hair that looks stylish, more sort of grey-blonde, gold glasses, wears jeans,' Toby said. 'She doesn't wear lipstick. Looks older than Mum but acts younger. Her house is kind of small, warm, crochet rugs. She's the manager of a hospice.'

'Like a youth hospice?'

'Most of the people are pretty old. Oh!' He realised her mistake. 'You mean a youth hostel. No, this is palliative care, for –'

'La la la!' Sophie put her hands over her ears. When Toby fell silent she shook her head. 'How strange, all this about the olden days. I've literally never heard about Helen. We've met Wally, obviously. Not that he was a proper housemate. But never Helen.'

Toby nodded. 'Her room was the tiny room, Dad's study? One day she got a letter from the landlord telling her to move out. She was packing all her stuff. Then her father had an accident or something, back in Wagga. Helen went straight home. By the time he was out of hospital it was too late. She just dropped out of uni and never went back to Greeves Street.'

'So who cares?' Sophie said. 'What's the point of all this?'

He never asked his sister to justify *her* stories. 'Helen had seen on the news about Dad and the Your Rights at Work campaign. She wrote to the main ACTU email address. It got lost among all the other emails. Dad went through them a year or two later, found her email and wrote back. She said Dad was in a bad way. Those were her words: *in a bad way.*'

Gratifyingly, Sophie stopped in her tracks. 'When was this?'

'Like, 2009? She said I was in grade twelve.'

'And what was his bad way, then? What was wrong with him? Just tell me.'

'Helen said he'd been in love with a girl who worked for him.' Toby spoke gently. 'So, yeah, I knew it wasn't just the love nest thing – it had started a lot earlier. In 2007, I guess, if that's what she told you. But they weren't together the whole time. After less than a year he broke up with her. Helen said he'd "chosen" us, his family. But it "hadn't been easy for him, the poor bugger". That's what she said.'

'Poor old John!' Sophie put on a man's voice to pretend to be her dad: 'I want to spend my whole life at work and with some other bitch! If only my dumb family never existed!'

'You'll like this though.' Sharing the information felt like a betrayal of his mum. But it was so rare to have Sophie's full attention – he wanted to prolong it. 'So all this was happening on emails between Helen and Dad. Guess who found one of Helen's emails to him and flipped out?' Toby laughed at Sophie's shocked face. 'I know. Mum was furious. She told Helen never to contact Dad again – if she saw any hint of correspondence between them she'd kick Dad out of the house.'

'God!' Sophie said. 'Dark.'

'Helen couldn't risk it. She just instantly stopped emailing Dad. She said when he turned up, the time I was in the car, he was asking why she'd stopped writing to him. Why, why, why, he said. But that wasn't the weirdest thing. Remember how in the *Good Weekend* interview, Dad said he hadn't known Mum owned the house? He only found out when they were engaged?'

'Yeah.' Sophie frowned. 'Why?'

'Well, think it through. Someone kicked Helen out of the house all those years ago, ruined her relationship with Dad and made her drop out of uni. It wasn't some random landlord. It was Mum.'

'How crazy,' Sophie said. 'Disgrace Clare. What a psychopath! Well, I suppose we all have secrets.' She punched Toby on the shoulder. 'Except you.'

*

Later, in Sophie's bathroom, Toby stood under the jets and let the water beat his body. He thought about Astrid every time he had a shower. Was he going to think about her forever? Too tall for the sofa, he arranged some towels on the floor in what Sophie had called 'the study', a tiny spare bedroom with a desk, an ironing board, a built-in wardrobe and a pile of laundry baskets. He missed the hospice and the Jolly Trolley. He missed Lawrence and Mrs Zhang. He missed eating Old Saigon off his knees on the sofa in the cosy little house in Campbell. He missed Turtle. He missed Helen. When Helen sat in silence she wasn't trying to make him guess what he'd done wrong. She was just happy being quiet. What would his life have been like if Helen had been his mum? The thought was too treacherous. He pushed it aside.

Toby was fitfully dozing when the sound of a car door jerked him properly awake. A key was scratching at the flyscreen; the front door opened with a bang. Footsteps dragged and staggered down the hall. A dark figure slumped in the doorway of the study. In the flickering light of the internet modem, Toby could see Sam, eyes half-closed, clutching a bottle of champagne. 'Sam!'

'Shit!' Sam jumped.

Toby scrambled to his feet. 'It's just me, it's Toby!'

Sam laughed in relief and clapped Toby's hand in a handshake. He smelt like an ashtray with beer poured in it. 'God, sorry, I forgot today was the big day! Siblings reunited.' He waggled the champagne. 'Another grateful client! Should I open this? You'll have a drink, won't you?'

'No, but I'll make you something to eat? Toast or something?'

Sam laughed. 'You think I'm wasted, don't you! But, yeah, that would be nice.' There was no bread, but there was a packet of spaghetti. He filled a saucepan with some water and set it on the hob. Sam sat in a perilous lean at the kitchen table. 'Toby Clare. The lawyer returns. How's uni?'

'How's work?' Toby parried. He tried to remember the last thing he'd seen on Sam's Facebook. 'I saw the stuff you guys did for the tennis, very cool.'

Sam looked pleased, and showed off for a while about various things. Toby stirred two egg yolks together with finely grated cheese. Perhaps he could tell Sam about Astrid. He was older, experienced. It could be good to have his advice. He tipped most but not all of the pasta water out when it was ready, and spooned the yellow stuff in with the rest. Combined, it made a lovely slippery sauce. Toby ground some pepper over it and laid it before Sam.

'Bloody hell!' Sam spoke with his mouth full. 'Amazing, proper cooking. Seriously.' He shook his head. 'Professional level. So how have you been, mate? With the bereavement?'

'Oh.' Toby shrugged. 'You know!'

But before he could continue, Sam dropped his head into his hands. 'I don't know how to help Sophie. She's not dealing with it very well. I've been googling it? I think she has some symptoms.'

'Of what?'

Sam spoke darkly. 'Mental health.' For some reason this made Toby laugh. He took Sam's plate to the sink to hide. An insect was tap-tap-tapping against the flickering fluorescent light. After a second Sam joined him. 'It's been more than a year,' Sam said. 'I've run out of things to say. Work does this thing, they'll pay for three sessions with a counsellor? I went to see how I could help her, and the counsellor said I *can't*.' Sam's friendly face was dragged down against his will. His chin wobbled and his eyes filled with tears. 'You don't know what it's like! To get a call from the station manager at Southern Cross! Come and pick Sophie up from his office, he's saying! She's been running around looking like she'll jump! She has to stop all that, I made her promise. I want my life back, my job, a house, a wife – kids! All my ducks in a row! I'm twenty-eight, Toby, I had plans for this year, look!' Sam reached up into the top kitchen cabinet and took down an old-fashioned black and red Arnott's biscuit tin. He opened it, took out a bundled-up tea towel and unfurled it to reveal a black velvet ring box. He clicked it open and angled it towards Toby. Inside was a delicate gold band with a single diamond poking up. 'But I just can't! I can't!' He snapped the box shut. Toby put his hand out and grasped Sam's upper arm to comfort him. Sam stiffened. 'You think I'm a bad person!'

'I don't, I don't.'

'I'm not coping, I'm drinking too much, I spend too much time at work, I need help, kindness and attention, Shalini – I have needs, okay! But I've stopped all that now, I know it's bad, I know!'

'Really, I *really* don't think anyone's bad,' Toby mumbled. *Except myself,* he thought but didn't say.

'I'm going to do it, okay! I'm going to propose!'

'Sam,' Toby said. 'I don't mind and it's none of my business.'

'I never said I was perfect!' Sam stormed off towards the shower. 'Life hasn't been perfect to *me*!'

With a tired sigh, Toby snapped the ring box shut, wrapped it in the tea towel, tucked it inside the biscuit tin, put the biscuit tin in the top of the cupboard, shut the cupboard, settled himself on the floor and tried once again to sleep.

29.

ON SATURDAY MORNING Grace and Girl stood together in the doorway to the treatment room and surveyed the stacks of lever arch files, wage cases, programs from historic ACTU Congresses and copies of old speeches that littered John's handcrafted wooden shelving. 'If the union or Labor need any of this stuff, they've had a year to come and ask me about it.' Grace kicked one of the boxes that lined the hall. 'As far as I'm concerned, everything that belongs to John can go. Are you sure you don't mind? It's not a very fun way to spend a weekend.'

'Really,' Girl said. 'I'd love to help.'

'Then let's toss it. You get started, Girl, I'll bring the vacuum cleaner up.'

Halfway down the stairs Grace was drawn from her house by a booming male voice. She concealed her injury with a hat and went to see what was happening. Fifteen or twenty people had gathered in Greeves Street outside the block of flats. A squat bald man in a suit was loudly declaiming the merits of the neighbourhood. 'Leafy Fitzroy! Melbourne's historic first suburb! Thick of the action but you can hear a pin drop!'

'Hmph,' Grace snorted.

'Kick back and enjoy the loife stoyle,' the man cried. 'My role is to guide, to assist, to facilitate you through this auction process today. What we have here, today! Is a one-bedroom!

Ensuite, extra toilet, main living room, meal-slash-kitchen area.' In a tone of special veneration the auctioneer began to talk about the 'artist, and his creative home'. Grace felt herself flush from her head wound to her chest. Was Anton there? It wasn't how she'd imagined the circumstances of their reunion. Yet after an absence of a year, she could ill-afford to be choosy. She wove through the crowd, searching. 'A beautiful day to buy your dream home. Do I see a start for Unit Nine, 93–97 Greeves Street? Good strong bidding.'

'Two-eighty,' someone tossed out.

The auctioneer sounded cross. 'All right, we can start there, but where do we go? Where do we go?'

'Two eighty-five,' someone called.

'Three hundred!' cried someone else. The crowd rippled with excitement.

'In or out, sir, in or out,' the auctioneer taunted. The first bidder shook his head in surrender. There was a long silence. Someone raised their hand. 'Another five! These are the bids that buy real estate!' The bids were faster now. 'Four hundred and ten,' the auctioneer whooped. 'Let me check with the vendor!' Grace's entire body was shaking. But another man in a suit passed the auctioneer a mobile phone. He held it up to his ear. 'Yes!' the auctioneer shouted. 'This property will be selling today!'

'Grace?' Girl was standing at the front door.

'Four-ten,' Grace said dully. 'A very good price.'

'And Anton?' Girl's eyes were red and brimming with tears.

'Oh no,' Grace said. 'What's wrong?'

'Nothing,' Girl said. 'It's just my allergies.'

'Sorry, sweetheart, it's so dusty in there, isn't it?' Girl nodded. 'I had to let the cleaner go, did I tell you? She stole

from me, some face creams. I've got some eyedrops, I think.'
She clasped Girl's shoulder and turned her towards the stairs.
'Head up to the bathroom.' There was a bottle of Visine in the
cabinet. She shook it: almost full. Girl still looked despondent.
'What's wrong? Worried it's a bit old? I don't think eyedrops
expire, do they?'

'No, it's just a bit stupid . . .'

'Say what you need to say,' Grace said sternly.

Girl smiled. 'Sorry. Spit it out, Girl, you say.'

'Exactly, spit it out.'

'I'm just scared of putting in eyedrops, that's all.'

'But not of having eyedrops? Just putting them in?' Girl
nodded. 'Come on then, silly sausage. Look at the ceiling.'
Girl looked up obediently. Her little face was almost heart-
breakingly clear and beautiful. She was like a boy chorister. She
could be twelve, younger even. Just a slip of a girl. Her mouth
was like a little flower, or perhaps she was pouting a bit about
the allergies. 'No, you have to open your eyes, silly. Gosh,
they're quite golden – your irises, I mean. Tawny, I suppose is
the word. How unusual.' She tapped a few drops into each eye.
Girl stayed gazing up at her. 'There you go,' Grace said.

Girl blinked and took a step back. 'Thanks.'

'Come and I'll help you do the rest,' Grace said. 'Oh, you've
got so much done!' The boxes in the hallway were nearly full.
The shelves were almost clear. On the desk lay two items, a
shoebox and a photo frame, facedown. Grace didn't recognise
the box. Kids' soccer boots? Baffled but curious, she lifted the
lid and gasped. Dozens of plastic animals lay jumbled inside.

'What are they?'

Grace pretended she hadn't heard. 'Oh, I didn't get the
vacuum, did I?'

'I'll get it,' Girl said.

'Thanks, sweetheart, we'll sort the dust out before we do anything else.' As Girl's footsteps grew quieter Grace dropped to the floor with the box in her lap, instantly transported to John's funeral. The service had gone superbly, just as if the final two weeks of John's life hadn't happened and he'd died very suddenly of a heart attack. Former prime minister Bob Hawke was there, strutting his puffed-out *le coq sportif* strut, dry white hair sticking out above his collar. He clasped her in an embrace. 'A lot going on here,' he growled into her ear. 'But, Gracie, he loved you.' And for a second, she believed him. Julia Gillard was a notable absence, negotiating with rural independents about hung parliament confidence and supply. Kevin Rudd came – well, he had time on his hands. Wally, John's friend of four decades, had got the guitar out and sung 'In My Life' with his two big sons. The only acknowledgement of John's difficult final end was the coffin, lid firmly kept shut.

'But you'd like to see him, wouldn't you? To say goodbye?' The funeral director almost wrung his hands after the service, so eager he was that she look.

'Not really,' Grace said.

'I hope you don't mind me saying, but I prepared your husband. You know, the injury was at the back of the head – the way I've done it, you can't really see it at all.'

She agreed to take a look at his handiwork, on the proviso that no one else would ever see. The last guest trickled out. Grace sent Toby and a dramatically sobbing Sophie on ahead to the wake at Trades Hall. She opened the door to the Family Room and found another woman mauling John's body. 'Gosh,' Grace said. 'Sorry to interrupt this intimate send-off.'

It wasn't strictly mauling, and she wasn't really 'another woman'. It was just Ingrid, John's veteran personal assistant. Her hair was a mess, her face haggard and distressed. She had a cardboard box with her. 'Oh, Grace,' Ingrid said, aghast. Her hand was frozen inside the coffin.

Grace frowned, her eyes dry. 'What are you doing, actually?'

'The animals, remember? The ones John got for me on his trips?' No, Grace didn't remember. 'Fifteen years we worked together,' Ingrid said. 'Always so kind.' Her face, soft and abject, collapsed on itself, and she cried. Grace was sickened by Ingrid bringing her grief into her private space, the *Family Room*. Why aren't you crying, you witch, Ingrid's tears seemed to say. Didn't you love him? Didn't he love you?

'Get out,' Grace shouted. Ingrid's mouth gaped. 'Get out! Get out! Get out!' When Ingrid was gone, Grace picked out all the animals she'd tucked between the red silk of the coffin lining and the rich navy of John's best suit and tossed them into the cardboard box.

'Mrs Clare?' The funeral director was back, staring at her like she was a freak. 'Did you want to come back to the crem and watch him go?'

'The crematorium? Burn, you mean?' He was the freak, not her!

'You don't see him burn, just see the coffin going in.'

'I'm fine, thanks.' Grace tucked the box under her arm.

'But what do you think? I remember him from TV, I put a bit of make-up on him to get his skin tone looking good.'

'Very nice.' Satisfied, he withdrew. Alone at last with the corpse of her husband. John was propped on a voluminous pillow, presumably to hide his wound. It tipped his head to the ceiling so his nose was in the air. He looked arrogant and handsome and (being dead) hard to get. She was surprised by a phantom thrum of desire. 'Funeral went well,' she said. 'Well, that's it, John.' He had left her, and in the most public way. First he chose Tessa over her. Then he chose death. It was a repudiation of everything they'd built together. The rejection of Grace herself had been total. To grieve someone you loved would be hard enough. But what if the world knew they didn't care about you at all? It was pathetic. Shockingly, tears bubbled up and choked her. Rushing for the door, she cried out over her shoulder, 'I tried my fucking best!'

And now once again her lovelessness and *unlovableness* was being mocked by Ingrid's box of animals. It was right to get rid of everything to do with John. She would not be a sitting duck for every memory and emotion that carelessly ruined her day. She wouldn't wait for the rubbish men to come, she'd walk down to Smith Street Woolworths right now and toss them in the skip. 'Girl,' she shouted. 'Girl! Where are you?'

'Oh, Grace,' she heard a little voice. 'I'm downstairs. Sophie and Toby are here.'

30.

SOPHIE WISHED SHE'D warned Toby to look less fragile and weak. Nothing appalled their mother more than a person in crisis. Sophie had bitterly predicted that Toby, unlike her, would be allowed to return home. Now she was worried that he wouldn't. 'You don't have a key, do you?'

Toby laughed. 'As if.'

That girl from next door opened the door before they'd even knocked. Her eyes were bright, almost glittering. 'Come in,' she said.

'Gee, thanks Jeeves. Thanks for inviting me into my own home.' Sophie hooked her coat over the bottom of the bannister. 'And what the *fuck*,' she said, 'is that?' Staring her in the face was the most insane shit she'd ever seen: YOU KNOW WHAT YOU DID YOU CUNT, right there on the wall. 'Toby, check this out.'

'Oh, it's okay, we've got the paint on order to touch it up,' Girl said.

'You've got the paint on order to touch it up,' Sophie repeated blankly. 'Mum,' she shouted, 'I love your crazy new Banksy!'

'This isn't a comedy club, Sophie.' Her mother descended the stairs. 'And that's not where coats go.'

'I'll decide what is and isn't funny, and the circumstances in which we joke.' But as she got closer, Sophie's laughter died in her throat. 'Mum, what?'

'Oh my God, Mum!' Toby sounded outraged. 'Your head!'

'For God's sake.' Their mum stormed down the hall. 'Girl, let's put some tea on.'

Toby and Sophie stood on one side of the breakfast bar while their mother and Girl fussed with the teapot on the other. Toby let his huge backpack slide off his back and onto the floor. He looked like he was going to cry. 'Mum?'

She clicked her tongue. 'Come here.' She opened her arms and Toby went to her. She rubbed his back energetically and patted it twice. 'There's no need to worry. I'm absolutely fine.'

That statement was factually incorrect. The whole side of her head had been shaved. There was a scar in the bald patch that was so thick and long and meaty it looked like a lipsticked mouth puckered for a kiss. When Sophie spoke, her voice was shaking. 'But what *happened*?'

Her mother withdrew to the kettle. 'A little senior moment! Basically I had a fall. In the bathroom. Whacked my head on the sink. Luckily I was able to make it to hospital.'

Girl had been spooning tea into the teapot. She paused now and looked at their mum with a strange expression.

'What's Girl doing here, anyway?' Sophie said. 'Is she your man servant?'

'That isn't funny,' her mum said. 'Girl is staying with me for a while, aren't you, Girl?'

'What!' Sophie cried. She felt herself shrink to the size and powerlessness of a child. 'But that's not fair! I wasn't allowed to stay at home!'

'You both had privileges Girl doesn't have.'

'But it's not fair! Toby, is it fair? What about Toby, can he move home?'

'It's all right,' Toby said quickly.

'But, Toby' – Sophie couldn't believe it – 'weren't you going to ask Mum if you could move back?'

'No, no. Like, I wanted to see Mum, obviously.' Toby was mumbling at the floor. 'Check she's okay. But yeah, no worries, it's cool.'

It took a moment for their mother to notice he'd picked up his rucksack and made off. 'Toby!' she cried, and chased him down the hall.

Sophie stayed behind. 'What's the story with the graffiti in the hall?' Girl didn't respond. 'Hello? I'm talking to you.'

Girl glanced towards the kitchen door. 'I don't really know.' She put on a pious face. 'It's been very difficult for her.'

'It's been very difficult for her,' Sophie imitated. The sound of shouting reached them from the front door. 'Come and fight in the kitchen,' Sophie called. Her mother burst into the room. Toby was pursuing her. Both their chests were heaving. Sophie leaned against the breakfast bar with her arms crossed. 'Okay, now do the fight again so I can hear.'

'Mum's pissed off because I've been staying with her mortal enemy.'

She rolled her eyes. 'I don't have *mortal enemies*.'

'I know you hate Helen. I know what you did to her!'

'And what was that?' She cocked her head dangerously. 'Because if you knew the full story . . .'

'Mum, do tell,' Sophie said. 'Who *is* Helen? What's the full story?'

'What about you, Toby!' their mother said. 'Does Sophie know why you're not in college?'

'I've been expelled for sexual harassment,' Toby sighed, just as their mum shouted, 'He's been expelled for sexual harassment!' Toby appealed: 'It was just from college, not uni, if that makes a difference.'

'I don't know,' Sophie said. 'Does it?'

All the fight had gone out of him. 'Anyway, I didn't come here for this. I just wanted to see Mum, check she was okay, say sorry, basically. That's it.'

'And are you sorry?' Now their mother's arms were crossed.

'Jesus Christ, Judge Judy!' Sophie said. 'As if you can talk about sexual harassment.' All three Clares suddenly turned to look at Girl, but her back was to them, her little shoulders drawn up in a hunch. 'You can just leave the tea now,' Sophie told her. 'Thanks.'

'Girl is a guest in this house,' her mum said. 'But, Girl, yes, the mop's under the hall stairs, if you want to keep going with the clear-out.' Girl scurried off.

'What clear-out?' Sophie demanded.

'The treatment room.'

'Dad's study! Where's all his stuff?'

'That's all sorted.' Their mother opened the fridge door. 'Milk?'

In the Clare house some things had always been off limits. Once, as a child, Sophie had barged into the tiny downstairs bathroom while her mum was on the toilet. Grace had slammed the door so fast that Sophie's fingers were caught in the hinge. Two of her nails had turned grey and fallen off; that was how zealously Grace defended her own privacy. Sophie took a deep breath. 'Are you going to tell us what really happened on the night Dad died?'

'Come on, Sophie.' Her mother turned away, contemptuous.

'But who did you have sex with on the sofa?'

Grace put her mug down wrong; it fell off the bench and smashed on the floor. 'Enough,' she cried. Sophie and Toby were children again, eight and three, caught gorging on Nutella in the utility. 'Enough! Enough!' their mother was shouting now.

'Mum, please, just be normal,' Sophie called over her shoulder as she escaped down the hall. 'We have to be normal and talk, we have to discuss things like normal people.'

'I would love more than anything to be a normal mum, Sophie.' She stood at the foot of the stairs, her eyes bright. Toby slunk around behind Sophie, trying to open the door. 'My daughter is the most despised millennial media figure in Australia. My son is a sexual harasser. My husband cheated on me and topped himself. How the hell am I supposed to behave?'

Casting about, desperate to grab for one last straw, Sophie's eyes alighted on two little feet at the top of the stairs. 'Good luck with your new daughter, Mum. Hope she's not as disappointing as us.' She ducked low and shouted up at Girl. 'And good luck with your new mum, Girl! I think you'll find she's a shit one!'

Sophie and Toby took stock as they walked along Greeves Street. 'That seemed to go pretty badly,' Toby said.

'But I'm not surprised, are you?'

'No.' Toby seemed to shudder under the weight of his huge backpack. 'That girl from next door – she's so weird.'

'When did she even become a thing? Where are you going, by the way?' They'd stopped on the edge of Brunswick Street.

'Southern Cross? Get the Greyhound back to Canberra, and the hospice. Helen said as long as I work there I can stay with her.'

'Wow, Mum would love that if she knew. I'll walk you to Parliament.' It was actually nice being with Toby. All along Brunswick Street couples strolled arm in arm, families where the dad was alive and the mum wasn't horrible, and big groups of friends too, happy people getting along. Sadness swallowed her up. She lived a very lonely existence, generally. She had Patrick and the shop, which was companionable. And she had Sam, when he was home and hadn't given up on her. That was it. 'Toby,' she said after a bit. 'What was the sexual harassment?' He looked like he wanted to walk in front of traffic. 'Like, was it bad?'

'I didn't do anything bad on purpose. But a girl was still hurt by me.'

'God, Toby. Anyway, you're supposed to say, "I hurt a girl" not "a girl was hurt by me". Did you at least say sorry?'

Toby stopped stock-still on the footpath. His eyes filled with tears. 'I've wanted to say sorry the whole time! It's all I've wanted to say! But I apologise too much, that's what people say, that's what Dad told me.'

'You're insane.' Sophie shook her head. 'Obviously it would be best not to be hurt at all. But I'm sure a sorry would be great, if the person meant it.'

Down near Parliament Toby cleared his throat. 'You know,' he ventured. 'I was thinking. Dad told me something else once. He said, like with relationships, that I didn't have to rush to settle down.'

'Really?' Sophie remembered the sea wall, the roar of the roller-coaster on the wind. 'Because he basically told me I was lucky to have Sam and I didn't deserve him, pretty much – that he was too good for me.' Toby looked sceptical. 'I'm serious, I can't remember the words, but I remember the feeling.

301

He made me feel like I *did* have to rush to settle down.'

'I can't remember the words, but I remember the feeling,' Toby repeated.

'I'm post-factual! I don't need evidence, I have intuitions, and they're pretty much always true.'

'I never learnt about that in Foundations of Australian Law.'

'You were too busy sexually harassing. Anyway, I'm twenty-five. It wouldn't be rushing to settle down – if Sam ever asked me to marry him, which he won't.'

Toby was studying her. 'I wouldn't be too sure about that.'

'Sam puts up with me, all my issues. He makes me laugh. He looks after me. He'll be a great dad one day.' Toby's expression was shrewd. She didn't want to know what observation or opinion he was formulating. 'But if I need advice from a uni dropout, you'll be the first one I call.'

'Okay. Do you really think I should apologise to Astrid?'

'*Astrid.*' Sophie raised her eyebrows. 'Toby, I do. If you mean it, you should.' They'd reached Parliament Station. 'This is me,' Sophie said. 'Are you going to give me a hug or what?'

Toby pulled her quickly towards him. 'Bye, then.' He released her and hid his face.

'Loser!' Sophie shoved him on the street. 'Are you having a cry?'

His long eyelashes were wet. 'You're the loser! You're having a cry!'

'As if,' Sophie scoffed. But as she turned away, smiling, tears sprang to her eyes.

She returned to a house that smelt like laundry liquid, the windows open and the bedsheets drying in the sun. Sam was invariably diligent about his share of the housework, but it was rare for him to take even the slightest sensual pleasure in his surroundings. Now a bunch of supermarket tulips drooped languorously in an IKEA vase on the kitchen table. A saucepan of pasta sauce bubbled away on the stove. *Where is Sam and what have you done with him*, she let her expression say.

'I don't know, it's the weather,' he said. 'The weather felt like spring.' It was the first time he'd smiled at her since he'd picked her up from Southern Cross on Tuesday night, given her his coat and driven her home in silence. Now he crossed to the fridge, pulled out a bottle of sparkling and gave it an encouraging little swirl. 'Do you want some?'

She hadn't been able to face sex with him for a long time. The prospect of being pinned down and loomed over in the dark snapped her body closed like a trap. But the sun was shining, and two glasses of champagne bubble-wrapped and cushioned her in the present. She was able to lead him over to the red couch and take his clothes off, to sit him down and hop on his lap, to kiss him in the light and be reminded of all that was good about him. Sam stared at her, dazzled. 'I'm going to come but I want *you* to come,' he said after a while. Sophie consulted her internal fantasy library, dormant for over a year. It would need a comprehensive overhaul, all the scenes of Matthew excised. Her own image needed an update too: she was different now, graver and more cautious. She leaned forward, reached down her hand, screwed her eyes shut and desperately called forth the erotic. Out of nowhere she was visited by a figure – Tessa Notaras in her smoky kitchen, topless. 'You did it,' Sam gasped. 'You're back. We're back!'

31.

In Alex Comfort's shocking manual *The Joy of Sex*, one section ('Sauces & Pickles') had run alphabetically through a terrifyingly advanced menu of lovemaking: *goldfish, grope suit, harness, horse.* Young Grace, dreaming of losing her virginity, had been equally thrilled and appalled. 'Never blow into the vagina,' Comfort warned. 'This trick can cause air embolism and sudden death.' *Blow* into the vagina? There was so much she needed to know. She'd studied the manual with the same care she took over her law texts. When the time came, she'd be ready.

One night, late in 1975, she invited John Clare for a pizza. The only table was in the very back of the Lygon Street restaurant, in a shabby lean-to near the outdoor dunny. They shared two carafes of red wine, sediment so thick John looked to be wearing lipstick. The owner had never seen a more beautiful couple, he said; he poured them each a free nightcap. On a bench in Macarthur Square, the sour tang of their first limoncello kiss. Back in her room, John was tentative, even shy, nothing like the masterful bearded man in Grace's book. She helped his penis slide inside her. Even then he moved only gently. He hadn't been that way with Helen – or had he? She cast back to Sunbury, the kombivan. Helen's hair, spread on the mattress. Helen's legs splayed open. The side of Helen's breast, shaking with John's thrusts. Suddenly, mid-memory, Grace climaxed. Afterwards, they lay in each other's arms, stunned. She only once, in all the years after, orgasmed with him again. Yes, it could be considered a tragedy.

By the end of the following year John had finished his history degree. Grace encouraged him to undertake an honours year. 'I started uni when I was twenty-one,' he said. 'I'm too old to be hanging round campus.' When she suggested he find a full-time job, he complained he was still too young. One day Wally ran into the kitchen at Greeves Street, waving his tickets for a round-the-world trip. Grace read the writing on the wall. 'If you want to go,' she said. 'Just go.' He disappeared from her life for almost a year, during which she won the Prize for Labour Law *and* the Prize for Contracts.

One night, so late it was almost morning, she was roused from her sleep by the repeated peal of the share-house telephone. It was Wally, calling from the Middleton Hospital for infectious disease in Singapore. John had become terribly ill in India. He was getting treatment; they just weren't sure what for. He'd been asking for Grace since he woke up. She boarded a plane and flew to his rescue. Hideously weak, really just skin and bone, John cried when she walked through the crowded ward. Once he stabilised, she arranged for his treatment at a private tropical medicine clinic in Hawthorn. When it was time for him to leave, he returned to Grace's room in Greeves Street. She'd been patient, and he'd come back.

Grace achieved her Bachelor of Law and Bachelor of Arts. She became an articled clerk and then a solicitor at Hector and Gross, going into the city every day, part of a new vanguard of working women, an early adopter of the power suit. John messed around, working as a carpenter. He became active in the precursor to the CFMEU, a trade union for guys on building sites. In 1983 he was offered a job as an industrial officer at the Australian Council of Trade Unions. It wasn't until 1985 that he found the motivation and wherewithal to propose with a very simple gold ring purchased from a mid-range jewellery shop in Brunswick. At the age of twenty-nine, Grace was a good six or seven years older than the average Australian woman at the time of engagement and marriage. She was also, by that stage, the youngest senior associate, of either sex, in the history of Hector and Gross. One day, John stopped in front of a real estate agents' window and invited Grace to identify her dream house. He'd saved a deposit for them on the sly. Grace was able to surprise him with a secret she'd kept for over a decade: the house in Greeves Street was hers. Theirs, after the wedding, and perfect for a family, which was lucky, because she was pregnant.

Babies had not played a role in Grace's life. As a young working woman, she'd socialised with other young working women, who by and large did not have children. Her male colleagues did, and they made it sound like quite a handful, but nothing she couldn't manage. She didn't have a mother; she didn't have a sister. She knew nothing about delivery beyond the leaflets at the doctor's. One of John's young colleagues at the trade union recommended a workshop called Embracing Active Birth. When they showed up to St Mark's Community Centre they discovered it was run by a *full-on* hippie: gold coins on her belt, chains and leather straps on her ankles, tufts of underarm hair escaping her crocheted vest. Grace at that point was wearing a (men's) suit jacket over the most formal of her shapeless maternity work sacks. She nearly turned and walked right back out. But the hippie spotted them and invited Grace to join the women on the carpet. The partners – even, rather scandalously, a female one – were encouraged to crouch behind. Labour was painful, the hippie admitted. But with massage techniques like these, the pain could be reduced. John stroked and prodded Grace's back, aching from a hard day's work. The hippie swept him aside and took over. Instantly Grace felt a great calm. The hippie was right: everything had become too medicalised. It was vital to remain upright for a long as possible in early labour: walking about, eating and drinking as she wished, listening to what her body needed. The hippie didn't call them contractions, instead favouring the term 'surge'. When the surges came closer together, Grace would assume a position that felt comfortable, preferably in water. She would not under any circumstances lie on her back. When the baby was born, she would ask for it to be placed on her chest so the baby could seek out and find the nipple. A close and natural feeding relationship would follow. Women had been giving birth for millennia, the hippie concluded. Stay strong, stay active, don't let the doctors tell you what to do.

All this had seemed so right to Grace at the time, so clear. But as her due date passed, the midwives became restive. There were mutterings about an induction, something the hippie cautioned her to avoid. When they offered her a stretch and sweep, she accepted. It was performed not by one of the midwives but by a consultant just back from lunch. He took off his jacket, rolled up a shirtsleeve, slapped on a glove and pushed her knees wide apart. When he leaned over her she could tell he'd been drinking. But her legs were already open, and she so badly wanted to meet her baby. 'I'll count to ten,' he said. 'One, two, three . . .' At three, he pointed his finger, jabbed a hand straight inside her, and scooped the rim of her cervix like an ice cream. Grace was still crying two hours later when she felt the first unmistakable surge. By midnight, her crying continued, but for a different reason. The contractions hurt so much she was certain she was going to die.

Afterwards, John accepted it was his fault. He knew she didn't want an epidural. When she begged, he should have said no. He was there when her feet were forced into stirrups – couldn't he have spoken up? She overheard the doctors telling him she needed an episiotomy. She used all of her remaining energy to make John leave the room. Her perineum was sliced through with garden shears. As she was stitched, her baby was taken away to be weighed, cleaned and wrapped in a blanket. Grace's lifeless limbs were contorted into a nightdress. She was encouraged to freshen her lipstick. 'And here's Dad,' she heard a nurse say, proffering the swaddled bundle.

'Stop,' Grace roared. Everyone in the room turned to stare. 'Give me,' she cried, 'my baby.' Sophie, her beautiful baby girl. Just to see her was to fall in love.

Only Grace could feed her, painfully, with her body. Only Grace was alert to the slightest sound from her bassinet at night. Only Grace could decode the different cries for milk, for a change, for a nap. Grace had thought she'd be back at work within a month. At that point she was still carrying around a rubber ring so she could sit. After six weeks she was still wearing maternity pads, and couldn't conceive of a future after them. Her pregnancy knickers were still her everyday knickers, so large she couldn't tell the leg holes from the waist. If Sophie missed a feed, Grace's breasts filled and leaked. If she showered, she could hear a baby crying, even when her daughter was asleep. The idea of returning to the office was laughable.

And then there was the *pull*, her daughter's magnetic allure. When Sophie managed to latch on, and her milk began to flow, it was like, Grace imagined, a junkie's first hit of smack. They were perfectly symbiotic, Grace anticipating her daughter's needs, Sophie accepting Grace's help. She couldn't farm it out to someone else. No one would get it right. Back at the office, her rival Stephen Rice was made the firm's youngest ever partner. After a moment's fury, Grace didn't even care. She gave in her notice without going back. When her farewell card arrived, she dropped it unread into the bin.

Grace thrummed with the drive to conceive a second child. But it was not an easy process. For one thing, John was out late or interstate three or four nights a week. For another, when Grace had stopped breastfeeding she plunged into a hormonal depression so black she could barely speak. Just as Sophie reliably slept through the night, Grace forgot how to sleep altogether. Lying in bed, her mind churned with horrors. Her mother's cancer was growing within her. Her mother's cancer was growing within Sophie. Sophie could read her mind and Grace's despair would harm her. Considered in the light of day, or verbalised haltingly to John, the fears lost their power. But at 4 am, she was not her analytical, judicious self. Sometimes, when her mind woke up but sleep still paralysed her body, she swore she could see the shears and feel the tugging of stitches in her vagina, sewing it back up. Get over it, Grace! Get a grip! *Women had been giving birth for millennia.* Three times she'd been examined by a female GP between Sophie's birth and her first birthday. Her stitches had healed perfectly; her perineum was seamless. 'A magnificent vagina,' her doctor cheerfully pronounced. 'Anything else?' She could howl and collapse in the doctor's arms. *I'm losing my mind*, Grace wanted to say. But if she lost her mind, she'd lose her baby. Her biggest fear was that her daughter would be taken away.

Then, as Sophie grew, she began to impose herself, insisting on her difference and separation from Grace, alienating her with her outlandish demands, harrowing her in public and private with dramatically illogical and wilful behaviour. Toddler Sophie could not be reasoned with, she could not be soothed. Grace's only option therefore was to absent herself. Not physically, obviously! She would never give her daughter up, or even admit that she needed a break. Just sort of . . . mentally. Blank mind, blank face. *Got to get through it* became her gritted teeth mantra. Only when four-year-old Sophie was firmly ensconced in a charming kindergarten could Grace climb out of her hole, begin to get reacquainted with John, and physically prise herself open for business.

And then the whole process began all over again with her sweet and precious Toby. By the time *he* was settled in kindergarten, Grace had been out of the workforce for nine years. He'd do whatever it took to help her back in, John said, if that's what she wanted: cleaners, babysitters, he'd cut back his own hours. Two parents, two jobs, two children, twenty-four hours in a day. It was not beyond the wit of man. She'd read magazine profiles of women who'd done it. But it was impossible, and grew more and more impossible every day. It was like the Enid Blyton she read to Sophie when she'd tucked her in at night: you climbed down the Faraway Tree after another exciting adventure. When you went back up, either the land had changed or the magic was gone. Grace had stepped out of her life as a lawyer and that life had moved on without her.

Having been a young gun, at the very peak of her game, it was intolerable to consider restarting at the bottom. *Never.*

And John knew it was impossible too, which was why he made free with his wild offers. His work consumed him, every part of him, leaving only the smallest husk for her at home. And, for her part, home consumed her, the children running roughshod over her body, soul and mind, treading every part of her into the ground. At least John got to be a husk! Grace was simply *dirt*. (She knew it was melodramatic; she couldn't help it! It was just the truth.)

'Why can't you just love me?' John's most common refrain during arguments.

'What's all this, then?' she'd reply, gesturing at the kids' bookbags on the breakfast bar, the PE kits with sewn-in labels, the warmth of the wood fire, the dinner simmering on the hob, the home she'd made for him. 'Is this not love?'

'But why can't you be *nice?*'

'Because it's *not fair*,' she'd say, and when the children were young she'd say it crying. 'It's not fair that you live a whole free life and have a home to come back to – and I just have the home. You can't have everything, and kindness too. You can't have all of me, my whole life dedicated to the family and you, everything done for you – *and* a kiss and a smile and a pat on the back. It's just *not fair*.'

She dumped *The Joy of Sex* at the op shop along with the children's baby clothes and toys. As for the other book she'd bought in London – *The Female Eunuch* had functioned as a long, very pointed, very personal denunciation of how Grace had chosen to lead her life. 'Dear Grace, your life is a joke, love Germaine' – that's basically what the book said. She'd tossed it in the recycling.

Years, this went on – years and years and years. Always she had this sense of waiting: for kindergarten to start, for a hectic period in John's work to be over, for a family holiday to start, for a family holiday to end. *Just got to get through it.* If she could just get over the next hill, she'd have some time to survey the horizon. That was the thing with the horizon: it kept moving. That was also the thing with time: it kept passing. Soon she was approaching fifty, and as that tremendous milestone loomed she became convinced it was her last chance. Fifty was time to take a breath, to be the person she always expected to be. John seemed to be in a similar frame of mind. Approached by Labor to run in the 2007 election, he shocked her by saying no. Grace had been stunned, hopeful. Was this it? A turning inwards towards home?

As the election date approached she allowed herself to dream: travelling together, socialising as a couple. The house was sometimes quiet, with Toby keeping a teenager's hours. Sex could be back on the menu – couldn't it? She planned a small election party, a celebration of John and the union's successful campaign, the beginning of their new life. It was ruined, her own fault. John put the seafood in the freezer, and she forgot to remind him to take it out. A small thing perhaps, but catastrophic to her. She lost her mind, she was atrocious. Her behaviour that night was a source of great shame.

She waited until he left for the union victory party before slinking down to make two sandwiches, smoothing foil over the one for John. He came home late, thoughtful and subdued. He'd had his head shaved by that fool Pat Benison; he looked like a handsome stranger. In their relationship, John was always the one who made apologies, for being late, for his thought-lessness, for so clearly prioritising others above his family.

But in bed that night, it was she who begged forgiveness, for allowing over the years a gap to open up between them, and for her behaviour that night with the Balmain bugs. He was moved, astonished – his eyes filled with tears. She slid her leg between his legs, their old secret code that she could be persuaded. He held her hand, kissed her forehead, and turned away. He'd always planned time off after the election. But the surprise of the Bali tickets failed to delight him. She'd left it too late. He'd looked like a stranger because he *was* a stranger. He didn't love her enough to try again.

After the ACTU barbecue she arranged her evenings so they went to bed at different times. She took her pyjamas into the bathroom and got changed in there. They touched so seldom she cringed when he rolled over and draped himself on her in his sleep. Each time she shrank away, it gave her a sense of relief, to have come up to the edge and withdrawn. It was better to be no one at all than to try and fail, to hope and disappoint. After a while she shrank so much it was just her, in her house, no future and no past. Germaine Greer had been right. Grace Clare was an idiot.

Yet it was to the writing of the iconic Melbourne feminist that Grace turned as her periods grew further apart, and she entered what Germaine called the 'climacteric'. Once again she felt subtly blamed by the author for her own condition. Her sleeplessness, rage, depression and tiredness – all symptoms more pronounced, Germaine implied, in women who hadn't done the necessary work of interrogating themselves, their relationships and their choices. One morning, in 2008, Grace found herself at three months past her last period. The gap between that one and the one before it had been nine months. The gap before that, eight. If she could just pass the magical twelve-month line with no period! It was such an awful feeling, to be in-between. It was like getting dressed in front of John: he could see her naked or he could see her clothed, but – God! – how she hated to be observed transforming. If it had to happen at all, change was supposed to be private. If she could just move from the uncertainty of 'menopausal' to the pristine clarity of 'post-menopausal', the autumn of her life could begin, a phase which Germaine said could be long, golden, milder and warmer than summer.

The day she'd been thinking about Germaine she walked into town feeling unsettled, nervy. Her mood was negative and black, like a depression. But, unlike traditional depression, she'd felt also a terrible, clashing desire for action. Drifting unthinkingly through the vast glass cavern of the atrium at Federation Square, she found herself in a gallery dedicated to Australian art. There was a queue for one of the rooms and she joined it. When she made it to the front, she was momentarily nonplussed. Manky bits and bobs littered the gallery like rubbish put out for the council. Some young art-school show-off, Grace thought. More comfortable with the objective than the subjective, she went over to imbibe the text.

Born in 1917, Rosalie Gascoigne spent the majority of her adult life as an astronomer's wife and a mother in the isolated scientific community of Mount Stromlo. Gascoigne spent her days pushing a pram around the futuristic white dome that housed the groundbreaking Oddie telescope, collecting items of interest from the inhospitable landscape and arranging them in her home. She made a formal study of the principles of ikebana but it was not until her children had grown up, and she'd moved to the Canberra suburb of Deakin, that she began visiting art galleries and reading art books. She began

314

to create, first assemblages of rusted iron and found materials, then assemblages in boxes. She was fifty years old.

By that point Grace was feeling so drawn in, so personally touched by the life story of Rosalie Gascoigne, that, bashful, she could hardly look again at the work. Turning, she took the plunge; she inhaled the art, consumed it. The gallery was not crowded but she felt the proximity of others as a personal affront. The art in that very gallery earned Gascoigne her first solo exhibition, aged fifty-seven, and a major survey at the National Gallery of Victoria only four years later. In 1992 she was the first female artist to represent Australia at the Venice Biennale. She died a colossus of the art world in her eighties. Imagine only beginning your life just when other people thought it was over!

Sculpture was beyond Grace: too elevated a form. It would be as absurd as announcing she was taking up ballet. She needed something earthbound, even domestic. That night, Grace angled the screen of her laptop on the breakfast bar so she could make her investigations unobserved. 'Learn pottery in Fitzroy,' she typed.

She had been welcomed to Johnston Street Pottery by Anton Mansell. He was a courteous teacher, quiet and gentle. For a long time he seemed less a person to her and more a functionary – a conduit to a new life. The new life was a long time coming. After months of sometimes daily lessons and practice, she still had trouble throwing a basic cylinder. 'I just can't do it,' she cried.

'Grace,' Anton said. He wore his dark brown hair swept back off his face in a half pony. 'You're asking the clay to defy gravity, to grow up, up, up' – he mimed with his hands – 'while keeping the walls delicate and thin. Even professional potters struggle. You mustn't despair.' But she did! Pottery would ennoble her existence and underpin her last decades on earth. Any obstacles to her plan felt devastating.

Everything changed when she got her first iPhone for Christmas. 'Anton, look,' she said, when the studio reopened for the New Year. 'Show me again; I'll record it with this.' She waved her new phone. 'Then I can watch it at home, and finally get it through my thick skull.' Anton stared at her. He reached out and briefly held her cheek. His thumb brushed her forehead. 'Be kind to yourself.' He sat down, tossed a ball of clay perfectly into the centre of the wheel, and began.

Reviewing the video later, she saw Anton's thumbs push into the spinning ball and open it out into a bowl shape. The walls were kept strong by his hands, effortlessly guiding the clay into a cone. No wonder she was awful at it. Her pathetic thin fingers were so dry! Now Anton prepared to open the mouth of the cone. By that point wet clay was all over his hands and up his hairy forearms. He tickled the water in the ice-cream container. Gently he slipped his wet fingers inside the spinning form. 'Small finger of the right hand, second smallest finger, right up to the knuckles,' he was explaining. 'Let the clay run up against it. Left hand, thumb and forefinger,' he said. 'Steady the clay as the mouth is opened.' At home, watching, Grace's heart was pounding. Her insides seemed to be melting.

'What have you got on you, lovey?' John's voice. She turned her phone over on the table. 'Something on your face?'

She hurried to the downstairs bathroom. Reflected in the mirror, like a cross on Ash Wednesday, she saw the smear of Anton's thumbprint on her forehead.

That night she found herself inching to John's side of the bed, breathing in time with his breaths, her chest to his back. After a long time he rolled to face her and put his hand up to her cheek. She slid her leg between his legs. She turned on her side with her back to him, her eyes clamped shut and her mind full of Anton. They moved together slowly, pyjamas against pyjamas, each preserving the other's privacy, politely not making a sound, even when they both shuddered and, astonishingly, came.

Grace didn't have a clue what to do with the feelings that swirled inside her. She tried to get closer to Anton in the way she'd always been intimate with or cared for others. She annexed his life, taking part-ownership, then steered and chivvied him to better himself. When the flat came up next door, she encouraged Anton to view it. She laughed in triumph at his flushed cheeks and evident excitement. 'I knew it,' she said. 'It's perfect for you.' He could move out of the rooms above his studio and use them for what he'd confided was his dream: a gallery space. She arranged the launch party for the first exhibition. Many, many people came, though not John. Still, her husband managed to ruin her night from out of town. Halfway through the party, red dots were added to the plinths of her own two pots, showing the world they'd been sold. She floated home, ecstatic. A few days later, the pots were installed in the library at Greeves Street. John had bought them. 'Why are you angry with me,' he kept asking her, over and over. 'Why are you angry with me?'

Was she *in love* with Anton or did she just *love* Anton? Shorter than John, though taller than her. Slightly out of shape. Hairy forearms, exquisite large hands. He was sensitive, zen. Quite literally: he meditated. When a student pulled out of a ten-week course after six classes, and demanded a full refund, Anton simply gave it. 'Let go, or be dragged,' he murmured to Grace. If she was in the studio over lunch he invited her to join him. Lunch for her was toast eaten standing up as she made calls and dealt with admin. During those studio lunches she watched Anton lay out multiple dishes of bright, simple vegetarian food; she marvelled at the time he took over it, his joy and care. She had existed in the world in one way for years: her way. Here was another way.

She esteemed Anton; she was fascinated by him, almost craved him. One day she was sensible about it, phlegmatic, accepting: 'Let go, or be dragged.' The next day she was tender, hopeful, wild with possibilities. She lay awake in the small hours imagining her head on Anton's chest, his hands in her hair. Other nights, detached and far-sighted, she emailed notes to herself about how he could scale up the studio, employ more tutors, earn more, spend less time teaching and more time making. Or what if he sold the big workshop, downsized to a personal one, and spent all day on his art? 'Indulge me,' she said. 'I'm great at this stuff.' He imagined a perfectly equipped personal studio, the brand of clay, the precise angle of the sink, the complicated requirements for the drainage system; she jotted them all down in her notebook. She ran the numbers on how many commissions he'd need to get by. He could do it, make a living from his art. Why wouldn't he? Why could men never envision the future? Anton's heel-dragging reminded her of John. If John had his way, 99 Greeves Street would still have the bath in the kitchen. Life took energy, imagination! She teetered like this, desire on one hand and frustration on the other, flip-flopping sometimes hourly.

Would the feelings have run their course or would love have blossomed in its own time? She'd never know. John had travelled to Sydney for a dinner celebrating the 2009 passage of the *Fair Work Act*, the final demolition of the Howard Government's brutal industrial relations regime. The next day he'd returned early enough to eat dinner with Grace and Toby. Afterwards, muttering something about emails, he disappeared into his study. When she and Toby had finished his modern history revision, Grace called through the study door to say goodnight, showered, put herself to bed, and was woken half an hour later by John's carelessly loud pulling of the bathroom-light cord. Sleep was hard for her; it had been since she had children. She had one chance per night to fall asleep, and she'd had it. She'd be up then until at least three or four. 'The light, for God's sake,' she snapped in the darkened room. Instead of his usual apology, he sighed and turned his back to her. Within ten minutes he was gently snoring. Grace put on her glasses, picked up her iPad, and composed an email to her husband.

John, you've just woken me up again. Ten-thirty I went to bed and at eleven you woke me up. I've had half an hour's sleep. I'll be lucky to get back to sleep at four. Five hours, that's how long I'll be awake, it's how long I'm ALWAYS awake, lying here listening to you snoring. Why are you so inconsiderate? You used to be away for three or four nights a week. Now you're constantly under my feet. Why are you always hanging around? Why are you always interrupting my routine and Toby's routine right before his most important assessments? If there's some project you're holding back on to spend more time with your family I would encourage you to take it up. Because I can tell you one thing for sure. Your family doesn't want you.

She pressed send. Immediately the anger inside her lowered and became tolerable. Even so, sleep eluded her. After an hour lying in the dark, she took up her iPad to once again google Hormone Replacement Therapy. The links on the first three pages of results had already changed colour from her repeated insomniac clicks. On the fourth page she found herself on a British chat room or some sort of website where women could share their experiences of the menopause. Many seemed to have found HRT helpful. Then she saw a post entitled 'A Husband's Plea'.

> Dear ladies, apologies from me, I am a man, and have no business here in this 'women-only space' and I hope you won't bite my head off for posting but I am eager for the opinion of women. My wife is undergoing the 'Change' currently and I have never felt more alone. She has said she is not interested in sexual relations with me and that is fine, I still find her beautiful and would like that kind of closeness with her but I would never force it. I just miss her so much, her arms around me and her kindness. She used to always talk to me and hug me but now she just wants to be alone or with our boys. How can I tell her that I love her and want her love again?

Grace cried and cried until she was choking on her own snot. She allowed herself to make a little more noise in the hope that John would wake up and she might talk to him, explain herself, tell him she still cared. She thought suddenly of her cruel message, burning a hole in John's inbox, waiting to hurt him. She ran into his study, the old treatment room. John had built the half-depth desk and the shelves himself, hours of painstaking measuring and cutting, his hands running lightly over the wood. She was hit by a wave of sadness so huge that she'd momentarily reeled back. John's iPad was charging in a nook above the desk. She took it down, swiped it open, and found Helen Macklin's message.

Oh Johnnie, my poor love. I'll write more soon but I didn't want to leave you hanging. When will you next be in Canberra? Lots of love forever from Hel.

Helen Macklin had loomed large in Grace's mind despite three decades-plus of no contact. As soon as Grace had learnt about the concept of googling she'd checked up on her former best friend. Sub five and a half minute kilometres in a women and girls' fun run in Canberra – could that be her Helen? A tiny dot in a large group photo from a Wagga Base Hospital nursing program reunion? If she had the same surname, did that mean she was unmarried? Was Helen in turn googling her? Did she notice that the only results for Grace Clare were in profiles of her husband or bulletins from her children's schools? *Helen Macklin, General Manager, Lally Hale House*, Grace read at the bottom of Helen's message. Only working women had email signatures. Grace's aorta twisted with envy. She scrolled down but the space below was blank. What could John have written to merit this passionate response? One thing was clear: 'Johnnie' had committed a painful infidelity. His blameless good-guy persona was revealed as a lie.

Grace deleted her angry message to John, and Helen's loving one too. In bed, on her own iPad, she carefully typed Helen's email address from memory. What followed was a simple warning: contact my husband again and I'll throw him out of my house. She would not do 'Johnnie' the favour of confronting him about his behaviour. No, she wouldn't allow him for one moment to think she was jealous. Toby would be leaving home in less than a year. Grace would use the time to prepare for her post-family life: a life of art, a life with Anton. She took the plans for the dream studio to an architect and made them a reality.

John's bafflement: 'You're the one who said Toby's grade twelve was everything. Now we have to live on the ground floor for five months?' Half a million dollars; her entire remaining inheritance from her father. The structural engineer alone cost a year of school fees. The back-fence neighbours tried to get the extension stopped at council. Don't kid a kidder: Grace lawyered up; won, of course. She had the whole thing clad in corrugated iron, a nod to Rosalie Gascoigne. Two potters' wheels side by side next to the vast window overlooking the backyard. The German kiln Anton suggested, much bigger than the one she'd thought she needed. 'It's when you're packing the glaze kiln you have to think of,' Anton said. 'You need plenty of space, because when two pots touch, in that heat, they can fuse. It's called kissing.' Waves of lust buffeted her; she'd briefly closed her eyes. 'Grace?' Anton's hand above her elbow. *Yes*, she'd thought. John would be in for a big shock. Grace was going to be reborn. And the man who would accompany her for the triumphant last phase of her life would not be John, but Anton.

Well, so much for that, she thought now. She ran a tentative hand across her shaved patch and lingered with disgust on her scar. Now she had no husband, no Anton. Her children had finally shown up – not to check on her! No, just to needle, accuse and snipe. They'd ruined her day, smashed Anton's special mug and scared the one person Grace could rely on for company in her increasingly hostile house.

*

Upstairs, in the big front guest room, Girl was lying on her stomach with her legs kicked up.

'Reading, sweetheart? What have you found?'

Girl lifted the book up so Grace could see: *Rebecca*.

'Don't let me interrupt,' Grace said. 'How do you like *Rebecca*?'

'I love it.'

That seemed to be the limit of Girl's feedback. Grace regularly consumed literature, performance, film, culture. She could review anything: synthesise it, contextualise it, argue that it was sexist or derivative or fallacious. Art seemed to bowl Girl over. Conversations on the topic were stilted as a result. Girl had sat up and swivelled her legs to the side of the bed, but she wasn't speaking. 'I'm sorry about the scene with my kids,' Grace said. 'They've had a hard time.'

'Of course,' Girl said. 'John. His death.' Grace grunted. 'I know it's not easy, Grace.' Girl's voice was wobbly. 'I know you took all those sleeping tablets. When you fell. I don't think people know how badly you hurt yourself. You could have died.' She was properly crying. 'And then I may as well die!'

Grace could have cried too but it would not be right or appropriate. Girl was just a girl. She cleared her throat. 'I'm sorry I scared you.'

'You did scare me!'

Grace needed some distance and to collect her thoughts. 'I'm just going to . . .' She started pulling the door shut without formulating an excuse. 'Finish tidying,' she concluded.

Girl looked away. 'Okay.'

Grace stood in the doorway of John's study and surveyed the empty room. The box was on the desk with its lid off; the plastic animals stared out in reproach. The truth was that Grace

323

had been envious of Ingrid's ability to cry at John's funeral. At her grief, so pure and simple. And what was in the frame? Grace picked it up and turned it over, expecting a piece of trade union memorabilia. Instead she was confronted by a photograph of herself, a picture she'd always hated. It was the one with Sophie and Toby in Callala Bay, the year Grace had almost refused to go on holiday. Turning forty and not too pleased about it, she'd been in her fourth straight year of Toby waking her before 5 am. Most days she'd have three breakfasts before ten, so she wasn't exactly in the mood to 'flaunt her curves' at the beach. She'd left her bathers at home on purpose. But April on the South Coast had been as warm as summer. In the photo, taken by John, they'd been paddling at low tide. Grace's long denim skirt was tucked up like pantaloons between her straddled legs. She'd felt like an old frump, a washerwoman, the skin above her knees wrinkling. Toby was next to her, his little hand in hers, his tummy still fat like a toddler's. On her other side, age ten, Sophie was lithe in her first bikini. All holiday Grace had felt powerfully negative and foreboding about the bikini and Sophie's tall, slim body inside it, the oldest and tallest and slimmest she'd be before puberty and the curse of womanhood crept up on her, with its breast buds and stretch marks and cellulite and discharge. Throughout the holiday – cooking in the unfamiliar kitchen, hanging out the washing on the rusty Hills hoist – Grace had felt Sophie judging her, swearing she'd never be like her. Sorting through the holiday snaps later, Grace had glanced at the picture of them on the beach and thrown it, horrified, into the bin. John must have rescued it, kept it all this time.

Now she studied the picture properly and saw, to her devastation, that she hadn't been old at all. She'd been young.

She'd been beautiful. She sat down, shaking. She saw that she'd been holding Toby too tightly. She saw that Sophie, staring at her dad through the camera, had been isolated, lonely, still a child. All holiday her daughter shunned group activities to read Agatha Christie and Sherlock Holmes, and when she wasn't gorging on pointless mysteries she was staring at Magic Eye books, picture books with colourful repeating patterns, surely aimed at children much younger than ten. 'You just look at them, and unfocus your eyes, just relax, and you see the 3D image,' Sophie tried to teach her. Grace tried: the images vibrated, and levitated slightly from the page. 'I can't do it,' she said. Sophie had looked so sad.

'Those bloody books are a waste of time,' Grace told John as they tapped the fine white sand out of the kids' sandals.

'Why, can't you see them?'

'No, the images just sort of shake, and levitate a bit, and come out from the page.'

'That's it, you silly goose!' John laughed. 'You're seeing them!'

Now, like a Magic Eye image springing into 3D, Grace saw the truth. Her whole marriage, her whole life, she'd been waiting for the good times. They'd happened, and they'd happened without her knowing. At some point, her husband had loved her enough to rescue a photograph of her from the bin and keep it until he died. She clutched the simple oak frame to her chest. Oh, Toby, she thought as she sobbed, I held your hand so tight because I loved you. Oh, Sophie, I kept you at a distance because I thought you didn't love me. And, John – I didn't show you love for the same reason I threw the photograph away. It wasn't that I didn't love you. It was because I hated myself.

John used to tell a joke, a joke she had laughed at the first time and rolled her eyes at the next twenty. It was something like this: a man falls off a cliff and ends up in the sea. 'God,' he cries to God. 'Rescue me, please, God!'

A boat cruises by. 'Hop in,' the captain says.

'I can't, God will save me.'

A helicopter flies overhead and lets down a rope. 'Climb up!'

'I can't,' the drowning man says. 'I'm waiting for God to save me.' The man dies and goes to Heaven. At the Pearly Gates he confronts God: 'I prayed to you to rescue me!'

'You bloody idiot,' God says. 'Who do you think sent you the boat and the chopper?'

All week she'd been desperate to see her kids. They'd come to her, appeared at her door, however imperfectly – instead of welcoming them, she sent them away. Grace's eyes filled with tears. She balled up her fists and pressed them to her face. 'You bloody idiot,' she cried silently. 'You bloody, bloody idiot.'

32.

RUBY DETACHED HERSELF with a smack, stared up at Tessa and smiled a gummy smile. Tessa smiled back then looked away. She wasn't embarrassed to see Yasmin's breast, the nipple dark and elongated, but she didn't know how Yasmin felt – and her goddaughter was supposed to be feeding. Ruby kept playing the game until, with a click of her tongue, Yas refastened her nursing bra and pulled down her t-shirt. Suddenly Ruby's face turned pink, her little rosebud mouth stretched into a rectangle, and she let out a long sad wail. 'Oh no, you *were* hungry,' Yas said kindly. She held the baby close, shuffled to the edge of the couch and stood up. 'If I can feed her a tiny bit more in her room I might be able to put her down,' she told Tessa. 'And then it's party time for me – for half an hour, at least.'

Tessa waved at Ruby. 'Bye, beautiful.'

Christian was still getting the brunch stuff at Preston Market. She washed the cups and plates in the sink and sat down at the kitchen table. Chris and Yas despised the brown and orange kitchen and couldn't wait to tear it out. But it was charming to Tessa, and somehow more correct, more right and good, than her own more considered and expensive interiors. The mess was charming too: the blocks on the rug, the water toys in a ring around the bath. She reached for one of the Sunday papers. Inside, veteran Fairfax reporter Michelle Grattan complained Labor had trashed two leaders in less than four years. How could the party win office in 2007 with a comfortable majority, then by 2011 be on a primary vote of less than 30 per cent? 'Some feat,' Grattan wrote. 'Julia Gillard is still PM, of course. But, unless you believe in miracles, she's a dead woman walking, to be dispatched by the people at the election or perhaps by her party before.'

There was a bang from the hallway and Christian came in with a big banana box full of shopping. Tessa jumped up. 'Is there more in the car?'

'That's it, Tess, you sit down.'

'Can you believe this about Gillard?' Tessa nodded at the papers.

'She made a huge mess of a lot of stuff,' Christian said. Tessa studied him as he unpacked cheese and yoghurt into their humming, ancient fridge. His movements were efficient but something about him gave her pause. He was jowly, and whiskered, and his belt almost disappeared under his flannel-shirted belly. Exhaustion maybe, a fact of life in young parenthood. Early parenthood, she corrected herself – Yas was thirty-three, like Tessa, and Chris was already thirty-five. But something about him worried her. His face wasn't just tired; it was set and grim.

'But the first female prime minister,' Tessa tried again. 'Think of all the sacrifices she made.'

'Sauce for the goose, sauce for the gander,' Christian said. 'She cut down Rudd, now Rudd will cut her down. What do you care, anyway?' He waved a tomato at Tessa. 'What did you think would happen? Rudd lined your friends the miners against the wall. Give us back what you stole, he said – our fucking money and our kids' futures. But you're like' – he raised his hands and put on a woman's voice – 'no, no, Kevin, leave the miners alone! No, don't do a carbon tax, Julia, my clients wouldn't like it! That's all you care about, flying Business Class and staying at the Hyatt.' He raised his voice over her protests. 'I mean, it's fine for you.'

Tessa was baffled. 'What's fine for me?'

He sighed and rested his forehead on his hand. 'Sorry, Tess. Sorry, okay? I just mean . . .' He shrugged. 'You're not the one having kids on a dead planet.'

Yasmin came out, a delighted smile on her face. 'Fell asleep on the boob! Tess?'

'God, Yas.' Tessa gave her friend a hug. 'I'm such a huge idiot. I forgot I have to work. I've got a presentation tomorrow, a huge one.'

'Tess, no!' she moaned.

Tessa got the big David Jones bag out of her tote. 'Look, these are for Ruby. So sorry I have to run. Love you,' she said. 'Message me.'

As she left the little weatherboard house, barriers seemed to grow up around her: walls to keep her safe, a shield against others and what they thought or felt. *Not my fault, not my problem*, she chanted as she walked to the tram. *Not my problem, not my fault.*

Back home, Tessa made herself a cup of mint tea, slid her laptop towards her, and for the first time began to prepare what she'd present in her meeting the next day. Sure, Anders, she could 'rebalance the conversation'. Pro-mining sentiments formed an organic part of free-flowing conversation on Miners' Wives.

They had data on all the users. Why not target them with stimulus calculated to harden their loosely positive views of mining into dogmatism? Facts could be presented – facts like how much the Australian economy relied on mining for GDP, and on fossil fuels for cheap and secure energy. Quantify the impact of any carbon tax on the cost of doing business and of running a home. Bar graphs, footnotes, stats and details – her women dealt in them with the ease of economists; Tessa had seen with her own eyes the way they compared health funds, tax rates and different makes of washing machine. That would be the first step, then. Making the raw material of arguments available. A website, Australian Resources Council–branded, stating the case. There we go, statingthefuckingcase dot com, she'd register it right now. She'd partner with an agency to build the site; she'd need copywriters and researchers on it for a year, a maintenance team to keep it updated, maybe a million up-front and four hundred grand per annum on a rolling contract?

But that wasn't the end of it. Facts don't win culture wars. Sure, you could present data on renewables versus fossil fuels. But why not simply produce a grainy JPEG of futuristic wind turbines looming over poppy fields and caption it GREEN ENERGY ZEALOTS DESECRATE DIGGERS' GRAVES? Then you could link to a bogus Facebook post on RENEWABLES: THE FACTS reporting that 'vast swathes' of 'the Western Front' were under threat from turbines, disinterring thousands of ANZACs who lay there dead, having fought for our FREEDOM! Sit back and watch the Facebook comments roll in: 'sickening', 'RIP', 'Coal forever, fuck these looney lefties', 'Is this how we treat our war heroes???' What would she need to engineer a covert campaign of that sort? A team of four, maybe six. Next time there was a power cut, she'd release them like flying monkeys to every newspaper comments section and Facebook group in the country to blame janky renewables for collapsing the grid. What would that bit of the strategy be called? Something noble: 'Operation Veritas.'

Last, there'd be the opposition research. Compiling dossiers on every green lobbyist and activist, logging every time they said 'cunt' in a tweet, forwarding it to their employer to get them sacked. That would need four people too. Two teams of four, pretty expensive. Three to four million a year. That was income, obviously, not profit. Maybe she'd have to ask for five.

She worked for so long the sun had gone down and she found herself sitting in the dark. Christian's red face, his sudden venom. *You're not the one having kids on a dead planet.* Dead planet? He made it sound like entire continents were being burnt to a crisp, like polar bears were right now digging through bins for a crust. It was 2011, not 3011. Labor was still in power – just. Barack Obama would be re-elected in the States. Around the world, slowly but surely, the legislative framework was being put in place to price carbon and mitigate greenhouse gas emissions. *Slowly but surely* was how change happened. As if Tessa Notaras could single-handedly halt the march towards better climate policy! Besides, in many ways, she took better care of the environment than most people. She'd pay her carbon tax, when the time came. She'd happily pay extra for renewable energy. She almost always selected the box to offset her flights. Could Christian say the same? He drove a car – she didn't! And how many disposable nappies did Ruby get through in a day? Her mind flashed to her goddaughter's little legs, her splayed toes. Christian's low blow was correct: Tessa didn't have a child. This is what she had instead – work that she was good at, work that paid well. Was it the life she would have chosen? No. But the life she'd chosen wasn't available.

Her phone flashed on the table beside her. A text from John's old PA at the Australian Council of Trade Unions: *Hello Tessa. I'd like you to come and see me in the morning. The Prime Ministers' Gardens in the Melbourne General Cemetery. Please meet me there at eleven. I have some information for you regarding John. Best wishes, Ingrid.*

33.

GIRL'S GRANDMOTHER HAD arrived from Poland with her husband in 1962. Already pregnant with Girl's dad, it took Elżbieta Zieliński only a few run-ins with ocker bureaucracy to register him with the translated version of their surname: Green. Always her father was special, Girl's grandmother reverentially told her. So handsome and so clever. Girl's mother, Belinda, on the other hand – Baba sucked her teeth. 'If she was pretty, she could be lazy. If she was clever, she could be selfish. But she is not pretty enough, not clever enough, to focus on herself. What is special about her? Nothing. She should be like me.' She jabbed her thumb into her chest. 'Family and the home. You, though, my girl.' And Baba would squeeze Girl in a hug. 'You are beautiful enough, clever enough for anything.'

On school holidays Girl accompanied her grandmother to giant old houses in Carlton and Fitzroy North. As Baba cleaned, Girl sat in the living room or kitchen, quiet as a mouse, reading or doing her schoolwork. 'You will have a house like this one day,' Baba said. 'This is what you deserve.' When Girl's mum and dad split up, Baba remained in the old family home in Coburg, outlawed by her son from any contact with Belinda. Not from contact with Girl, but Girl didn't want to see her anyway. Yes, they'd been close when she was a child. But she was no longer a child, and there was no need for her schoolmates to know she was related to a cleaner. If Grace or Millie ever found out, Girl would die.

All weekend she'd waited for Grace to make her intentions known. Saturday had been taken up with cleaning out John's old room and dealing with Toby and Sophie. Sunday morning, Grace had appeared preoccupied, even sad. Suddenly she jumped to her feet. 'Just popping out,' Grace said. 'To see John's old assistant. You're happy here, aren't you?' Before Girl had a chance to reply, Grace snatched her keys and hurried out to the Saab. Girl wandered from room to room, her eyes filling periodically with tears. When Grace got home, she would ask, properly and formally, to stay. If she had to, Girl resolved, she'd beg. She took up position in the big front bedroom to oversee the street. After a few hours, the Saab jerked to a halt in a car space. Behind it pulled up her mother's battered Ford. Soon she heard Belinda's voice from the hall. 'Girl, get your stuff!'

'It was my pleasure to have her,' Grace was saying as Girl descended the stairs with her pillow, her bag and Big Ted. 'How did the house-hunting go?'

'Great,' Girl's mother said. 'Wodonga's much nicer than you think.' She spoke about Girl across her head like parents do in front of toddlers. 'I know Girl will be very happy there.' Girl could read her mother's expression. She was furious.

Back at the flat, her mother tossed her bags on the kitchen counter. 'All Friday I spent rushing around the high schools for you.' She shook a plastic folder out of her bag. 'Your teachers put together your assessments. Profoundly gifted, Mrs Taylor said. The new school had to know what they're dealing with.

Nothing too good for Girl Green. How was I supposed to explain this?' She slapped a piece of paper down on the bench. Girl's own handwriting filled the page, fluent and ornate.

Je m'appelle Geraldine Green. J'ai quatorze ans. J'habite dans une grande maison à Fitzroy avec ma maman, Grace . . .

'Well?' she demanded. 'What does that say?'

Girl cringed. '*Je m'appelle* . . .'

'In English!'

'My name is Geraldine Green. I'm fourteen years old . . .' Girl's voice started to tremble.

'Why did the only French teacher in Wodonga ask me if I'm really your mother?'

'Oh,' Girl laughed. 'Because she couldn't read my handwriting. She probably thought this said *ma maman*, but no, look!' She pointed with a trembling finger. 'This says Grace is *ma marraine.*'

'And what's that when it's at home?'

'Kind of like . . . guardian?'

Her mother snatched the paper and shoved it back in the folder. 'I was always a fourth-class citizen. Your father, then you, then bloody Baba, then me. That was the pecking order. I was always last. I thought when Gabriel left and we finally moved out, it would be my turn. *Our* turn. Mother and daughter! But I'll never be good enough for you. Well, it's your loss. And one day, if you have kids, I hope to God for your sake they don't treat you like you've treated me. More boxes are coming tomorrow. I'm going to need you to pack up your room. We're leaving at the end of the week.' She held up her hand. 'End of story. No arguments.'

Her mother took a towel from the drying rack in front of the heater. As soon as she heard the wrench of the shower turning on and the hot water throbbing, Girl rushed next door to ninety-nine. Grace answered the door in her dressing-gown. 'Girl?'

The tears came easily because her anguish was real. 'Please, Grace. You don't have to answer now. But I'm begging you. Please let me stay with you when my mum leaves. Please.'

34.

Monday morning and Sophie was bathing in the warm glow of Patrick's admiration. 'I don't know how you did it,' he was saying. '*The one with the red and black cover*. Madness.'

'I don't know!' Sophie said. 'I just closed my eyes and it came to me. Michael Connolly – *The Poet*!'

'That book's about fifteen years old. Incredible.'

'The customer thought I was magic, or psychic, did you see?'

'You *are* magic,' Patrick said. 'We in the beleaguered second-hand crime book trade must take our victories where we can. Today we feast on vanilla slice. No, you stay, I'll go.' He got his jacket from the back of the chair.

'Patrick?' Her boss spun around. 'I don't know if I ever said thank you,' she said. 'For taking me back into the shop . . . after I left, and after I was a dick to you.'

'That's another thing about us,' Patrick said, 'those of us in the beleaguered second-hand crime book trade. I may not get out much, not in real life. But between these covers . . .' He gestured wide to take in the whole shop. 'I've seen it all. Once you've read a few novels it's almost impossible to be unforgiving. Don't give it another thought.' As he left, a woman entered. Patrick nodded back towards the counter. 'She'll sort you out,' he told her happily. 'Anything you need, ask Sophie.'

In Sophie's mind, her mother was a giant, as solid and immutable as an Easter Island statue. But the woman who entered the shop was tentative and small, preoccupied and sad. Had Sophie grown or had her mother shrunk? 'Hi, Mum.'

Her mother peered about, a fedora covering her scar. 'You seem to be doing well.'

'You don't think it's a bit pathetic? Age twenty-five and working in a shop?'

'It wasn't what I expected, but nothing in my life is.' The sudden sting of criticism. She meant Sophie wasn't what she expected. 'I've made a bit of a mess of things,' she said.

'What – *you* have?'

'Why, what did you think I meant?'

'Mum. Everything you wanted for me I've ruined. I wore my retainer, like, one night a week. I dropped out of honours and still had to pay the fees. I ruined my amazing job by making a dick of myself in public. Dad killed himself because of me –'

'What?'

Sophie wouldn't tell her mother about the sex-thing video-thing for a million dollars. 'It's hard to explain, but I know he was ashamed of me.'

'Good grief, Sophie.' Her mother was shaking her head. 'I've read that before, about divorce. Children will find any way possible to blame themselves for adult problems.'

'Why were you reading about divorce?'

'Ha.' She went over to the window seat and stared out at Little Collins. 'I always thought the way to make children feel safe was to make the adults adults and the children children. I could never believe those women who said "my daughter's my best friend". I thought, let your kid be a kid. Shield them from all the adult stuff. I didn't want you to think I was a human being who "had feelings" and second-guessed myself. It would be unsettling, wouldn't it? I wanted to be strong, and to protect you.' Sophie had felt like crying the second her mother said *my daughter's my best friend.* That might not have been what her mother wanted. Sophie would have taken it, had it been offered.

'So, yes,' her mother went on, oblivious. 'I'd read about divorce, but never considered it. The newspaper front page was a shock to me. Tessa Notaras – God, I'd met her! I didn't think a single thought about her. She wasn't even on my radar! All my adult life I thought John and I were locked in a titanic battle. John versus Grace. I didn't realise there were any alternatives.' She gestured out the window at the multi-storey carpark. 'Any off ramps.' Sophie had never heard her mother speak like this, interrogating herself and her life. She kept silent so it wouldn't stop. 'John lost the seat of Melbourne – shock,' she continued. 'Then he went missing – selfish and annoying. Then there was the front-page story – obviously humiliating. And then suicide. What's worse than being widowed? Well, I can tell you. Being widowed by someone the world knows didn't love you. It's a very, very lonely place to be.' A mere metre separated Sophie from her mother, a few footsteps at most. Should she cover that ground, go over there, reach for her, hug her? But now her mother was angry. 'I should have seen your dad was unhappy. I should have been kinder. Softer. More gentle. But if he was suicidal, nothing I did could have helped! It's what everyone says to people left behind. Don't I deserve that comfort?'

'Mum,' Sophie said. 'He wasn't suicidal.'

'He jumped off the roof of our family home!'

Sophie generously let *our family home* go through to the keeper. 'Backwards?' she said instead. 'Why? Seriously, why?'

'Sophie, at some point in our marriage I pulled the shutters down. I just couldn't seem to do it – to give him whole-hearted, proper love. I've done so much wrong in my life. Bad things I've done I've never told anyone!' She turned back from the window. 'I don't know if Toby mentioned Helen Macklin?'

'He did, yeah.'

'I was able to put things right with her this morning. I called her. I apologised.' She waved her hand vaguely. 'Toby's staying with her, did you know that?'

Sophie nodded. 'Did you really pretend to be the landlord and evict her?'

'Yes.'

'And send her a bitchy email saying if she wrote to Dad again you'd kick him out?'

She peeped at Sophie from under her hat. 'Yes.' After a second, they both laughed. Her mother's laugh turned into a moan and she covered her eyes briefly with her hands. 'I feel like I'm in some kind of program. I had to say sorry to Toby about the weekend. I had to call the cleaner and apologise for accusing her of stealing.'

'What, Ivanna?'

'Face creams or whatever . . . I had to visit Ingrid and give her back some *animals* she'd been given by John . . . And, Sophie. I did sleep with someone else the night your father died. Just once, and never again. I've been punished for it, don't worry.'

'Mum,' Sophie said slowly. 'I don't want you to be punished. And I *do* worry about you.'

She batted this away with an impatient noise. Instantly their connection was severed. 'I don't want you to worry!' her mother said. 'I want you to be happy!'

'I know!' Sophie shouted. She glanced back towards the shop door and lowered her voice. 'I know you want me to be happy. You made that very clear when I was growing up. I couldn't cry for a second without you being like, you're fine! You're fine! Stop moaning, you're fine!'

'I didn't say stop moaning.'

'Whatever, you actually did. You couldn't let me be sad, or weak, or embarrassing, you couldn't let me fuck up.' Her mother clicked her tongue. 'See,' Sophie shouted. 'It made you feel sick, it made you hate me!'

'Sophie! I never hated you. Never.'

Sophie put on a mean voice. 'Grow up, Sophie, you're a disgrace, no, you can't come home, Sophie, nobody wants you.'

'Sophie – I gave you everything.'

'You love to say that, but what did you give me, actually? And don't say school fees and braces!'

'I showed you how to roast a chicken, how to use the washing machine, how to find a tradesman in the Yellow Pages!' Sophie gave a snort. 'You may laugh!' her mother said. 'But I was motherless, I had no one to show me that stuff!'

'I was, and *am*, laughing,' Sophie said bitterly. 'Sometimes it's all you can do.'

'It's not a joke, Sophie, it's life? It's called standing on your own two feet.'

'You try standing up when you're always being pushed away.' Triumph shot through her: she'd nailed it.

'Wow.' Her mother exhaled. 'What a talent you have with words.'

Sophie put on her Grace voice again: 'What a shame you waste it.'

'Anyway, it's not about what I gave you.' Grace turned back towards the window. When she spoke, her voice was low and muffled. 'It's what I *gave up* for you.'

'What?' *It's what I* gave up *for you?* Is that what she said? She always did this, switched off halfway through a discussion and became completely impenetrable. 'Mum, what? I just didn't hear, say it again?' But her mother stayed silent. After a second she adjusted her hat like it was hurting her. Feeling pity made Sophie furious. 'Why don't you take off that fucking stupid hat? Why do you hide everything? Why didn't you tell me you'd been hurt?'

'You don't have a phone!'

'Don't blame me! You have Sam's number! You're like, *I don't want you to worry*, but I do worry, I do care. All my care and worry goes towards you and you're literally like –' Sophie crouched behind a pretend shield. 'You fight it off, you repel it!'

'Now I'm repellent.' Her mother rolled her eyes.

She *always* did this, turned a comment into a criticism, a criticism into an attack, she ducked and twisted until she was the blameless victim and Sophie was the perp. 'All my life you've said *I'm* selfish.' Sophie's voice was shaking; she spoke more fiercely to cover it up. 'But what comes first, me being selfish or you literally pushing me away, turning down everything I *ever* try to do for you? When I hung out the washing I'd look out later and you'd be like –' Sophie mimed frantically adjusting the pegs.

Grace shrugged. 'You didn't hang it out properly!'

'So nothing about me is good enough! What about you? You couldn't even vote for your own husband. You shagged someone else the night he died! Who was it? Did you tell the coroner? I should call the police!'

'I know he's your favourite and he could do no wrong. But, Sophie, your father ran away with Tessa Notaras for a *week*.' There was a sword in Sophie's hand, the knowledge that her father betrayed her mother for years. She could run it through her right now. But Sophie noticed, appalled, that her mother's eyes had filled with tears. 'He abandoned us,' she cried. 'He abandoned me, Toby, you. That was his choice. I don't think my one transgression really stacks up.'

'Who wrote that graffiti in the hall?' Sophie said. '*You know what you did you cunt* – who's accusing you, what do they know?'

'Well, what do *you* know? How do you know what I did the night John died? What were you doing that night, skulking in the garden like some kind of psycho?'

Sophie stood back behind the shop desk. 'That's my business.'

'I'm your mother, there's no such thing as *your business*.'

'All my business is my own business; you don't know anything about me.' Her mother was leaving, walking towards the door. Sophie couldn't use the sword but she reached for a final dagger. 'And you know how you were moaning earlier about being motherless?' The door was open, her mother halfway out. Sophie raised her voice to follow her down the stairs. 'We actually do have something in common! Because I am too!'

She stood there, heart pounding. Why had she even come? The shop phone rang and she lifted the receiver. Her voice was shaking. 'The Unique Crime?'

'Possum Magic! What's wrong?'

'I've just had the most insane fight with Mum.'

'Oh no, really?'

Sam never disagreed with Rosemary, his earthbound and practical mother. There was disapproval in his tone. Sophie walked it back. 'Not a fight exactly, it's more that I found out something crazy. About the night Dad died.' She waited for Sam to ask what. He didn't.

'Dinner,' Sam said. 'I want to take you out, that's why I rang. Where would you like? Your choice.'

'Marios.' On the other end of the line, Sam moaned. 'Sorry,' she said. 'I *know*.' All the waiters at Marios were handsome, even the old ones and the women. They all had the ineffable confidence born of working in an institution. Sam felt, rightly or wrongly, that they disliked him. Sophie privately thought the truth was worse: they simply didn't recognise him or think about him at all. She, by contrast, had gone to Marios with one or other of her parents every week for the first eighteen years of her life. 'I just love it so much. But why? Why dinner? Are you breaking up with me?' She spoke in a lighthearted way, but a cold wave passed through her chest.

'No, the opposite! I have something I want to say.'

'Is it about the weekend?' Sophie said confidentially. 'Are you pregnant?' She was still laughing when Patrick came in, her date fixed with Sam for eight.

35.

Tessa strolled up to the big black marble monument memorialising Australia's leaders, past and present. *Julia Eileen GILLARD*, read the most recent inscription. A dead woman walking. Would Tony Abbott's name be next? She turned away. *Not my fault, not my problem.* Ingrid was late. If it got to eleven-thirty she'd just have to jump in the cab to Travallion, whether Ingrid had shown up or not.

Just then, a hunched figure shuffled into the garden. Ingrid looked like she'd climbed out of a crypt. Her formerly thick hair was wispy and frizzed. There were blistering red patches on her nose, chin and cheeks. Tessa could see a long tube protruding from the underarm of her sleeveless top. It led to a plastic pouch in the pocket of her woolly cardigan. Ingrid saw her looking and shrugged her cardigan shut. 'It's a port-a-cath, isn't it?' Tessa recognised it from KathyCat's posts about cancer on Miners' Wives. One of the Port Hedland women had made her a special belt to hold her IV infusion pump. KathyCat passed away in June. More than fifty internet friends had shown up at her funeral. Was Ingrid going to die? *Not my fault, not my problem*, Tessa tried to think, but her not-caring barriers didn't seem to work.

'Don't you cry.' Ingrid smiled. 'I didn't invite you to a pity party.'

'I tried to call you a couple of times,' Tessa said. 'At the ACTU. But you weren't there.'

'I know, they sent your cards on. I couldn't write back, not then, but I kept them. Come on. I'll show you John's spot.'

Tessa took Ingrid's big shoulder bag for her. 'How are your lovely nephews? Milo and . . .?'

'Thomas. High school now. Great boys.'

'What about Ajax? Your puppy? I always remember that photo you had on your computer.'

'Puppy! He's an old boy now, with silver hair like me. I had to give him away. He was a good dog, but I couldn't walk him anymore, tugging on the lead. Manny has him, Manny Rahman? Takes him for runs on Merri Creek. I see him every week, Manny brings him round for a chat.' They walked past ranks of rose bushes, some already budding, some even newly in bloom. Tessa wasn't a plant person, but seeing them flower so early gave her a chill. 'You've never seen John's grave, have you?' Ingrid said. 'You didn't come to the funeral.'

'I wasn't invited.'

'Yes, I saw the papers. Well, this is John.' She crouched down and ran her hand over the plaque.

In loving memory of
John Courtenay Clare
22 May 1953 – 27 August 2010

Tessa didn't want to look. 'Sorry, Ingrid. It must have been a shock to you. To read about our relationship in the press.'

Ingrid looked up. 'It wasn't a surprise. I knew you'd been together. Can I have my bag, please?' Tessa handed it down.

Ingrid tipped the bag on its side and arranged, one by one, two dozen little plastic animals.

'From your desk,' Tessa said. 'From John.'

'Grace's had these since the funeral. Came round yesterday to give them back to me. Have you been watching *Downton Abbey*?' Tessa shook her head. 'Well, Grace was like the lady of the house, come to visit a servant.' The animals were in a neat semicircle at the foot of John's rose bush. Ingrid got to her feet, waving away Tessa's help. 'She said sorry.'

'What about?'

'Oh, this and that. She yelled at me at the funeral. Took these guys away.' Ingrid pointed her foot at the menagerie. 'I know John would have wanted them near him.'

'She used to call us John's guard dogs, do you remember?'

Ingrid didn't seem to hear. 'I accepted her apology. But I was disappointed. It meant I couldn't take my revenge. All this time I'd planned it, imagined it. Then she was nice to me, and now I can't.'

'What revenge?'

'When you left at the end of 2008, John was heartbroken. He didn't eat, couldn't work. He came into his office and sat there with his door shut. Sometimes it would get to be seven or eight. I'd have to go home. He'd still be in there.'

'First of all, *he* left me,' Tessa said.

Ingrid didn't seem to hear. 'Remember the emails from the public that used to come in to him through the website? You always badgered him to reply. One day – it was months after you left – he went through them and started to respond. My email was set up so I saw all of his going in and out. One day I saw a reply much longer than the others. It was to someone called Helen, in Canberra.' Tessa stared at her, baffled. 'She was from his uni days, you know. Before he and Grace got together. They used to be an item. They were just friends when they wrote to each other, don't worry. He only had eyes for you. But they wrote a lot, personal stuff. He always deleted them after a few days. I had to print them out, you see. If I didn't, they'd be lost.'

Ingrid was like a sleepwalker Tessa was afraid to wake up. She said gently, 'Did he know you were reading all his emails?'

'He knew about the IT set-up, my filing system, that I sometimes replied as him. So, yes, he did. He relied on me.'

'He did, he did rely on you.' Should she chance it? 'He loved you.'

'He did love me,' Ingrid said. 'He did.'

'He did.'

'It wasn't just you who knew him, you know,' Ingrid said fiercely.

'I know.' Sometimes Tessa wondered if she knew him at all.

'The emails ended a few months after they began. Her emails to him. His kept going. *Why aren't you replying, Helen? Is it something I've said?*

'When was this?'

'John was so sad, Tessa. So sad.' Ingrid was staring at the animals. 'I went back to the union after my first operation, just to look after him. But then the cancer came back. The whole time in the hospital I was thinking: *I must get better and get back to John. He needs me.* By the time I was on my feet, he'd left. Running for election, remember. As an MP. No more ACTU for either of us. Probably for the best. I don't think I could have worked again, anyway.'

'Oh, Ingrid.'

'Grace was horrible to me at the funeral. Horrible. And

because of that I kept having an idea? It would just come into my mind all the time. The idea was that I'd pop all the emails through her letterbox. Show her how sad he'd been.' Ingrid angled her poor raddled face to the sun. 'Lots of times I went round there, knocked on the door, waited, my emails in my bag. Last weekend the door just opened like it was opened by a ghost. The house was empty, Grace wasn't there. She was careless of John and careless of her big beautiful house. She had everything, but she *didn't even care*! I did something bad, Tessa. I got my pen out, I wrote on the wall. I wanted to make her feel awful. I hated her so much I felt like I had two cancers.'

'What did you write?'

Ingrid looked away. 'I can't say it out loud. When Grace came over yesterday, she surprised me. She'd fallen in the shower, banged her head up. She doesn't look how she used to look, you know – smug. She said sorry. About the funeral, about how she treated me. She seemed to mean it.'

'That's good,' Tessa said. 'I don't know how anyone could ever be mean to you, Ingrid.'

'I've decided what to do with the emails instead,' she said. 'You loved him, didn't you? You loved John?'

'God . . .' Tessa shook her head.

But Ingrid seemed satisfied. She nudged her bag with her foot. It fell open to reveal a manila folder. Tessa knelt to pick it up. One of Ingrid's usual neat labels was on the front: EMAILS TO HELEN MACKLIN, 2009. Suddenly Ingrid put her hand low on her belly. 'Got to find the bathroom. Don't leave, okay? I have more to say.'

'Do you need me to come with you?' But Ingrid had rushed away in pain, bent nearly double.

Tessa found a bench in the sun. Inside the folder were about thirty stapled pages' worth of emails. Tessa began to read.

Dear Hel,

> *What a turn-up for the books. Helen Macklin! Terrific to hear from you. You'll be interested to know that a couple of times in the past few years I borrowed my son Toby's Facebook so I could search for you! Sadly, to no avail – there are many, many Helen Macklins in Scotland and Canada!*

Tessa smiled. She scanned through pages and pages of reminiscences about university and their share house. John had always been more stilted on the page than in person. Helen's writing was so vivid she made the old days come alive. A few weeks in, the tone changed abruptly. In what seemed to be a throwaway line, John wrote, *Imagine my surprise when I discovered the whole time I lived there, Grace had owned the house!* Helen responded, furious. *I'm so very sorry,* John wrote back a few minutes after receiving her email:

> *I didn't think how finding out about Grace owning Greeves Street would affect you. In my mind, you left to take care of your dad. I had forgotten about the 'eviction'. I think Grace would be the first to say that she had some unhappy times in her past. I'm sure it was due to some unhappiness on her part rather than anything you had done. My young former colleague Tessa once said that sometimes I'm set on 'send' rather than 'receive', and I don't properly consider the impact of what I say on those close to me. So I'm really sorry about how I broke the news about Greeves Street, and earlier for just assuming you'd be married now and have kids. I totally understand why,*

once you have your life set up perfectly to your liking, you don't want to upset the applecart by introducing a romantic partner. I sometimes imagine what living on my own would be like. If it was something one chose, I think it could be very fulfilling. But if it (a solo existence) was thrust upon one, or there was an individual one hankered to be with, it might be isolating and challenging. I think you must be braver than I am, going your own way as you have. I admire your philosophical approach about not having children. It's true, there are many ways to care for and about others.

It was all Tessa could do not to flick immediately forward and search for further mentions of her own name. She glanced around for Ingrid. What if she changed her mind and took the emails back? She quickly scanned Helen's long, elegantly formulated reply. It ended in an observation. *My dear Hel,* John wrote back:

I will have to take your count of 'at least one sorry per email' as gospel. For some reason I tend to delete these emails after I have read and re-read them. Not because they aren't important – perhaps because they are. As for the apologies, I suppose I've been trying to learn, perhaps belatedly, how my behaviour affects others.

I'm writing this very late as you can see. Toby is doing his homework and Grace is helping him. (Even though he's nearly eighteen! If I could get into university on my own, Toby definitely can. My head was in the clouds at his age. He has always been a wonderful, focused, calm boy, very bright and aiming for law at ANU. Perhaps you'll see him around the nation's capital?)

Tomorrow I meet with industry super funds and fly to Sydney for a union conference. Travelling on my own can be lonely. I used to fly with my former close friend Callum, who worked for me here at the ACTU. Then Tessa stepped into his large shoes. Unfortunately, without her, I don't have anyone to travel with. Outside of a very intense campaign period, my working life is quite solitary. It's not that I'm ever truly alone, it's just that I don't have company. I don't know if that makes sense. I wonder if you would ever like to meet up next time I'm in Canberra? Johnnie xxx

Hi Hel, his next email began:

Sorry, I didn't mean at all to place pressure on you about meeting up! Although I'm slow at typing, I'm absolutely happy to communicate in this way if it suits you best. There's another sorry. Sorry! I have never heard that word 'mentionitis' before. Did you make it up? Very clever. I do mention Tessa often, don't I? She was a special part of my life for a long time. She has moved to Sydney to go corporate and has left quite a large hole. I'm in Sydney myself, just having a glass of red in my hotel room. Big dinner tonight to celebrate the repeal of WorkChoices and the victory of the fair go, blah blah blah! I find it hard sometimes to build myself up to attend these large, mainly social, functions. It would be different if I had a campaign on, or someone to persuade.

You asked about Sophie. I worry about her. She's always been very sensitive. But she has a lovely young man in her life. Head over heels for her, nice bloke. Moving out to the suburbs, saving for a house. Doing what young people in love should do, building a future together. Both my kids could do with more time at home but Grace was adamant they make their own way. The thing is, I had to 'make my own way' because I was alone in the world. It took me ages and I made my mistakes, but I had total freedom – I got it together in the end. Whereas we loaded up our kids with expectations and rules, then turned them out onto the street. They were unsupported without being free.

Whoops, this is a bit of a therapy session! I'd better send this now and reply to the rest of your email later.

Johnnie xxx

Tessa could see Ingrid making her way back through the roses. She rushed to finish the last few pages. John's next email looked instantly different, dragged out shapelessly across the page with typos and jumbled punctuation.

Hel, yes, I am back from the dinner . Say one thing for the labour movement, we can sink a red or two .! I don't think I have been this far gone in a long time. I do drink almost a bottle of wine most evenings. gin and tonic. But this was another level.

Now Iam back in my hotel. It's lucky for me I have you to write to. makes me feel less alone. Talking to Gillard tonight opened up many regrets for me. She and Rudd asked me to run as a Labor MP in 2007. If I had, Iw ould have been playing a role. Now I am just wheeled out for speeches an d functions. I haven't made a single difference to anyone's life since the 2007 election. I have only brought misery to those I love.

Grace doesn't love me. Maybe she never has. Perhaps she sensed from me some hesitance at the start. But that was just me being young, callow. When Sophie was born I was on board, totally & completely. By the time Toby was born I'd lost her, she'd pulled away. I've made a mess of my marriage and my family and it's too late to fix it. Her mother died when she was so young, her dad left her, abandoned her. It wasn't on purpose, but I did too.

I dilly dallied on the Labor safe seat , because I couldnt leave the ACTu, couldn't leave Tessa behind. Won the campaign in 2007, couldn't even enjoy it. Finally I got her, Tessa. My beautiful serious girl. The last love of my life. But I messed that up too. kept her waiting. Unforgivable. Told her I couldnt leave the family. Because of what it would do to my poor kids. I gave Tessa up for my family and they don't even care. They would'nt notice if i never came home again. Now I'm crying in a hotel alone. I just hate hotels and travelling and never being home. But when I am home I don't feel 'home'. I'm never at home anywhere. My home was a person, Tessa. but I lost her.

If she would send me just one signal I would run to her. one message, any sign. But she wants nothing to do with me. who can blame her. Feeling sorry for myself is a bad look when others are struggling. i shouldn't send this to you as you will worry about me. But it has taken me so long to type I don't want to waste it.

lots of love from
Johnnie xxx

The next email was sent the evening after:

Oh Hel, I'm mortified, sick with shame. I'm sorry for laying all that on you. I'm a bad friend, man, husband and father for letting it all hang out like that last night. I don't know what got into me, apart from buckets and buckets of shiraz. But that's no excuse. Please just ignore that email and let's continue as friends. I miss hearing about the patients and their families and the Jolly Trolley.

Love Johnnie xxx

A few days later he tried again:

Dear Hel, has it been a very busy time for you at the hospice? I wonder if maybe you've gone on holiday or your email is down? I still really want to correspond with you.

Your friend John xxx

And again, a week after that:

Helen, I'm so sorry, I asked the girl to put me through to you. I'm not surprised you hung up, it must have been a shock – but please, Helen. Where are you?

J x

His last email was dated June 2010:

Dear Helen,

I'm so sorry I just turned up on your doorstep. I'll never understand what I did that upset you and drove you away. I will regret it always.

Sometimes I get the feeling that I'm running out of time. Once, before me, my future stretched out, unlimited. Now I have a sense of blackness, the end rushing closer. I'll be running for Labor in the next election. I hope I get the opportunity to make a difference. But there's a terrible problem with politics.

Parties, unions, activist groups – even lobbyists, non-profits, businesses big and small – they're all made up of people. And voters, voters are people. People unloved, people hurt, people rejected, people in pain. How are we supposed to do the work? To imagine a better world and make it happen? The answer, I suppose, is love. Love is what allows us to change, to free ourselves from the past, to let go of mistakes and of shame. But we never get it when we need it. Or we want it from the wrong person. Or sometimes we don't get it at all.

You. Grace. Tessa. Even my children. I never got love right. I would do anything to have my time over again. I won't bother you anymore and I hope you can forgive me. With best wishes from your old friend,
John

Oh, John.

When Tessa looked up, Ingrid had joined her on the bench. 'I was there at the election party, you know.' Ingrid said. 'Last year, when he lost. I could always read him like a book. Even before the polls closed I was worried. He needed a cup of tea and a sandwich, some sugar. Grace didn't care, she didn't even vote for him! And the young man they sent from Labor spent the whole night on his phone. He wheeled John out in front of the cameras for that little exchange with Kerry O'Brien. It wouldn't have been so bad if he didn't say 'wank'. He was a pretty good communicator but not everyone talks like a unionist. Afterwards he dashed off and no one knew where. I took a guess and went up into the stairwell. He was sitting in there like' – Ingrid hung her head – 'I said not to worry, it's not the end, he could do any job in the world. He said there was nothing left for him. Tessa, I was scared. He never used to

356

talk to me like that. Like – he cared about me, but in the way I loved Ajax, just as someone to walk beside him while he did what he did. I put my arm around him. He never really had a mum, you know,' Ingrid said. 'Any of the spare love went on Daniel.'

Apart from their brief conversation on the plane, John had never talked to Tessa about his disabled brother, about his home life growing up, his single mum in Essendon. She'd had to cobble together even those bare facts from a newspaper profile. 'I never realised,' Tessa said.

'John was staring at his hands.' Ingrid turned her palms to the sky. They were raw and red and sore. She saw Tessa looking at them and tucked them into the folds of her cardigan. 'Finally I said to him: John. If you want to be with Tessa, go and get her.'

'I suppose you knew about us from the emails.'

'Oh, Tessa. I knew about you from the beginning. I knew about you before it even happened. You're a witch, John said to me. You're a mind-reader. He showed me a text from you. You said you were thinking of him. I said, call her. He said he couldn't. He said, what if she's with a new boyfriend, and they see me calling and feel sorry for me? What if she cancels my call? I said, John, she's texted you. If you're waiting for a sign, here's a sign. I had your address in my book from your cards, remember? I gave it to him. I said, if you love her, go to her.'

'And he came to me.' Tessa's memory turned like a kaleidoscope; the pieces swirled and slotted into a new pattern. Their love had been real. Whatever happened that night on the roof, he had loved her. She put her arm around Ingrid, careful not to pull her off balance. 'Thank you.'

Ingrid went back over to look at John's resting place. After a moment, Tessa joined her. Ingrid gestured at the neighbouring plant. 'I've reserved this spot,' she said. 'Please don't think I'm weird. I asked Grace yesterday. She said it was fine.'

'I can't think of anything nicer, Ingrid,' Tessa said. 'John always liked having you next door.'

Ingrid was regarding her patiently as she struggled not to cry. 'Do you know why I asked you to come here?' Tessa frowned to hide her tears. 'Because you're kind.'

'Oh . . .' Tessa's mind flicked back to Christian, his judgmental face and bitter words. 'Not a single person in my life thinks I'm kind.'

'You are,' Ingrid said. 'You always were to me.'

'I feel like I'm hated wherever I go. I only work, and my work is terrible.'

'Now you're fishing for compliments. Put my folder in my bag, will you?' They walked together to her car. 'I'll tell you who's got a soft spot for you,' Ingrid said. 'Why don't you respond to Manny's messages?'

Now that she thought about it, Tessa didn't know. 'I do, to some of them! They just kept coming at the wrong time.'

Ingrid looked at her sharply. 'Well, when's the right time?'

'I don't even know what the time is . . .' Tessa pulled out her phone to take a look. It was ten minutes past midday. Her phone showed two missed calls from Christine James at Travallion.

'Do a dying woman a favour,' Ingrid said. 'Text him back and say hi. Do it right now so I can see.'

Tessa navigated to the message Manny had sent a week ago. *Hi Tess, just realised it's been a year since John died. If you ever want to hang out, get a coffee and have a chat, I'd really love to see you. Manny.* She looked at Ingrid. Ingrid nodded at the screen.

Sorry to take so long to reply, Tessa quickly typed. *And yes, Manny, I'd love to see you too.*

It was a beautiful day so she walked home, along Rathdowne Street and across Carlton Gardens. What was it, the approach of spring? Some new clarity? The world looked different, higher contrast: beds of waving red tulips stood out almost painfully against the grass. Birds were trilling and chatting – all different sorts of birds. An insect flew past her face with a *zip*! Ingrid's kindness, the new certainty of John's old love. Manny, his friendship and constancy in the face of her despair. Something was changing inside her. Her barriers were falling, the walls were coming down. She collapsed onto a bench under a tree with a dense canopy and stared up the vast grey trunk. She could feel the power of the sun. There was a plaque and she rose to look at it. Many legendary Aboriginal speakers addressed gatherings under this Moreton Bay fig, the plaque read. 'The leaders spoke of justice and rights for their people . . .' There was more, but her eyes filled with tears. Mere metres away, on Nicholson Street, idling cars filled the air with fumes. What was happening to the Earth? What was she doing? *Not my fault, not my problem.* For so long she'd pushed away reality. Now, fortified by love, she could heave up her portcullis. Truth rushed in, and she welcomed it home. There was just one world. She had only one life. And when Christine James rang again, Tessa was ready with a message for Anders Nielson. Politely, firmly, she told him to get fucked.

36.

At the Aveda salon on Brunswick Street, Grace wondered why she'd bothered. The harshness of the black hairdressing gown against her drab old face – she was hideous. Grace had always felt out of step when it came to beauty. When she was young she looked very young; people would often call her 'sweet'. In her twenties, she felt that if people were to look at her, they would find her pleasant. The problem was they didn't look. As a mother, she didn't exist. In middle age, she was a mark for every lost person looking for directions and charity mugger looking for money. It was only when her hair began to properly grey that Grace began to feel slightly ahead of the game. She'd thought, with a small boost in confidence, that she looked rather pretty for 'an older woman'. Then she'd fallen in love, lust, fascination, *whatever* with Anton. All at once she was desperate for allure. Back to the salon, back to the dye. She went in looking young for a woman in her fifties. She came out an anxious forty-eight. Like everything else to do with Anton, it was a mistake. And now here she was, back at the hairdresser. She'd invited a stranger to critique her appearance, perhaps even butcher it further. 'Well, there's a lot going on with my hair, as you can see.' She made eye contact with the man in the mirror. He was studying her. Would he be gentler or more awful because he was about Grace's age?

'I suppose I need to deal with my grey roots, and with the very short patch on the side.'

She thought the man would ask about her scar, but he didn't. He ran his hands through her hair until it was smoothed out around her face. Immediately she looked better than she had in about a year. 'Do you know who you look like?' he asked. God, here we go. Grace braced herself for humiliation. 'Do you remember that great little show on the ABC? *SeaChange*? The lawyer, her husband cheats on her. She moves to the coast or something?'

'Yes, yes, I remember that!' Grace didn't dare to hope.

'That's who you remind me of, her. Sigrid Someone.'

'Thornton!'

'That's it. Well, I saw her in *New Idea*? She had her hair cropped for a role. That's what I'll do for you. Why bother with dye and long hair at all? Why disguise the scar? Disguise yourself? Look at this beautiful face. Own it. What do you think, Sigrid?'

'Own it,' she said.

Snip, snip, snip. Was she mad to think Anton ever cared about her? But she wasn't, she wasn't mad. The conversations they'd had were some of the most intimate of her life. She'd faced the window, looking down at her spinning pottery wheel. Anton had faced the window and looked down at his. One Friday afternoon Grace idly brought up the previous night's episode of *Q&A*. 'It's fine for artists,' she grumbled. 'They just get on TV and say "free the refugees". But who has to deal with the details and make the hard choices? Not them – the grown-ups in the room!'

'But, Grace,' Anton said mildly. '*You're* an artist.' She'd been stunned.

She told him the story of her life growing up, salvation in the form of Greeves Street, her decades with John, every detail. How she'd experienced her relationship with John as an act of shrinking. Shrinking the parts of her she thought he didn't like or respond to. Zapping away anything that made her feel uncomfortable, vulnerable or ashamed. John didn't ask her to do this; she just did it. Why?

'I'm imagining Grace the plant,' Anton replied. 'Born shooting out in all directions, free. It wasn't your fault your mum got so ill, and that your dad only let you grow in one way. You were very tightly pruned when you were younger. Then, as you grew, you tightly pruned yourself. What if you put down your shears? What if you simply stopped?' At that point in the conversation, she'd heard Girl's footsteps running up the stairs. Whether on purpose or not, Grace knocked over her water bucket. By the time she cleared it up, she'd managed to compose herself. Inwardly, however, her heart was galloping. Was Anton saying what she thought he was saying? To let herself be free, to feel what she felt, to love him?

She had done it – she put down her shears. She allowed herself to yearn and plan. At yoga, she submitted to the formerly intolerable humiliation of being a beginner – she bent and stretched and became something new. She had treated John with a hitherto unknown lightness of touch. They'd had some quite nice times together, touring Toby's university, dropping him off at college. Once her life had become full, fuller possibly than John's, she rather enjoyed their evenings together, when Girl and Anton hung up their smocks to go home, and she and John chatted or worked their way through an American box set. When he approached her with the idea to appear in the pages of the *Good Weekend* magazine, she saw how important it was to him and immediately agreed.

Before she knew it a young woman with a digital voice recorder was inviting her to 'open up' about her multi-decade history with the 'universally admired' John Clare. Sitting at the kitchen table, Grace recalled a comment from the ACTU Legal Officer, Liz Eccles, the only one of John's colleagues she'd made a personal friend. It had been after John's speech at a Christmas work barbecue: 'Gosh, he's an inspiration,' Liz had said. 'It must be impossible to hold your own in a marriage with someone like that.'

Grace had looked at her in utter shock. 'But you don't understand,' she'd replied. 'He's not like that at home.' She'd heard him hawk and cough in the shower, watched him totter to his wardrobe with a towel wrapped around him like a skirt, the trembling skin of his pecs and jowls. She'd seen how the whites of his eyes were almost yellow the mornings after a bottle of wine. She watched him grimace and stretch his back when he'd been on lots of flights. When he was called upon, increasingly rarely, to give TV and radio interviews, she saw him flick the switch to autopilot. John Clare wasn't 'John Clare', the political figure, playing a part in the life of the nation. John Clare was *just a man*. As the journalist waited, expectant, Grace flashed her husband a supportive smile, did the interview, posed for the photograph, and that was that.

The day the 'Two of Us' column came out, Grace prepared a light lunch of chickpeas flavoured with paprika, which she served with avocado and brown rice. Anton was vegan and had been since the nineties. He wouldn't dream of imposing his own principles on others, but Grace had found herself voluntarily adopting them, cutting out almost all meat from her diet and a lot of dairy products too. John walked in, frowning at his phone. 'I'll open a bottle of red, shall I?' They lunched together, chatting amicably. Callum Worboys had asked John if he could return to Melbourne and work for him again.

'Oh, now he comes crawling back!' Grace said cheerfully. 'I hope you told him no.'

'In no uncertain terms,' John replied.

They talked about Sophie, how fortunate she was to have Sam's calming influence, how lucky they were to pass the mantle of Sophie's day-to-day care over to someone so energetic and enthused. It was so nice to have the house to themselves, both of them agreed. By the time John was on his third red wine, Grace's mind was on her studio. Keen to get back, she gathered the dishes. He followed her to the sink. 'We'll do them later,' she said, meaning the dishes.

'And what should we do now?' John was looming into her space, his hands around her waist, nuzzling her neck. She could smell the red wine on his breath.

'What are you doing?' she demanded.

He took a step back. 'I thought – we were talking about how nice it was? To have the house to ourselves?'

'I meant so I could be alone. To work!' ('My work' was what she called her pottery, being too shy to say the word 'art'.)

Up in her studio, Grace pulsed the wheel. Her leather-hard vessel spun ever so gently as she used a bent-wire tool to shave off imperfections. ABC Classic FM fought against the torrential rain beating against the skylight. Melbourne's weather had always been unpredictable, but it was not an exaggeration to say it was getting more extreme. Grace must have missed John's usual discreet tap at the door. She didn't notice him till he'd reached the edge of the big worktable. The surprise made her scream with shock. 'I knocked,' he said, wounded. Grace wasn't in the mood for his emotions. 'Look.' He pointed at the ceiling. 'You've sprung a leak.' She got up from the wheel with a sigh. Rain was dripping from the corner of the skylight onto the pine worktable beneath. 'It's the skylight.' John stared up. 'What's the warranty like?' He was second-guessing her management of the builders, and her choice to have a studio at all. He was implying she'd made a mistake, that she didn't deserve the space, that she was worthless.

'Please.' She saw him notice how she was gripping her turning tool. She tried to stay calm. 'This is my space. This is my life. I was happy to do the interview for you. Happy to have lunch. But I must be allowed to get on.'

'Is this because I wanted to make love?'

Her jaw was clenched and she spat out the words. 'I simply. Want. To get on.'

'That's it, we're over as a couple? This is the rest of my life? Being ignored?'

She shrugged. 'We could swap, if you like. I spent the last twenty-five years being ignored. I had to raise the kids at the same time – you should consider yourself lucky. Even ignored, you're still free.'

'But I don't want to be free. I want a family. I want love.'

She couldn't be calm. Above the rain, her voice had risen to a roar. 'I'm sorry, it's too late.'

After the fight in the studio they once again become strangers. John flew to Canberra to visit Toby and didn't ask if she'd like to come. When Julia Gillard took over and the Member for Melbourne resigned, Grace had to find out from Liz Eccles that John was the new candidate. She sought no role in his campaign and was not offered one. When the election was called and John's literature was printed, she and the children weren't featured. She barely saw him as the election drew closer. He chose to tell her about polling day when Girl was in the kitchen, using her as a buffer to keep the conversation light. 'You'll need to come and vote with me.'

'Of course I'll vote,' she said.

'No, *with* me,' he said. 'For the cameras.'

Grace sighed. 'Really,' she said. 'It's no problem.'

'And the election-night party? You'll come to that?' Of course. The truth was she'd begun to see 21 August 2010 as her independence day. Attending the party would be her last official act as John's wife. If he won, he'd disappear to Canberra for weeks on end, and she'd hardly see him from one day to the next. If he lost – well, why would he? The seat had been held by Labor for one hundred and six years.

When she woke early on the morning of the election, it was with a sense of calm finality. Next to her, John's side of the bed was empty. She put on her new dressing-gown and strolled downstairs to get the day started. To her surprise, John was nowhere to be seen. Maybe he'd left already, to meet up with his callow adviser Jason, to crisscross the electorate, crawl some malls and press the flesh. She opened the front door – the Saab was still there. Something drew her upstairs, up the new staircase and into her pottery studio. John was sitting at a stool at the big worktable, his head resting on his hands. 'Oh, Gracie,' he said. 'There you are. I was just looking at this lovely life you've created for yourself.' Something made her cross over to him, lean into him, wrap her arms around him. He mumbled in a low voice. She asked him to repeat himself. He said, 'I think I'm going to lose.'

'Surely not,' Grace said soothingly.

'No, that's what the polls say.'

Grace stepped back from the embrace. 'You can see why people are fed up with Labor, can't you?'

John rubbed his eyes. 'Of course I can.'

'Rudd had his shot. We were all with him – he had the whole country in the palm of his hand. Now look at us.'

'I know,' John said. 'I know.'

'You politicians, you men. We gave you all the power in the world and you squandered it.'

'I know.' John spread his hands. 'God help me, I know. But it doesn't help to have this kind of negativity from our own side. We all have to knuckle down, pull together, get Julia across the line.'

'All you care about is Newspoll. *Take the people with you,* that's what you say. *One step at a time!* It's all a joke. You had your shot to make everything better. You blew it.'

'Grace.' John looked up tiredly. 'When you say the system's broken, when you say there's no more hope, the only people who win are the conservatives.'

'That's fear talking,' she said. 'What we have *is* broken, that's the truth. Hope comes back when you imagine something new.'

After all, that's what her conversations with Anton had made so clear to her. Pruning back her instinctive natural responses had kept her scared and ashamed in her personal life. It had also kept her political ambitions small. But change was possible. Change was good! As a voter, as a citizen (despite Anton's kind permission, she couldn't bring herself to say 'as an artist') it was not her job to *do the numbers* to get Labor elected, or to deal with the *nuts and bolts* of public policy. Her job was to stand up and be counted. She was ready and willing. Anything the future asked of her, Grace Clare would do!

'Is that what you think?' John said. 'That we're broken?'

His eyes were bloodshot, he looked ghastly. No one would vote for a man that tired. She patted his shoulder gently. 'I'm going to make you a tea.'

Her vote wasn't *for* Jonas Banks or *against* John Clare. But her privacy was breached and her ballot photographed. Clicking the link Sophie sent her on her phone, Grace's fervent radicalism gave way instantly to embarrassment and regret. The number two next to his name? Was that what pushed John over the edge? He stormed out of the live-cross with Kerry O'Brien and went AWOL at his own party. When Grace returned to the house in a taxi it was to find a quarter of John's wardrobe empty and the Saab gone.

Oddly she'd felt not worried but relieved. The end of their great joint enterprise: the Clare family. The relationship had been able to sustain one career, one life after the birth of their children: his. However complainingly, she had dedicated herself to it. Once it was over, and the children had been launched, there was no need to carry on. Men didn't go through menopause but a mid-life job loss would serve the same function. Who was he without his power? He'd have to look inside himself and find out. For her part, she knew who she was and who she wanted to spend her future with. Why wait? She'd had her hair done for the election party, she was wearing black trousers, cinched in at the waist, her silky black boatneck top showed the soft skin of her shoulders. She'd looked out of her bedroom window and over to the furthest of the next-door flats. Anton's blinds were closed but his lights were on. She applied her lipstick and went over.

God, even thinking of the events of that week – the pain of it. She'd tapped on the high window of Anton's kitchen, afraid that knocking on the door might lure out Girl or Belinda. Anton had taken a long time to answer and when he did he looked surprised. It was not the reaction she'd expected. Tears rose to her eyes. 'What's wrong?' Anton said. 'Is it John? I saw he lost. Come in, Grace, come in. Would you mind if I just cleared up? Could you put the kettle on for us?' And so there she was, on her seduction mission, making tea in Anton's kitchen. No, that was not how she wanted it to go! Grace was so flustered, so devastated, she burst into tears.

'Don't worry about it,' she sobbed. The next morning she received a visit from a penitent Anton, not to see her but to drop off a handwritten letter on elegant Italian laid paper:

> *My dear Grace,*
> *It has been so long since I had a visitor in my home. I'm afraid I forgot my manners. Please make a return visit tonight, if that would suit you.*
> *Yours truly,*
> *Anton*

That evening they sat together on his simple linen sofa, their knees pointing together. 'Anton,' Grace began.

'Grace,' Anton said.

'I don't have much experience in these matters.'

It was not what she'd planned to say. Oddly it made Anton inch closer. He moved his beautiful big hands around to indicate – what? His empty home? His lack of family? 'Obviously, neither do I.'

'So you know why I'm here?'

'Oh, Grace, when two people get on as well as you and I . . . All throughout our time together, time we spent as close friends, I've been asking myself if we could be more.'

'But –' Grace knew she sounded bitter.

'But, Grace, I'm afraid you'll have to believe me – you'll have to believe me when I tell you. I'm not the man for you.'

'You don't know that, you can't know that, why don't you let me choose what I want?' She remembered herself, aged sixteen, her plea that her father allow her to stay on at Campion and move to Manna's house. He'd given in – but he was a bad person who hadn't loved her. Anton was a good person who did love her, she could tell. Anton reached out and held her hand. She moved closer until she could rest her head against his shoulder.

'Grace,' he said into her hair. 'If anyone had told me as a young man growing up – that I would one day have a woman like you in my arms . . . I wouldn't have believed them. You're like – Juliette Binoche to me, or Catherine Deneuve. You're a cut above, Grace Clare. A cut above.' He sandwiched her hand in his to stop her speaking. 'It's not that I think you're too good for me. I don't believe I'm a bad person. I don't think I'm particularly special either. It's that I'm not the right man for you, or for anyone.'

Why? What did he mean? The rejection was delivered gently, but it was firm. She fluttered around her house like a bird that had flown inside. By the Monday, John had not returned. Anton seemed to think she'd bounce straight back into their old friendship. Well, he was wrong. She had to text him: *STAY AWAY.* She put the chain on the door so Girl couldn't let herself in. 'I'm not well,' Grace told her through the crack, and she was in her dressing-gown to prove it. It was on the Wednesday that she started getting texts from people she knew. Had she seen the item on Jeepers? It said John was missing, had 'gone underground' since the election loss. She replied to every single one: *Hello, all fine. Best wishes, Grace.* The coverage reached page three of *The Age.* Journalists somehow found her number. She turned her mobile off and unplugged the home phone.

On Friday morning she couldn't take it any longer. She made a visit to Johnston Street Pottery, where Anton was hosting Studio Time. He waved her into the little room he used as his office and leaned against the desk; she sat on a small wooden stool. 'No, this isn't right,' she said.

'No, you're right,' he agreed. 'You stand and I'll sit.'

He sat down and she towered over him, smiling at the change. He looked up at her. His face was perfect. She held it in her hands. 'Anton,' she said. 'For twenty-five years I've been with a man whose biggest problem in life is that his wife's not happy. It would be a great joy to me to really see you, get to know you, and – whatever you struggle with – to love you.'

Anton's face was streaming with tears. 'Grace, I'm sorry,' he said. 'I can't.'

She'd thought that was that until, like a dream, he turned up at her door that night. She'd gone to her yoga as usual. When she got home she went straight to the shower and cried and cried and cried. A towel wrapped around her, she lay on her bed in the dark, heartbroken, pillow soaked through from her tears. Then: a knock at the door. What now? She tied on her dressing-gown. In a rage, she stomped down the stairs. It was Anton. He was trembling all over. 'Is it too late?'

She led him to the sofa: 'It's never too late.'

Grace was the desirer. She was the one who consumed. She climbed on Anton's lap and held his beautiful face in her hands.

She suddenly understood the kissing on television. She made her mouth part of his mouth, and his mouth part of hers. She undid the buttons of his shirt. She could feel him growing hard and she climbed off his lap to draw his trousers down his thighs. 'Grace,' he said, and clasped her by the wrists. 'I've never . . .' *Felt like this*, she completed in her mind. Or *done this before*, he might have been saying. And as she was taking his penis into her mouth she could reply, truthfully on both counts, 'Neither have I.'

All that time, her husband had been propped up around the side of the house, dead. And it hadn't been the start of her life with Anton. It had been the end. God, she was a fool. A tragic old fool. She wiped her eyes with shaking hands.

'Don't be scared,' the hairdresser said. 'Wait till I've run the dryer over it.' Grace hadn't been worried until he warned her not to be. She screwed her eyes shut as the hairdryer warmed her whole head. He snipped a few last snips. 'Now look,' he said. There she was, framed in the mirror. The fuzz of new growth around the scar harmonised artfully with the charcoal and ash of her new crop. For the first time in a year she looked into her own eyes. She was still in there. However painful it was, she was alive.

Grace wove and swayed through the afternoon crowds, past Klein's Perfumery and beautiful Brunswick Street Bookstore, past Marios, where two lanky tweens sat with their mother in the window, stirring their ice chocolates and laughing at the same joke. What was love supposed to be? Grace had tried so hard, devoted her life to it, to the exclusion of all else. She'd kept the home fires burning and used herself as kindling. Still her entire family found her wanting. And Anton, of course. Anton too. Two tall, graceful Sudanese boys stumbled out of 7-Eleven, hooting and skipping and hitting each other with schoolbags. Girl would be home by now, but Belinda would be at work. Was there anything in the flat for dinner? At Vegetable Connection Grace picked up enough salad for both of them, avocados, bread, buffalo mozzarella. *She has no one now*, Ivanna's husband had said – but that wasn't entirely true. One person in the world was keen for Grace's company, grateful for her meagre care. As she walked up Greeves Street she saw a small figure in the black slacks and neat jumper of the Parkville High uniform. 'Girl,' she called out, and the little face turned to her, lit up with hope. 'Come for dinner,' she said. 'And tonight I'll talk to your mum. I'd like you to move in with me – for good.'

37.

ARE YOU BREAKING up with me? *No, the opposite*, Sam had said. As she tidied the shop and reconciled the till, Sophie found herself pondering the *opposite* of a breakup. Getting back together? But – miraculously, given her past behaviour – she and Sam were not apart. She recalled Toby, bowed beneath his huge rucksack, ever so gently lecturing her that it was too early to settle down. He seemed to think a proposal could be on the cards. Sam was twenty-eight: it was proposal age. The truth came to Sophie in a flash. It would happen tonight at Marios. A bargain would be made, whether spoken or unspoken: no more questions about her father's death, no more bad behaviour, no insanity. If she agreed, there'd be a ring on her finger by the end of dinner. A wedding zeroed the clock. All her mistakes would be in the past. And she'd do it properly this time, stay on the straight and narrow. She remembered her old share house in Pigdon Street, the ritual bingeing of all the chocolate and ice cream because the next day they'd start a *regime*. There were still two hours before the beginning of her new, good life. 'Bye, Patrick,' she called up to the storage loft.

'Bye, Sophie,' he called back down.

She raced around to Collins Street and the packed rush hour 109. The tram inched painfully towards the Black Bream and *The Age*. She got out and sprinted before her pounding heart and bursting lungs caught the attention of her brain, and she cried out loud, in the middle of King Street, 'STOP!' What would she even say to Matthew if she saw him? She'd ask him why, maybe. But why *what*? She needed to get out of there. She crossed to the opposite tram shelter and rested her face in her hands.

'Sophie?' It was a small woman with glasses. She was carrying a loaded shopping bag. 'It's me, Marilyn? The Sinister Spinster, you called me. The nickname was not original. You remain the only person who's said it to my face.'

'*Marilyn.*' Sophie groaned with horror remembering the last time she saw her – she'd climbed onto Gavin's lap at the newspaper's Friday drinks. 'I'm so sorry.'

'Not a problem,' Marilyn said. 'You were having a rough time.' She peered down towards Docklands and frowned. 'Now tell me. What are you working on?'

'Working on? I've got my job at a bookshop?'

'And – your writing?' Sophie looked at her blankly. Marilyn exclaimed, annoyed. 'Sophie! You always have to be working on something. Always. No matter what's going on with your personal life. You were only getting started in journalism when you hit the skids. I sacked you from the blog, not from *writing*. I sacked that horrible prick Matthew Straughan – couldn't meet a deadline to save himself – do you think he's slunk away, hidden himself, hung his head in shame? No, he's moved to the *Herald Sun*. You were twice the writer he was, Sophie – for God's *sake*. So many ideas, it didn't matter if some were terrible. Are you at least *thinking*?'

Sophie gasped a laugh. 'All I'm thinking about is my dad. Why he died, whose fault it was.'

'What would you do with the information? If you knew?'

'Um? Get some resolution?'

'Some revenge?'

Sophie stared at Marilyn, intelligent eyes in her plain face. 'No,' she said slowly. 'Not even that. I just wish that I could *know*.'

'That's what writing's for, Sophie. To work out what you know. Give it a go, why don't you?' A tram dinged. Marilyn nodded towards Parliament. 'Are you heading up?'

'Oh – yes.' Sophie dug in her bag for her wallet.

'Well, do me a favour and get on at the back door. I can't do any more chitchat, I've said what I have to say.'

Sophie laughed, she couldn't help it. 'So what should I do?'

'Work on something! If it's crap, start again. If it's good, send it to me. If you want some advice about getting a job, a real job, as a real journalist – give me a buzz.' Marilyn mounted the tram steps. 'And stop being so bloody full of yourself. Everyone makes mistakes. Why should you be the one who disappears? You're no better or no worse than anyone else. Get your shit together and get on with it!' Marilyn was halfway up the front steps. Sophie ran down the platform and got on at the back. The doors slammed shut and the tram cruised off.

It was nearly seven by the time she reached St Vincent's. Sophie watched her stop approach and fall behind as she continued up Victoria Parade. She rushed through Powlett Reserve exactly one week after the first time. On this occasion, unlike the previous two, she knocked on the front door of the tasteful apartment and waited on the step. After a moment, Tessa appeared.

'I'm so sorry, I'm a complete psycho, but I'm not here to cause trouble,' Sophie gabbled.

'What *are* you here to cause?' Tessa said. 'Offence? I don't have dandruff, by the way. It's just a tiny bit of a dry scalp. I get it when I'm under stress.'

Sophie laughed. 'I'm so sorry I said all that.'

'Come in, wipe your feet this time.'

'I actually love your flat so much.' They settled on the sofa, each with a glass of red wine. 'I haven't really got anything to say,' Sophie admitted. 'Apart from sorry for being a freak.'

'I'm not exactly *not* a freak myself.'

'Well, cheers!' Sophie held out her wine. They clinked and drank.

'So have you solved the mystery? You said you'd been doing some detective work, remember?'

'I can't believe I thought I could solve it. I've made zero progress – every time I try I just get sucked into a bad place. I'm going to have to give up.'

'That's a pity,' Tessa said. 'I thought if anyone could work it out, you could.'

'Okay, let me ask you. Did *you* ever think he was suicidal? That he'd kill himself?'

'I don't know,' Tessa said. 'Sometimes he looked so sad, unfathomably tired and sad. He sometimes felt he was reaching the end of the road. But he was also so vital, so powerful and alive.'

'He wasn't powerful when he died. He had no job, nothing to live for.'

'I have no job, as of today, and actually I find it quite liberating,' Tessa said. 'Anyway, he had me. And he had you. But did *you* ever think he was suicidal?'

'I never did. But he never told me anything about himself. And, Tessa – I never asked.'

'I thought I was close to him, as close as you could get,' Tessa said. 'But I'm still finding out new stuff. I don't understand why he had all these people who loved him – me, you, some woman he emailed in Canberra, your mum, Ingrid, Toby – but he wasn't his full self with any of us.'

'Who wants to show anyone their full self?' Sophie shuddered. 'It's fine for you, with your perfect silk shirts and perfect flat. But as you yelled at me outside – and you were right, by the way – I was a huge embarrassment to him. And Mum was a massive bitch. Why would he want to be around us?'

'Sophie, I was a bitch to him as well, and quite often.' Tessa angled her long legs out to cross one over the other. 'If multiple women want to murder the same man, it's the man who should look within.'

'You were there that night, you saw my mum shagging someone. She did, by the way' – Sophie put on a dumb voice – '*make love* to someone on the couch. She wouldn't tell me who. But you must have been furious if you thought it was Dad. Are you sure you didn't murder him?'

'As sure as I can be,' Tessa said simply.

'You don't think my mum did, do you?'

'I really doubt it. They were together for decades; she'd had plenty of opportunity.'

'So what do *you* think happened?'

Tessa stared into her unlit fire. 'It said in the coroner's report that there was a note, so I know you weren't lying to me. Was that all it said? *Dear Grace, I'm so, so sorry.*'

'Yeah, that was it.'

'I think . . .' Tessa trailed off.

'What?'

'I think it had become second nature for him to apologise to the women in his life. I suppose it would make sense for him to write it to her – about me. I suppose he would be apologetic, and perhaps ashamed. So on the one hand, I understand it. On the other hand, if not for the note, I would genuinely believe it was an accident. That something or someone made him go out on the roof and he just – fell. It's the only way it all makes sense to me. Because I swear, Sophie, he might have felt bad about hurting your mum, but I don't think he felt bad about us. We loved each other. Our week away together – it was the happiest we'd ever been.'

'But you're forgetting the other thing,' Sophie said. 'My video. You said he died of shame about me. What if you're right?'

'Sophie.' Tessa sighed. 'I loved your dad since he asked me about photocopier paper in 2005. We got together in 2007 and had a beautiful – what? – eight months together? Then you were having some personal problems of some kind, I don't know. You broke your arm or something? And he dumped me! He *chose you*. After that I didn't see him for more than two years. He came back to me the night of the election, we went away for a week. *Finally*, I was thinking: my turn. He's in the house packing his bags. I'm in the car, waiting. An email comes in showing his daughter –' Tessa must have seen Sophie's twisted, devastated face. She slowed down and looked Sophie in the eye. 'His absolutely, one hundred per cent *beloved* daughter he would do anything for, who's clearly struggling, in trouble and needing help, I'm a strategist by trade, Sophie. As *if* I would ever let him see that video. I deleted it. Instantly. He never saw it.'

Sophie covered her face with her hands and sobbed. Tessa disappeared for a second and came back with a piece of paper towel. Sophie blew her nose. 'You're being much nicer than I deserve. But I don't understand. Why did Callum send it?'

'Oh my God, you had sex with Callum Worboys? I hate that guy.'

'Well, *he* had sex with *me*. I hate him too,' Sophie said. 'Obviously.'

'He absolutely despised your dad. He never understood why John was the boss and he was just the offsider. But the email wasn't from him. I'll never forget the name. It was like a joke: Gavin Purves.'

Of course. Gavin at the Black Bream, holding down the ice cubes with his thumb. His food-court stir-fry, the bitten-off prongs of his plastic fork. She'd thought she had his measure. But she'd played in the shallow end of his needs and entitlement, unaware of the lurking depths. Gavin walking towards her, the flip of his belt from its loop. Tipping her out of his lap at the work dinner, his round face contorted and stained. He must have sent the email straight after she left. She put her wine down on the floor. 'Is it okay to use your bathroom?'

Tessa nodded down the hall. 'I'm sure you know where it is.' Sophie ran a warm tap and pumped some cleanser into her hands. When her face was clean she used Tessa's moisturiser. She combed her eyebrows with Tessa's little brush and put on Tessa's eyeliner and mascara. She carefully applied Tessa's lipstick and kissed a tissue twice to blot. When she came out, Tessa was waiting for her. 'Make-up looks nice.'

'Imagine if you were my step-mother,' Sophie said. 'I could use it all the time.'

'Don't joke.'

'Ugh, I hate it when people say that to me.'

'I don't mean you're not funny. I mean it's a bit of a sore

point.' Tessa opened the door and Sophie stepped out into the night. 'Look, I just want to tell you something quickly,' Tessa said. 'I saw Ingrid today, Ingrid from the ACTU. She really blames your mum, unfairly in my view. She visited the house and scrawled some sort of threat on the walls.'

'You know what you did you cunt,' Sophie quoted.

'Wow.' Tessa laughed. 'No wonder she wouldn't tell me what it said. But I thought it might be nice if you and Toby looked her up. I know how much she cares about you.'

'We will.' Sophie nodded and walked down the path. 'Thank you for not ringing the police.'

'By the way, Sophie?' Tessa called after her. 'A man having sex with you when you don't want sex with him? There's a name for that.'

Sophie cocked her head. 'Being a slut?'

Tessa clicked her tongue. 'Don't make me give you a feminist speech.'

'Thanks for the wine.'

'Thanks for not breaking in.' The door closed.

If Sophie jogged, she'd still get to Marios on time.

38.

It was her grandmother Girl was thinking about that afternoon as she walked home from school and towards an uncertain future. 'You are beautiful enough, clever enough for anything,' Baba had said. Well, was she? What hung in the balance wasn't just her education and her social life but her very identity as a person. Was she special? Or was she not? Suddenly, out of nowhere, the question had been answered. Yes, Grace had been saying with her invitation. Yes! The linseed floors. The whorl of the staircase. The cool of the utility, its hanging plaits of garlic, exposed copper pipes snaking up the wall, its crackled ceramic sink. Doing her homework at the breakfast bar that evening, Grace flipping idly through Girl's science textbook – she couldn't believe it was real. 'What's a lithosphere?' Grace said.

Girl blinked, surprised. 'It's like the Earth's outermost layer?'

'Global systems, including the carbon cycle, rely on interactions involving the atmosphere, biosphere, hydrosphere and lithosphere,' Grace read. She discarded the book and cleared away their empty dinner plates. 'You know, if you asked me to explain climate change – the science, I mean – I think I could get maybe . . . halfway there?'

'Really?' Girl smiled, politely disbelieving. 'You with your no plastic bags, and your hundred different specialty bins?'

'At the risk of sounding like Sophie . . .' For a moment, Grace's face clouded. 'I don't need the facts to know the truth. I can feel the climate is changing. I can see it with my own eyes.'

A prickle of defensiveness rose within Girl, as if Grace was charging her with not caring. 'Last month we had the highest August mean daily maximum temperature on record,' Girl said responsibly. She reached for the print-out Mrs Chu had distributed that day in science. 'In Melbourne, I mean. Average maximum temperatures were 1.5 to 2.5 degrees Celsius warmer than usual. Most stations received less than half their usual August rainfall totals.'

'Awful,' Grace muttered. 'Sounds about right.'

Later, in the tiny hall bathroom, Girl looked at her own face and felt she was seeing it anew. Her skin was perfect, like airbrushed skin from a magazine. She had almost finished the second pot of Grace's La Mer. They cost hundreds of dollars. How would she get another? She would manage, she felt sure. Nothing was out of reach. After all, she'd managed to make Greeves Street her home. She could stay there for the end of grade ten, the whole of grade eleven and twelve, and what was to stop her from making herself indispensable and staying there throughout her years at the University of Melbourne, where she would study – what? God, her whole life she'd been focused on working out who she was good enough to be. Now she'd have to consider what to *do*.

'Girl!' Her reverie was interrupted by a shout. 'God! For God's sake! I must call Sophie.' In the hall Grace was holding her phone to her ear with a trembling hand. 'Oh, Sam! Sam! It's Grace. Sam, you must tell Sophie, I need to speak to her. Urgently. It's about her dad.'

39.

'WINE, GARLIC BREAD?' the waiter said in greeting.

'Yes to red wine, yes to garlic bread.' From where Sophie was sitting she could survey the entire front half of the cafe. Marios had looked almost exactly the same her whole life. She could have been five and stealing her dad's coffee froth with a spoon. She thought she'd known her father inside out too, but she hadn't. Disappointments lay just below the surface – secrets and regret. Sophie surveyed the couples and families chatting brightly, enjoying themselves; the woman alone with a novel and the man alone with his phone. Everyone was so deep, so complex. It was impossible to know the truth about anyone or anything. Could she go on, knowing she'd never know? Sam came in, nervous he'd have to ask for a table. 'Sam!' she called, and the waiter waved him over. In Sam at least she'd found someone she could see through. Or had she? Even inside him, mysteries must lurk.

'Your garlic bread, *bella*!' The waiter dropped a little basket on the table. 'Your wine.' He slid it over.

'Oh, um . . .' Sam said to the waiter's disappearing back.

'Sam, did you want some wine?' Sophie said loudly. The waiter turned with an arched eyebrow.

'Just some house white,' Sam said in a small voice.

When the coast was clear, Sophie leaned forward for his hand. 'They don't hate you.'

Sam laughed. 'Were you here long? It's impossible to park. Eight's so late for dinner, I want to eat my own face.'

The waiter returned and plonked down Sam's wine. 'Ready?'

Sam plucked up the black menu but Sophie said, 'Lasagne! Just two lasagnes!'

'Was the menu thing annoying?' Sam asked quietly afterwards.

'It basically hasn't changed since we were born.'

'Fair enough,' he said. 'Now can you explain why twenty bucks went out of the account last week, to something called THE EARTH?'

'No,' she said, surprised. The penguin on Lonsdale Street. *Get a job*, Tessa had spat. Sophie laughed, remembering. 'Wait, I can. It's a donation, ongoing. Like a regular one, to stop climate change.'

'I've cancelled it,' Sam said. 'Poss! We'll never buy a house like this. Leave charity to the rich!'

'Is that why you invited me here? To lecture me about money?'

'No, God no.' Sam reached for her. 'I'm just nervous.'

They held hands loosely over the table. Sophie swallowed the last of her wine. 'I was thinking about how we can never know the truth of anything.'

Sam was suddenly watchful. 'Yeah?'

'Just like – how we can't even know the truth about ourselves. New stuff comes up and surprises us.'

'I'm kind of hoping there won't be any more surprises. With me *or* you.' Sam's phone was facedown on the table but it began to buzz and vibrate. Sam flipped it over. 'That's weird.' He picked it up. 'Grace?' Sophie opened her hands in a question, which Sam ignored. 'But we've just ordered down here.'

'Lasagne?' The waiter set down two steaming plates.

'The dinner's just come,' Sam said. 'And I've got something I want to ask Sophie.'

'Let me talk to her,' Sophie said. Sam passed the phone over. 'Mum?'

'Oh, Sophie, it's crazy, I think I know what happened to your dad.'

'*Sophie*,' Sam insisted.

'Sophie!' her mother almost shouted. 'I know why he was on the roof!'

'Mum, I'm in Marios, I'll just run up and see you.' She hung up the phone and got to her feet, but the family at the next table was leaving, and she was momentarily trapped. 'I'm just running up to see Mum.'

'Sophie, our lasagne's here. I've got something to talk about, something I think you'll like. You don't even care about your mum, why are you running off to see her?'

'I never said that! I do care about her!'

Sam shook his head. 'It's not even going to see your mum that's the problem. *Of course* you should care about her, it would be great if you guys were close. It's just – I thought you said there was no point wondering why your dad died. That we can never know the truth.'

'There's every point *wondering* – I'd given up finding out.'

'Sometimes you have to give up to grow up.' When Sophie looked in the mirror, her own reflection wavered and disappeared. But Sam was so unchanging, so solid. She bent down and gave him a kiss on the cheek. It was smooth, real and warm. Sam's boundaries never faded in and out. He never dispersed into the atmosphere like a gas. When his arms were around her they kept her together, but only in the shape of his embrace. 'Sophie . . .' Sam held both her hands and squeezed them.

'I just want to live a nice, normal, quiet life with you. Please, I thought you were over all that.'

She squeezed his hands back and let go. 'I'm not over anything.' The family had started to trickle out onto the street. Sophie's path was clear. She didn't want to be the negative of someone else anymore. She just wanted to be herself.

'If you go,' Sam said, 'we won't just pick up where we left off. It's not like the last time. You can't just leave and come back. If you leave, you leave. Sophie?'

Five minutes it took, less. She hadn't even knocked before her mother was dragging her inside, her eyes bright and huge. They held each other's elbows in the hall. 'Mum,' Sophie said. 'Your hair, it looks so good.'

She laughed. 'I forgot about it! I'm so sorry about today.'

'*I'm* sorry about today!' There was a flicker of movement at the top of the stairs. 'Ah,' Sophie said neutrally. 'Girl is here.'

'Hi, Sophie,' Girl said.

'Girl's moving in with me properly, for good. At least until she finishes her grade twelve. But, Sophie!' She gave Sophie's arms a little shake. 'I've done it, I've solved it, I know why he was on the roof! The weather, it confused me. But now I know!' Her mother turned and jogged up the stairs. 'Come and see! Look!'

Girl stepped aside to let them pass. 'I'll put the kettle on.'

Sophie and her mother emerged into the third-floor studio extension. Sophie had been up there just a handful of times. Now she saw the stool on the worktable, the skylight lying open. She looked at her mother, afraid to disappoint. 'I don't know what I'm seeing?'

'It's what you're *not* seeing,' she said. 'When your father was running for Parliament, this skylight sprang a leak. I've hardly been up here for a year. But can you see water damage?'

'No?'

'That's what he was doing!' Her mother's voice vibrated with passionate conviction. 'Can't you see? He was up there fixing my skylight – for me.'

Sophie stared at her mother. 'But, Mum – the note?'

'Dear Grace, I'm so, so sorry.' Tears were running down her mother's cheeks. 'He was sorry he went away, that he left me like that without a word.'

'Oh, Mum, wow.' Sophie put her arms around her. 'Let's get that cup of tea. Careful down the stairs.'

'God, I'm shaking.' Her mother's knees buckled and she had to sit down.

'You're shivering, you're freezing. No, stay there, I'll get you something warm.' Sophie jumped down and went into her parents' room. She would always call it that, even though her father was dead. Was her mother right? She remembered Tessa: he'd got into the habit of apologising to the women in his life. If not for the note, she'd think it was an accident. He had a reason to be up there, her mum said. Fixing the skylight. The pieces fit together, but they didn't make a whole. They were facts, but they didn't feel true. She opened her mum's side of the cupboard but nothing looked comforting enough. She opened a drawer and found an old cashmere cardigan, tattered and full of holes. Her mother joined her in the dark. 'Here,' Sophie said.

'Do you remember this cardigan?'

'No?'

Her mother sat down next to her on the bed and held out

her forearms to show the ragged cuffs. 'It was what I wore when I fed you at night. When you were a baby.'

Sophie stared at her. 'You kept it?'

Her mum shrugged. 'It was special.'

'You mean . . .' Sophie said, slyly winkling out a compliment. '*I* was special.'

'You were always special.' Her mother rolled her eyes. 'I wouldn't have bothered with any of this if you weren't special.'

'Some people might say,' Sophie hedged, 'that love is not love if it comes dressed up as criticism.'

'Some people might say,' her mother said, 'that born failures have to make the best of what they're dealt.'

'Do you mean me?'

'Paranoid!' she scoffed. 'I mean me. Other people were sent out into the world filled to the brim with love. Somehow I was always empty. But, sweetheart – I really tried my best.'

'It was nice you taught me to roast chicken,' Sophie agreed. 'But look at us now, chatting, being real. Why weren't you always like this?'

'Weak, you mean? Bereft? Totally alone and broken?'

'Honest! Human!' Sophie laughed at her mother's appalled face.

'Oh, sweetheart,' she said. 'Maybe it's time to explain something to you. Explain why I'm like the way I am. It's about shrinking, no, it's about . . .' She made a scissor cut in the air. 'It's about pruning.'

Her mother saw Sophie's confusion, and her face, which had been alive, fell suddenly into deadness. 'Mum,' Sophie clutched her hand. 'Don't switch off, don't turn away. Tell me. Please, tell me.'

'God, it was so hard, having a daughter like you. A star, Sophie. You were a star – you still are. You felt things, emotions went into you, they vibrated, they came out as expressions on your face, as actions, things you did and said. I wasn't allowed to be like that when I was young, to feel things and do things.'

'You were all alone in the world,' Sophie said.

'I was, but even when I wasn't, I kept myself locked away in a box. It was a very small life, Sophie. Very small. But it was safe. When I saw you *living large*, doing and saying whatever you felt like, making mistakes – part of me wanted to lock you away too. Part of me felt like you were doing it all on purpose, just to upset me and hurt me. Part of me – well, I envied you!'

'Me?'

'Look at you.' Her mum held her out and inspected her. 'You're a beautiful, special girl. You're just at the beginning of your life. Your promise, your potential – you could do anything, be anyone.'

Perhaps Sophie hadn't ruined everything. Maybe her life wasn't over. Twenty-five wasn't so old. Suddenly, she laughed. 'Mum, I'm just thinking. All that stuff with Helen. Flipping out at the cleaner. Anonymous graffiti calling you nasty names. Shagging someone else!' She jumped up and pulled open the cupboard door to reveal the mirror inside. She dragged her mother over so they were both looking at their reflections. 'I've got some bad news for you, Disgrace Clare!'

She groaned. 'What?'

Sophie put her face next to her mother's face. 'We're much more alike than you realise!'

As they laughed together the atmosphere changed. Sophie's mother glanced over her shoulder at the window. A light had come on somewhere. She ran over and looked out. 'Oh, it's nothing.' She sat down on Sophie's dad's side of the bed, her face hidden.

Sophie put her arm around her. 'It was that pottery guy Anton, wasn't it? Your *one transgression*.'

'God.' Her mother stared up at the ceiling as tears pooled under her eyes. 'I haven't seen him since the night your father died. He's sold his flat – he skipped town rather than see me again.' She sobbed. 'He said he wasn't the man for me, that he had personal problems, that I deserved someone better. But I wanted him – I loved him. Why didn't he love me?'

Sophie's mind floated free, up and out of her parents' bedroom, beyond Smith Street and towards Matthew and Flat E, his single plate and fork and wine glass in the dishwasher. 'Sorry, Mum.' Sophie rubbed her back. 'Shit happens.'

'But why?'

Sophie laughed. 'I ask the same thing every day.'

'I don't think I can do it anymore,' her mother said. 'Live here in this house. What if I moved out? Left all this behind? Could you forgive me? If I moved to a little house by the sea?'

There was a crash at the door and a cry, almost a howl. Girl was there, stricken. She'd dropped three cups of tea.

Girl was lying on one of the spare beds in what used to be Sophie's room, her scalded foot elevated and wrapped in a wet towel. Sophie's mother felt her forehead and stroked her long hair a few times. 'Are you sure I shouldn't call your mum?'

'She won't care,' Girl muttered.

Sophie turned away. 'I'm just going to call Sam.' But downstairs, when she dialled his number on the home phone, it went straight to voicemail with an implacable click.

Her mother came into the kitchen, shattered cups balanced on the tray. 'Four in a week.'

'You could probably fix one or two of those.'

'Sometimes it's better to move on. Anyway, I'll use them in the garden. Go and keep an eye on Girl, will you? Poor little love.'

Sophie rolled her eyes. Upstairs, instead of stopping at the landing, she felt herself drawn to her mother's studio. Steadily she mounted the floating oak stairs. Quietly she climbed onto the pine worktable and up the stool to the roof. She lay sprawled on the mossy plants and waited. Her mind was empty, completely clear. It was as if she could see each individual star and feel the slow rotation of the Earth. After who knew how long she heard a cautious footfall in the studio below. She raised herself onto her elbow and peered over the edge of the open skylight. Girl was creeping up to the big silver storage locker. Sophie watched as she opened it, dropped to her knees, pulled out a crate, selected a book and turned the pages until something fell out: light, white, a folded-up note. 'What's that?' Sophie called.

Girl looked like she was going to pass out. 'Nothing.'

'Bring it up.' Girl glanced towards the door. 'Bring it up,' Sophie said. 'Or you can show me downstairs with Mum.' Reluctantly Girl obeyed, and climbed to the roof to join her. Sophie held her hand out for the paper. *GRACE*, it said on the front in John's writing. Sophie sighed. 'Do you want to explain why you have this?'

'I just found it then, in the clay cupboard?'

'Girl, you didn't just find it, you knew it was there, I saw you.'

'I didn't do anything wrong.' Girl pouted. 'I was protecting Grace. Why are you even here?'

'This is my home,' Sophie said. 'Why are you here?' Girl got to her feet. She walked towards the side John's body was found. Filled with a bad premonition, Sophie scrambled up and hurried to her. 'Be careful.'

Girl wheeled around. 'You be careful,' she hissed, and took several fast strides towards Sophie.

'Fuck!' Sophie stumbled back and collapsed in the sedum.

Girl turned and stood again by the edge of the roof overlooking the flats. 'You think you own everything! You Clares. Why should I wait for you to tell me if I'm in or out, worthy or not worthy?'

'What do you even mean?' Sophie gazed up at her, astonished. 'We've barely spoken. Girl – please. Come away from there. Whatever's happened, it'll all be okay. Everyone makes mistakes, everyone in the world. Whatever you've done, you won't be in trouble.' Sophie had been slowly getting to her feet. 'You're just a child.'

Girl's face crumpled. She staggered towards Sophie, who caught her in her arms and danced her away from the edge. Was Girl angry? No, she was moaning, covering her eyes with her hands, then clenching her hands into fists and banging them at her chest and forehead. Sophie pulled Girl's hands down and crushed her in a hug until she calmed. Finally they sank to the dirt and moss and crouched there, panting. Sophie reached for the folded note, held it gently in her fingers and sighed. Answers were coming. The end was in sight. She lay down, arms behind her head, staring at the sky. After a second Girl did the same, two best friends swapping confidences at a sleepover.

'I was following the election coverage.' Girl sounded far away, indistinct. 'I saw Grace didn't vote for John. I saw him flip out on TV. I lay on my bed that night, waiting. Twenty minutes later the light comes on in Grace's room. It's John. He's sitting on the bed and I could see his whole back shaking.

He fills his bags and storms out. By the time I got down to the road, the car's driving away. I went back up to my room; again I waited. Suddenly the light flicks on. There's Grace. But she's not worried, she's fine. She's putting lipstick on in the mirror. She comes right up to the window, she looks over the fence, but my light's off – I could see her, but she couldn't see me. I ran into the kitchen, expecting her to knock. But she walked right past me and went to Anton's door. Then all week she avoided me, didn't want me around, said no, Girl, not today. Do you know what that's like?' Girl wrapped her arms around her chest with a shiver. 'All my life I've felt bereft, exposed, a snail without a shell. When I was here, when I was with Grace, I felt like . . .' Girl drew a square in the air with a triangle on top. 'I was somewhere. I was someone. I was safe. I was home.'

'It must have felt like everything was falling apart.'

'It did,' Girl said gratefully. 'I *cried*, Sophie, it was painful for me. All I could do was wait. On the Friday, I lay on my bed, I watched her getting ready for yoga, I held my breath in the dark.' A shiver ran down Sophie's spine. 'Then the light switched on again. Your dad was back.' Sophie squeezed her eyes shut as Girl went on. 'I let myself in with my key. He wasn't downstairs, he wasn't upstairs – he must have been in the studio. But when I opened the door I couldn't see him. The stool was on the table, I climbed up onto the roof. He was sitting there, just like, *in the dirt*, with a notebook and a pen. Where were you? I said. Where have you been? He looked at me like – like an object had just spoken to him, or an animal. He said he'd been *away*. Away with who? And Sophie, he said it was *none of my business*. He was breathing like . . .' Girl's chest heaved. 'He said, look, I'm leaving, but I couldn't go without fixing the skylight. Something was blocking the drainage.

I've unblocked it, he said, it'll be fine now. Then he sort of cried out, like *ugh*, and ripped a page out of the notepad. He folded it up really small and put it in his pocket. He goes, Girl, please. You need to go home.'

Sophie made an almost imperceptible agreement noise, a little encouraging 'Mmm'.

'So I started to climb back down,' Girl said. 'I got off the table, I started to get all shaky, I had to sit on the studio floor. It was like the words had gone inside me, *you need to go home*. Who did he think he was? He was the one leaving, not me. It was my home now, not his. I got up, I climbed back onto the roof. He was folding up another sheet of paper, he was writing Grace's name on the front. He tucked it in the notebook and stood up. I was crying, I didn't even realise. He put his arms around me. I said, *John* – he kind of took me by the arms and held me back to look at me. *Oh, sweetheart.* Oh, sweetheart, he said, like he was sorry for me. You poor girl, let me take you home. I pushed him away. I *am* home, I said. His face was all sympathetic: you're so very welcome here. Grace cares about you very much. For a second I started to relax. You're a terrific young woman, he said, and we've all loved getting to know you. But Grace is a grown up with her own life and, Girl, you're just a girl. I shouted, I can't remember what, and he *raised his voice to me*: she doesn't need you! She DOES, I said. Girl, he said. Please. Just go home. I couldn't hear those words. Not again. I ran towards him, he shouted STOP –'

'You pushed him,' Sophie said.

'He made me feel bad!' Girl shouted. 'People shouldn't make other people feel bad! I didn't mean for him to die. I just wanted the badness to stop.'

'And did it?'

Girl stared at the sky. 'Only for a second.'

Sophie covered her eyes. What would you do if you knew, Marilyn the Sinister Spinster had asked. Get revenge? Sophie could bash Girl, push her off the roof. She could scream downstairs and get her mum to call the police. The cops would arrive, handcuffs snapped on. Girl would be marched out to the car. She'd be punished. A terrible rage surged inside Sophie. Her dad, her father, was gone. Girl should pay. She should pay with her life. But after a moment, Sophie uncovered her eyes, and forced herself to speak calmly. 'Then what happened?'

'So Grace was going to come home any minute. I had to make a quick decision about the note.' She nodded towards Sophie's fingers. 'I put it in my pocket. I sprinted back to the flats and waited. I waited for Grace to come back from yoga, I waited for screams, for sirens, the police. But there was only silence. What if Grace had found him, lying there with a broken leg? What if he was telling her what had happened, but his side of the story, not mine? I'd go round there, check everything was okay. Then I heard the sound of a door opening outside. I looked through the kitchen window. Anton was leaving the house. I crept out, and I followed him. He was going round to visit Grace. Her hour of need – it should have been me, not him. I couldn't make my mind up. I wanted to go in, I was going to. But then a woman rushed up the street. I didn't want her to see me.'

'Tessa Notaras,' Sophie said.

Girl nodded. 'I saw her picture in the paper the next day.'

'Then what?'

Girl shrugged. 'Then nothing. I went home. I waited in

the kitchen in the dark. Anton came back. His face was . . .'
Girl beamed her hands round her head like the sun. 'It was
like . . .' Girl stared up at the sky, disbelieving. 'Here we go
again. That's what I was thinking. Another man taking my
place.' Sophie kept her face blank but these words blew up
inside her like a bomb. Girl was obsessed with Grace, that
much was clear. But was she *in love* with her? Did Girl herself
even know?

'Anyway!' Girl was cheerful. 'I woke up the next day to your
screaming. My mum ran round, remember? I got dressed and
followed behind. Anton came out of his flat. John Clare's dead,
I said. There were sirens in the distance. His face went grey like
clay. I said, *Anton*, I said.' Girl waved an admonishing finger.
'I saw you go round there. I saw you with Grace. I saw you up
on the roof with him. I saw you push him off. You've got one
chance. I'll keep your secret if you get out of town. Anyway!
He left. That took care of that.'

Sophie's poor, poor mother. 'Then you came round?'

'Yep, I went round, it was all *Sophie, Sophie, Sophie*.
Everyone was paying attention to you. No one was looking
after Grace. I couldn't believe how alone she was. She really
needed me, she needed my help. I knew straight away I'd done
the right thing.'

'To my dad?' Sophie chose her words carefully. 'Pushing
him?'

Girl gestured at the piece of paper in Sophie's hand. 'No,
taking the note. It said he was *leaving her*! Imagine her reading
that! I couldn't let it happen. All morning I was freaking,
worried about the note in his pocket. But it was nothing, just
a fragment. And it was good for me – it made it seem like
he'd jumped.'

'Dear Grace, I'm so, so sorry,' Sophie said. *It was second nature for him to apologise to the women in his life.* Tessa had been right.

'Yeah.' Girl seemed relieved. 'So I couldn't keep the other note at home, in case my mother found it. It was safer here, in the clay cupboard. I hid it for when I needed it.'

'And what were you going to do with it tonight?'

'Just let Grace find it.'

'But why?'

'Just to remind her that she's weak, and hurt, that her husband left her, that men are bad news, that she needs me, and I love her. Over the last year, we've really made it work, just the two of us. She can't live without me, and I can't live without her. I can't let her move to the coast.'

Dad *had* been thinking of Mum up on the roof. He'd been mending something broken. Just that thought had cracked her mother open. She'd talked with Sophie about her real self, her real feelings. It had made her consider, for the first time, properly moving on. What would happen if she was dragged into a legal process, all this horror rubbed in her face? What was justice anyway? If justice was punishment, there wouldn't be any of that. Girl had been barely fourteen. She hadn't planned to kill him. She was clearly unwell. She'd never see the inside of a cell. Sophie swapped the folded note from hand to hand. Her father was gone, and he was never coming back. Her duty now was to the parent still alive. Sophie pushed herself up and sat cross-legged. Girl did the same, eager to hear her fate. They faced each other in the dark. 'This is what you'll do,' Sophie said. 'It's my turn to offer you a chance. Go downstairs. Don't say anything to my mum – don't speak to her ever again. Go home.' Girl's eyes flared briefly with hatred. 'Your real home,' Sophie went on calmly. 'With your real mother. Pack your stuff, and wherever your mum's going, go.'

'You can't make me. If you had any proof, you'd call the police. You haven't, because there's none.'

'I can't make you,' Sophie agreed. 'And I'm not going to call the police. But I am going to tell Belinda. I'll tell her what you did. She'll get you the help you need. Because, Girl, you do need help.'

'Of course I need help,' Girl said. 'But nobody ever gives it to me.'

'You'll get it,' Sophie said. 'I promise.'

'Is that it, then? I just walk away?'

'It is for now. Walk away and stay away.'

'What do you mean, *for now*?'

'Well, something's happened to me, hasn't it? My father was murdered. Everything that's happened to me is part of my story, the good and the bad – and my story belongs to me. It might be in five years, it might be in ten. But if I want to write it one day, I will.'

Girl knelt. 'Sophie, please.'

'Girl, now,' Sophie said. 'No more talking. Just go.'

Girl disappeared down the skylight. Sophie slipped her hand into the envelope and angled the note towards the light. *My dear Grace*, she read.

Our lives here together have come to a natural end. I will be starting a new one with someone else, and for the past few years I have observed, with bittersweetness, you starting yours. It has been my privilege to work on our love together for more than three decades. Some things we didn't get right. Some things,

like our beautiful children, we really did. I will always think
fondly of our time in 99 Greeves Street.
    With love,
    John

Sophie held the note to her chest. Up on the roof, for the first time since his death, she could feel her father's presence. *Wherever you are, whatever you do.* That's what he'd said to her. *I'm looking after you and loving you.* Now she said it back. The words hovered there, aglow. He could hear her, she was sure of it. When her voice faded away, so did the connection. Alone again, her eyes filled briefly with tears. She lay down and stared at the stars. She'd done it. She'd cracked it. She knew.

40.

Almost a year later

The TV presenter and his wife had sent her the loveliest letter. Themselves 'longtime Fitzroy residents' – four years – they *loved* the house, its well-worn patina, its heritage. They dreamt of raising their own family there, doing pottery together in the beautiful rooftop studio, and beginning what they hoped would be their own multi-decade 'journey' in 99 Greeves Street. Grace had accepted their offer and become a millionaire more than twice over. Settled in her beautiful bush shack, high up on Red Hill, she checked her iPad one day to find Sophie had sent her a link. There was the wife of the TV presenter: long flowing hair, long flowing dress, baby on her hip. She was sharing what the design blog called her 'stunningly updated home' – in the same family for decades, the text read, it had become tired and needed some love. The exquisite renovation had been completed against the clock before the couple welcomed their first child. Grace clicked through the photographs. The walls were white and the floors poured concrete. Ceiling roses – gone. The open fire had been replaced by a levitating glass cube. The studio was now a 'media room'. You had to laugh!

These days when Grace rolled into town she stayed in the Country Women's Association bed and breakfast in Toorak, for the very civilised price of sixty dollars per night. Her modest single room contained a copy of the Country Women's collect, which began:

Keep us, O Lord, from pettiness;
let us be large in thought, in word and deed.
Let us be done with fault finding and leave off self-seeking.
May we put away all pretence
and meet each other face to face . . .

She'd started to read it out loud to Sophie on the phone that morning. The words after 'Let us be done with fault finding' were drowned out by her daughter's laugh. 'You found fault with me one second ago!' Sophie protested.

Grace mentally rewound the tape: 'You mean the Instagraph thing?'

'It's Instagram,' Sophie said, 'and, yes, it's rude to ask me if all the photos have to be of my face! That's what it's for! I post food too – and funny stuff.'

Not that funny, Grace thought. 'Anyway, sweetheart,' she said. 'I wasn't complaining. I love to see your face, and all the glimpses of your new life.'

Grace was placating her, but she wasn't lying. Sophie had moved back home after she and Sam called it quits. During those hectic months, sorting through years of family stuff, downsizing and packing, Grace had become quite used to having Sophie around. Now her daughter was completing a journalism traineeship at the *Northern Daily Leader*, and writing front-page stories about break-ins at the Bowling Club. Toby had driven seven hours from Helen's house to see her on the weekend. At least Grace had managed to raise two children who liked and cared about each other – she can't have done too badly.

She found herself humming as she drove down Queens Parade, the windows open in the Saab. Why had John chosen to die just as the Melbourne winter was ending and the days becoming glorious? It made her feel guilty celebrating spring. She felt especially guilty this year. Temperatures were at least 1.6 degrees warmer than average. The papers were full of warnings about the summer of misery to come, weeks and weeks of forty-degree days. In the past, the collision of all these feelings would have sent her round the twist. Manacled to her ankle and dragged everywhere with her were a lifetime's worth of grievances and grief. John's death – she'd never understand it. The mysterious chasm that lay between her and Anton – his brief and tentative email still lay in her inbox, marked as unread. How had Sophie found him? Did Grace dare write back? But her burdens were getting lighter, and sometimes she forgot about them altogether – when she swam in the ocean, when the phone rang and it was her children, when she welcomed visitors to her new house and life. Already she'd hosted Sophie and Toby, and Brendan and Ned, her old neighbours. Helen was due soon for a long weekend. Wally lived nearby, had dropped round firewood and eggs from his hens, and had built her kitchen when she moved in. The only person who hadn't responded to her invitation had been Girl. Wodonga must be going well – good for her. Soon Grace would get back to Red Hill, the rustle of the bush, the smell of salt in the air, to her flourishing garden, and her tranquil, independent new life. But first, she had something she needed to do.

Grace parked near the gate of the cemetery and cradled both the heavy bouquets to her chest. She could hardly see to stumble from the car and into the Prime Ministers' Garden. She found as she approached she was scared to go further, scared to let the reality of bereavement overtake her, worried her green shoots of happiness might be stamped out instantly by the wrong memory. She put down the bouquets and sat for a moment, surrounded by the names of Australia's leaders. The country would be better if John had made it into Parliament, if his name had been engraved on this wall – of that she was certain, at least.

She stood, picked up the flowers and arranged them in her arms, and the movements called to mind a baby, but which one she couldn't think – Sophie? Toby? She realised what she was imagining was the future. She found herself blinking away tears. Thank God she'd rescued her bond with her kids. One day, if she stayed healthy, and did her ten thousand steps a morning; if she kept doing her recycling, and helped to save the world; if she stayed patient, and stopped making fun of Sophie's new Instagram – then, perhaps then, she would hold a grandchild of her own in her arms. A fresh start. She could look back over her life, every wrong choice and mistake, every triumph and sacrifice, and know it had all been worth it.

She'd been stock-still, eyes up. Suddenly there was a whirling at her ankles, a displacement of the air; a wet nose touched the bit of foot exposed in her nice new sandals. She held the flowers up out of the dog's way and said a warm 'Hello!'

'Ajax!' The call came from somewhere else in the cemetery, a man's voice.

'Ajax!' A woman that time.

The dog disappeared, and Grace went on her way. At the edge of the garden she stopped. Two figures stood near John's rose. One was Manny Rahman, the sweet boy from the union media team. Grace's heart stalled and jammed: the other was Tessa Notaras. She wore her hair long in a plait down her back. Manny hugged her to him. Tessa righted herself, smiling, and flicked her plait out from the embrace. She tucked back under his shoulder. Together they stared down at the line of roses. Ajax lunged and danced like a puppy. 'Car, and *then* park,' Manny said clearly. The dog let him clip on the lead. As they turned to walk away, Grace was instantly apprehended by a startling new fact. Tessa was pregnant. Grace was pierced, tears burst to her eyes.

Oh how horrible it was to feel more than one thing at once. Emotions were combining again; she couldn't make them make sense. Pregnant, clearly in love, Tessa was only in the foothills of a great and arduous journey, as many bad days ahead as there were good. Having summited, Grace couldn't envy someone starting out. She couldn't turn back the clock. Even if she could, she wouldn't. She stared at the flowers, cradled in her arms. She felt the warmth on her short hair, summer-hot already in spring. What was in store for her? For her children, her grandchildren? Love, given and received. Moments of joy – she would be alive to them, she would notice them when they came. She breathed, the waves crashed – the shore washed clean and new. The feelings passed. She had survived. Absurdly, for no rational reason, she found herself suffused with hope. Alone, she walked on. At the graves, Grace laid down Ingrid's flowers. She crouched on one knee and set down John's. Words came to her. She spoke them from the depths of her heart. Thank you. I love you. Goodbye.

Acknowledgements

99 Greeves Street may be fictional, but Melbourne is real, beautiful, fertile and complex. The city is built on the unceded land of the Wurundjeri Woi Wurrung people of the Kulin Nation. I pay my respects to their Elders, past, present and emerging, and acknowledge their ongoing, deep-rooted tradition of storytelling and their enduring connection to and stewardship of the land.

I'm eternally grateful to Alison Jenkins, Sophie Braham, James Ross-Edwards, Lisa Owens, Meaghan O'Connell and Emily Gould for their friendship, knowledge, guidance and inspiration as I worked on this book over the course of many years and drafts.

Thanks too to Mathilda Imlah, Victoria Hannan, Emma Capps, Ana Kinsella, Sean Kelly, Noah Erlich, Anthony Jones and Adriana Edmeades Jones for informed and invaluable early feedback; to Shahidur and Eve Rahman for the kind loan of their surname, and Natalie Smith for the kind loan of a space to write; and to Anna Littler, Helen Manis and Debbie Zimmerman for their indispensable support.

I'd also like to credit two teams of people whose creativity and hard work transformed my Word document into a real novel: from David Higham Associates, my agent Lizzy Kremer, as well as Maddalena Cavaciuti and Kaynat Begum; and from

Picador, my publisher Cate Blake, copy editor Emma Schwarcz, senior editor Danielle Walker, cover designer Laura Thomas, publicist Allie Schotte, and everyone at Macmillan Australia.

I was helped in the writing of this book by the work of Sally Weintrobe, especially *Psychological Roots of the Climate Crisis: Neoliberal Exceptionalism and the Culture of Uncare* (2021).

Most of all, I want to thank my beloved family: my husband Jude and our three beautiful children.